THE
SACRIFICE

THE
SACRIFICE

William X. Kienzle

Andrews McMeel
Publishing

Kansas City

01 02 03 04 RDH 10 9 7 8 6 5 4 3 2 1

Library of Congress Cataloging-in-Publication Data

Kienzle, William X.
    The Sacrifice / William X. Kienzle.
        p.cm.
    ISBN 0-7407-1226-8
    1. Koesler, Robert (Fictitious character)—Fiction. 2. Catholic Church—Clergy—Fiction.
    3. Detroit (Mich.)—Fiction. I. Title.

    PS3561.I35 S23 2001
    813'.54Z—dc21

                                                    00-050433

ATTENTION: SCHOOLS AND BUSINESSES

For Javan,

my wife and collaborator

ACKNOWLEDGMENTS

Gratitude for technical advice to:

James Bannon, Deputy Chief, Detroit Police Department (Retired), Detroit, Michigan

The Reverend Dr. Barton De Merchant, Benedictine Oblate and Episcopal Priest

Inspector James Grace, Director of Professional Standards, Department of Public Safety, Kalamazoo, Michigan (Retired)

Sister Bernadelle Grimm, R.S.M., Hospital Pastoral Care (Retired)

Jerry's Gun Shop, Rochester, Michigan

The Honorable Timothy Kenny, Third Judicial Circuit Court of Michigan

James Macy, Director, Oakland County Food Bank (Retired)

Thomas Petinga, Jr., D.O., Chief of Staff, St. Joseph Mercy Hospital, Pontiac, Michigan

Andrea Solak, Chief of Special Operations, Wayne County Prosecuting Attorney's Office (Retired)

Robbie Timmons, Anchorperson, WXYZ-ABC-TV

Inspector Barbara Weide, Detroit Police Department (Retired)

Any error is the author's.

IN MEMORY OF
THE REVEREND GEORGE WIDDIFIELD

ONE

"T HE CATHOLIC CHURCH IS DEAD. It just doesn't know enough to lie down and roll over."

Father Daniel Reichert recoiled as if he'd been struck. "How can you say such a thing! You, of all people!"

"Just look around you," Father Harry Morgan responded, with an all-encompassing gesture. "Everyone running about like chickens who've been relieved of their heads." He turned back to Reichert. "And what for?"

What for indeed, thought Reichert. The ceremony that was about to begin was meaningless at best and heretical at worst. But that it threatened the very existence of the Church—the One, Holy, Catholic, and Apostolic Church? Certainly his boon companion, Morgan, had to be hyperbolizing. Harry knew as well as he that the Catholic Church was indefectible. Jesus had said so. "Behold I am with you all days. Even to the end of time."

No, the one, true Church could not be dying, let alone dead. "You ought to have a more open mind," Reichert rebuked.

Morgan's lip curled. "You should talk!"

In effect, each priest had just accused the other of being narrow-minded. If truth be known, it was simply a matter of degree.

Reichert and Morgan shared an epoch. Born in the twenties; parents staunch Catholics; the priesthood looked upon as an exalted calling. The two had entered the seminary a couple of years apart; Morgan was the elder by two years.

They advanced through the seminary—high school, college, and theologate—in what would later be known as the pre-Vatican II era. The transformation that rumbled through the Church when the beloved Pope John XXIII opened some windows and let the present in affected Catholics variously. Where once Liturgy, law, and theology had been marked by a universal rigid sameness, after the Second Vatican Council indisputability was replaced by uncertainty. Gradually, two camps formed.

One was the conservative wing: fundamentalist, dedicated to a counterreformation, committed to a return to the pre-Vatican II Church. The other held to a liberalism that would not be static no matter how uncompromising the Vatican remained.

Fathers Morgan and Reichert were devoted to a fairly firm conservatism. Even so, they could and sometimes did differ between themselves.

This was such an occasion.

The Archdiocese of Detroit was about to receive into its presbyterate a former Episcopal priest. His wife and a younger son would follow the priest into the Roman Church. The other son and a daughter (middle child) were quite another matter.

The decision as to whether to accept such ministers or priests into the Roman Catholic priesthood was left up to each individual diocese. If such a judgment was affirmative, there were still many bases to touch, steps to be taken. But in any case, the matter clearly was controversial.

On the one hand was the incontrovertible fact that Catholic priests were in critically short supply. And that shortfall was pretty much worldwide.

In Detroit, for instance, parishes that had once been assigned as many as three or even four priests in the fifties and sixties now commonly were staffed by only one. And many parishes that had held one or two priests were now closed for simple want of a pastor.

Recruitment was one obvious avenue toward a solution. Detroit, as well as other dioceses, gave that possibility a professional shot—to little avail.

Priests who had become inactive, in many cases choosing married life rather than celibacy, had a snowball's chance in hell of being called back to priestly duty.

Offering ordination to married men and/or to women was a proposition that the Vatican had shot down repeatedly.

In fact, Rome considered the latter two potential solutions dead issues. Proponents kept insisting that there was life in the concepts yet. But those who wanted to reactivate priests and/or invest women and those living in matrimony were not in charge of making the rules.

Then, seemingly out of the blue, came an unforeseen phenomenon. A trickle of Episcopal priests left their Church to seek refuge in the Roman Church. By no means was such defection of gangbuster proportions. But it was interesting, if not noteworthy.

Ordination to the priesthood, which some Roman Catholic feminists desired, was accorded to women in the Episcopal Church and then to women in the Church of England—mother church of all who call themselves Anglican.

Such a drastic turn of events had its own reverberations. Many male Anglican priests took extreme umbrage at what they saw as a betrayal of tradition. As a result, many of these men now wanted out. They felt there was no place for them in a priesthood that included women—let alone female bishops, a development that followed inevitably on the heels of the breakthrough.

But these men had given their lives to the Anglican Church. What were they to do? The toothpaste was out of the tube. A female clergy was now part of the Anglican Communion. That would not revert to a former discipline. Some of these aggrieved men felt impelled to abandon their denomination. But where could they go?

For some, the obvious path led back to the Roman Catholic Church, pre-Henry VIII version. But would they be welcomed by Rome?

The answer was—what else?—the creation of a commission . . . to address this specific matter. In 1980, the Vatican, responding to petitions from both Episcopal priests and Episcopal laity, created a Pastoral Provision to give the question special pastoral attention.

These Episcopalians desired full communion with the Roman Catholic Church. In this Provision, former Episcopal priests accepted as candidates for ordination in the Roman Catholic Church would undertake theological, spiritual, and pastoral preparation for such ordination.

Thus, ordination of married Episcopal priests as priests of the Roman Catholic Church was made possible. The Provision also authorized the establishment of "personal parishes" in Roman Catholic dioceses of the United States.

This was the response to the request of the former faithful of the Episcopal Church that they might be permitted to retain certain liturgical practices proper to the Anglican tradition.

Since 1983, close to one hundred former Anglican priests had been ordained for Roman Catholic priestly ministry. Just under ten personal parishes had been established wherein the Book of Common Prayer was authorized.

However, news of the Episcopalian migration—not to mention the Pastoral Provision—qualified as trivial in scope. The parade of a handful of Anglican priests toward Rome might be reported in religious publications at most. The secular media generally overlooked the story.

But now this event was a first for the Detroit archdiocese as well as the metropolitan area. As was the case with most premier events, this ordination attracted some attention.

In addition to this being a first, there was the fact that the priest involved was a local celebrity. A string of accomplishments fattened Father George Wheatley's curriculum vitae. His relevant activities included a weekly column on the op-ed page of the combined Sunday edition of the two metropolitan papers, as well as an hour-long weekly radio program on CKWW, a Canadian station serving Windsor and Detroit. He was sought after as a lecturer and after-dinner speaker. His every church function, whether it be the Eucharist or an informal prayer service, was well attended. Before committing to a specific service, people phoned to ascertain which Liturgies he would be celebrating so they could be sure of having him in the pulpit. Far from objecting to the admission of women into the diaconate or the priesthood—not to mention the hierarchy—Father Wheatley had supported this feminist cause long before it became a reality. Indeed, his only daughter was now in the seminary studying for Holy Orders.

As was typical within the Anglican community, he was able to inject a good many of his personal beliefs into his sermons, columns, speeches, and teachings.

In short, from those who knew him well, to more casual congregations, he had his world on a string in the Episcopal Church. Why would he want to switch from a religious organization that allowed him to put a bit of bully into his pulpit to one that was top-heavy with autocratic authority figures?

There seemed no apparent reason for the step he was about to take. Nor had he volunteered any rationale to fascinated news media.

All that seemed apparent was that he was a big fish and, for whatever reason, the Roman Catholic Church appeared to have caught him.

The movie *Guess Who's Coming to Dinner* featured actor Sidney Poitier as an affluent, handsome, well-spoken African-American engaged to marry into a white family that preached all the proper liberal doctrines of the age. Now, white parents were to have their professed values tested. Would they accept a black man as their son-in-law?

It helped that the color question rested on the indisputable fact that Sidney Poitier would be a catch in anybody's game.

Until this moment, the Archdiocese of Detroit had shown utterly no interest in having an Episcopal priest join their local presbyterate. Not until the many-talented Father George Wheatley appeared on their doorstep. Then it was *Guess Who's Coming to Dinner* at the altar table.

Now, in Old St. Joseph's Church, Fathers Reichert and Morgan, while contemplating the consequences of admitting Anglican priests into the Roman presbyterate, were exchanging their barely divergent views on the subject.

Neither could see much point to it. But Reichert was open to considering an option, whereas Morgan's mind was inexorably closed.

Some years back, a Jewish man with no personal connection to the Catholic Church had been waked in the very church building in which the two priests were now standing.

Father Reichert had bitterly opposed this liturgical favor and loudly condemned the move. But when the possibility of a miracle occurred during the event, he had spun 180 degrees and championed the cause. Even after the Church dismissed the miracle claim.

Had it been Father Morgan at that scene, he would never have changed his mind, nor believed for an instant the claim of a miracle.

So it was by no means peculiar that Reichert left the door of his present conviction slightly ajar, while Morgan saw the matter as an unalloyed tragedy.

"Uh-oh," Reichert, leaning toward Morgan, stage-whispered against the crowd's noise, "here comes Bob Koesler . . . and he's heading straight for us."

"No need to be concerned," Morgan replied. "He's the Enemy. We know that. We just keep our guard up."

It did not occur to either Morgan or Reichert that it might be considered odd for any priest to look on another priest as "the Enemy." Ostensibly, all were united in their goals. Their attitude was, rather, a testimonial to the intensity of feeling left in the wake of Vatican II.

The three priests were contemporaries, in their early seventies. Two had dug in their heels and evolved not a whit from each and every lesson learned in their seminary days over fifty years before. The third, Robert Koesler, lived in both eras eclectically, choosing the better insights in both traditions.

Whether from coincidence or not, the three differed likewise in their physical appearance. Reichert and Morgan were of moderate height and slim to the point of ascetic moderation. Koesler remained tall and robust. It fact, it wouldn't have hurt him to lose a few pounds.

"Dan . . . Harry . . ." Koesler greeted them.

"What happened?" Morgan responded. "You come back out of retirement?"

" 'Out of retirement'?" Koesler was puzzled. "What's that supposed to mean?"

"We've been watching you work the room," Morgan said. "You look for all the world as if you were still pastor here."

Koesler laughed. "Nothing of the sort. But I *was* pastor here a bunch of years. You know how it is: Returning to a parish where one has pastored brings back memories, old friendships, catching up on what's going on in each other's lives . . ."

"No," Reichert snapped, "the way we heard it, there's no going back."

Morgan's approving smile ratified Reichert's correction.

"Well. . ." Koesler left the word an orphan. From long, hard experience he knew that it was only a matter of time before disagreement would insert its ugly countenance when liberal and conservative met head-on. It was like trying to mix oil and water.

On this occasion the bristling had risen a bit earlier than usual. In this case the contentious matter was the place of residence and the theoretical need to separate and distance oneself from one's previous parish. Following the letter of the law, a pastor who retired from the active ministry was expected to move elsewhere and to divorce himself from the management of his former benefice. The purpose of this direction was to forestall possible whipsawing between a former and a present pastor by any interested and usually meddlesome parishioner.

If one were to interpret the direction literally, which priests like Reichert and Morgan were likely to do, a former pastor would not even talk to—or indeed even admit the existence of—such former parishioners.

Koesler well understood the problems that could crop up in these circumstances. Such awareness, coupled with the prudence that came with age and experience, could derail any such problems.

Besides, Koesler was very close to Father Zachary Tully, the present pastor of St. Joe's. Indeed, Father Koesler had arranged that Tully succeed him as pastor. There was no problem in this arena that the two had not handled or could not handle in the future.

But Koesler also understood that there would be no settling disputes between himself and the other two priests. That might have been possible had he been able to consult with Reichert alone. But as long as Reichert was guided by his mentor, Harry Morgan . . .

After an awkward silence, Reichert spoke. "How come you're having the ceremony here at St. Joe's? I mean"—he gestured toward the TV cameras and newspeople positioned throughout the church— you've got the media here. But why not go to the top—why not the Cathedral?"

"First," Koesler disabused, "let's get something straight: This is not *my* idea. There was a lot of discussion on how to handle this—"

"You were in on this discussion?" Morgan interrupted.

Koesler hesitated. This was nobody's business but those who were personally involved in the matter. And that very definitely included him. He had been Wheatley's initial contact, and the one who had steered the Episocopal priest through the tortuous process.

But Koesler was nothing if not polite. "Yes, I was in on the planning. And, as a matter of fact, the Cathedral was the committee's first choice. But the consensus was that this would have been like waving a red cape at a bull. We felt the media would be all over this event if we held it in the mother church of the diocese."

"Well," Reichert almost sneered, "you certainly solved that problem, didn't you?" He pointedly turned to stare at each of the TV cameras as well as the reporters who were hustling about interviewing members of the congregation and searching sedulously for any VIPs who might be present.

Koesler shrugged. "The best-laid plans of mice and men . . ." He didn't complete the quotation. "I suppose it was a mistake. It was foolish of us not to anticipate there would be leaks here and there. In the end there were just too many people involved. And when that many people know what was intended to be a secret"—he shrugged— "the news media can't be far behind.

"Anyway, I think—I hope—avoiding the Cathedral maybe sent a message that this ordination is not intended to be a sensational event. There are some—maybe a majority—who think it bizarre. But we can point to this ancient but modest church that puts the ordination in perspective."

"We'd like you to know," Reichert said, "that Harry and I are among the majority who consider this whole fiasco to be bizarre."

Then why are you here, you—

Aloud Koesler said only, "I would never have guessed it." He silently congratulated himself for concealing every sarcastic nuance.

"But once the 'brain trust' "—Morgan avoided concealing his own sarcasm—"decided to skip the Cathedral, why St. Joe's? Hasn't this poor parish suffered enough?"

Koesler did not share the opinion that St. Joseph's parish had suffered, certainly not any more than any other modern-day parish coping with the problems of its parishioners. He assumed that Morgan was referring to Koesler's term as pastor here. Still, he avoided being drawn into an altercation. "We chose St. Joe's," he explained patiently, "because of George's family."

"His family!" Reichert's amazement was all too evident.

"Well, of course, there is his family—"

"What's his family got to do with the selection of St. Joe's for his ordination?!" Reichert was almost foaming.

"It just seemed appropriate," Koesler said, "that his ordination take place in the parish where he and his family will be living."

"Will be living!" Reichert's voice rose to a near shout. Several people standing nearby turned to see who was so agitated.

"He's got three kids," Koesler said calmly. "Two of them are away just now. But they'll certainly be here frequently. Then, in the course of time, there'll undoubtedly be grandkids. He's got to have room.

"Besides," Koesler continued, "Father Tully wants to move into one of the nearby town houses. So, rather than create a new rectory—another white elephant—we offered George the rectory here. He was very satisfied."

"I should think he would be," Reichert said. "A house so large and spacious."

"It creaks," Koesler commented.

Reichert ignored the comment. "And I suppose it's rent-free."

"As free as the rectories you or any priests lived in as assistant and pastor."

"That's different!"

This conversation had developed into an exchange between Reichert and Koesler.

"What's different about it?"

"We are priests. Full-time!"

"So is he. Or so he will be. Look"—Koesler was getting a bit agitated himself—"even if you don't care to recognize the validity of his orders in the Episcopal priesthood, you've got to consider today's ordination ceremony as valid."

"As far as the Anglican Church is concerned, their orders are worthless," Reichert spat out. "Pope Leo XIII settled that for all time."

"I wouldn't be too sure of that."

Koesler was pushing the envelope. There was no widespread agreement among Catholics as a whole that would contradict Leo's conclusion. Which had—at least in Leo's day—pretty effectively put the kibosh on anything remotely resembling the present situation. Koesler had, on occasion, wondered how traditional Catholics could claim that anything and everything a Pope said was "infallible" when history proved irrefutably that what one Pope said in one century was quite likely to be overturned by another Pope in a later century. Not unlike, he thought wryly, the U.S. Supreme Court, which certainly had done an about-face on more than one issue over the years.

"In any case," Koesler said after a moment, "he'll have the stamp of approval when he gets reordained in just a few more minutes."

"And I wouldn't be too sure of that!" Morgan reentered the conversation.

"What?" Few things surprised Koesler any longer, but Morgan's statement did. "Surely you can't quibble about this program that accepts converts for ordination. It's tied into the Vatican. Rome controls it, for God's sake."

"They're taking advantage of the Pope's debilitated physical condition."

"Who? Who's taking advantage?"

"You and your people, who won't quit until you've changed everything our Church stands for."

Now Koesler *was* steamed. A rare state for him. "Harry, how can you justify that statement? You, of all people, have got to believe in the

Pope. In traditional thought there isn't any time when the Pope ceases to be the successor of Peter, Vicar of Christ."

It was clear that Morgan, and even to a greater degree Reichert, found such a position incompatible, to say the least.

"There are times . . ." Morgan spoke deliberately, as if experiencing how painful it was for him to even question a decision that emanated from Rome. "There are times," he repeated, "when it is clear that the Pope has been harboring traitors. And that these traitors have led him astray by giving him incorrect information."

"And such a time is now?" Koesler was incredulous.

"Exactly."

"Like what, for instance?"

"Celibacy!" Somehow the term gained singular importance, greater weight, as Morgan pronounced it.

"*Celibacy?*" It seemed a non sequitur, but Koesler knew in what direction this was heading.

"You people have been insisting on an optionally celibate clergy." Morgan shook a finger at Koesler. "Each and every time you have attempted to inflict a married clergy on Holy Mother Church the Pope has beaten you back. But now, you have sneaked in through the back door. You're ordaining a married man!"

"What? Do you expect a man like George Wheatley to abandon his wife and family because he is about to enter the Roman Catholic priesthood?" Early in this conversation Koesler had regretted having greeted Morgan and Reichert. Regret had evolved into thoughts of near murder. Of course, all he had to do was walk away. But there was always the chance of straightening out what he considered to be fuzzy thinking.

"No," Morgan said, "I don't expect Wheatley to abandon his family. I expect him not to be ordained. I expect him to beat on the walls of the Church in vain. I expect the response to his request for ordination to be a resounding 'No!'"

Koesler sighed deeply. "You do know, Harry, that the Uniate Churches—which are recognized by Rome—have married priests who are every bit as ordained as we are."

"Then let them get out of here and move to Greece or Russia or wherever. Let them try to be accepted by any one of the Eastern rites.

Let them leave the security of this country. And then let them get married and enjoy sex until their prostate glands fall out. But let them leave us—the Latin rite—the hell alone so we can give witness to the world of a love greater than mere humans can achieve on their own."

"You know where this is going, don't you?" Reichert decided he'd been silent long enough. As in an Australian Tag match, he came on in relief of Morgan. "Everyone in your camp of diehard liberals will bide his time until this practice of welcoming so-called Protestant priests into our clergy becomes rampant. Then you'll say: 'See, it works. It's perfectly natural to have a married clergy. We must get rid of mandatory celibacy.' And," he concluded, "you will have destroyed a sacred tradition." If he had been at a desk or a table, he would have thumped his fist upon it.

"The Holy Spirit acts in wondrous ways." Koesler could think of nothing more basic and absolute.

In response to which statement, the two friends, Koesler feared, were going to suffer simultaneous strokes.

"How dare you say such a thing!" Morgan had mounted the battlements. "It's as we said: They are taking advantage of this ailing old man. It's on public record! The Pope has said so at his every opportunity. He has banned the topic from speculation. An unmarried clergy is of divine ordinance."

"And the Greek rites?"

"Though there are numerous different Greek rite churches, all in all, they comprise only a mere handful of members compared with the Latin rite. When we in the Western world speak of the Catholic Church, we're talking about the Roman Catholic Church—the Latin rite!"

Koesler shook his head. "Look, I believe the Church is here to stay. I believe that as truly as you do. But the Spirit may be directing us through uncharted waters. At the bottom of it all is the shortage of priests. Now, it cannot come as a surprise to you that we're running out of priests."

"The Holy Spirit will save us," Reichert declared. "It doesn't matter how desperate the situation becomes. And the solution will not lie with taking in the leftovers of Protestantism."

That reached Koesler. "Surely you can't refer to a man like George Wheatley as a 'leftover.' He's one of the finest Christian gentlemen I've ever known."

"Well. . ." Reichert began.

"Besides," Koesler broke in, "I am willing to grant you that there hasn't been any sort of wholesale movement toward the Catholic priesthood by Episcopal priests. I'll expand that opinion to say that most of the converts so far might have been motivated by less than noble reasons."

"You mean," Morgan said, "that they are protesting the practice in their own Church of admitting women into their clergy. Whereas that protest is the only good thing to emerge from this entire fiasco."

"And," Reichert added, "your friend Wheatley doesn't bring even that saving grace. He supports women's ordination. Why, his own daughter is studying for their priesthood!"

"You," Morgan stated, "have managed to do what I've always thought was impossible: You and your ilk have forced a Pope to contradict himself. Or seem to. After all, he is only permitting this practice of ordaining Protestants. That's far removed from his apostolic teaching in this matter.

"But I must thank you for one thing, Father Koesler." There was no reason for the formal address other than sheer sarcasm. "This conversation has served to clear my mind. Before we talked this out I feared that our Holy Church was actually dead and didn't know it. Now I see that there is hope after all. As long as we who enjoy the *vera doctrina* survive this attack. Except that we must be overwhelmingly militant. And I assure you: This militancy is already being mobilized. We shall endure!"

As Morgan finished his bellicose statement, Reichert groaned and clutched at his chest.

Both Koesler and Morgan, concerned, immediately moved toward him. But Reichert waved them off as he fumbled in his breast pocket.

"What is it, Dan?" Morgan asked urgently. "Your heart?"

Reichert retrieved a small vial containing tiny white pills. With a practiced hand he extracted one pill, popped it into his mouth, and carefully folded his tongue over it.

"It's his nitro," Harry Morgan explained. "He never goes any-where without it. It's been a lifesaver."

Gradually, Reichert returned to normal.

"Let's get out of here, Dan," Morgan said. "We'll go back to my rectory and you can take it easy . . . I'll be there to watch over you."

"No, no. I want to stay here."

"It's only going to get worse. They're going to ordain the guy. It'll drive you up the wall."

"Maybe, maybe not. Let's stay and watch."

Morgan shook his head. "If you insist."

"You know, of course"—Reichert leaned heavily on Morgan's arm—"that I would give anything to prevent this. I mean, the fact that I want to stay doesn't mean I approve."

"I understand, Dan. I understand completely. Why don't the two of you go over there where there are some empty chairs." Koesler ges-tured to the recessed grotto where a religious statue stood. The sight-line wouldn't be the best. But at least they could sit down, relax—and be more comfortable than they were now.

TWO

FATHER KOESLER WATCHED THE TWO MEN as they haltingly made their way to the grotto, Reichert leaning on Morgan.

Their behavior and their reaction to what was about to take place in this church brought to Koesler's mind the militia movement that was struggling to become popular.

The Constitution of the United States made reference to the right of citizens to bear arms as members of a well-regulated militia. As Koesler understood it, the militia man considered himself constitutionally correct.

This present movement attracted people who had serious apprehensions regarding the government. Particularly the federal government as exemplified by the Administration and its bureaus, such as the FBI, ATF, the Secret Service, and so on.

The more militant among such detractors had formed paramilitary units, complete with firearms, bombs and like weapons. In effect, they considered themselves at war with the authorities of the nation. And, in a sense, they were. No two events would better bear out this situation than the bombing of the government center in Oklahoma City and the Davidian holocaust in Waco.

This sort of fatal confrontation was kissing cousin to a brand of religious militancy that motivated people who bombed abortion clinics and murdered physicians who performed abortions.

Koesler had never, to his knowledge, met a militia person face-to-face. Yet he had the feeling that he had, in some sense, just talked to the prototype.

Reichert and Morgan stood for all who felt similarly about the state of their Church. They were faithful people who were intensely dedicated to a religion that claimed to stretch back to Jesus Himself. Reichert and Morgan had been inducted into this faith more than seventy years ago. For the past approximately fifty years they had been priests. During that time, an event—Vatican II—that took place in the mid-sixties had turned their world topsy-turvy. And they were bitter as bitter could be.

The analogies between the militia people and Catholic traditionalists seemed to Koesler inescapable. Of course, there had been no extreme violence on the part of Catholic conservatives. Was it possible the movement might fester into such a tragedy?

Lost in these thoughts, Koesler only gradually became aware that someone was standing next to him and, in fact, had been standing there for some time. Slowly he turned to look at this silent companion.

It was a priest. At least he was wearing a black suit with clerical collar. A fair assumption would make him a Catholic priest. But, on this occasion, he might just as easily be an Episcopalian. He was bald, with a shadow of facial hair. At about five feet six, he was a dumpy figure, and his clothing was rumpled. The latter condition swung the assumption toward his being Catholic.

In simplicity, Koesler supposed that an Episcopal priest had a wife to see to it or at least remind him that he be well groomed. Catholic priests, generally, had no such buffer.

As Koesler continued to study his companion, the man grinned broadly. Clearly he had no intention of identifying himself.

Koesler hated that. Life held too many needless games without playing Guess Who I Am. So he broke the ice by extending his hand in greeting. "Am I supposed to know you?"

The grin widened. "Bobby, Bobby, Bobby . . . you don't remember me."

The statement was rhetorical. Of course Koesler didn't remember him.

The grin metamorphosed into an expression of fake solicitude. "No need worrying that you're having a 'senior moment.' It's been twenty-some odd years."

Perhaps it was the proffered date . . . twenty-some years. Or maybe that miracle of memory which even at his advanced age occasionally kicked in. But the scales began to fall. "Joe . . ." Koesler reached for a last name. "Joe Farmer! Son of a gun. Has it been that long?"

"You probably thought I'd died."

"Not really. The truth is, I haven't been thinking of you at all." No reason Koesler should have been thinking of Farmer. Still, there was a semblance of guilt.

"But you remember me now?"

"Yes." Koesler had known Farmer briefly many years ago. Joe belonged to a religious order: the Society of the Precious Blood, sometimes known by the casual sobriquet Precious Bleeders. The aim of their founder was to establish a missionary order. In time many in the society served in parishes much the same as diocesan priests such as Father Koesler.

Father Farmer had carved out a life somewhere between that of a secular priest and a missionary. He traveled around the Ohio/ Michigan territory generally conducting one- to-two week spiritual crusades in various parishes.

He'd been at this occupation for these twenty-five years and more. Koesler guessed that in all that time Farmer had not radically altered his presentation. His guess was correct.

Still portraying God as a vengeful being just waiting for some poor soul to sin grievously so he could be plunged into hell. Farmer would then get graphic about the pain fire can cause, especially when it does not consume.

"And how long does hell last? Imagine, my dear sinners"— Koesler could in his imagination hear Farmer's summation—"a solid steel ball, larger than the earth. Every thousand years a small bird flies by, just brushing that ball with its wings. Well, my dear sinners, when that little bird has worn down that ball to nothingness . . ." Pause for effect. " . . . eternity *has not even begun!*"

Confessions usually were pretty heavy after that no-holds-barred threat.

The exhortation had lost a lot of its punch with the passing years. Catholics of today were more apt to appreciate God as infinitely compassionate and merciful. But it had worked in Farmer's heyday. Back then one could never lose by overestimating a Catholic's capacity for guilt.

As he stood there recollecting, Koesler remembered that Joe Farmer had a penchant for gadgets, practical jokes, and funny if occasionally vulgar stories. The stories regularly lost a lot of their effect since Joe always broke himself up, effectively smothering the punch line.

Now, giving Farmer his full attention, Koesler asked, "What brings you to town, Joe?"

"This!" A sweeping gesture encompassed everything and everybody in the church.

Koesler feared a reprise of the confrontation he had just concluded with Reichert and Morgan.

"An abomination!" Farmer judged it.

"Joe, why do you do this to yourself? You must be retired by this time."

"No."

"No?"

"One can't retire from the priesthood."

"I did."

"You may have taken leave of the active ministry. But no priest can retire."

"Ah, yes: 'A priest forever.'"

"You can't tell me . . ." Farmer shook a finger at Koesler. It was the second time today that he had been finger-whipped. He couldn't recall that happening to him before, ever. "You can't tell me," Farmer repeated, "that you've stuck yourself on the shelf. I'll bet you're plenty busy."

"As a matter of fact, I am. But, I assure you, if I got as worked up over any event as you are over this ceremony today, I sure wouldn't voluntarily attend it."

"I've got reason."

"Oh?"

"Next month I'm going to conduct a retreat for what you might call a conservative group: Project Faith. Ever hear of them, Bob?"

"Uh-huh. There aren't many members, but they sure make a lot of noise. They know how to get publicity, too."

"Well," Farmer said, "that's why I'm here. This is research. I'm going to come into that retreat armed with the latest propaganda the enemy is using."

The second time the word "enemy" had been uttered this afternoon. Could the Church survive all these enemies?

"Joe"—Koesler rested a hand on Farmer's shoulder—"what you're saying reminds me a lot of a conversation I just had with a couple of priests here. Did you see them?" He inclined his head toward Reichert and Morgan. "Do you know them?"

Farmer looked directly at the two priests huddled in the grotto. "Sure, I know them. Fine, upstanding gentlemen. I didn't interrupt your conversation with them . . . you looked like you were having too much fun." The mischievous gleam was back in Farmer's eyes.

"Yeah," Koesler said with some disgust. "At least you've got a better reason to be here than they do. You're preparing a talk. They're here mostly out of curiosity."

"Damn straight!" Farmer stated forcefully.

A lingering silence followed.

"Joe," Koesler said finally, "you go back as far as I do . . . and more. Can you remember . . . what was it we used to talk about?"

Farmer's brow furrowed. "Hard to say now. After the damn Council, we went through a bunch of changes." He shook his head. "I must admit I didn't pay much attention to the thing . . .

"I had no idea it would go as far as it's gone," he said, after a moment. "It didn't have as much immediate effect on me. I was going around our neck of the country, doing my thing, preaching retreats. Not very much that happened during the sixties and seventies affected me personally." He looked up at Koesler. "But I was watching you guys. And, man, it was pitiful.

"In most parishes, there was a fresh wall between the priests and the people. Especially when the parish councils started up. Nobody knew what the hell was going on. Who was running things? For as long as anyone could remember, the pastor had been boss. But with the parish councils, there was a grab for power. For the first time, parishioners not only had a say in what went on; they grasped the reins."

"You make it seem so sinister. As if the laity—at least those who were active enough to be interested in a parish council—were plotting a takeover."

"Maybe there was no conspiracy. But when they saw the barn, they really headed for home. And by home, I mean the books, the expenditures, the budget."

"I didn't have that problem. We didn't have any course in fiscal management when I was in the seminary—and neither did you. Hell, I was happy that competent people could take control of the finances. No, my problem was with council members who wanted to take over the altar and the pulpit.

"But, hell, Joe, that's all water under the bridge. We've moved a long way over the years. Back then the place was crawling with priests. Nowadays you could shoot cannons off in Catholic churches and hit very few clergy."

"True, true. But we certainly aren't going to fill the vacancies with the likes of Reverend Wheatley and his wife and children."

Koesler couldn't argue with that conclusion; he let his silence stand for agreement.

"But," Farmer went on, "you were wondering what we used to talk about. Priestly conversations have changed, Bob—along with just about everything else. It used to be real, genuine, good old-fashioned gossip: Who was running for bishop . . . or even who was bucking for monsignor. Who was doing what to whom. Whose parties were the best. Vacations. What parts of Florida could best stand an influx of priests.

"Now all we hear about is who's retiring early, who's taking a leave. Resigning pastorship and sliding back into the assistant category. The young squirts getting to be pastors before the oil of ordination is dry behind their ears.

"The stories used to be funny—a reflection of our lives. Most of it was lighthearted. And, like the song says, the livin' was easy.

"Now there's little—if any—fun; nothing to look forward to but old age—sitting on the shelf, waiting to die."

Farmer seemed to have said just about all he wanted to, and lapsed into silence as he continued offhandedly scanning the growing crowd.

Koesler reflected that he had begun this day in high spirits, excitedly anticipating the ordination that would be unique, at least in Detroit—and in all of Michigan for that matter. Now, after talking with Morgan, Reichert, and Farmer, he found himself depressed—more depressed than he'd been in recent memory.

"I guess," Koesler said at length, "our conversation just coincides with what's affecting us at the time. It's only natural to be preoccupied with all that Vatican II has done. And it's done a lot. But that would have to differ from one diocese to another, don't you think?"

"How's that?" Farmer asked more in politeness than in interest.

"Well, take Detroit, for instance. Our archbishop simply took the Council as God's message to the Church of today. There isn't a liberal bone in Cardinal Boyle's body. But—just because his loyalty has always been with the Church, he has the undeserved reputation of being in the liberal camp.

"And because Boyle implemented the decrees of the Council, we really had a confrontation here. I suppose that's why the fluff talk has deserted us.

"You ought to be able to speak to this theory, Joe. You're forever traveling from state to state, from diocese to diocese . . ."

Farmer needed little time to respond. "I think you've got something there. I hadn't really thought of it. But just last month I gave a weeklong mission at a parish in Toledo. For the closing, the pastor held an old-fashioned open house, with lots of the old geezers like us in attendance."

"No kidding. How'd he keep the youngsters out?"

"Simple: He didn't invite any. It was just a grand bash. Drinks and finger food at four on a Sunday afternoon; dinner at six; closing of the mission at seven-thirty—and afterglow with a hell of a poker game for as long as anybody cared to stay." His face and his tone spoke volumes: "It was a page from our past. The booze flowed freely and so did the stories. One of the guys had one I hadn't heard before."

"That right? Usually it's old favorites."

"I could be wrong," Farmer disclaimed. "Stop me if you've heard it. Anyway, so the story goes, this took place a good many years ago in New York.

"Seems a priest needed an emergency appendectomy. A flu epidemic had filled the hospital to overflowing. But it was a Catholic hospital, so there's always room for Father.

"The operation went off without a hitch. But post-op was bursting at the seams; the wards were filled, and the private and semiprivate rooms were all occupied. Where could they put him?

"Finally, they located an empty bed in the maternity ward. So, rather than leave him in the hallway, they put him in there and, because he was still groggy from the anesthetic, he didn't know the difference.

"Then there was a complication. Every crib in the nursery was taken and another newborn baby made his appearance. As a last resort, the harried nurse decided that it would be safe to put the kid in bed with the priest." Farmer grinned. "He was, after all, in the maternity ward."

Koesler made a face in disbelief. "This is apocryphal, right?"

"A story is a story. This one may have a moral."

"Okay."

"Well, eventually, the priest came to. He was bewildered and appalled to find a baby in his arms.

"Just then the doctor came in to check on his patient. Of course he put two and two together right away and figured out what had happened.

"The priest looked up at his doctor in confusion. 'I don't understand . . . what's this baby doing in my bed?'

"The doctor, run ragged, overworked to the point of giddiness, and a practical joker to boot, gave his fancy free rein. 'Well, Father, it's this way: We opened you up and got your appendix out just in time. Then we noticed this other problem: Your baby had come to term. So we removed the little boy in a sort of cesarean section. And there you have it.'

"The priest was totally unnerved. He was so obviously hysterical that the doctor attempted to reassure him. But now in near panic, the priest said, 'But you don't understand! Okay, okay, so it's my baby, but you don't realize . . .'" The laughter started near Farmer's navel, moved up through his chest cavity, and wheezed and rumbled out his throat. "'Cardinal Spellman is the father!'"

Koesler reflected on Farmer's new ability to finish a story without totally breaking himself up and demolishing the punch line. This was one of Farmer's cleaner offerings. And Koesler thought it at least amusing. "Joe, you know the old saying, *Nil nisi bonum de mortuis.* Besides, you said it had a moral."

"I said this story *may* have a moral. There's one in here someplace. Each listener has to come up with his own.

"Besides," Farmer added, "Spellman was archbishop of New York. That alone should make him fair game. Sometimes I think that just about every priest in America—or at least those of our generation—has a Spellman story. How about you?"

Koesler smiled. "Not personally. I never met the man. The closest I got was through a friend of mine who was at St. Aloysius, downtown. I guess Spellman visited Detroit with some frequency. On one visit, Spellman was going to offer Mass at St. Al's. My friend was helping the Cardinal vest. Spellman asked where he was assigned. My friend replied, 'I'm assistant pastor of this parish.'

"Well, Spellman turned right around, glared at him, and snapped, 'Father, in my archdiocese that word is a noun, not an adjective!'" Koesler chuckled, but Farmer's only reaction was obvious bewilderment. "'A noun, not an adjective'?"

"He meant that no priest dare claim the word 'pastor' unless and until he was indeed an actual pastor. Until such time, the word 'assistant' was to be used as a noun only, and the title 'pastor' could not be claimed by the assistant in any way, shape, or form."

"Pretty nitpicky."

"Yeah. But doesn't it sort of illustrate the changing times? Nowadays, there are very few assistants. And they're called *associate* pastors now. It's hardly worth getting a business card made when a man is ordained these days. The title 'associate' is going to disappear in a very short time for today's newly ordained. As a matter of fact, George Wheatley is never going to be a pastor."

It took several moments before Koesler's statement sunk in. "Wheatley is not going to be a pastor? Never?"

"That's right."

Farmer scratched his head. "Am I hearing you correctly? What's Wheatley's position in the Episcopal clergy?"

"He's a pastor—what they call rector—in one of the suburban parishes."

"That's what I thought. He's plenty old enough to be a pastor in any one of Detroit's parishes. We used to need assistants. Now we need pastors. Hell, we need everybody. So why is Wheatley not going to be a pastor?"

"He's not going to be a pastor or an associate. Quite simply, he's not going to be in any parish ministry." In response to Farmer's obvious puzzlement, Koesler held up a hand, traffic-cop-like. "Why? Because it's a rule."

"A rule!"

"You know as well as I, Joe, that we have rules like Carter's has little liver pills. As far as I can tell, this is just another in a long series of 'em."

"Does that mean the guy can't say Mass in parishes? If it does, why in hell would he want to be a diocesan priest? I mean, I'm fighting to hold on to my mission work. Everybody's pressuring me to settle in a parish.

"I admit the old firing line is nearly empty. But there's a need for missionary work, too. So here's a guy who wants on the firing line . . . and they're not going to let him?!"

Koesler shrugged. "Don't look to me for an answer. These rules come right from HQ—from the Vatican.

"But I admit I can't make sense of it either. He's done everything they demanded of him: He's been accepted into our Church; he's met all the requirements, completed all the assignments, been ordained deacon—in short, he's done everything necessary to become a Roman Catholic priest in good standing. Obviously he would want the same sort of ministry he had as an Episcopalian. But he's not going to be able to have it. And I can't conceive of a single rational reason why he can't. When you think of how desperately we need parish priests . . ."

"So what's he going to do?"

"Some chancery work—at least to start with . . . and maybe some jail ministry on top of that. And he will be able to help out at parishes on weekends. But he'll never be able to establish the special bond that seals the relationship between resident priests and parishioners."

"Well . . ." Farmer shook his head. "Doesn't that beat all! I started out being prejudiced against this heretic joining us. And now I feel sorry for the poor guy. I just don't know . . ."

After a few moments of silence, Koesler said, "It's about time to start this ceremony. Are you going to join the procession?"

Father Farmer smiled. "Didn't bring any glad rags. I think I'll just get down there close"—he inclined his head—"so I can have a ring-side seat. Is the Old Man going to do the honors?"

"Cardinal Boyle? No. We asked for him, but he's not well."

Farmer grinned. "What he is is *old*! Like Methuselah. Why don't they turn the guy out to pasture? He's too ancient to be of any use as a stud. Why, he's even older than the Pope!"

This, Koesler knew, was leading up to one of the most widespread and oft-repeated bits of scuttlebutt in the archdiocese. Koesler wanted no part of it now. "Well," he said, as Farmer started to move toward the sanctuary and a ringside seat, "I'll see you afterward at the reception." Farmer's only response was a grin.

Koesler looked about. He was reminded of his visit many years before to the Sistine Chapel. It was a long distance down many corridors from the out-of-doors to the extremely popular viewing site. A series of wall plaques informed visitors that they were nearing the sacred chapel and reminded them that they should maintain a reverent silence when they entered.

When Koesler had, at long last, entered the chapel, the scene was bedlam. Tour guides were showing their groups the priceless walls and ceiling. Almost everyone was talking and because there were so many people speaking in so many tongues, each group had to speak more loudly than the next in order to be heard. And since it was an enclosed space, the sound was amplified.

So it was now—almost—in the interior of Old St. Joe's. Granted, the walls and ceiling here couldn't hold a paintbrush to the Sistine. But a lot of people were milling about. What little effort there was to hold down the noise was largely unsuccessful.

Koesler made his way toward the rectory where the clerical guests were assembling. He was thinking of his conversation with Father Farmer.

What, indeed, kept Cardinal Mark Boyle from retirement?

Koesler subscribed to the theory that keeping the Cardinal in harness, though he was well past the maximum age for retirement and had submitted his resignation annually since becoming eligible, was this Pope's way of getting even—as political as that seemed.

Even for what? Some clerical pundits had it that Boyle had been a closet liberal all along and had just been waiting his chance to change everything. The Council gave him that chance.

For Koesler this was an easily discarded theory.

As former editor of the diocesan paper, Koesler had known Boyle rather better than the average Detroit priest. The Cardinal was the newspaper's publisher . . . even though he rarely seemed to advert to that fact.

Koesler knew that among Boyle's strongest commitments was his dedication to fidelity. Faithfulness to the Roman Catholic Church. However, one of the Cardinal's chief virtues was an ability to coexist comfortably with and hold no animosity toward those who did not share his view or opinion. It was this virtue that Koesler most admired in Boyle.

With dissidents, Boyle was prone to listen to them, respond to them, reason with them—whether the disagreement was profound or pro forma.

He held strongly to his own conviction. But he was willing, as had been noted, to live with the opposition.

This was not exactly the Vatican's *modus operandi*. In the wake of Rome lay any number of fractured theologians. Some forbidden to publish or to teach. Some excommunicated. Or, as in the case of the famous Galileo Galilei, forced to deny what their own scientific eyes saw.

Boyle's un-Vatican-like response to opposition—his aversion to squashing those with whom he did not totally agree—made it only natural, in Koesler's view, that Boyle's name would appear on the Vatican's Enemies List.

Thus, when it was time to name a new auxiliary bishop for Detroit, Boyle would submit an honest list of candidates. Rome, in response, would select the most conservative of the candidates.

Sometimes, the Roman Curia would ignore all on the list and name an archconservative of their own choosing.

This selection of the conformables—those most compliant and loyally submissive to the Vatican—was not invariable; a few rare mavericks did manage to sneak through—but it definitely set a discernible pattern.

In Koesler's view, a similar motive led the Vatican to consistently reject each of Boyle's offers to resign. It would have been a simple matter to accept one of these offers and allow this bothersome Cardinal to retire to the shelf. Instead, he was left to twist slowly in the breeze.

If Koesler's hypothesis was correct, the Vatican, in this instance, was not the epitome of Christianness.

Koesler heard his name called. Not unusual; he knew a significant number in today's congregation. He stopped and turned. It was Father Zachary Tully. He was standing in a group consisting of his brother, his sister-in-law, and George Wheatley's wife, Bernadette, known to her friends and relatives as Nan.

During the process of Wheatley's conversion to Catholicism, Koesler had come to know the Episcopal priest quite well. But not so his wife. Bernadette Wheatley kept her own counsel. Toward Koesler she was neither reserved nor effusive. Tentatively, their relationship might be described as congenial.

Mrs. Wheatley, a strikingly handsome woman, gave the appearance—probably because she was so slender—of being taller than she actually was. Her gracious smile had a plastic foundation.

"Plastic" was Koesler's word for Nan Wheatley. And one would have a difficult time getting emotionally close to plastic. Her mutation into something like a Stepford automaton took place gradually over the period when she and her husband entered in stages the Roman Church.

Her Anglican world crumbled as former parishioners and friends fell away. Seemingly in the "Whither thou goest, I shall go" mode, she appeared to be following uncomprehendingly the path set by her husband.

And then there were her children. But that was another story.

Koesler hesitated to respond to Tully's invitation. The time for the procession leading to the ordination ceremony was nearing. He checked his watch, something he did often, day and night. Things should get under way within the next fifteen minutes.

The musicians in the choir loft were playing divertimenti so softly they scarcely could be heard over the muted hubbub of the congregation.

Would it seem impolite not to respond to Tully's invitation? Koesler was acutely sensitive to Nan's feelings; above all, he wanted her to feel accepted in her new, unaccustomed situation.

He joined the group.

THREE

FATHER TULLY CHUCKLED. "I saw you checking your watch. There's plenty of time. They wouldn't dare begin without the former and present pastors."

Koesler winced. "Was I doing that? Sorry. Just a long-standing habit. But we'd better get in there pretty soon."

"Trust me," Zachary said. "I'll get you in procession on time. At least we won't have to get you to the church on time. You're already here."

Lieutenant Alonzo—almost everyone knew him as "Zoo"—Tully headed one of the Detroit Police Department's seven Homicide Squads. He was becoming legendary for his speedy arrests leading to a high percentage of solid convictions. Part of the secret of his success was his development of snitches and sources. The other not-so-secret formula was total dedication to his work.

Coincidentally, Father Koesler had become Tully's most reliable expert source when a Catholic aspect arose in any of the lieutenant's murder investigations.

It had not always been so. Koesler's involvement in some of the early investigations had been more or less accidental. Perhaps even providential—although that was up for debate.

In any case, by now Koesler was securely in the saddle as a prime resource.

Only a few years before, Lieutenant Tully had discovered he had a half-brother who was, incredibly, a Catholic priest. Incredibly in that the police officer had no connection whatever to organized religion. Zachary and Zoo shared a common father, but had different mothers.

Zoo's African-American parents had been Baptist. Both Zoo and his father had backslid from that affiliation early on.

Then, one day, without warning, Mr. Tully moved on.

In New Orleans he met and fell in love with a woman who happened to be white—and a fervent Catholic. They had one son. They named him Zachary.

Shortly thereafter, Mr. Tully died. His son, a mulatto, could easily pass for white.

Not knowing he had family in Detroit, Zachary thought he was an only child. He went through the stages common to boys growing up in committed Catholic families of that era. He learned by rote the Latin needed to be an altar boy. Encouraged by his mother and her relatives, he attended a seminary and was ordained a priest.

Some years later his order sent him to Detroit to acknowledge the generosity of a wealthy layman. Before he left on the trip, his aunt—sister to his late mother—told him for the first time about the family he had not known.

In Detroit he met his half-brother, Alonzo, and his wife. The three quickly became so close they might have grown up together.

Zachary knew little about police work, but he was fascinated by the murky world of homicide. Alonzo knew even less about Catholicism—even though his wife was a faithful Catholic.

Zoo's first wife had left, years before, taking their children with her. Later, Zoo's significant other had also walked out. In both cases the breakup occurred because neither of the women could compete with Zoo's first love—his work.

His present wife understood his priorities; she was content to play second fiddle to killers who needed to be tracked down.

Anne Marie taught primary grades in the Detroit school system. She had been married before. That marriage was a disaster. A sympathetic priest overlooked the disaster and witnessed the canonically awkward marriage of Anne Marie and Alonzo. The couple had no children. They lived for each other. They opened their symbiotic union just wide enough to include Zachary, their brother the priest.

Zoo was in attendance at St. Joe's today for two reasons: At the moment, no homicide case demanded his immediate involvement. And, free of such demand, he wanted to be with Anne Marie and Zack.

There was no other reason for him to attend this ceremony. What was so big a deal about switching Churches? George Wheatley had been a priest in one Church and now he was going to be a priest in another Church. Zoo couldn't understand the fuss. But, as usual, he was willing to learn whatever he could.

Koesler noted that Nan Wheatley was twisting her handkerchief between her fingers. "Are you nervous?" he asked.

Her eyes darted toward him. "A little," she admitted.

"It's probably normal," Koesler said. "This is a very important day for George, and for you and the kids . . . for the Catholic Church in Detroit, for that matter."

"Without becoming a nuisance," Anne Marie said, "I told Nan I'd be happy to help her get settled in any way I can."

Nan smiled at Anne Marie. Koesler noted the smile was sincere.

"Just knowing she's going to be there has been a comfort," Nan said. "I've gone through something like this before . . . I mean, we've been in a number of parishes . . . there's always something new; new people to meet, new Church officials, a new place to live . . . things like that.

"But"—her tone was almost mournful—"this will be vastly different."

Koesler felt a pang of sympathy for the Wheatleys—particularly for Nan. So much to get used to. So foreign an experience that could overwhelm one. George at least would be occupied with his new position—whereas Nan was, as it were, merely along for the ride.

Occasionally, Koesler felt a similar sympathy when meeting or saying good-bye to a traveler in an air terminal. He himself was going nowhere. He was home. His charge was going or coming. The trip probably had been or would be miserable, commercial air travel today being what it was.

"Oh," Anne Marie exclaimed, "I hope your coming here to live and minister here won't be that bad!"

"It won't be that bad," Father Tully assured. "We won't bite."

Nan returned to her handkerchief twisting. "You don't understand. I'm afraid you just don't understand. Before when we were called to new positions, it was always an Episcopal congregation. There would be differences, of course, but usually only small variations.

"Settled parishes often reflect their pastors. Or rather, they reflect the relationship of pastor and parishioners. The relationship might have been nurturing and tender. Or it might have been adversarial and unpleasant. One accepts such a call mindful of the circumstances.

"But," she emphasized, "we all were Anglican Episcopalians! By that very fact, we were bonded together.

"Now . . ." She hesitated. "There are so many differences . . ." Her voice trailed off.

"There's one thing that unites us," Anne Marie said. "We are Christians—at least we're trying to be Christians."

"That's right," Father Tully said. "And we'll need that common bond. It just may help that you'll be taking over the rectory. Rectory living won't be a novel experience. You've done enough of that."

Nan's expression grew troubled. "Yes. After looking over this rectory, I thought yes, indeed: We've had enough of rectory life."

"Not to worry," Anne Marie said. "Before you even move in, we've enlisted the help of lots of volunteers who are going to clean, paint, and repair the old place."

"It's so . . . enormous," Nan said wistfully.

"We thought both you and George would appreciate the space," Father Tully said. "Unlike any of the previous occupants, you have a family."

"Three children," Koesler said. "Two of them are away at the moment. As Nan says, that's a lot of space. Once upon a time there were almost that many priests living here. And they had lots of room to rattle around." Father Koesler had not been comfortable at the thought of his former rectory housing a family. But since Mrs. Wheatley had not previously indicated any opposition to the plan, Koesler's had been the only nay in the voting.

"We hope," Anne Marie said, "that the Wheatleys will be with us a long, long time. A few more years and the three children will increase and multiply. What a grand place this will be for family get-togethers."

"By the way," Zachary said, "where are the kids?"

"Richard is here . . . somewhere . . ." Nan's tone was almost distracted. "The other two couldn't make it."

"Couldn't make it!" Zachary intended to discover what could be so important that the two older children wouldn't break a previous commitment to be with their parents for such a momentous occasion. He was about to press the question when he caught a high sign from Koesler to drop the subject.

Anne Marie didn't catch Koesler's sign. "I suppose this is a particularly awkward time for the older children . . . one an Episcopal priest and the other in seminary."

Nan's reaction left no doubt that she found this topic uncomfortable. Anne Marie, seemingly unaware, continued. "Are many of Father Wheatley's former Anglican priests here today?"

"Not many, I'm sorry to say." Zachary, since his sister-in-law was pursuing the topic of mixed religion, felt free to join in, Father Koesler to the contrary notwithstanding. "We made it abundantly clear that this was intended to be an ecumenical affair. Clergy of all denominations were welcome. Of course we were particularly eager for a goodly turnout of Anglicans. But unless things in the rectory have changed a great deal in the last half hour, there's just a sprinkle of Anglicans. Probably the biggest group of non-Catholic clergy are some neighboring Baptists."

"Why is that?" Anne Marie wondered.

The identical question was on her husband's mind. So much of what was going on in this building and in this conversation was utterly foreign to him. He did not even know what questions to ask. So far, listening to the questions and answers, he was picking up interesting information.

"Why so many Baptists? Or why so few Episcopalians? Or both?" asked Zachary.

"So few of his own former colleagues?" Anne Marie clarified.

"That's understandable," Nan said. "If George were taking a stand against females as priests—a practice we . . . I mean they . . . favor, then a good number of that persuasion would be here today. And, I'm sure, a goodly number—if not a clear majority—oppose women priests. We have them, of course—oh, I'm sorry: Identifying with the Episcopal Church is a habit I haven't yet got under control. What I meant to say was that the Anglican Communion ordains women to the priesthood—even to the office of bishop.

"I think the vast majority of Episcopal priests who cross over to the Roman priesthood are taking a stand. They are protesting—they are Protestants, after all—the ordination of women.

"That is not George's purpose. He is making this move as, in his words, a sort of coming home. I think his reasons for changing will become more clear, more evident, as time goes on.

"The point is, among Anglican priests who come over, very few would share George's motive. If, on the other hand, he were protesting a female clergy, we could expect the presence of at least some of his colleagues who share that view."

"That clears things up for me." Anne Marie seemed satisfied.

Koesler once again consulted his watch. It was perilously close to starting time. He would stay only a few moments more. Nervously, he looked around the church.

In the choir loft, the singers and musicians were leaning over the railing, trying to see if the procession was about to start. Indeed, the altar ministers, holding the crucifix and a candle per server, were awaiting a signal to begin.

Two of the servers were girls. The boy carried the crucifix.

At least, thought Koesler, we've come that far. Now it was perfectly permissible for females to serve at the altar. But even that small concession had been hard-won and was by no means universally embraced. And—*who was that?!*

In the sanctuary, near the altar, a black-clad figure was bent over examining something . . . something to do with the altar.

The figure was no less than Father Joe Farmer.

Now—Koesler borrowed from Gilbert and Sullivan—here's a howdy-do! Just a few minutes ago, he and Farmer had been deep in conversation. Farmer had concluded by announcing that he would not join in the procession. He was just going up front to get a ringside seat, he'd said. He would eschew a position in the sanctuary, a position he had every right to occupy, in favor of a place of less distinction.

All well and good. But what in tarnation was he doing poking around the sanctuary? He might have been investigating anything from a mouse—a church mouse, of course—to an altar stone. Joe's mind worked in strange ways.

Koesler's stream of consciousness led him toward his appreciation of Farmer's essence. When Koesler thought of Joe, the first word that came to mind was not "priest." Nor was it "religious," nor "missionary." No, at first blush, Koesler thought of a salesman. The title character of Arthur Miller's *Death of a Salesman*. Yes, a traveling salesman.

Thirty or forty years ago Joe Farmer had been relevant. He came to town to deliver a message. And then he would move on to another territory. At every stop, he would conduct a mission. In the early days, the mission would last two weeks. The first week was for the parish women. For the second week Joe depended on the grace-filled wives to hound their husbands to go to church five or six consecutive evenings after putting in the usual workdays. If there was a parochial school, the pupils would be subjected to a mini-mission. They were excused from class to attend.

After the week or two everyone seemed satisfied that the spiritual life of the parish as a whole had been ratcheted up several notches. All felt better for the experience. Except, of course, those who did not attend. They might feel a pang or two of guilt for favoring television with feet up on the ottoman instead of Joe's scary exhortations and an unforgiving kneeler.

But those parishioners who faithfully attended felt they had sacrificed and profited spiritually.

The only one who did not attend, yet felt great, was the pastor, who, with an additional missionary priest present, took the opportunity for a well-deserved vacation.

Joe Farmer had begun his specialized vocation many years ago by laboring very hard to work up about a dozen spiritual talks designed first to frighten, then to offer hope, and finally, to conclude with the promise of salvation.

The story was told of one parishioner who, in the best missionary spirit, talked his non-Catholic neighbor into attending the parish mission with him. True to form, the five sermons delivered Monday through Friday concerned death, judgment, hell, purgatory, and, finally, heaven.

After the first few talks, the Protestant gentleman confided in his thoughtful neighbor, "I have never felt so depressed in all my life!"

To which the neighbor replied, "Not to worry. It's all downhill from here on."

Koesler smiled as he recalled Father Farmer and his missions. The point of it all was confession. That's what all the scary stuff was about.

In the early days of Koesler's and Farmer's ministry, confession—or the Sacrament of Penance—for most Catholics became routine. Frequency was routine. Catholics confessed twice a year: Christmas and Easter. Or once a year: Christmas or Easter. Or once a month. Or once a week. Or for the dyed-in-the-wool scrupulous, as often as possible.

In any case—with exceptions—there was little insight into the state of the penitent's soul. Anger at home with the spouse but particularly with the children. Gossip. Petty theft. Bad language. The standby for children: disobedience. The standby for nuns: failure in promptitude.

Things have changed, thought Koesler. The name now: Sacrament of Reconciliation. The format: no kneeling on a board and no anonymity-providing door and curtain. Those who had once used the sacrament frequently now used it rarely.

There was some movement toward linking confession to a drastic change in life and/or lifestyle. And yet there still existed a push toward confessing at Christmas and Easter; the vast majority of penitents confessed because it was the appropriate time, not for good reason.

Koesler was so lost in thought that he was startled when someone touched his arm. "I hate to disturb you," said a smiling Father Tully, "but even by my watch, it's pretty late."

Koesler glanced at his watch. It was as if he had overslept and was late in starting Mass. Embarrassed, he blushed. Onlookers were amazed.

"Oh, I am so sorry. I don't know what I could have been thinking of." He looked toward the church entrance. There were the altar ministers, patiently standing as stiff and attentive as little soldiers.

For once he was grateful that something was starting late. This delay might enable him and Zachary to vest and get in line for the procession. At least they stood a good chance of not having to hurry to catch up.

Fathers Koesler and Tully turned to go. They had taken only a few steps when it happened.

Later, when he had time and leisure to piece it all together, the sequence of events became clear. At the time, everyone was so confused that no one knew what had taken place.

First there was a powerful whoosh. That was followed by a sharp, explosive crash. For an instant Koesler thought—hoped—that these sounds had come from the musicians in the choir loft . . . possibly turning on the old pipe organ and then giving out a crescendo of the timpani.

But even as he tried to find an innocuous explanation for this untoward thunder, he knew something far more serious had to be the cause.

For one thing, the orchestra did not continue what it had not begun.

For another, the interior of the Gothic church was clogged with dust. Dust that hitherto coated remote places had been dislodged, lifted, and wafted about. Koesler and many others covered their noses and mouths with handkerchiefs.

Screams and shouts rose from throughout the congregation. Something terrible had happened; as yet no one knew what.

Koesler was tall enough—and he was standing on a raised platform—to see over the heads of the crowd. People were running from the sanctuary. It all fell into an inescapable conclusion: A bomb had gone off. It had exploded somewhere in the front of the church.

Everyone, bent on escaping, was fleeing from the site of the blast. No one seemed to be assisting anyone else. Koesler could not imagine everyone escaping without trying to help others in need. Surely, if anyone was seriously injured, someone—or some few—would risk his or her own safety to rescue someone in need.

As the dust began to settle, Koesler could see pretty well throughout the church. Thank God! he whispered. No one hurt. With the racket that had occurred, it was a miracle.

Then he remembered. Joe Farmer.

Farmer had been investigating something in the sanctuary. Something in the vicinity of the altar.

The crowd was spilling out of the church. Almost all of them were coughing and blowing their noses.

But in the crush of survivors who had brushed by him on their way to fresh air Koesler did not spot Joe Farmer. He pulled his cassock above his knees and ran full tilt toward the sanctuary.

Somebody was running with him. A sidelong glance identified Lieutenant Tully headed in the same direction and pulling ahead of him.

Koesler briefly thought of the original Easter when, having heard of the Lord's resurrection, the Apostles John and Peter ran to the tomb. John, by far the younger man, won the race, but waited for Peter to be the first to enter and find it empty.

Tully clearly was going to be first. But Koesler was fearful that they would not find an empty sanctuary.

FOUR

THE SCENE IN THE SANCTUARY WAS SURREAL.

Several statues were tipped over. Some had toppled to the floor. Their eyes, which had never been alive, were freshly dead. Cracks like drunken spiders' webs crazed the stained glass windows.

But structural damage was not the prime interest of Father Koesler and Lieutenant Tully. While Father Tully was ministering to those panicky people who had been in his general vicinity, his brother and Father Koesler were looking for victims, fervently hoping there were none. Lieutenant Tully wanted to find anybody who might have seen and survived. Koesler was concerned about one particular person who, he feared, had been in the epicenter of this explosion.

As it turned out, Zoo Tully was the first to locate Father Joe Farmer.

The officer had seen death in all of its various guises: murder, suicide, natural causes, gunshot, strangulation, execution, drowning, asphyxiation—and explosion. He knew what he was looking for. And he found it.

Koesler hurried to the lieutenant's side as Tully halted before a pile of clothing. It looked as if someone had dumped a bundle of soiled laundry that waited inertly to be picked up. If Koesler had not been looking for Farmer specifically, he doubted that he would have recognized this pitiful heap as being human.

Zoo knelt alongside Farmer, bending over the priest's body. The officer's mouth was no more than an inch from Farmer's ear. Then he turned his head to put his ear to Farmer's lips.

Koesler could not tell what was being said. Tully was not whispering, but there was so much hubbub that even at this proximity verbal communication was problematic, if not impossible.

Evidently whatever information Tully was trying to get from Farmer wasn't forthcoming. Tully kept shaking his head in obvious frustration.

The lieutenant finally straightened up and, seemingly for the first time, became aware that Father Koesler was kneeling beside him. As Tully began to raise himself from the unforgiving marble floor, he said, "He wants to go to confession."

Wordlessly, Koesler inched nearer. The closer he crept the more obvious was the extent of Farmer's injuries. The very capable emergency staff at Receiving Hospital just minutes from St. Joe's church would do their best to patch Humpty Dumpty. Koesler hoped only that they would be able to relieve the priest's pain.

As Koesler gingerly bent low over Joe Farmer, Lieutenant Tully traced a path of blood that stretched from the altar to where Farmer's broken body now lay.

The poor bastard, Tully silently commiserated. He must've been right on top of the damn thing when it detonated. Tully moved away from the victim. As he did so, he said to Koesler, "Ask him if he saw who did it. Ask him if he knows who did it." Questions that Tully had pumped at Farmer. Questions that had met only with a plea for a priest to hear his confession.

"I'm here, Joe," Koesler said into Farmer's ear. He would hear Farmer's confession first; only then would he treat with Tully's concerns for information. "You wanted to go to confession, Joe. This is Bob Koesler. You ready? Go ahead when you're ready."

"This is it, isn't it, Bobby?" Farmer mumbled. "I'm dying . . . I'm dying . . ."

Probably, Koesler thought, that would be the best thing that could happen to you now, you poor guy. You're too old—as am I—to go through all this just to exist immobilized and in agony . . . or at least trying to cling to life while undergoing attempts to deal with constant pain. "It's too soon to know whether this is it, Joe. Now, is there anything on your mind? Anything you want to set straight?"

Slowly, agonizingly, Farmer shook his head. "Just that from here my life seems such a waste," he murmured. "I didn't do anything with my priesthood. Just those same old sermons, over and over. Things changed . . . I didn't. Maybe I should have."

Koesler was acutely conscious that valuable time was slipping by. If this was going to be the end, he wanted Farmer to leave comforted in and by his priesthood. He deserved to be thus comforted. If only he would let it happen. "Joe"—Koesler's lips were almost pressed against Farmer's ear—"put yourself in the welcoming arms of Jesus. In a few moments you may be judged by Love. God is full of mercy and compassion. Lose yourself in Him."

Koesler raised his head slightly. He saw one lonely tear finding its way down Farmer's face. In its wake it carried blood and black powder. The track of that tear was the only white spot on Farmer's exposed flesh.

It was almost as if Father Farmer was there one minute and in the next he was gone. In that brief span, a team of well-trained paramedics lifted him as gently as possible onto a gurney and began to roll the package toward the door. As with a thought placed out of due time, Koesler realized that he had not absolved the priest. He did so now. He finished the rite just as the gurney reached the outer door, turned to the left, and passed out of sight.

The thought crossed his mind that he should accompany his colleague to the hospital. But immediately he realized that he would only be in the way. He had heard Farmer's confession; he had given him absolution. All was now in the hands of God—and the emergency room staff. Koesler turned back to Lieutenant Tully.

"Did he have anything to say about who did this?" Zoo Tully asked.

Koesler realized that he hadn't quizzed Farmer on what he'd seen. There was a slight guilt, washed away quickly by the reality that there had been neither time nor opportunity to do so. He shook his head.

"Damn!" Tully said.

Koesler stood and looked about him. Where had all these cops come from? Before the blast he had been peripherally aware of a considerable number of uniformed officers outside the church. But they had been busy mostly with traffic control. Now they were very definitely on graver duty.

They were, in police parlance, securing the area. And, along with that, interviewing the members of the congregation, in hopes of finding someone, anyone, who had seen something, anything.

But these witnesses had seen everything and nothing. Unfortunately, none related anything even remotely helpful.

Most had paid no attention to what was going on at the altar; they had been busy renewing old as well as recent friendships. Others had been occupied in securing a prized vantage for the ceremony. This was not the usual group of church attendees who filled the back pews first and only reluctantly allowed themselves to be herded toward the front. Today the pews starting at the sanctuary had filled first.

Thus the police hoped to find somebody who might have noticed some sort of activity adjacent to the altar. But their frustration mounted as it became increasingly clear that most of those present had seen no one in the sanctuary—neither near the altar nor anyplace in the immediate vicinity. At best, they might have noticed a florist making last-minute arrangements of floral pieces. A few recalled some young men who were adjusting the sound system.

Those who'd been aware of any activity whatsoever gave their names, addresses, and phone numbers to the police. They would be contacted later and interviewed in greater detail.

All this Koesler noted and took in. There was a lot going on. From the selfsameness of the questions, it was obvious that a similar routine was going on throughout the church.

Personally, he was just beginning to recover from the numbing shock of it all. Out of the corner of his eye, he was aware someone was beckoning. Lieutenant Tully. Koesler moved mechanically to where Tully was standing with another man, whom he introduced as Officer Lloyd.

Koesler's first impression was that Lloyd—"Call me Gil"—was heavily padded and hung down with equipment—the walking equivalent of an armored vehicle. It was a safe guess that Gil Lloyd was with the Bomb Squad.

"Stick close to me, Father," Tully said. "In a little while I'm going to be questioning some priests and even a bishop. You may come in handy." With those few words Tully made clear what Koesler's role would be. Koesler didn't mind; it was something like being a translator at the United Nations.

For now, this would be a meeting between the Bomb Squad and the Homicide Squad. Koesler would be kept on ice. He would be needed later.

"There's no doubt, " Lloyd stated, "where the seat of the blast occurred."

"The altar," Tully observed.

"Check."

"What did he use?"

"Gimme a break. We just got here." *Detectives!* thought Lloyd; *they want everything yesterday. If we gave 'em what they wanted when they wanted it, they'd still have only half a package.* From experience, he'd learned the simplest way to handle a dedicated professional such as Tully was to take the detective along on the painstaking investigation. He invited Tully, who invited Koesler; the three made up a small procession.

They started at the "seat of the blast"—the altar. The Bomb Squad had already begun its work, starting at the altar and fanning out in concentric circles, establishing the perimeter of the blast.

So far, they had established that the force of the blast had not traveled beyond the front of the altar area. The space between the altar and the first pew was not affected. Dust and debris had settled over the surface, but no damage had been done. Not even to the many religious statues and paintings outside the altar area.

So, very quickly, the squad had narrowed its focus. Although there was almost no damage in front of the altar, there was plenty of wreckage to the rear of it.

"The perp," Lloyd pointed out, "must have laid the device against this corner of the altar. You see"—he pointed to his team who had worked themselves to the end of the sanctuary and were checking the walls—"my squad is following the path of the explosion."

With that, one of the crew brought over a box containing a variety of objects that had been all but pulverized by the blast. He placed the box atop the altar and began to reassemble the pieces as best he could.

"Where'd this stuff come from?" Lloyd asked.

"Pretty much a straight line from this table to the rear of the church." The officer pointed in an imaginary line to the rear wall.

"Okay," Lloyd said. "Where are we in here?" He looked expectantly at Koesler. "This part of the church has a name, doesn't it?"

"Sanctuary."

"Sanctuary. I thought that was a place you could go for safety."

"The name goes a long way. It can mean a particularly holy place in a church. Or a place where you can be safe from the law—but that's mostly medieval. Or a refuge for wildlife—" Koesler stopped, aware that all this information was considerably more than the bomb expert wanted.

"Yeah, okay . . ." The other officer was taking notes. As he wrote, he spoke aloud. " . . . found in direct line from altar to rear of . . . uh . . . sanctuary."

"Let's see what we've got," said Lloyd.

Both men continued to spread the fragments across the altar top. Koesler noted that it was with a look of satisfaction that Lloyd set certain items apart. "This thing is coming together faster than I thought it would." Lloyd was enjoying their success and making no bones about it. "This," he said, "is 'The Building of a Bomb 101.' I'm looking for a timing device and what do I find? The face of a Big Ben pocket watch. Here's the winding stem."

"And look here," the other officer said, "here's a battery and wires." That said, he headed off in search of additional pieces to fit into the puzzle.

Lloyd's latex-clad fingers turned what was left of the battery over and back again. "Plenty of energy to get this limited job done. From here on, I know what I'm going to be looking for. The whole thing fell into place the instant we found the watch. There was a hole drilled in the face and the face is bent, but there's no doubt it's a Big Ben. And that's what gives this business its character."

"You're sure?" Tully asked.

"Yeah, sure," Lloyd responded. "What are you looking for when you find a timing device in a bomb?"

"A time bomb!" Koesler had not realized that the question had been rhetorical as far as the other two were concerned. After a brief, awkward silence, Tully tried to redeem the situation. "That's right, Father: a time bomb."

Lloyd scratched the day-old stubble on his chin. "This puts me in mind of something . . ." His voice trailed off as his brow knit in an evident attempt to recall—what?

"You've seen your share of bombs," Tully said. "Something peculiar about this one?"

"Maybe it's the placement . . ."

Oddly, this scene rang a bell in Koesler's mind. Having just made a virtual fool of himself answering an obviously rhetorical question, he was in no mood to repeat the performance. But, since neither of the other two was offering the elusive example, he thought he'd get his feet wet again. "Could it be," he ventured hesitantly, "that attempted assassination of Adolf Hitler?"

Lloyd nodded thoughtfully. "World War II, wasn't it?"

"Yes." Koesler nodded. "The placement of the bomb. As you said . . ." He paused to allow one or the other of the officers to continue.

Then he recalled ruefully that the incident had taken place almost sixty years ago—in 1944, toward the closing of the European segment of the war. He couldn't count on either of these younger men coming up with the particulars.

Koesler had a singular reason for remembering this attempted murder of the Austrian-born dictator. He preferred that interpretation of history which posited that the war in Europe would have been over much earlier had not Winston Churchill wanted his pound of flesh. The British Prime Minister wanted to make Germany pay for the destruction it had wreaked on England.

Many Germans, particularly of the military, had grown convinced that the war was lost, and wanted to sue for peace. As part of the bargain, the Germans would eliminate Hitler. When the Allies rejected this offer, a core group of German officers concocted a plan to assassinate the Führer, thus presumably clearing the way for a surrender.

The mechanics of that plot had caught Koesler's memory.

Since it was obvious that neither of the others remembered it clearly. Koesler decided to recount that event. He sensed some relevance to the present situation.

He explained first the German need to eliminate Hitler, then how the plot was supposed to work. "It was early on a July morning and Hitler summoned members of his military high command to a meeting at his field headquarters. One of those summoned was a member of the conspiracy—a Colonel von Stauffenberg, if memory serves.

"Stauffenberg carried a bomb, much the same as we have here. It was in a briefcase. The staff assembled around a huge granite table covered with battle maps. Stauffenberg carefully placed the case containing the bomb against the table leg near where Hitler was standing. Then the colonel casually stepped out of the bunker.

"The bomb exploded shortly after that. Stauffenberg assumed he had carried out his part of the plan and that Hitler was dead."

"Yeah," Lloyd said, "but somehow Hitler survived it."

"Yes, he did. Just before detonation someone had moved the briefcase to a spot farther away from where Hitler was standing. He was burned and bruised, but he was alive. Alive and enraged enough to carry out a purge that wiped out several in his high command, including Field Marshal Rommel—probably his most brilliant general. And Rommel was not even actively involved in the murder plot, although he had known about it."

"Wow!" Lloyd exclaimed. "What a memory!"

Koesler smiled self-consciously. "It's not so much a good memory. I lived through that era, though, thankfully, not on the spot. I was fifteen at the time it happened. It impressed itself upon me as one of the most memorable incidents in twentieth-century history.

"And," Koesler continued, addressing Lloyd, "when you talked about where the bomb was positioned, it brought back that memory. I mean, in both cases, the bomb was placed so that it would focalize, sort of, the maximum destruction."

"So"—Tully had become fascinated with the story and its theories—"the colonel wanted to get rid of Hitler. The others in the headquarters didn't matter. It didn't matter how many got killed as long as Hitler bought it . . . that the idea?"

"Well, I don't really know about that," Koesler admitted. "If I recall correctly, there was only one death from the bomb. And, while I don't remember who was killed, it certainly was not the intended victim. So, one fatality. And, I think, ten or eleven others were injured."

"It must have been a time bomb," Lloyd observed. "No one was near it to detonate it."

"I assume that's right."

Tully began to pace in small circles. "And it didn't reach the intended victim because the briefcase containing the bomb had been moved."

"Right."

"And," Tully continued, "ours was a time bomb."

"That's what this leads up to." Lloyd fingered the remains of the bomb. "And—what's this?" One of Lloyd's assistants had presented him with more misshapen debris.

Lloyd nodded. "Just what I was expecting . . . some pipe and synthetic black powder. The 'ABCs' of Bomb-Making." He studied the materials. "Look here: See all these surfaces that look discolored. These areas were originally raised. And the raised surfaces carried information that would be vital in identifying where these pieces were made, how they were delivered. In short, the bomber took great pains to make it near impossible to trace any of this stuff back to him.

"And, if he went to the trouble of filing down the raised surfaces, I'd be willing to bet my pension that there won't be a fingerprint anyplace on this stuff.

"Same undoubtedly will go for where he brought the parts. We'll look into various distributors, retail and wholesale stores. But our guy probably bought the stuff at different stores in different states.

"In short," Lloyd concluded, "what you see here is probably what you're going to get. It's a time bomb. Very simply constructed. Probably could learn how to put a thing like this together in high school. Also very carefully disguised so it couldn't be traced back to our perp."

"But it didn't work . . ." Tully had ceased pacing and was studying the bottom corner of the altar that had been gouged by the blast. "What do you think, Gil? How close do you think this bombing could come to being almost a copy-cat replay of the bomb that was intended to take out Hitler?"

Lloyd resumed scratching the stubble on his chin. "I don't know, Zoo. It would pretty much depend on how powerful the bombs were. We assume Hitler's table was pretty solid. We know what we've got here. We don't know what was put together there. We could try to find out for sure. Maybe the Germans kept some sort of record . . ."

"Give it a try, would you?" Tully stood and brushed the dust from his suit. "I've got a hunch—although I may never get to check it out. I've got a feeling that the guy who put this together did his homework on that field headquarters and the MO for getting rid of Hitler—"

"But," Koesler broke in, "neither bombing worked the way it was intended to—" He stopped short; how could he know what the present bomber had intended?

"Well," Tully said, "we know why the Germans failed: The bomb was moved. As far as the human damage was concerned, the body count was at least one dead and"—he nodded at Koesler—"ten or eleven injured."

"But our bomb failed," Lloyd said, "because there wasn't anyone here. Except for that unlucky bast—uh, priest. I saw them carry him out, poor guy. He gonna make it?"

"He was alive when they took him," Tully said. "But he didn't look good." He turned to Koesler. "A friend of yours? I saw you talking to him."

"An old friend," Koesler said. "I hadn't seen him in ages." Koesler was startled that Tully had been aware of their conversation. Either the lieutenant was extraordinarily perceptive or he had been bored out of his mind. Or both, Koesler concluded.

Tully turned back to Lloyd. "Let me know, will you? I mean, whichever way it turns out. Whether you come up with any parallel between the German bombing and what we've got here? And, whatever you turn up in this bombing. Maybe the perp overlooked something. He wouldn't be the first to figure he thought of everything, but goofed up."

Gil Lloyd nodded and returned to his investigation as Tully and Koesler left the scene and headed for the rectory.

As they passed down the aisle of the church they noted many police officers, some in uniform, others in plain clothes, interviewing possible witnesses. The police were being fed more than they ever wanted to learn about the cataclysm that was the Second Vatican Council, how the Church had abandoned the spirit of that Council, and the pros and cons of ordaining women. But as time went by, it was becoming increasingly clear that virtually no one had seen or heard anything helpful.

For now, Tully and Koesler were going to talk to the main players in this drama.

As they excused themselves through the crowd, Tully mused, "Hitler escaped death because the bomb was moved—by someone who didn't know that the briefcase he was moving contained a bomb. Whoever was the target of today's explosion just wasn't there when this bomb went off." He turned to Koesler. "Why was that, do you think?"

The thought crossed Koesler's mind that they were taking it for granted that Father Farmer had not been the intended target—that his maiming had been unwitting. There was that word again. The bomb meant for Hitler had been unwittingly moved, putting Hitler out of harm's way—presumably Joe Farmer had unwittingly moved into harm's way. Or . . . ?

"QED," Koesler said to himself . . . that would have to be ascertained.

For now, he returned to Lieutenant Tully's question. "They were late. I don't know why. But for some reason they were late."

"I thought so. You seemed nervous about missing the procession."

This guy, thought Koesler, is really observant. "It certainly wouldn't be the first time a church service started late."

"I suppose that's true," Tully agreed, without any real experience in church services, late or otherwise. "But this time, being late saved X numbers of people from injury or even death. I think it would be helpful to know who or what caused the delay."

"So do I," Koesler said.

FIVE

WHAT MIGHT BE TERMED THE CORE GROUP was assembled in the combined living-dining room of St. Joseph's rectory.

Nan Wheatley was on the couch next to her husband. She sat at an angle facing him, as she held his hand. Father Wheatley was ashen-faced. Seemingly in shock, he sat passively as his wife gently stroked his arm.

Father Tully had been standing motionless, gazing out a window at the late winter landscape. He turned when his detective brother entered the room along with St. Joseph's former pastor, Father Koesler.

Then there was auxiliary bishop John Donovan. It was difficult to ascertain exactly what was going through his mind. His face had a faint reddish glow. It might have been anger. Or, perhaps, impatience. Or vexation at having his plans for the day disrupted. Or perhaps a tad too much port taken to brace himself for George Wheatley's formal ordination.

The ordination rite—of course canceled, or at least postponed now—would have required little of the bishop. An alert master of cer-emonies, in this case Father Tully, would have handled everything. He would point to the spot in the missal where the bishop was to read, and the bishop would read. He would direct the bishop where to go, and the bishop would go. It was all so simple; all the bishop had to do was relax and follow directions.

As for Father Tully, there was a certain satisfaction in telling a bishop what to do and where to go. Even if it was only for a short time.

Whatever, about half an hour before the procession was to start, Bishop Donovan had surprised everyone by accepting the pro forma invitation from one of the caterers to partake of some port.

How could the bishop have known about the goddam bomb?

Now Bishop Donovan sat torpid, trying to clear his mind of all fuzziness.

A police interrogation was bad enough. But there were all those reporters and TV cameras just outside. Slur one word and you'd be nothing more than an auxiliary forever.

"Was it a bomb?" Father Tully asked his brother.

The lieutenant nodded.

"Is the priest dead?"

"I don't know," Zoo replied. "They took him to Receiving. He was alive—barely—when I last saw him." He turned to Mr. and Mrs. Wheatley and asked without preamble, "Where are your children?"

"Richard's with us," said Nan. "He's . . ." She turned to look vaguely in the direction of the hall. "He's indisposed. He's in the washroom." She turned back to Lieutenant Tully. "He knows he's expected. He should be out here shortly."

"And the others?"

"Ronald . . . Father Ronald is on his way. I reached him on his car phone. And Alice is also en route."

"Where was she?"

"In her room at the Pontchartrain downtown."

Zoo Tully, from the first moment he'd learned that the two older children would not be present at the ceremony, had been curious. Why weren't they attending? After all, this would seem to be a moment of triumph for their father. Why would his children not be there?

Back to that later. For now, Tully accepted the premise that the younger Wheatleys would soon put in an appearance. Meanwhile, he had a problem that might easily be solved, but which, were it left unaddressed, would continue to bother him. "Since my wife and my brother have been involved in the plans for this ceremony for the past few weeks," Zoo said, "I've heard the terms Episcopalian and Anglican tossed about as if they were identical. I heard the same thing from others here today. Anybody tell me the difference between the two terms?"

Silence. The consensus seemed to be that George Wheatley had spent a good part of his life in that communion, so he should be the one to explain. But he sat motionless and silent.

"I'll give it a try," Father Koesler said finally, with a slight nod toward the Wheatleys. Turning back to Zoo, he added, "I assume you'd like an explanation in twenty-five words or less."

"It's just that it would help if I knew: Are they the same or not?"

"Yes and no." Koesler smiled. "If you go far enough back, we're talking about a 'Christian' Church. When you get to the fourth century and Constantine, we're talking about the Roman Catholic Church . . . as in Holy Roman Empire," he explained in an aside. "Then came schisms and the Reformation. Then King Henry VIII claimed that the monarch of England, and not the Pope in Rome, was head of 'the Church of England.' And that's when the Church throughout the considerable British Empire became Anglican.

"Certain territories—such as the United States and Ireland—in a move to gain more autonomy, took on the added title of Episcopalian. So, for instance, the proper title for this communion in the U.S. is 'The Protestant Episcopal Church in the United States of America'— otherwise known as the Episcopal Church."

"And the Anglicans?" Tully pursued.

"It's sort of a generic name." Koesler pondered for a moment, searching for a simple yet valid explanation that would satisfy Zoo Tully. "It's like this, Lieutenant: All Episcopalians are Anglican. But not all Anglicans are Episcopalians. And for the modern example of how this works, it was the Episcopal Church in this country that first ordained women priests. At which point, the broader Anglican Church was forced to deal with the fait accompli. So now, throughout the Anglican Communion, women now can be priests—even bishops."

"But it's okay to use either name?"

"I suppose so," Koesler said, after a quick glance at George Wheatley. "Unless in some given instance there's some sort of variance. At the outset, you'd have to say that the Episcopal Church in the United States approved the ordination of women. However, the Anglican Church did not—until the Anglican Communion endorsed what their daughter Church had done."

"Okay," Tully pronounced as he looked around. "Everyone clear on that?"

All heads nodded. Tully did not advert to the fact he was the only one present for whom the appellations were subject to question.

All eyes turned to a sound at the door. After a short, peremptory knock, the door opened. Koesler thought it odd that someone would knock at a door and immediately come in without being invited to do so. And if someone was going to enter in any case, why bother to knock?

The priest had only a brief moment to ponder this as a tall, bulky man strode into the room. Koesler's eyes widened and his mouth dropped open.

Walter Koznicki.

Inspector Walter Koznicki.

Walt Koznicki had retired as the very long-term chief of the Detroit Police Department's Homicide Division several years ago. For the past couple of years he had indulged his wife's great desire to travel. "Around the world and more," as he enjoyed describing the grand excursions they were taking.

What with one thing and another, Koznicki and Koesler had seen little of each other in recent years. The priest had been unaware of his friends' return from their latest trip. So the inspector's presence here now was truly a surprise.

Koznicki surveyed the group. His eyes met Koesler's; he winked, and smiled for just the briefest moment. Then his gravely serious demeanor returned. He bent to whisper in Lieutenant Tully's ear. The lieutenant's face remained impassive, but when Koznicki straightened up, the lieutenant announced to the others, "I have bad news." He had their attention. "The priest who was injured in the bombing has died. We are now talking of murder . . . Murder One."

Then, indicating the newcomer, "This is Walter Koznicki. Formerly inspector and head of the Department's Homicide Division." He turned back to Koznicki. "How about it, Walt: Want to sit in?"

"If you do not mind, I would very much like that." Koznicki lowered his bulk into a chair next to Koesler. The two old friends beamed at each other.

At that moment, two caterers entered the room and proceeded to lay out a coffee service on the dining table. Father Tully stood. "Coffee, anyone?"

Bishop Donovan sprang from his chair as if catapulted. Coffee, yes! Hot, strong, and black.

That's the way he got it. If truth be known, the preceremonial port had not been his first alcoholic drink today.

Most of the others lined up behind the bishop. Nan Wheatley poured for herself and her husband.

Koesler, recovered from the surprise of seeing his old friend again, was sobered by the news that Joe Farmer had passed on. After seeing the horrible injuries inflicted by the bomb on Father Farmer, Koesler's assumption had been that death was the only possible outcome. Even Receiving's renowned Emergency Services personnel could not put the priest together again. Father Koesler prayed silently for Joe Farmer's journey into the next life.

Koesler was brought back to the present by a conversation between Koznicki and Zoo Tully.

"When did you get back?" Tully asked Koznicki.

"Just a few days ago. I have been experiencing a severe case of jet lag. Wanda . . . well"—he chuckled—"she enjoys travel so much that jet lag doesn't seem to touch her . . . or so she says."

"I didn't see you in church. And even with that crowd, I couldn't have missed you."

Koznicki smiled. "I had no idea there'd be this much traffic here today. I got caught in the congestion, and then had trouble finding a parking spot. Actually, I would have been even later, but one of the uniforms recognized me and waved me through. I was coming up the steps just as the explosion occurred.

"I saw them carry out that poor priest. It was confusing; he did not at all resemble the Reverend Mr. Wheatley. So I began asking questions that led me to the sanctuary. And," he concluded, "from there to here.

"But," he asked, "are you sure I will not be interfering with your investigation? I no longer have any ties . . ."

Lieutenant Tully smiled broadly. "It'll be fun working with you again, Inspector." He paused. "You and the good Father here."

Koesler felt self-conscious at the intended compliment. He fully understood that whatever help he might provide would be as a resource person. In effect, he had already entered into that office by giving his explanation of the difference between the terms Anglican and Episcopalian. God knows he'd played this role often enough in the past couple of decades . . . almost every time the Detroit police had investigated a homicide in Detroit that had Catholic overtones.

Briefly, Tully brought Koznicki up to speed on this, the commencement of yet another investigation of what Tully, Koznicki, and Koesler would, among themselves, term a Catholic Murder Case.

"Okay," Tully said loudly, "let's get back to where we were."

They all resumed their seats.

Bishop Donovan had removed his liturgical vestments, leaving his black clerical suit and his Roman collar circled by the silver chain of his pectoral cross. Clearly, he was eager to depart and make his way home. He'd had his share of excitement for this day and more.

The lieutenant understood the bishop's wish to get out of there. "Do you know, Bishop, did the advance publicity for this ceremony today mention that you would be presiding?"

Donovan thought for a moment, then shook his head. "No, it didn't. As a matter of fact, I was a last-minute substitute. Bishop Anderson, who was supposed to preside, came down with the flu."

"Whoever did this," Zoo said, "planned very carefully. If you were the target, the perpetrator would have to have known that you were going to be here before you yourself knew it. From what you've just told me, that's highly unlikely, if not impossible. So I think it's safe to cross your name off the list of possible targets."

Until this moment, Donovan had not given a thought to the possibility that someone might want to hurt him. Hell, it was a bomb they were talking about! Someone out there wanted him dead!? He came close to losing the little food and the larger amount of spirits he'd ingested.

Tully was still talking to him. But Donovan was no longer listening. He had become absorbed with a gigantic distraction. Coming back to the present, he heard Tully's voice " . . . but I wish you would give this some thought, Bishop. Try to think of any enemies you might have. Especially anyone who might be violent."

The bishop sat lost again in macabre reverie. Of course he had enemies. If a man in his position—a priest or a bishop—didn't have any enemies, that was a sure sign that he wasn't doing his job properly. But someone who'd want to kill him—?

"Lieutenant"—Donovan's voice cracked slightly—"you just said that I was an unlikely target?" His voice rose again, making a question of the statement. "That the guy would have to have known that I was going to be here today even before I myself knew. I mean, I'm not afraid or anything . . . but I would like some reassurance that I was simply at the wrong place at the wrong time. I mean," he repeated, "I'd like to know that I don't have to spend the rest of my life look-ing over my shoulder and being supercautious—"

"Nothing like that, Bishop," Tully assured. "For one thing, we're gonna get this guy. In the meantime, though, in a situation like this y— uh, one can't be too cautious. Although, as I said, it's highly unlikely that you could have been the intended victim.

"But you are a prominent figure . . . not one of the crowd. So it's not beyond possibility that someone might have known . . . some-body, say, in your headquarters. The . . . uh . . ."

"The chancery," Zack Tully supplied.

"Yes, the chancery," Zoo picked up. "There are any number of ways security can be breached. All we're saying is that it is most unlikely that you were the intended target. However, that doesn't mean it is totally impossible. I'd hate to see something happen because we thought it was impossible when it wasn't."

"*You'd* hate it!"

"Just keep your guard up"—Tully smiled reassuringly—"and try to think of some names."

"I may go now?"

"You may."

The bishop left, dodging the few media people still at the scene.

Lieutenant Tully turned back to the group. "Who was in charge here today?"

"What do you mean 'in charge'?" asked Koesler.

"In charge of the ceremony itself? All that was supposed to take place in the sanctuary?"

After a brief pause, Father Tully spoke up. "I was in charge, I guess."

"You!" A note of surprise in Zoo's voice. "How come I didn't know that? This ceremony was just about the only thing you've been talking about the past couple of weeks."

Zachary shook his head. "I must have been very boring. But now that I look back on it, I guess I must've talked about what we expected to take place without mentioning who was going to direct traffic."

Zoo Tully sighed deeply.

Walt Koznicki suppressed a smile. He, more than most, had appreciated the irony of Zoo Tully's suddenly learning he had a Catholic priest for a brother.

Inspector Koznicki—those who knew him still accorded him his preretirement title—was confident of Zoo's ethical standards. But there was no doubt whatever that the lieutenant steered clear of any institutional religion. Koznicki found it amusing to see this Baptist backslider struggling to cope with organized religion as it was alive and well in the Tully household.

"Okay . . ." Tully turned his total attention to his brother. "We want to get the chronology as accurately as we can. Now, excepting the priest who was killed, no one was injured because no one else was at the altar when the bomb went off. And no one was at the altar because the ceremony was late in starting. In other words, probably nothing was wrong with the bomber's timing. Something went wrong with your timetable, Zack."

Father Tully nodded. "True enough."

"What time was the ceremony scheduled to start?"

"Four-thirty."

"Yes, I remember you kept mentioning that over and over."

Father Tully winced. "You don't have to keep reminding me." He looked up at his policeman brother. "Next time I get on your nerves, just tell me."

Zoo ignored the digression. "But it didn't start at four-thirty. Exactly what time did it get under way?" Actually, Zoo had a pretty good idea; at the time, he had been glancing at his watch with some impatience, wondering just when the program would start. But for purposes of this investigation, he had to be exact.

Father Tully glanced around at the others. No one volunteered to supply a time. "I hadn't reflected up till now," he said finally. "But as far as I can tell, it never really did get under way. I—and Bob—started for the sacristy to see what was holding things up. For all practical purposes, Father Koesler and I were wearing what we needed for the ceremony—our cassocks. All we needed to do was slip on our surplices and we could have easily gotten into the procession that was already moving into the church. As for exact time . . . ? I suppose we headed back there sometime between four thirty-five and four-forty. But, as I said, I couldn't swear that the procession had in fact begun even then. Only that Bob and I began walking over.

"Actually, I wanted to find out what was holding things up."

"Well," said Zoo, "let's suppose for the moment that things actually had started on time. You said the procession was scheduled to begin at four-thirty. Suppose it did."

"Okay," Zack agreed.

"How long," Zoo theorized, "would it take for the procession to enter the church and reach the . . . the, uh, sanctuary?"

"Hmmm . . . I'm not sure. But one way or the other—whether it started on time or it was late starting—it probably would have taken five to ten minutes to reach the sanctuary—"

"Five to ten minutes? Why the discrepancy?"

"Oh, yes . . . well, it just depends on how many people take part . . . how many are in the procession—and how fast or slowly they walk."

Lieutenant Tully, satisfied, nodded. "Okay. So if the procession had begun promptly, it would have reached the altar at approximately four thirty-five to four-forty. And what time did you say you and Father Koesler started for the . . ." He hesitated again, searching for the correct term.

"The sacristy," his brother provided.

"Yes, the sacristy. What time did you start for there?"

"About . . ." This time it was Zack who hesitated, trying to pinpoint the exact time. " . . . about four thirty-five to four-forty."

"But you didn't reach the sacristy—your destination. Because . . . ?"

It was as if Zachary was playing into his brother's hand. "Because the bomb exploded."

"And what time was that?"

"Between four thirty-five and four-forty." Zachary was growing increasingly certain where his brother was going with this line of questioning.

"Now," Zoo said, "you stated that whether or not the ceremony started on time, it would still take five to ten minutes for everyone in the procession to reach the sanctuary." Fathers Tully and Koesler both nodded agreement. "Now, let's suppose the ceremony *had* begun on time. What would be happening at the altar?"

Father Tully knew exactly what would have been happening. He himself had planned it all after consulting with the Liturgy Department of the Archdiocese of Detroit. "Well . . ." Zack closed his eyes and envisioned the aborted ceremony as it might have been. "There were only ten visiting clergy—three women and seven men." He further explained that six were Catholic priests and four were of other denominations. Of course the three women would be members of these other denominations.

"They—the visiting clergy—would have taken their positions in the rear of the sanctuary. Actually," he said after further thought, "I would have directed them. As it turned out, they might have been pretty well out of harm's way. Depending on the power of the blast, they at least had a better chance of not being seriously injured—"

"Who," Zoo interrupted, "would have been at the altar?"

No hesitation here. "Three. The bishop would be seated. His ceremonial chair would be several feet from the altar, on a slightly raised platform. And standing together at the middle of the altar would be George Wheatley and me.

"At that point, the ceremony would have begun."

"At that point," Zoo said solemnly, "the bomb would have exploded."

A reflective silence fell over the group. The realization sank deeply into their consciousness that in all probability, if the program had gone as planned, at least two people—Wheatley and Father Tully—would now be dead. Possibly also the bishop. Additionally, others would have been injured—perhaps even one or two fatally. Anyone in that sanctuary, from the bishop to the altar servers, would have been in jeopardy.

"Now," Zoo addressed his brother, "you can give us all this information because you yourself planned the ceremony."

"From the procession to the recession," Zack replied.

"But *you* didn't plant the bomb. How could anyone else know in advance what was going to happen? And they'd have to know what plans were made. I mean, the bomber would have to know the timing just about to the minute before he set the timing mechanism. Who else, besides you, Zack, would know what was going to happen and when it was going to happen?"

Father Tully shrugged. "Just about anyone who was familiar with this type of Liturgy."

"I've got to understand this," Zoo said. "Explain it, please. Better yet"—he turned to Father Koesler—"since you were not responsible for planning this ceremony—would you, Father, explain how the ritual could be more or less common knowledge."

"Well . . ." Koesler gathered his thoughts. "I guess there are two prescribed ways of entering the sanctuary for a Liturgy. We're talking about Mass, usually . . . but also benediction or novena or rosary devotions.

"Anyway, for less solemn occasions, the priest and the altar ministers enter the sanctuary in the simplest possible way. Maybe from the side or rear of the sanctuary, if there's a sacristy in that area.

"But in any case, usually, whether it's devotions or daily Mass—or Sunday Mass, for that matter—the procession starts in the rear of the church, processes up the center aisle, and enters the sanctuary, circling around behind the altar. The celebrant—or main concelebrant plus any other priest or priests who are part of that procession—advances to the altar—facing the people—and bends to kiss the top of the altar, thus reverencing it.

"And that's the usual way the celebration of Mass begins."

"And that's common knowledge?"

"Yes," Koesler asserted. "Ask somebody—anybody—who attends Mass, even irregularly. He or she may have to give it a little thought. But unless that person is comatose during the ceremony, he or she knows that the participants enter from the rear of the church, they process down the center aisle, they enter the sanctuary, they go immediately to the altar, reverence it, then they stay pretty close to the center of the altar. The whole thing takes about five to ten minutes—depending on how many people are in the procession.

"I'm sorry the procedure seems so cut and dried. I know it would narrow the field of suspects if insiders were the only ones familiar with the Liturgy. But the ritual is so predictable that almost anyone could have had the knowledge . . ." His voice trailed off.

"Well, all right," Zoo grudgingly agreed. "But there's got to be a margin for error."

"And now"—Walt Koznicki spoke for the first time—"we have seen that margin filled. Many, many things could go wrong with such a plan. The ceremony might have begun earlier than scheduled. The ceremony could have been only slightly delayed. Or the procession could—as it did today—suffer a significant delay."

"That way," Koesler said, "if poor Father Farmer's curiosity had not been piqued, no one would have been hurt, much less killed. There would merely be some damage to a portion of the sanctuary."

Silence. "But what," said Zoo, after a few moments, "if the procession had started on time? The bishop and my brother would have arrived at the altar just a minute or so before the explosion. Wouldn't one of them have noticed the bomb . . . or any out-of-the-ordinary object?"

"Possibly," Zack conceded. "But speaking personally, I doubt I would have paid any attention to it. As I heard one priest express it recently, this is the age of the Plastic Church. In the old Tridentine Mass that most of us grew up in, one large missal held all the words that would be used for any Mass throughout the year. It even contained all the sung prayers for the celebrant and his assistants.

"Nowadays, there's a lectionary for the readings, another book for the Mass prayers, and another containing the prayer of the faithful that takes place just after the homily.

"My point is: It is not strange that there would be objects in the sanctuary whose purpose would be known only to whoever put them there."

"A good point, I think," said Koznicki. "We are, after all, acting as Monday morning quarterbacks, in that we know there was a bomb and that it exploded, killing one person. To us now this is all a fait accompli. In retrospect, it is natural to think that we would be alert and suspicious about every small object that might appear strange or odd. Whereas, in actuality, as far as those who were participants in the ceremony and had places reserved for them in the sanctuary, they probably *would*, I think, tend to overlook objects we might now consider foreign to the ceremony.

"But," Koznicki added, "that is not to say that choosing this method to commit murder didn't involve a heavy risk of failure."

"Right," said Zoo. "Our presumption is that somebody wanted to kill someone who was part of this service today. Centering and focusing on that one person—whoever it may be—the perp could have simply shot the man on the street, in his home, wherever. We read about such things in the papers every day: So-and-so was shot while standing on his porch, while walking down the street, while driving his car, while at work. Or so-and-so was found drowned in his bathtub; the police suspect foul play.

"Murder—or attempted murder—by bombing a church simply doesn't happen every day, or every year, or even every decade." He held up one hand as if to forestall dispute. "I did not say that church bombings do not occur, or that there are not deaths as a result. What I am saying is that church bombings as a means of killing one specific target are so rare as to border on the nonexistent.

"Of course, there is always the possibility—although I think it is exceedingly remote—that this bombing did not target any specific individual—or individuals. It is possible as in the bombings of Southern black churches, for instance, that the perpetrator wanted to make some sort of general statement, send a message, express some sort of nasty attitude.

"In which case," he concluded, "in being concerned with specific timing we could be barking up the wrong tree.

"Besides, an attempted murder like the one today can go wrong more often than not.

"We've explored some of the ways it could fail. And there are many more possibilities. In any case, the perpetrator is taking a big chance with a bomb. Yes . . ." He nodded as if to himself. " . . . the use of a bomb is a special consideration in this case.

"Now," he continued, "it's too bad—for our purposes—that so many people appear to be familiar with how a church procession works. That opens the door to lots of possible assassins.

"So"—Zoo turned his attention to George Wheatley—"it'd be a good idea to take a closer look at what happened with the procession. It was fortunate the delay occurred. But why was there such a late start—"

A hesitant knock at the door interrupted Zoo's question.

"Come in," Zack Tully invited.

Judging from his appearance and demeanor, the young man who entered had to be one of the Wheatley clan. Indeed, it was the younger son. In his mid-to-late teens, he was the only one of the Wheatley progeny who had chosen to attend his father's ordination.

Nan Wheatley had explained that Richard was indisposed. And, he did appear to be under the weather. His shirt was unbuttoned at the neck. His tie hung askew. His hair was rumpled and his countenance was marked by a deathly pallor. In short, the young man gave every evidence of having very recently been very sick at his stomach.

"This is Richard, our younger son," Nan Wheatley said, smiling at the lad encouragingly.

Richard hurriedly scanned the room, nodded, and took a seat next to his mother.

SIX

I N THE AWKWARD SILENCE THAT FOLLOWED, Richard finally coughed nervously. "Sorry I'm late. Got a little shook up. Actually, I was doing pretty good until I saw that guy on the stretcher. He was so messed up I guess I just lost it." He hesitated. "Did he . . . does anyone know . . . uh, did he make it?"

"No, dear," his mother said in a consoling tone. "He died."

"Oh. I'm sorry. Was he Roman?"

"Yes, dear."

Koesler was not the only Roman Catholic in the room who felt strange being identified by an adjective rather than the accustomed noun.

"Is everybody else okay?" Richard inquired.

"As far as we know, yes." Nan was now holding one hand of her husband and one of her son.

"Where were we?" Zoo said.

Koesler picked up the ball. "I believe we had determined that a great number of people would be familiar with the procession that opens nearly every liturgical event. At least in the Roman Church." He was beginning to find it somehow refreshing to be Roman rather than Catholic. It seemed to level the playing field. The Episocopalians felt justified in calling themselves Catholic. And, in fact, they did so at Mass and in their prayer life. So if they could tolerate being designated as Anglicans, Koesler, for one, could live with being known as a Roman. It *was* refreshingly different. And since there was going to be a good deal of talk regarding the two communions, things would get cluttered if both sides constantly referred to themselves merely as Catholics.

"Okay," Zoo said, "let's get on to the next, and maybe the crux of this business: Why the delay? What held up the procession? It was thanks to that delay that there was only one death instead of multiple deaths and injuries—"

"Excuse me," Father Tully interrupted. "I think I know where you're going now: George—Father Wheatley—was to be the star of today's show—"

"We're taking this step by step," Zoo broke back in. "And yes, the next logical step is in Father Wheatley's direction."

"And I'm suggesting that there's someone else you should consider first."

"And that is—?"

"Have you forgotten that according to the Liturgy, there would have been more than one person standing directly in the bomb's path?" It was strange, when Zack was assuming an authoritative role, how much the two brothers resembled each other.

There was a moment's pause.

"You?"

"Me."

"How do you figure? As far as I'm concerned you could have been in the classical wrong place at the wrong time. What would motivate anyone to murder you?"

"Race." Zack's voice was emotionless.

"Race?" Zoo sounded slightly puzzled.

"We do have the same father."

"Well, yes, but—"

"True, I can pass. But I've never done so. I'm mulatto, and to some people that means I'm a nigger."

That word once allowed in otherwise polite society by now was used meaningfully only by the rankest of bigots. The word enunciated here by Zachary Tully, a priest, jolted this group like a stinging slap to the face.

"You're saying," Zoo stated, "that you could have been the target. That the bomb could have been meant for you?"

"Yes. That's very possible. And if the supposition is true, it would be a fatal mistake to overlook it."

Zoo shook his head. "You've been here, first in residence, then as pastor, for—what?—three years now. Why would any nut wait all this time to attack you? You've never had any trouble along these lines . . ." Zoo's forehead knotted in sudden suspicion. " . . . have you?"

Clearly, Zachary was deeply concerned. "Yes, I have. I just haven't told you or Anne Marie about it."

Zoo found this revelation difficult to swallow. "But . . . when? Why? How long has this been going on?"

"I didn't get any feedback while I was filling in for Bob Koesler when he went on vacation. But"—he turned to Koesler—"after you retired, Bob, and I became pastor"—he turned back to Zoo—"maybe three or four months after—the letters and phone calls began."

"What sorts of letters and calls?"

"The letters consisted of words cut out of newspapers and magazines and pasted on notepaper. The calls were from some man whose voice was muffled so I could hardly understand what he was saying, let alone identify him."

"How often would he contact you?"

"I don't even know for sure if it was the same man every time. There was no regularity, no routine. Usually, if we had anything out of the ordinary . . ."

"Like . . ."

"A festival. A novena in honor of St. Joseph—the parish's patron saint. But especially if we sponsored a program that had something even peripherally to do with race: social justice, mixed marriages—that sort of thing. It was as dependable as sunrise: I'd get a letter or a call."

"Have you got any of those letters? Did you keep them?"

Zack's reaction was as one who had failed at something very important and vital. "No . . . none." He was crestfallen.

Zoo was both angry and frustrated. "We could have helped you. By this time, we could've had that bas—" Zoo caught himself. " . . . that guy—locked up in Jacktown." Zoo was almost clenching his teeth. "Zack, what were you thinking of? You know you should've given that stuff to me!"

Now Zack was like an adolescent being lectured. "I didn't want to worry you. Particularly, I didn't want to worry Anne Marie. Besides, as time went on and nothing happened, I thought maybe the guy had given it up."

"Not likely," Zoo said. He shook his head. "In light of what happened today, you're right, Zack: This gives the situation an entirely different slant." He turned back to the others.

"I was given to understand that there were strong feelings against Father Wheatley and his move to join the Catholic Church." His tone was now near belligerent.

Koesler almost winced. He knew he was going to have the devil's own time trying to be conscious of that term "Catholic." But he had entered upon the process of becoming sensitive to the terms "Catholic" and "Anglican" or "Episcopalian."

"He did seem the overwhelming choice as designated target," Zoo went on. "But we still have to account for the delay in starting the procession. You may or may not have been the intended victim. But why didn't that ceremony begin on time—"

Once again a knock. This time a uniformed officer opened the door to admit two people, a young man and a younger woman.

Nan Wheatley dropped the hands she was holding and rose to greet her other two children.

The young man was Ronald Wheatley—"Father Ron Wheatley," as Nan referred to him. He was "Ron" to his immediate family and familiar friends. But whenever there was the slightest chance that his professional status would be unclear to strangers, Nan always tacked on the "Father."

Nan crossed the room to put a protective arm around her daughter's shoulder. "And this is our daughter, Alice."

Father Koesler was the only one present who was familiar with the entire Wheatley family. He had worked with George in touching all the bases in the elder Wheatley's quest to become a priest in the Roman Church. During that process, Koesler had met Nan Wheatley about the minimum number of times. And none of those times was it a purely social visit.

Koesler was aware that Ron was an Episcopal priest and that Alice, too, was preparing for that vocation. However, were it not for their relationship to George Wheatley, Koesler undoubtedly would have been unaware of their existence.

Ron physically resembled his mother. Both were tall and slim, with chiseled features. They were attractive people.

Ronald's clerical suit was impeccable; his trouser creases looked as if they could cut steel. Just the right length of French cuffs peeked correctly from the sleeves of his fitted jacket. Silver cuff links in the shape of a cross were occasionally visible.

Keeping in mind his vocation, Ronald—Father Ronald Wheatley—was power-dressed.

Alice, on the other hand, resembled her father. Even her voice, deep for a woman, had the same sonorous quality. Neither father nor daughter seemed concerned with their appearance. George Wheatley had gone to pot early on. He was by no means gross or obese. Nan chose to look upon her husband's waist as nothing more than left-over baby fat. His girth was not muscular or particularly flabby; it was just . . . there. George was comfortable with his bulk—and with his life, for that matter.

This unconcern with appearance did not work as well for Alice.

In her early twenties, she could charitably be described as being on the far side of zaftig. Less charitably, she clearly was overweight. At that young age she should have been as attractive as she ever would be. Instead, she just didn't quite make it. A solid program of exercise and diet would have done wonders. Instead, most of her time was spent studying and snacking.

The heavy, black frames of her glasses didn't help. Her face was round and full, making her resemble a female Charlie Brown. Or, per-haps, a triple-decker snowman.

This, Father Koesler's initial appreciation of the young woman, may not have been kind. But it was incontrovertible.

Alice's entire demeanor seemed to indicate that she was missing out on the fun of being young. Koesler put himself in her place and regretted the course she had chosen. After college, she had embarked on a seminary career that would require three additional years of study. She was now completing the first of those years.

Ron and Alice seemed breathless, as if they had been running, or at least walking rapidly.

"Are you two all right?" Ron was addressing his parents.

George nodded.

"We're fine, dear," Nan said.

"Was anyone badly hurt?"

"A priest was killed," Lieutenant Tully said. "The priest who was murdered"—Tully used the verb deliberately—"was Father Joseph Farmer."

"A Roman?" Ron asked.

"What?" Even though the term had already been used during this gathering, so unfamiliar was Tully with this subidentification that he could not have provided an answer to Ron's question.

"A Roman, as distinct from an Anglican," Father Tully explained to his brother. And then, to the young man, "Yes, he was a Roman."

"Anyone else seriously injured?" Alice asked.

"Not as far as we know just now," Zoo replied. Then: "Where have you two been?"

The identical question was on Walt Koznicki's mind.

"You mean Alice and me? What right have you—" Ron Wheatley was on his way toward being defiant and uncooperative when he thought better of it. "I was driving around," he said calmly.

"Going nowhere?" Tully asked.

"As a matter of fact, yes: going nowhere."

"You did not intend to attend your father's ceremony?"

"That's why I was driving around—aimlessly."

"Which was . . . ?"

"I couldn't make up my mind whether to attend.

"The time to begin the *ordination*"—evidenced in his tone was an abundance of distaste—"came and went. And that settled things as far as I was concerned. I would have driven home. But my mother called my cell phone number. Of course, the bomb had just gone off so she couldn't tell me much more than that. But it was enough to get me over here."

"You came here directly?"

"No, not directly. My sister is staying at the Pontchartrain. It's just a few minutes from here. So I picked her up."

Zoo turned to Alice, who still stood in the protective embrace of her mother. "What were you doing at the Pontchartrain?"

"I flew up from Dallas. I'm a student at a seminary there."

"So you're an out-of-towner. It seems probable that you would stay with your parents . . . or your brother."

"Yes." Alice seemed impassive. Being questioned by a police officer in a rectory where a bomb had just exploded didn't seem to rattle her.

"So why didn't you stay with one or another of your relatives?"

"The main reason is that I wasn't sure I would attend my dad's *ordination*." Her tone was almost identical to her brother's. Was she parroting his sarcasm, Zoo wondered, or was the sentiment her own?

"I knew she was in town," Ron volunteered. "I phoned her. We talked about what Dad was going to do. We agreed that we both were uncertain about attending. She didn't want to stay with our folks and feel pressured to accompany them.

"Likewise she didn't want to compromise my decision. So she stayed downtown. The idea was that the Pontchartrain is close enough so that she could wait till the last minute to decide and still taxi here in time. Matter of fact, I wasn't even sure I'd catch her in. But I did. We came straight over. And"—with a gesture—"here we are."

"So," Zoo said, "I assume you both were alone at the time of the explosion. You have no one who could testify that you were in transit and not at the scene?"

"What!" Ron's anger was instant. "If we had been in the church then, don't you think someone would've seen us? We don't need an alibi for being alone and away from this place. We simply weren't here."

"There were a lot of people milling about," Zoo suggested.

"This is purely outrageous!" Ron's anger was escalating. "I am a priest. My sister is a seminarian. And we're talking about our father. You are suggesting that we tried to kill our own father. Killing *anyone* is out of the question. Killing our *father*—patricide—why, the very idea is a gross insult to both my sister and me." The words were uttered as if they were bullets.

"This is a murder investigation, Father," Zoo said calmly. "We ask questions . . . lots of questions. You're going to have to get used to this. You are not the only ones who may get angry about being questioned. We are going to get whoever did this. And, in order to do that, we must ask questions. Get used to it, Father; it's going to happen."

Father Ron Wheatley and his sister looked daggers at Lieutenant Tully. They were furious . . . and deeply insulted. The lieutenant didn't care. His mind was occupied with bringing the bomber to trial. And it didn't help that his brother the priest had just revealed that he'd been the target of threats to his safety and even to his life.

This investigation had too many loose threads. Zoo dedicated himself to tying up these loose ends and getting to the bottom of this. "Now . . ." He took a deep breath and dived back into the cause of the delay in the ceremony—a delay that seemed to grow more important by the minute. "Now," he repeated, "we were just at the point of determining what caused the delay . . ."

"You must know," Zachary Tully addressed his brother, "that delay is mother's milk in churches. Just drawing on my own experience, I'd say that far more ceremonies start late than start anywhere near on time."

"I know, Zack. But we can't dodge the fact that this delay made a lot of real difference."

No one picked up the verbal ball. Everyone seemed to be waiting for someone else to either take responsibility or suggest some hitherto unsuspected cause.

At length George Wheatley said quietly, "I'm afraid it's my fault."

All eyes turned toward him. No one was more surprised than Zoo Tully. He had never heard George Wheatley speak.

But the others were more than conscious of the resonant quality of that voice. There were those who, with some humor, called it, "the voice of God." The implication being that if God were to speak in human voice, this was what it would sound like. The phenomenon was that such a stentorian instrument should be packaged in so unlikely a box.

To look at the hitherto silent George Wheatley, one might expect his voice to be reedy, perhaps even shrill, possibly even not particularly attractive. But when George Wheatley spoke—even merely cleared his throat—it was, indeed, "the voice of God."

Koesler was interested in what George had to say. He also was content to sit back and listen to this magnificent organ.

Still, no one had asked the obvious question: Why did George think he had been responsible for the seemingly all-important delay?

Zoo Tully, who, with no challenge from former Inspector Koznicki, was heading this investigation, shook off his amazement at the quality of the man's voice. "Why do you say it's your fault?"

"Well," George said, "it was the phone, really."

His children—all three of them—broke up in laughter.

It must be an inside joke, thought Koesler. Certainly there was nothing intrinsically funny about answering a phone.

Lieutenant Tully experienced the same bewilderment: What was so funny about answering a phone?

"You must excuse us." George Wheatley too was chuckling. "It's a bit of an inside joke. I have a nasty habit of answering a ringing phone."

"Whenever it rings," Alice said.

"No matter what's going on," Richard added.

This interrogation had been so deadly serious, literally, that everyone was grateful for the levity.

"The classic example," Richard said, "happened when we were in a rural parish, up around Port Huron. It was eleven o'clock on a cold evening. We kids had gone to bed. Mother had taken our two dogs—two *big* dogs—out for their final run of the night. Suddenly she called to my father—so loudly we kids woke up. Dad went running out—"

"We were living on about two acres—fenced in," said Alice.

"Right," Richard continued. "It was pitch dark . . . big oak trees all over the place, so there was not even any moonlight to see by. It was almost impossible for Dad to see where Mother was. She couldn't have jumped that fence unless one of our lives depended on it. But that wasn't the case. Mother and the dogs were out there somewhere."

"We wanted to go out and help, but we knew better," said Alice. "And then we heard Mother yell, 'George! The dogs! They've cornered a possum!' It was obvious she was at wit's end."

"And then," Ron joined in the story, "the phone rang."

The Wheatleys broke up again at the memory.

George grew sober. He was not at all proud of his contribution at this point in the story. "I know it sounds silly, but I couldn't help it. I went back inside to answer the phone."

"He left Mother, the dogs, and the possum out there in the dark, and came in to answer the phone!" Ron summed up.

"I regretted it," George said, "the very instant I got back in the house. I knew I had made the wrong decision. I knew it. But by that time there was no turning back. So I picked up the phone . . ."

"Was it worth your while?" Father Tully had been caught up in the flow of this incident. "I mean, who was on the phone? An emergency? A sick call?"

"Well," said George, "that's just the point. I had no way of knowing whether it might be a sick call or some other emergency. That's why I was so torn over which way to go."

"So, who was it?"

"A wrong number."

Now everyone, including even Nan Wheatley, laughed.

"And then?" Father Tully prompted.

"Well, of course, I got back outside as quickly as I could. From all the racket—Nan yelling and the dogs barking loud enough to rouse the dead . . . well, I started wondering whether we were waking the neighbors.

"Whether or not we were didn't really worry me at the moment. I finally located the foursome. It appeared to be a tableau: a lot of noise, but not much movement.

"Nan was trying to hold the snarling dogs back. The possum, cornered up against a pile of logs, seemed willing to wait for the first one of the three dumb enough to dare those bared razor-sharp teeth.

"I took hold of the larger dog's collar in hopes that that helpful gesture might win me a bit of absolution."

"Did it?"

"It did not—at least not then. Informing my wife that it had been a wrong number didn't help either. Not until much later. It took years before we were able to laugh at it all." He turned to his wife. "Nan was the last to find any humor in the incident."

Lieutenant Tully looked thoughtful. "Who beside your immediate family knew of your compulsion?"

Wheatley likewise looked thoughtful, then smiled. "Almost anybody who knew me or worked with me. As I recall, I've even written about it in my column, and mentioned it on my radio program. Now that I think of it," he added, "I've heard from several readers and listeners who say they suffer from the same addiction."

"Did you ever," Zoo asked, "discover what in your past might trigger such a compulsion?"

"No . . ." George looked around the room, stopping to focus on Fathers Tully and Koesler. "I thought you two priests might have the same difficulty."

"Not this kid," Tully said.

"Yes," Koesler admitted. "I suffer from the same compulsion . . . though I've never had a wife to bring me to my senses."

Everyone laughed.

"It may," Koesler said thoughtfully, "just be that it was a different era. When I was ordained there were a lot of priests around." He paused. "We didn't think there were all that many at the time . . . we didn't know what was to come.

"Anyway, my first assignment was to a large parish with three active priests. So you were on duty for emergencies every third month. But when it was your month to take calls, you were expected to go when called . . . false alarms and all.

"So I, for one, can understand why you went for the phone.

"On the other hand," Koesler said, "I can well understand that your wife wasn't just yelling for you to come and see how mystical the moonlight was." He smiled. "It was a difficult call. I'm only glad I didn't have to make the decision."

Everyone seemed a bit more relaxed. The anecdote seemed to have loosened up the group.

Lieutenant Tully brought them back to the present. "You were going to tell us about a phone call that came just as today's ceremony was about to begin."

"Yes." Wheatley grew grave. "It rang about seventeen after four—a little more than ten minutes before the procession was due to start."

"Four-*seventeen*? How can you be so certain—so precise?"

"When the phone rang, I glanced at my watch. I do that often . . . consult my watch . . . or a clock. It's another of those compulsions, I guess."

Koesler was beginning to like George Wheatley more and more.

"So," Tully pursued, "by your time it was a little more than ten minutes before starting. Why would you answer a ringing phone in a house that, at least for the present, was not yours?"

"Oh, I didn't answer it, Lieutenant." He smiled. "I admit it took all my resolve not to pick it up. But I didn't."

"Yes . . . ?" Tully encouraged.

"A young lady in a white jacket . . . one of the catering crew, I guess. She answered the phone."

"You know her name?"

"Not the slightest clue. Just one of the caterers."

"Okay."

"She told me the call was for me. That struck me as odd. But remember the dogs being held away from potential suicide while I opted for the phone."

"Was this call from someone you knew?"

"That's what I assumed. But I couldn't tell: Something was wrong with the voice."

"The voice? You couldn't tell whether the caller was male or female?"

"Unh-uh. There was something vaguely familiar about it . . . but it sounded . . ." His brow knitted. "Well, it sounded sort of like—you know: those electronic gadgets used to disguise a person's voice. The ones they use on TV to protect someone's identity. They backlight the person so you can't identify him or her by sight. Then they mix up the sound. The result is that the subject is shielded from identification.

"But as I say, Lieutenant, our conversation was not long enough for me to get a fix on who it might be. It could, I suppose, have been somebody who had a congenital problem with his voice . . . or maybe someone with a vocal cord injury—or someone covering the mouthpiece with a handkerchief. The end result, in any case, was that I had no way of knowing who it might be."

"You said 'his.' It was a man?"

Father Wheatley sat silent in recollection. "I think it was . . . I assume it was." He looked up at Lieutenant Tully. "All I can tell you is that it didn't sound like a woman."

"Okay," Tully said. "Someone—we don't know who, just yet anyway—phoned you shortly before the procession was about to start. What did this person want?"

"To go to confession."

"That close to starting time?"

Wheatley shrugged. "Yes. We in the ministry"—again he nodded to Fathers Tully and Koesler—"must be pretty used to that sort of thing." He turned back to Lieutenant Tully. "It can't be all that different for the police. Your time is their time. It doesn't matter that you're eating or going off duty or busy on another case. There's this person who needs you *now*. Then you're faced with the decision: Shall I listen to this insistent person, or go on with what I'm doing?"

"You agreed to hear this person's confession? I mean, you could have taken care of . . . that person . . . let's suppose for convenience the caller was male: You could have taken care of him after the service."

"I am well aware of that, Lieutenant. But this person—he—sounded truly distraught. At the end of his rope . . . perhaps literally."

"You thought he might be suicidal?" Koesler asked.

"I really thought he was. I can't remember all he said verbatim. But I got the definite feeling that he was at the point of doing himself serious harm. Yes"—he nodded—"to the point of taking his own life."

"But," Lieutenant Tully said, "the ceremony was only minutes from starting."

"I know. And I knew that then. But"—Wheatley shrugged—"remember the dogs and the ringing phone.

"He assured me," Wheatley returned to his narration, "that it wouldn't take long. As a matter of fact, he insisted it would take no more than a couple of minutes at most. The urgency concerned where he had to go and what he had to do next—after confessing to me. His meeting with me was of eternal significance. Heaven and hell. He said he was calling on his cell phone from just outside the rectory.

"I didn't hesitate. After all, what is a moment or two on earth compared with eternity? So the procession would be delayed a few minutes. It wouldn't mean the end of the world. But denying him those few moments meant to him—apparently—salvation." Wheatley looked almost stricken at the thought.

"I hope," he said after a moment, "that I have adequately described what went on in my mind. You have to realize, Lieutenant, none of us had the slightest inkling that there was a bomb. Furthest thing from anyone's thought. For me, the scales were clear. On one side, a soul in agony. A person, a human being, an immortal soul redeemed by Jesus Christ, was crying out in agony for a hearing. On the other side was the minor inconvenience of a patient congregation, most of whom were accustomed to services that began late."

"So," Zoo summed up, "you agreed to see him."

"Well, not so much *see* him. I told him I would wait for him in the office immediately to the right of the rectory's front door. I told him I would be seated with my back to the door so he could protect his anonymity if he wished."

"And then?"

"And then I told Bishop Donovan that I was indisposed—which, by then, was the truth. I told him I would be back in a few minutes. And I added lightly, 'Don't start without me.'"

"Just out of curiosity," Father Tully asked, "what did the bishop say to that?"

"He said mine was not a very auspicious beginning in the Roman Catholic priesthood."

"Did he smile?"

"*Does* he smile?"

"And then?" Zoo prodded. "What happened then?"

"I went to the office and took my position with my back to the door. And I waited. I watched the time pass on the clock on the mantelpiece. If the caller was indeed just outside the rectory eager to consult me, he was taking a strange way of keeping his part of the bargain.

"I waited for almost fifteen minutes. If the caller had any intention of consulting me, I had given him ample opportunity. Keeping a congregation waiting a few minutes was one thing; this wait—particularly since it now seemed that the delay was a hoax—was completely unwarranted.

"Still, I was perplexed—and concerned. Maybe my caller had gotten cold feet—but maybe, just possibly, even after all his pleading, maybe he had done himself harm—or even actually committed suicide. Should I just assume he'd had second thoughts—or should I check outside and make sure there wasn't somebody dead or dying out there . . .

"Finally—it was *not* my finest hour—I recalled Nan and the dogs. So—I left the office and joined the group assembled for the procession. As soon as Bishop Donovan saw me coming, he gave the high sign and we began to move forward.

"And that's when the bomb exploded."

Silence.

"A most interesting account," Inspector Koznicki murmured, just loudly enough to be heard in this quiet room.

Silence.

"Well," Father Tully said finally, "one thing is for sure: There's not going to be an ordination today."

"If not today, then when?" George Wheatley wondered.

"A good question," Father Tully responded. "I think the ball is in the Cardinal's court now. And I couldn't begin to guess what he'll do."

"Our Cardinal can be spontaneous," Koesler commented, "but he's seldom, if ever, capricious."

All heads turned as Anne Marie Tully entered the room. She had not knocked first . . . a sign of how at home she felt in her brother-in-law's residence. Even though Zack was now merely keeping it occupied for the Wheatleys.

"What's going on out there, honey?" Zoo asked.

"The crime scene's been marked. The tape is up. Pretty near everybody's been interviewed. Things look pretty organized. The caterers have been sent home." She paused a moment. "And I'll bet you guys are hungry."

Everyone looked around the room to catch the others' reaction to the suggestion of food. Heads nodded.

"Well," Anne Marie said, "I'd like to invite you to our house. It's in the neighborhood—not far from here. It'll be a little crowded, but we can manage."

Walt Koznicki stood, a commanding figure. "With all due respect, I would like to offer my home. I am sure that Anne Marie would do a magnificent job. But with our house, there is no lack of space. It is one of those old Detroit homes that, along with our neighbors', has been well kept up.

"Besides, it would come as no surprise to Wanda, my wife. She is expecting me to return for supper."

"You weren't going to stay for the reception?" Koesler asked.

"No. My plan all along was to dine with my wife." Koznicki smiled. "For all the many years I was a police officer, I seldom had the luxury of dining with my wife and children. We are trying to make up for those years by being together as much as possible now.

"I would not even be here had not Wanda almost pushed me out the door. She knew that I would want to witness this ceremony." He turned to the Wheatleys with the hint of a bow. "I offer you my warmest welcome. I am sure the department will ensure that nothing like this will happen again . . . not with Lieutenant Tully in charge."

"But, Inspector," Koesler said, "you and Wanda only just returned from an extended trip. Wouldn't this be too much of an imposition?"

"Not at all. Wanda always listens to our police band radio. She will know what happened. She will expect me soon. And she would not be at all surprised that I have invited you to our home. Even as I speak, I am certain she is making preparations for an abundance of food. But, to be certain, I will phone her now and make this invitation official."

He smiled as he looked from one to another of those present. "Does this meet with your approval? And how many may we expect?"

Anne Marie, since she had initially issued the invitation, was first to accept Koznicki's offer. "As long as Wanda is up to it, I'm sure it will work out for the best."

Koznicki beamed. "Fine. And how about the rest of you?"

Koesler raised a hand. "I'll go. Gladly."

Zoo Tully's first reaction was to stay at this site until he was satisfied that he had milked every nuance that the crime scene contained. But, on second thought, he had complete confidence in his squad. And it was quite possible that he would pick up some helpful understanding of all that was going on in this Anglican-to-Roman switch. "I'll come, Walt."

Alice Wheatley didn't look all that interested. "What with one thing and another, I think I'll just go back to the hotel and rest."

"You go to school in Dallas, right?" asked Zoo.

"Yes, the seminary."

"Were you planning on leaving Detroit soon?"

"Yes. I have a flight tomorrow . . . mid-morning."

"We would appreciate it if you would cancel that flight. Postpone your departure. It's possible that you may prove essential to the investigation. If that happens and you're not here, you'd have to make a return flight from Texas. All in all, it would be an expensive trip."

Alice studied the floor. It was obvious she was displeased. Reluctantly, she agreed to stay. "Is it all right if I stay with you and Gwen for the duration, Ron?"

"Of course."

"Good. It's too late to check out tonight. I'll be ready in the morning."

Ron nodded.

Koesler noted a spasm of anguish pass over Nan's face. To a lesser degree the same was true of George. They were embarrassed that their daughter, even in an emergency situation, would choose not to stay with them.

"Please," Ron said, "hold me excused also. I have a couple of meetings that need my attention."

Several of those present wondered at that: parochial meetings on a Sunday night?

George patted Nan's hand. "This has been a long, hard day. I think we need an opportunity to stretch out and get some shut-eye."

Father Zach Tully wanted very much to accept Koznicki's invitation. But he felt his place should be at his wounded church. If there were any questions, especially on the part of the police who were still at it, searching for evidence and, hopefully, gaining new information, Zack felt he should be available.

So he tendered his regrets and left the group for his first look at the damage now that the dust had settled.

Richard Wheatley had not expressed his feelings. By this time, several options were open to him. He could, of course, ride along to the Koznickis'. Or, he could go home with his parents. Or, stretching it a bit, he could ask to stay with his sister and keep her company before she returned to the hotel.

Finally, he decided his best chance for a good time was in the Koznicki household.

He had the grace to ask his parents' permission, after being assured that Zoo and Anne Marie Tully would drive him to and fro.

It would be a restless Sunday night for nearly everyone.

It was barely possible that someone in this group might let drop something that would be helpful. Or . . . was it possible that one of these people was responsible for the whole thing?

SEVEN

ALL THE LIGHTS HAD BEEN TURNED ON. Still, it was difficult to see inside the church. Particles of dust and powder seemed suspended in air.

Police officers and members of the Bomb Squad stirred up even more debris as they probed and assembled what was left of the damaged area of the sanctuary of Old St. Joseph's church.

A small but fixed smile lingered on Father Harry Morgan's face. His companion, Father Daniel Reichert, was tired to the point of exhaustion.

"It's like God vomited," Morgan stated.

"I beg your pardon?" It seemed that Morgan was bent on trying to shock Reichert. First that remark about the Catholic Church being dead, and now this. "Harry, don't you ever get the feeling that we humans push God beyond the point of endurance?"

"Well, not really. I've always thought that, in the end, God can take care of Himself."

"Yes, I suppose. At Judgment time. But take the Flood: God decides that His creation has fouled everything up. So He saves the nucleus of His creation and lets the rest perish in the Flood."

"You have a point."

"Or, take Sodom and Gomorrah. The two towns are steeped in unspeakable sin. So He destroys them with hellfire and brimstone."

"But you're forgetting, Harry, that He always anointed someone—Noah in the one case, and Lot in the other—to survive and build again."

"I'm not forgetting, Dan. That's us."

"Us?"

"Certainly. And if not us, then others who will restore sanity and holiness. But sometimes we go so far wrong that God's infinite patience is exhausted."

"How can infinity be exhausted? That's an Irish Bull."

"A figure of speech."

The two slight men, all in black, were so camouflaged in their obscure nook that both the police and Bomb Squad were more or less unheedful of their presence.

Father Zack Tully knew they were there, but didn't feel drawn to conversing with them.

Tully actually was helpful in explaining to the officers exactly what had been destroyed and where certain objects had stood before the explosion displaced them.

"Why did you say this reminds you of God's being nauseated? What a revolting metaphor!"

"Think it through, Dan. This is one of the oldest parishes in Detroit. It's been designated a historical site. Think of the good priests who've served here over the years. Noble men. Faithful to the Church and its infallible teachings. Then think of what's happened since the sixties. Think about that."

Reichert thought about that. "The Council. That damned Council! Upset everything."

"But God's been patient. He gave us a Pope who could see all the value that was lost. Most of all, he picked men who would return us to so many things that had been discarded . . . men who became good and faithful priests, bishops, Cardinals."

"True. But what's that got to do with what's happened here?"

"Think it through, Dan . . . think it through. Think of the pastors they've had here. Koesler didn't make too many mistakes. But he gave away too much power to the people."

"A mistake. A very definite mistake."

"Then they bring this Josephite priest in from Dallas, and right away they have to have guitar Masses, folk Masses. For all we know he may be holding Masses with pizza and Coke!"

"Would we know about that if he did?"

"They couldn't keep it a secret forever."

"Lord, God!"

"But the worst was yet to come. And it happened this very day. And that's why I think we have sickened God. If God had not intervened,

George Wheatley would have been transformed from a heretic to a Catholic priest. And just think of the package that he would've brought with him."

Reichert's face betrayed uncertainty.

"He is married." Morgan was impatient. "He brings his family with him. There goes the sacred institution of celibacy.

"Ordinarily, the saving grace would be that he opposed ordination for women. But this guy . . . his daughter is only a little more than two years away. And Wheatley supports her ordination . . . along with any others of the weaker sex who want to desecrate the Sacrament of Holy Orders.

"And that, Dan, is the reason the power of God was manifest here today. We have so turned away from God's evident will that we have sickened Him. Remember what the Lord said: 'I will vomit you out of my mouth.' That's what He did today . . . in a symbolic sense, of course."

"Fathers . . ." Zack Tully startled Reichert and Morgan, who had been intent solely on their own conversation and nothing more.

"Fathers," Tully repeated. "The police are concluding their investigation. It's time for us to clear out."

Reichert and Morgan started to stand. But they had been seated so long and the damp cold had so penetrated their bones that both of them evidenced difficulty. Tully reached to assist them. Reichert was realistically grateful. Morgan was stubbornly fussing. "We can get along very well on our own. You've got us on the shelf now. But you just wait: There's a new breed of priest, and a new kind of bishop who will return this one, true, holy, and Catholic Church to its own. You wait and see!"

Tully was taken aback. He had stayed in his own section of the church, up near the front where he could be of help to the police. Also, that had given him the perfect pretext for not talking with the pair.

But it was time to leave. And that was the straightforward announcement that he was making. Only to be hit by an admonitory warning that, as far as he was concerned, was gratuitous and ad hominem.

Tully sensed their reluctance to leave. Of course he could always ask the police to ease them out. But perhaps, with a little patience . . . "Exciting time today, wasn't it?" he commented, offering entree to more innocuous conversation.

"It certainly was," Reichert agreed.

Morgan, however, was unappeased. "Do you suppose that you and your knee-jerk supporters will heed God's warning and turn away from this heinous sin?"

"To which heinous sin are you referring?"

"Why . . . why . . ."—Morgan was incensed—" the ordination of a Protestant minister into our priesthood. A person whose aim is to destroy celibacy and ordain women!"

"You're getting yourself all worked up over some possible conclusions of a procedure that is entirely kosher."

"What do you mean?" Reichert asked.

"*Our* Catholic Church"—Tully stressed the possessive—"has created a Pastoral Provision that makes it possible to ordain priests and ministers of other denominations into the Roman Catholic Church. All we were about to do today was to follow the procedure sanctioned by Rome to accomplish this."

"Mark my words," Morgan warned, "you will live to regret what you're trying to do."

Reichert was tiring noticeably. "Come on, Harry," he urged. "We've had a long day. Time to mosey on home."

"I suppose you're right," Morgan growled.

"You've had a long day, all right," Tully said, ushering them toward the exit. "You must've been among the earliest to arrive."

"Yes, we were." Reichert shook his head. "I had the damnedest time trying to find the john in this place. When you get to my age, the old bladder makes demands that you can't ignore. I finally had to use one of the bathrooms in the rectory. I left Harry here to find us a good vantage for the event."

"I got the impression," Tully said, "that you went by yourself to find the john. Harry made of sterner stuff?"

"I can hold my water," Morgan stated.

"He certainly can," Reichert agreed. "We probably wouldn't have gotten such good seats without Harry's self-control."

"I recall seeing you two in conversation with Bob Koesler," Tully said.

"Yes. Bob directed us to an even better location," said Reichert. "But it really is time to go." He turned to Morgan. "Better check and see if we've got everything. Got your breviary?"

"Didn't need it. Got my prayers said before we started. How about your coat?"

"Oh, yeah. How about that box you brought along?" He looked about uncertainly. "I don't see it."

"The box?" Morgan seemed suddenly perturbed. "Oh . . . that was an alb I'd borrowed and used here at St. Joe's for old John Marshall's funeral. Took it home and had it laundered. I returned it today. Come on . . . let's go."

They left. Tully started to lock up. So, he mused, Morgan was on his own for some minutes early in the afternoon. And he was carrying a box. Interesting . . .

Whoever set off that bomb undoubtedly brought it into the church in much the same way that Morgan had returned the alb. Or said he did.

Is that what we're looking for—some sort of a container that could conceal a bomb?

Was that a clue? Tully thought he'd better ask somebody on the Bomb Squad exactly what he should be looking for in the way of such a container.

EIGHT

ALICE WHEATLEY chose to walk from St. Joe's to the Pontchartrain. The weather did not invite walking. But Alice's innards were churning. She thought the air, fresh and brisk off the Detroit River, would help calm things a bit.

Among the events and circumstances she had very definitely not anticipated was that she would have to stay over in Detroit for an indefinite period before she could return to Dallas and her studies.

Now she would have to phone the seminary to get an extension of her leave. Ordinarily that would not be a problem. The dean, as well as the faculty and staff, ordinarily bent over backward to be helpful. But, ordinarily, the occasion was not a parent who was converting from the Episcopal to the Roman Church. That fact, plus the caliber of the man they were losing, had put some noses out of joint, making things most awkward for Alice.

She recalled her nervousness and hesitation when she'd knocked at the dean's door. She entered, to be confronted by a stern and disapproving clergyman.

She explained how she felt her presence at the event was required, even though, when she'd first learned of her father's plans, she had been bitter and livid. So angry had she been that even if she were in Detroit during the ordination ceremony she was not certain she could bring herself to attend.

She said she had given this a great deal of thought over the months that her dad had been studying Roman Catholicism and jumping through hoops. She felt there was something she must contribute to this ordination ceremony.

Finally, and most convincing, she felt the seminary would lose some credibility in ecumenical circles should the dean refuse permission for her to attend.

But the understanding had been that she would return on Monday. "No later than Monday," he had stressed.

Now she felt trapped.

She had planned and expected—and wanted—to return, but Lieutenant Tully had not minced words. Further, she faced the risk of having to come back to Detroit whenever her testimony was needed in the investigation.

She would simply have to convince the dean that, while in no way could it have been foreseen, she had to stay over. The decision was out of her hands—as it also was outside the seminary's purview.

She didn't doubt that when she explained all this, eventually the dean would agree. She just didn't relish having to ask for permission.

As she walked along Jefferson Avenue, she pulled the collar of her coat tight around her neck. Not only did that give added warmth, it hid her seminarian's collar. People were prone to stare at the sign of her religious garb.

She was proud to be in seminary. She was eager to become a priest. And she hoped that one day soon the sight of women clergy would be taken for granted. Just as it was with men. But for the time being, particularly when she wanted to be left alone, she raised her collar as much for privacy as for warmth.

So lost in thought was she that before she was aware of it, she had reached the hotel.

As she entered her room, she heard the shower running. A voice called out, "Hungry?"

Alice dropped her purse and her coat on a chair. "Hard to say. I should eat something. But I don't feel like it."

A head peered around the corner. "What was that? I couldn't hear you."

"I said I don't think I have an appetite. But I ought to eat something. Do you want to go downstairs—or shall we order in?"

"Room service sounds good."

Alice kicked off her shoes and dug her toes into the deep carpet. "Fine with me. Got the menu?"

"In the desk drawer."

"Okay." Alice opened the drawer and took out the menu and began to scan it.

"I didn't know what happened to you. You were gone when I woke up."

"Yes . . ." Alice hesitated. "I went for a walk earlier. I was trying to make up my mind about several things."

"Including whether to attend your dad's ordination?"

"Yes. Then I decided I wouldn't. I *couldn't*. But . . ." She leaned back in the chair. ". . . by the time I decided not to attend, it was too late anyway. So I came back here."

"And then the bomb exploded."

"Yes. And then Ron phoned and took me over there." She looked up. "I'm surprised the phone didn't wake you."

There being no immediate response, she closed her eyes. Then she opened them again. "It was on TV already?"

"Yeah, they cut into basketball and hockey games for the breaking news. A lot of jocks were pretty angry, I'll bet. But you were there—"

She reacted unexpectedly. As if she were going to deny being there. But she said nothing.

"You were there. How are your mom and dad—and Richard?"

"They're all okay. None of them was hurt."

"Did the cops question you and Ron?"

"Uh-huh. And that's where we've got a problem."

"A problem? *We've* got a problem?"

"Yes. I've got to stay in the vicinity. Seems they need to have everybody—and that includes me—immediately accessible."

"You mean we're not going to be able to return to Dallas tomorrow?"

"Not exactly . . ." She shuddered as if all that had happened was catching up with her. "I've got to stay here. You don't. I have to cancel my reservation. You can use yours."

"You've got to be kidding. I'm not leaving you . . . especially under the circumstances. You know how air travel is. You never know when the next one will go down. I don't want to leave you . . . and I don't want you to leave me."

Alice sighed. "I feel exactly the same. But it just doesn't make sense any other way. You'll have to go back without me."

"Nothing doing. This is going to be rough on you as it is. My place is at your side . . . through it all."

"That can't happen. I had to cover for us when they told me to postpone my trip. I asked Ron if I could stay with him. He said yes."

"What did you do that for? We could scratch up enough dough to extend our stay here."

"That's not quite half the problem."

"You mean . . ."

"Yes." She shook her head again. "The larger problem is that your name is Sue."

Sue's lips tightened. "We aren't back in the dark ages of a few years ago. Our people are, by and large, coming out of the closet. When are *we* going to join them?"

"I don't know." Alice ran her thumb along the menu. "I don't know."

An impatient Sue tapped the tabletop. "It's not like you've got a religious problem."

Alice shook her head. "It's not like *I've* got a religious problem. But there *is* a problem. *We've* got the problem."

"You mean because I'm Catholic and you're Episcopalian!"

"That'll do for starters."

"I thought we'd settled on an ecumenical wedding. You surely can get one of your Anglican priest friends. That's can't be too much of a problem. And I think I can solve the Catholic angle."

"Yeah, sure." Alice's voice was flat. "The best thing you could possibly come up with would be one of the inactive guys. Somebody who's retired from the active ministry."

"It's better than nothing. I can't walk away from my Roman roots any more than you can shed the Anglican life you've led."

Alice didn't respond. She merely sat with closed eyes as if waiting for a sword to descend.

Tears formed in Sue's eyes. At twenty-one, Sue was not seductively attractive. With a little effort, she could've been. She hardly ever wore makeup, and when she did it was no more than lipstick. Her hair hung to her shoulders. It was periodically cut, never styled. Her clothes covered her modestly, without accentuating her well-proportioned figure.

There was no compelling evident reason why Alice and Sue loved each other. They just did. Indeed, that might be one of the unfathomables about people falling in love: They just do.

Alice and Sue did.

"Let's talk about it," Sue said finally.

Alice shook her head. "We've talked about it so much."

"But we shouldn't stop."

"What?"

"Talking." Sue dropped into a chair. The menu had been forgotten.

"Where do we start? At the very beginning?" Alice sang the latter words in the melody from *The Sound of Music*. "That would be a year and a half ago . . . roughly . . . at Western Michigan."

Sue smiled at the memories evoked by the name. WMU. The flagship of the college-heavy town of Kalamazoo. "We managed to pass each other as the proverbial ships in the night."

"For three years, anyway. And then, in our senior year . . ."

"We met . . ."

"In the temperature-controlled library . . ."

"Of the Medieval Institute . . ."

"Carefully rummaging through the rare books section."

The two women had relived their initial recognition of each other so frequently that they could recite the event antiphonally. Both were now smiling. This was a joyous memory. A pivotal memory.

"We ought to be more grateful to the Cistercian monks who donated so much to that marvelous collection," Alice said.

"That was the beginning."

"Then we began to learn how much we had in common."

"It helped that neither of us had a boyfriend at the time."

"That opened the way for us to be girlfriends."

"And then we discovered why we never seemed to be satisfied with any of the boys we dated."

"And then"—Alice concluded that episode in their young lives—"came love."

They paused, recalling what had turned out to be the last uncluttered period of their life so far.

"We graduated," Sue said. "Same class."

"We spent that summer as counselors at the CYO camp," Alice said. "Your connections got me the job. And then you decided to come with me to Dallas."

"Yes. There was no way you were going to pass on attending seminary. And I couldn't bring myself to even consider life without you. So, there I was at the University of Dallas.

"Which turned out to be a Catholic university, owned and operated by the Diocese of Dallas." Sue smiled broadly. "And although you were attending seminary, I was at least rubbing shoulders with seminarians, with Hungarian Cistercians as teachers."

"Right," Alice concurred. "We really owe the Trappists a vote of gratitude. They've played an important part in our lives without even knowing how important."

There was an extended silence, during which they sat and silently reminisced.

"Then we woke up . . . gradually," Alice said finally.

"We should've known that religion was going to be a problem."

"It's more my fault than yours or anyone's," Alice said. "I was far more aware than you of the coming conflict. Mixing the Roman and Anglican Churches is like stirring oil and water: It may look promising, but it doesn't work."

"I don't see it," Sue said. "I don't see it because, probably, I can't see it."

"Look at it this way, sweetheart: There is no possible way we are ever going to be able to marry in the Roman Church. They are not—emphasize not—going to ordain women. They are not going to accept married Roman Catholic men into the priesthood. They are not going to ordain married women. And they are not going to allow inactive priests to return to the active ministry.

"Some of those prohibitions are stronger than others. But even if the Roman Church somehow decided to do any or all of these things, they still wouldn't accept our marriage. Not because we are of different—"

"—slightly different—"

"Okay," Alice admitted, "when it comes to Episcopal High Church, 'slightly different' religions. It *is* possible to get a dispensation for an interfaith marriage. But not between two men or two women. I think you know the 'official' teaching of your Church regarding homosexuals—gays and lesbians."

"It's 'an evil.'" But that was conjecture on Sue's part.

"That used to be the official word. In recent years it's softened somewhat. Now, the 'official' teaching is that the state of being gay is not a sin. It may very well not be a gay person's 'fault.' But note the words: *Sin. Fault.*"

"I didn't know the teaching had gone that far," Sue said.

"Yes, it has. The bottom line is: Gays can be gay. But they may never express that externally. In other words, it's okay for a woman to love a woman or a man to love a man. But they may not have sex."

A long silence followed, during which both women sat, eyes closed, each going over in her mind that which they had gone over, verbally and mentally, many, many—too many—times before.

Sue was the first to open her eyes. "Look, Alice . . ." She leaned forward. "Here's where my bottom line is: I wish with every fiber of my being that we could be an ordinary couple, as the song says. I wish whatever worries that enter our lives would just be the same worries everyone has. Like health, security, peace. But maybe we can't have that. Not now, apparently. Maybe sometime.

"But if we separate because we can't be an ordinary couple, I think we will miss the whole point of our lives. If we split up now, we may never be together again. And I don't want that to happen.

"At the same time, I'm talking about sacrifices I would be willing, more than willing, to make. If push comes to shove, I could at least compromise my religion. I know some theologians who suggest a pastoral solution for people like us. People who are prohibited from a Church-sanctioned marriage because Church law hasn't caught up to today's understanding of human nature.

"Maybe, with the guidance of the right priest, I could learn to live with you in good conscience. But we want to be totally honest

94

tonight. We want to be perfectly candid with each other. Could you live with me that way? In good conscience?"

Alice shook her head. Not in the manner of one saying "no," but rather as one just overcome by the enormity, the immensity, the seeming insolvability of it all.

❧❀❧

"I'm trying to marshal my thoughts," Alice said finally.

"The priesthood is a wonderful but complicated calling, at the very least. It is a marvelous vehicle for helping people, for leading people in worship, for patching marriages—where that's possible.

"It also puts a priest in a goldfish bowl. Parishioners expect perfection. They're never going to get it, but still they expect it. You're constantly being evaluated and criticized. The hours are long. In reality, it's not anywhere near nine to five. It's around the clock.

"The point I'm trying to make is that the priesthood—and I'm primarily thinking of the Anglican priesthood, though all this is the same with the Roman priesthood—the point is that it's a demanding profession. And that's just the ordinary everyday demands of this priesthood.

"Let me explain it this way: Suppose two people get married. And I'm not considering a gay couple. A pair of straights. Let's say the man is an alcoholic, or almost one. She marries him because she's confident she can change him.

"So, on top of all the new demands and lifestyle of a newly married person, she has to reform her husband. What would you guess would be the odds that she could carry it off?"

Sue sat back in her chair and folded her arms. She could tell the general direction in which this was heading. She wasn't sure she wanted to hear the concluding argument. But the question had been asked. A response was expected.

"The chances are not good," she admitted. "They're not good for her working a cure for her husband's drinking. And, partly for that reason, chances aren't good that she or anyone could save the marriage.

"But," she continued, forestalling a further statement from Alice, "neither of us is addicted to anything. It's not us."

"It is and it isn't. My point is that a conscientious priest faces plenty of pressure just to do his or her basic sacerdotal job. It's demanding and unrelenting. A good marriage can be very helpful in relieving much of the stress."

"Do you have any doubt that we would have a happy marriage?" She was pained at the implication that their marriage could fail.

"Not for a moment," Alice replied. "What I suggest we do is factor in all the added concerns that we—no, make that I—would have to face."

"Okay. Let's hear them."

"Well, I can't stress this too much." Alice leaned forward as if to better gauge Sue's reaction to all this. "Just about the main thing that could complicate everything is the bishop. Bishops come in all sizes and strengths. Some bishops flat-out refuse to ordain a gay man or a gay woman."

"They can do that? In this day and age!"

"Uh-huh." Alice nodded. "What with one thing and another, they can do just about whatever they want when it comes to the essentials of priestly life.

"Now, granted, my bishop—I say 'my' because he has already virtually accepted me—anyway, he's in charge of the Diocese of Central Michigan. The See city is Lansing. My bishop, by past performance, does ordain gays. He demands a close and meticulous scrutiny before he confers orders. He never gave me the impression that he is open to this across the board. Each case is examined as unique. So, before I get into the ordinary, run-of-the-mill-type priestly ministry, I'll have to pass muster because I'm 'different.'

"Nor does all this mean I will forever serve the bishop of Central Michigan who ordains me. The bishop can and will retire, if he lives long enough. Or he may be translated to another See. In which case, if I were openly gay, I could be in some trouble."

"How?" Sue thought this was cruel. That the bishop's successor could change the rules of the game to suit his own beliefs seemed unfair.

"How could I get in trouble?" Alice was about to clarify her statement. "Honey, in some ways, placement can be more important than ordination."

"Placement?"

"I want a parish ministry. I stand a very good chance of getting such an assignment. But what if the bishop gets angry? What if a bishop wants to punish me? What if he removes me from the parish and puts me into a jail ministry, or seminary assignment—or places me on his own staff at the Diocesan Center?"

"Isn't there anything you could do if that happened?"

"Remember now, I'm gay."

"How could I forget?"

"I emphasize the gay issue because of what might be termed an 'official' stand of the Episcopal Church."

"Which is—?"

"Which is that the Church is, theoretically, guided by the biblical ideal. It's not a position carved in stone. Very few things in Anglicanism are inflexible. And nothing in Anglicanism is infallible in the Roman sense.

"But, for instance, there's the question of experience in the matter of gay priests."

" 'Experience'?"

"It's been fairly constant that when a gay priest is accepted in the average parish, a number—sometimes a goodly number—of parishioners walk."

"So let them walk."

"Easy enough for us to say. But there's been a steady drop in attendance and membership in the Church. For reasons as diverse as gay pastors to the changes in the Book of Common Prayer.

"To try to sum this up, there is an element of risk in what we face. Not completely unlike that married couple we were talking about a little while ago.

"No matter how beautiful a marriage may be, there's always an element of risk. All of a sudden, a couple is asked to give up a lifestyle peculiar to the single state in favor of a radically different lifestyle peculiar to the married state.

"It's a gigantic leap. And it involves a risk. When you complicate that by one partner's having an alcoholic addiction, the risk increases tremendously."

Sue rose from her chair and began to pace. "So what you're saying—what you want me to understand is that the bare bones of the priesthood is very demanding."

"Exceptionally so."

"Okay, I can see that. So are lots of other jobs. Police, firefighters, doctors, nurses—and most of the other service positions, as well as marriage and parenthood—all of them are demanding and involve risk."

"A cop straps on his weapon and walks out the door. He may never return. Same with firefighters. The special demands of living intimately with another person or having the responsibility of nurturing a child—all of that involves risk—"

"And now you're going to tell me that people accept these risks, most of them successfully."

"Yes."

"But I'm trying to tell you that our case is different. Our problems multiply because we are gay. Just being as we are might not carry too heavy a burden were we to occupy almost any position in life excepting the priesthood. Remember: Self-righteous parishioners reject the entire ministry of a person, no matter how much dedication and special talent, just because his or her orientation is different."

Sue stood still and faced Alice. "Yes, I understand all that. But I submit that for what we will gain, we can accept all the challenges they can throw at us. Alice, sweet, how many chances will life give us to find the perfect partner? You and I, we've got that now. We can't let it slip away."

Minutes passed in silence. Each woman tried to carefully pick the next direction of this brutally candid conversation.

Finally, Sue spoke again. "So far, just about all the negative things you've said involved the consequences should we come out of the closet. We've talked about marriage and we've talked about being open for all to see.

"We've talked about the bishop's reaction. We've talked about parishioners. I take it it's pretty well certain that some of your prospective congregation would leave the parish if not the Church. And that's a consideration the bishop would have to deal with.

"Now . . ." Sue began pacing again, this time more slowly and deliberately. " . . . now let's suppose that we go right back to the beginning—"

"The beginning?"

"To just after you came in the door a little while ago."

"Oh . . . okay."

"Your proposition was that you stay in Detroit for as long as you're needed, while I return to Dallas."

Alice nodded.

"The unfairness of that is what set me off: Why should you be forced to shoulder this burden by yourself when I could be here to help you?

"What I propose now, dear, is a return to the status quo. I'll go back to Dallas tomorrow. We'll keep in touch by phone until you return. And after that we go back in the closet and stay there to the best of our ability."

Another long silence.

"The best of our ability," Alice said slowly, "may not be enough."

"What can you mean? Not being pushy, keeping our distance, respecting the sensibilities of others—even if they are modern-day Pharisees—should be enough for any bishop or parishioner.

"I know you want me. And I know you want to be a priest. And I assume there isn't that much difference between the degree of desire. What I'm suggesting is a delicate balance . . . for everyone's sake."

"There's something more, Sue." Alice spoke deliberately.

"What?"

"My father."

❧❀☙

Sue realized her mouth was hanging open. "Your father?"

Alice's face was squinched as if she was searching for words. "It started very slowly and very long ago. I didn't say anything to you about it. I thought it would blow over.

"Daddy began his inner journey to Rome sometime before I was accepted into seminary. He kept his plans very quiet. At first, and for

99

a long while, Mother was the only one who knew. Then, as it came close to the time when he would leave the Episocopal Church to join the Romans, he told me and my two brothers.

"Naturally, we were shocked. Richard took the news better than Ron and I did. Of course, Richard wasn't as intimately affected. But then that was to be expected; Richard was never really involved in any organized religion.

"Ron was knocked for a loop. Mostly, I suppose, because he's been running for bishop for a long while. But that's another story.

"I must confess, I was livid when Dad told us. My reactions were totally negative. I regarded him as a heretic, a traitor! I hated him. I hated him because he had been the model for my vocation. I wanted to grow up to be like him. We even resemble each other." She shrugged. "So, okay, we're not that great-looking—"

"You are as far as I'm concerned."

Alice's lips turned in a downward smile. "That's what love will do for you.

"I wanted to have a radio show," she went on after a moment. "I wanted people to come to church to hear me. Everything Dad did so well, I wanted to do, too. Here I was, entering seminary, and he dropped this bomb.

"Eventually, at seminary, word got around. I don't think it was deliberately cruel, but they really started to hit on me."

"Who?" Sue was surprised that people who were studying for the priesthood could be so mean-spirited, so . . . so *unchristian*!

"Just about everybody. A teacher would say something like, 'The apple doesn't fall far from the tree.' Or classmates would ask me when I was going to nail my theses to the church door—

"Oh, not all of them; many were quite decent; others seemed unaffected.

"Why would they do such a thing? Your dad doesn't threaten them. It's *his* life to lead." Sue stood facing Alice, legs apart, hands on hips, in a combative stance.

"He *does* threaten them," Alice insisted. "First, his departure is a gigantic loss. Dad is famous—at least on the local scene.

"I suppose, with one thing and another, he is well known and recognized through the radio show, the newspaper column, his reputation as a top-notch speaker. At least much of the state of Michigan knows of him. He's known far more widely in the whole country as far as the Episcopal Church is concerned. There was a time when he was being seriously considered for a bishopric."

"He was? But he didn't get it, obviously. What happened? Did whoever runs that process guess right, that he was going to defect? That's a remarkable feat of foreknowledge . . . or did your dad tip his hand early on?"

"No." Alice shook her head and stared steadfastly at the carpet. "He could have had the position if he had wanted it. But he didn't. It was clear to us, his family, that he wanted to remain a simple priest.

"My point is that the Church considers him an exemplary churchman. They—clergy and laity—feel a great loss at his leaving. You know," she said after a moment's thought, "I doubt they'd hurt so badly if they could just understand the impetus behind his move."

"You mean, if he were leaving like most of the others—as a protest against the ordination of women."

"Yes, I think so. It's just . . . not being able to understand his reason. You see, he has no problem with women priests. He was the first to encourage *me*. There's no scandal either. He hasn't taken advantage of women or children. He has no evident problem with any of the theology of the Episcopal Church. And, so far, I don't think he has explained his position in any clear way.

"Even those who want to understand him can't seem to. So a goodly number of Episcopalians deeply resent what he's doing."

"Even so," Sue said, "that's between them and him. It doesn't have anything to do with you."

"His opponents—clerical and lay—have made it my business. I was as surprised to be treated the way I have been as you are to hear about it.

"This is the bottom line. The effect of my father's journey to Rome is spilling over on me. So, all the hesitation I've felt about us—

you and me—particularly our potential coming out—is intensified immeasurably.

"Not only would we face the risk of alienating future parishioners—if I were called to a parish by an understanding bishop—but I'm afraid there would be a lot of mistrust. People would tar me with the same brush they'll use against my father . . ." Her words dwindled off into an uneasy silence.

"It doesn't matter," Sue stated finally. "Even if you said you never wanted to see me again—"

"I couldn't do that. I know that's the direction I was going in . . . but I couldn't do that. What I felt had to happen—that we had to go our separate ways—I hoped would come from you. I hoped that after I painted as black a picture as possible, you would take the initiative and call it quits. I couldn't do it myself."

"What I was about to say . . ." Sue moved to Alice's chair, bent over, and embraced Alice protectively. "What I was about to say," she repeated, "was that if you told me to get out of your life, I would respect your wish. But I would never really leave you. We would always be together. In some way."

Tears trickled down the cheeks of both women.

Sue stood, and brushed her tears aside. "Isn't there anything we can do about your father? I mean, there really isn't anything we can do about us. Except, maybe, try to stay out of the spotlight, as it were, and in the closet.

"But your father . . . you know him much better than I. Is there anything possible that might change his mind . . . change his situation?"

Alice bit her lip. "I thought something was going to happen . . . but it didn't. On top of that, I'm quite sure that he doesn't know about us. Oh, he knows that we're close friends. But if he knows we're lovers, he certainly is keeping it to himself."

"Maybe he's keeping quiet on purpose," Sue argued. "Maybe he's waiting for you to say it's time. He might even bless our union, even though that would be pressing things, especially in the Roman Church."

"Nothing so convenient," Alice responded. "As a matter of fact, I'm quite certain that he disapproves of a gay relationship. I never asked him. I was afraid if I showed any obvious interest in this lifestyle, he might guess that I'm gay. I've heard him argue the question. His stand is: If someday scientists can say without hesitation or question that some people are genetically programmed toward gay relationship and sex, he might . . . in fact *would* reconsider. But, until then . . ."

Sue shook her head. "He's the only movable piece in this chess game. We've got to find some way of handling him."

"Let's forget about Daddy," Alice said, as she took Sue by the hand. "We've got tonight. Let's not waste it."

NINE

WALKING HAND IN HAND WITH SUE toward the bed brought back a long-forgotten memory.

One of her earliest recollections was being put to bed by her father. She needed nothing more to bond with him. Of course there were many other occasions when the two grew close.

The Wheatleys were a family that visited during meals. George encouraged his children to talk about what was going on in their world, to discuss events with their parents and with each other. Nan listened, corrected, and loved.

All three children wanted—even vied for—their parents' attention. But Alice, particularly, felt that she was her father's special favorite. That feeling was reinforced at bedtime. Nan was always there to tuck them in. George made it a point to do likewise as often as possible—when there were no parochial meetings or banquets to address.

But he always made special time for Alice. And somehow he managed to do this without making the boys envious.

It became routine. When she no longer needed to be carried, he would take her hand and accompany her up to bed. He would tuck her in and then tell her stories. Stories often from books she would later read when she grew older. They meant so much to her when she read them because from babyhood they had been served up to her with love and in the most beautiful voice imaginable—her father's voice.

Sometimes he would sing to her. He sang all sorts of melodies. The pop songs with which he'd grown up. Snatches of operatic arias. Everything but the music of her age. He told her—and she never forgot—what Jimmy Durante once said to Frank Sinatra: that rock and roll consisted of three chords, and two of them were bad.

Those memories were evoked now as she held Sue's hand. But not just those memories; a flood of images washed over her—images of her parents, especially of her dad.

As a child, only gradually had she begun to understand what her father was doing in church. At first she was dumbfounded and mystified to hear the churchgoers calling him "Father." She was afraid to voice this puzzlement. Her big brother was not hesitant to poke fun at her. She waited, and listened for someone, anyone, to ask the question, and satisfy her curiosity.

Eventually, she came to perceive that he was Father to his congregation, leading them in prayer, in eucharist, and through life's trials and crises.

But she would always be his special girl.

She was endearing in so many ways. But she was not a beautiful child in the accepted sense. Her peers, with characteristic thoughtless cruelty, sometimes picked on her. She always found refuge and support in her father's lap.

If she had been born just a few years earlier, she would have bumped up against the iron curtain that blocked women from the Episcopal priesthood. But, as it happened, she was born in the late nineteen-seventies; the barrier had been breached in the mid-seventies.

The walls came a-tumblin' down when eleven courageous women were ordained without official approval by a retired bishop or two, who at that stage of the game had little if anything to fear. Up till that time in the Anglican Episcopal Church, girls could yearn all they wished to follow in their priest father's footsteps, but their wishes were for naught. As for the Roman Catholic Church, a girl's chances were definitely less than nil.

Once ordained, the original eleven posed a problem that nagged for a solution. After some little thought and a lot of prayer, the House of Bishops acknowledged the validity of the women's orders and they became the charter members of a growing society of female priests. This solution also was ratified by the Anglican mother Church.

The Roman Catholic Church stands fast in its prohibition of women as priests for the specious reason that Jesus did not ordain any women, and that women do not resemble men.

Alice Wheatley was spared all this folderol by the accident of her birth date.

She never knew the initial frustration of being unequivocally barred from the priesthood. Like many of her generation, she was oblivious of the bravery and determination of the women and the bishops who had brought all this about simply by not asking permission. They just went ahead and did it. And changed history.

Thus, in practical terms, Alice was free to select the priesthood as her vehicle for life. And, following the example of her dad, she did. She graduated from Western Michigan University cum laude and went about the business of selecting a seminary for the three-year training that would lead to ordination.

First, she discussed the selection with her father. She explained that she wanted to attend a seminary far from home. He was so popular and so successful that she feared she would always be compared with him to her detriment. There was enough pressure being a woman seminarian without the added association with her father.

He tried to talk her out of this. He did not share her concern over comparisons. On the contrary, he felt he could help her in many ways. But in the end she had her way.

She was accepted by the Dallas seminary. She was happy. Her life was on track, proceeding nicely, as planned.

And then her father dropped the bomb.

Alice and her brothers knew something of great importance was in the offing when their father invited Ron and his wife, Gwen, over for dinner, and said he had something to tell all of them, but not till after they'd eaten.

That meal was not easily digested. Nor was there much chitchat.

After the dishes were cleared, the family gathered in the living room. George was in high spirits. He had fought a painful and lonely battle within himself over the future course of his life.

That battle was concluded, and he was at inner peace. He wanted to share that peace with his loved ones.

He had already talked it all out with Nan. Naturally, it had come as a shock to her. Her life had settled into a rewarding routine that fulfilled her. She voiced her opposition vigorously. Her resistance was overwhelmed by his conviction. Reluctantly, she promised to support him. Hers had always been the motto, "Whither thou goest, I shall go." George's startling deviation was proving the most difficult test of that maxim yet.

The conclave, following The Last Supper, as Alice and Ron later christened it, began with a prologue by Nan. After which, George, with measured enthusiasm, spelled out—as best he could in one sitting—the reasons for his decision.

Ron and Alice were stunned. Richard seemed merely bemused. Gwen, who one might have supposed would be personally unaffected, mirrored her husband's reaction.

Alice would argue she herself was hit hardest. On the threshhold of preparing for a career—a career that had been planted in her heart by her father—she had subconsciously been relying on her dad for support through seminary and into the priesthood. Now, in just a few minutes, her hope—her expectation—had been demolished.

Betrayed! Betrayed by the one person she held most dear in all the world.

Her joy turned to sadness. Her erstwhile tears of happiness were now bitter, burning drops.

Once George had finished his explanation, Ron and Alice quickly abandoned substantive questioning and turned to pleading, begging for a change of heart. Gwen, "the outsider," quietly but incisively echoed their pleas.

To no avail. George was the soul of understanding and compromise in all considerations except the bottom line. Which was that he was leaving the Episcopal Church to become a Roman. If all worked as it should, within a year he would be ordained a deacon, and then a priest in the Roman Catholic Church.

He expounded on what a tortuous journey this had been; in a sense, somewhat similar to that of a domestic priest who becomes a foreign missionary. George hoped that his children would try to understand and, one day, even come to share his sense of satisfaction in having made the right choice.

Richard, when he could get a word in edgewise, assured his father that the move was perfectly all right as far as he was concerned. A typical teenager, he tacitly wondered how his life would be altered—if, indeed, it would be affected at all.

Ron's fury was unabated. He snapped on his clerical collar and stormed from the house, leaving Gwen to follow after observing the niceties of departure.

Alice, sobbing, ran, almost blindly, up to her room.

George looked helplessly to Nan. He had expected a measure of negative reaction. But nothing like this. Had he erred in his presentation? Had he not expressed himself adequately?

Nan could have taken this occasion to once more dispute the wisdom of his decision. She might have supported Ron and Alice, and asked him to reconsider.

But she knew him too well. While he had agonized over his course, he had not once consulted her in arriving at this decision. He didn't want to pull her into this murky world he had created in his mind. He'd gone through it alone, except for his prayers to the Almighty, and emerged exhausted, but content, with his mind at rest.

Once she determined that he was convinced he was on the right course, she knew he would not, could not, turn aside.

She would not stand with her children against their father. She would be at his side. She would assure him: Ron's and Alice's reactions were merely temporary. It was natural and to be expected. They would come around. Give them time.

Having bolstered him, reassured him, alleviated his doubts, she would be the sounding board for the children. She would, as she had so many times before, be the conciliator. It would drain her. But she saw herself as the adhesive that held the family together.

Later that night, all was quiet. Only the faint sound of contemporary music could be heard. This was long after Ron had slammed out of the house and after Richard had gone up to his room to listen to CDs and further weigh how his father's action might change his own young life.

Nan puttered in the kitchen until she could delay no longer, then went wearily up the stairs, spent from this evening's discord.

George, as was his wont, made certain everything was locked and secure. He paused before the closed door of Alice's room. What sounded like low, broken sobs reached his ears. He knocked lightly. He wanted so to tell her a story or sing her a quiet song. He waited, but there was no response to his knock—although the soft sobbing seemed to have stopped. He hesitated. But he would not violate his daughter's privacy.

He moved on down the hall, heartened by his wife's assurance that all would be well. Time would heal.

But all wasn't well. And time would not heal.

TEN

They sat in silence. The sort of silence that all too often was the routine conclusion to angry, bitter words.

He was lost in his own thoughts, she in hers. But their thoughts, their daydreams, were similar. They dreamed of what they'd diligently planned for many years. For both, thoughts of his becoming a bishop had been on their minds from the beginning: It was manifest destiny.

Not only Gwen and Ron, but most of their friends—several of whom were Anglican clergy—simply took it for granted that Ron would not only be a bishop but that he would minister to a significant diocese. Chicago, Los Angeles, or even New York.

The couple had what it takes and they were utilizing those faculties to the utmost.

Gwen toyed with a spoon while memory led her back to her childhood. She saw the small farm in central New Jersey where she had grown up, an only child. Her father ran the farm with the help of his wife and, eventually, his daughter. She saw the primitive building where she had attended grammar school.

Not only did her father own and operate the farm, he was the pastor of the only church in that farming community. Those who preferred one of the mainline religions could drive some distance to one of the villages or larger towns that were not a natural part of the farming life. Gwen's father knew his Bible—and could relate the biblical teachings to life on the farm. So many of the Gospel stories involved fields to be planted, crops to be harvested, trees that were fruitful or barren, and many like examples that were second nature to farming families.

Clem Ridder, Gwen's father, was addressed as "pastor." He possessed neither diploma nor ordination. He was the only one in that backwoods farming community who had read the entire Bible. Cover to cover. Three going on four times.

It was for this feat that he had been acknowledged—not elected—leader of this ragtag congregation. He received no salary for his preaching. He was given the collection money, which might buy a plump chicken for Sunday dinner—except that the pastor already had chickens on his farm.

Gwen's Sabbath memories were of a day devoted to worship. She would slip into one of her cousin's hand-me-down dresses, all of which were far and away measurably better than anything Gwen owned. Then it was off to the small decaying shack that served as a church.

The Ridders would meet with ten to twelve other families—give or take a few—and conduct their services.

Clara Ridder led the hymn singing. She had a lovely, clear voice with only a hint of vibrato. Gwen accompanied her mother on the ancient pump organ, half of whose stops were inoperative. Gwen was, by and large, self-taught, although her mother had given her a few lessons to begin with.

Clara was a mousy woman. She was continually reminded of the many biblical passages about woman's place. Rumor had it that Clem Ridder beat his wife—just to get and keep her attention.

For cause or groundlessly, he would also switch or strap his daughter. "Spare the rod . . ."

The Ridders' income was roughly the median income of that community. Gwen didn't realize they were poor; she had nothing to contrast it with.

Gwen's grammar school comprised three rooms—three grades to a room, from kindergarten to eighth grade. As older students learned the multiplication tables, history, English, etc., Gwen, with her quick, retentive mind, learned them, too. By the time graduation neared, she was tutoring her classmates. This practice of helping her fellow students would continue throughout high school.

Every Christmas the students drew names to exchange presents. In the sixth grade, one classmate, a loutish boy who was always picking on her, drew Gwen's name.

Part of Gwen's morning routine included milking the two cows, gathering eggs, and, in the winter, breaking the ice in the watering troughs. What with all that, Gwen barely had time to wash up and grab a quick breakfast. Thus, more often than not, she looked a little grubby, her clothes a bit untidy, her hair unkempt, and her fingernails badly in need of a manicure.

That was the reason—and it did not escape Gwen—that her spiteful classmate's Christmas "gift" to her was nothing more than a large but flimsy kitchen matchbox filled with dirt.

The little monster's "present" gave added meaning to the maxim, "Kids can be cruel."

Gwen kept her face emotionless; she wouldn't give the rotter the pleasure of knowing how much he'd hurt her.

Two years later, Gwen went off to high school. The boor took his eighth-grade education and went off to work in his father's gas station.

At first, high school was frightening for Gwen. It was so large. Each class even had its own room.

Gwen may not have had a carefree childhood, but she had a significant number of pluses. By anyone's standards, she was bright, even brilliant. She had learned well many lessons, some from the schoolroom, others from the school of hard knocks.

Something else happened gradually over the years, with some subtlety. Gwen had grown into a smashingly attractive young woman.

She started slowly. For years she was as skinny as the proverbial rail. Pert, with straight blond hair and icy blue eyes, she participated in every sport available, from softball to field hockey. Still, she was, as another nasty classmate observed, "as flat in front as she was flat behind."

All that was to change. Gwen was about to fill out like an inflated balloon and grow curves in all the right places.

By the time she graduated from high school, as valedictorian, she was almost incredibly beautiful—a knockout. Motion picture perfect.

Now, she could call her shots. The very first was to leave home. As soon as she stowed her mortarboard and packed her suitcases, she was out of there.

One of the girls Gwen had tutored had become pregnant in her junior year. She left school, married the baby's father, and moved with him to Detroit.

That couple, Dan and Frieda Young, now were a foursome with two young babies. They lived in an upstairs flat in Detroit's inner city. The flat was too small for the Youngs and their children, let alone another adult. But Frieda remembered with gratitude Gwen's patience and help.

The Youngs had a verbal battle that almost ended in a Mexican standoff. But Frieda had the last word, and Gwen became a nonpaying boarder. At least for the time being.

About a week after Gwen moved in, Frieda had to take both children to the doctor for a checkup. Gwen, wary of Dan, volunteered to accompany them. Frieda wouldn't hear of it. The doctor's visit would use up the entire morning, and Frieda knew that Gwen's job-hunting schedule was full.

By the time Frieda and the kids left, Gwen was dressed and almost ready to go. She was applying her lipstick when, in the mirror, she saw his face behind her.

It happened so quickly. He was all over her, forcing her toward the bed as he spewed the filthiest language at his considerable command.

She managed to turn and drive her knee into his crotch. He fell, moaning, to the floor. She gave him one final contemptuous glance, stepped over his writhing body, grabbed her purse, and ran out the door.

As she left, she knew that this day had to be it. She would have to find work *and* somewhere else to live. Staying here after this was unthinkable.

Luck was with her. She found a secretarial position with an up-and-coming law firm. And, that afternoon, she took a room at the Y. Not that much better than the Youngs' flat, but without Dan. That in itself was worth the price of admission.

She returned to the flat to retrieve her clothes. She figured correctly that Dan would have recovered sufficiently to go to work. In any case, Frieda was there with the kids. She was thrilled about Gwen's job and her new residence. She helped Gwen pack and all but pleaded with her to come back for visits.

Gwen would have agreed to almost anything if it would hasten her departure before Dan's return. But privately, she was certain she would never darken this miserable hole again.

Gwen settled into her work and went apartment hunting. She found a nice enough place in short order. Now she had to plan the rest of her life. What was she aiming for on a long-term basis? Admittedly, there were many opportunities for a person with her talents, not to mention her looks.

One of the most memorable moments she had experienced in high school was career day, when successful adults visited the senior class and talked about their occupations. One of these visitors was an author who told the teens how difficult it was to make a living as a writer.

The piece of blank paper, he explained, was "the enemy." The young people discovered that just gazing out the window could constitute work; they wouldn't be daydreaming, they would be creating. Then there was the infamous writer's block. At such times, the professional does not put his or her work aside—not if he or she is truly a professional. The truly professional writer works through the "block."

Then there were questions. The author was asked to clarify his statement that the empty sheet of paper is "the enemy."

He confessed that he had never seriously or successfully written nonfiction. If he had, he said, then the paper would not have been a blank. In nonfiction there's always something there . . . something that has dimensions. In a biography, for instance, the writer does not have to create Abraham Lincoln; Lincoln had actually lived. There was something: a person, a slice of history, a war, a dynasty, etc.

It was fiction that was his subject. It was fiction that depended wholly on the imagination or the author's experience.

If that be the case, the visitor was asked, what advice would he give to the prospective writer of fiction or nonfiction—but especially fiction? He answered in one short sentence—a sentence that Gwen never forgot: Go with what you know.

She had not put that maxim to work in her life so far. But now that she was searching for something that would constitute a vehicle for her life, she wondered if she might profit by testing this advice against her own existence.

What had she learned from personal experience?

First and foremost she had learned "religion." On an organ or a piano, she could play nearly all the mainline religious music . . . hymns of almost all faiths.

She knew the Bible, cover to cover, as well as or even better than her father did. From the time she was a tiny child, her father had read to her from the Good Book. And once she herself was able to read, her parents saw to it that she read every word in the Bible—again and again.

This backgrounding so formed her maturation that it was overwhelmingly "what she knew." If she were going to follow that author's words to live by, she would have to learn just how she should "go with what she knew."

The bottom line: Somehow or other, she had to find a religious vehicle to carry her through life.

Admittedly, her experience was a mixed bag. Her father's was a hellfire-and-brimstone, pulpit-pounding faith. That he had read the entire Bible many times did not necessarily mean that he had profited spiritually from it.

Indeed, take the Bible from his hands and he would have been as mean a person as anyone might encounter.

"Go with what you know." She knew how brutal, unforgiving, and selfish "religious" people could be. From that, she felt she could aspire to the opposite extreme. She would know how attractive, kind, forgiving, and unselfish truly religious people could at least strive to be.

So she would shop around. She sensed that this might be the turning point for her. Her next decision could be crucial.

She didn't even bother investigating Roman Catholicism. No matter how good, how warm and welcoming, a specific parish or priest might be, there were all those rules. Besides, there was every possible reason to believe there was no future for women in the Roman Church.

She tried Methodist, Lutheran, Presbyterian, Baptist, and a few other Protestant and even Orthodox Churches, but none seemed compelling.

She was saving one for last. Underneath it all, the closest she could come to the ideal, for her, was the Roman Church . . . except that she could not tolerate Rome's discrimination against women.

Of equal consequence was their celibacy rule for priests. Gwen did not need to become a priest to achieve fulfillment in faith. Though it did appear vital for her plans that she have a priest for her husband. But not just any priest. She had to be attached to one who was, within his Church, going places.

This final point was crucial and, she thought, was possible under the Anglican—or, in the United States, the Episcopal—Church.

There was one final distinction. In the Episcopal Church there were three divisions: the Low Church, which everyone acknowledged as a Protestant Church; the Middle Church, which seemed to float between Low and High; and finally, the High Church.

That, she concluded, was the one for her. Particularly after the changes that followed the Second Vatican Council, High Church Episcopal was considered more Catholic than the Roman Catholic Church.

Having found the proper arena, she now had to find the proper priest.

In her recently amassed circle of friends were several young female Episcopalians. Gwen, the silent guest at every possible gathering that included these women, plugged into them. As often as possible, she primed the pump to get a lead on any possible consort.

It was bridge night at Gwen's.

Just as Gwen was disciplined in planning her life, she was disciplined in living her life: Her apartment—a place for everything and everything in its place—was always spotless. Gwen was not neurotic about it; she merely preferred to be ready for any eventuality; after all, you never could tell who was going to come to the door. Visitors, contrasting Gwen's apartment with their own living quarters, always left feeling a whit second-rate, occasionally even downright intimidated: Each knew her own housekeeping would never measure up to Gwen's.

If truth be known, the girl who had once shoveled out cow barns and chicken coops now considered housekeeping beneath her. When, eventually, she married wealthily, all that would be seen to by housekeepers or maids, or at very least, a cleaning lady.

Roughly half an hour ago Gwen's three guests—Rose, Beth, Mary—had arrived within minutes of each other. Of this number, only Mary was actually there to play cards. Gwen could take or leave parlor games. Rose and Beth preferred conversation; cards merely provided a gathering point.

Gwen set out finger food she had picked up at the deli. Her guests sat around the small coffee table chatting. Which was what Gwen wanted them to do. Mary eyed the card table eagerly. She wanted to play. But what else was new?

Gwen had recently picked up a Book of Common Prayer, and placed it on the lower shelf of the coffee table. Since the table's top was glass, the book could be easily seen.

"Oh," Rose exclaimed, during a lull in conversation, "you've got the Book!"

"Thinking of coming over to our side?" Beth kidded.

"Really, Beth," Rose said, "before we get to proselytizing . . . we've never talked religion. For all we know, Gwen may *be* Episcopalian."

"We have, too, talked religion," Mary replied. "We've just never gotten deeply into it." Mary could testify to the truth of this statement; the talk had too often interrupted their bridge hands—even on occasion interfering with bidding.

"As a matter of fact," Gwen said, "I have been getting interested in the Episcopal Church. I just got the Book to see how you pray."

"Come to any conclusions?" Rose asked.

"What I've read I've liked, I can tell you that," Gwen said.

"This is a swell snack," Mary said. "Maybe we can bring it over to the card table," she segued hopefully.

"They tell you," Beth said, "that it's a good idea to steer clear of talking about religion. But since you introduced the Book into this evening, just what religion are you? I mean, we're all Episcopalians. But you know that."

Gwen smiled. "That's a tough one. I guess I belonged to the 'Church of Where It's at Now.' My daddy was the preacher man. And I'll give him this: He did know his Bible. And he made sure I did, too."

"So, you're a Bible thumper." Rose laughed lightly.

"I guess. But what I'm interested in is finding a church that makes me feel at home."

"There are any number of those," Beth said. "The only way I can think of doing this is to shop around."

"I've done that. With every other religion but the Episcopal."

"Well," Rose said brightly, "that's right up our alley. We should be able to help you . . . even suggest a shortcut or two."

Mary picked up the snack tray and moved it to the card table.

The others grinned. They knew when it came to cards, especially bridge, Mary was a no-nonsense player. Without further comment, they relocated, placing their chairs around the card table. Gwen got a tray table for the hors d'oeuvres.

It was Beth's turn to be Mary's partner. Mary flipped cards to all four players. She dealt herself the first ace. She would deal the first hand. And so she did, after a quick shuffle.

"We might just start right at the top," Rose said, returning to the subject at hand. "The best of the Episcopal parishes."

"And that would be . . . ?"

"St. John's in Ferndale," Rose replied.

"It's not far from here," Beth added.

"One thing about St. John's," Rose said. "It's crowded . . . especially the Masses and services that the rector conducts."

"He's that good?" Gwen wondered.

"Every bit as good and better than any other priest you could find."

"His name?"

"Wheatley. George Wheatley," Beth identified.

"Oh . . ." Gwen tapped the tabletop. " . . . that name is familiar. Where have I heard it?"

"He has a radio program," Rose said "A call-in talk show. It's very popular. And he's got a column in the paper every Sunday."

"That's it," Gwen said. "I haven't heard the radio show, but I do remember reading his column. It's really quite good, isn't it?"

"I think so," Rose agreed. "I like it that before he reminds you that you're a sinner in need of forgiveness and repentance, he tells you funny little stories, anecdotes, some of his experiences—"

"One club," Mary bid.

"Is he married?" Gwen asked.

"Oho . . . o . . . o," Rose and Beth exclaimed simultaneously.

"So *that's* what you're looking for," Beth said.

"You should've told us that in the beginning," Rose said.

"One club!" Mary drove home her point.

"You're not looking for the father." Beth giggled. "You want the son."

"I beg your pardon?"

"George Wheatley is very much married," Beth explained. "Mrs. Wheatley—Bernadette—is very much his wife. They have a teenage daughter who plans to attend seminary herself. And a younger boy, the Last of the Mohicans . . . I think he's in middle school—"

"But the one you want," Rose interrupted, "is Ron Wheatley, a priest."

"He's George Wheatley's son?" Gwen asked.

"George's and Bernadette's. Yes," Beth said.

"Are we playing bridge or not? I bid one club!" Mary was definitely serious about her game.

Rose studied her hand for a few moments. "Pass."

"It took all this time for you to pass?"

"Anyway," Beth said, ignoring Mary's sarcasm, "Ron is not married."

"What a waste!" Rose said.

"A waste?" Gwen asked.

"He's a hunk!" Beth enthused. "Oh, don't get me wrong: He doesn't belong on Muscle Beach. But . . ." She grinned like a cat considering a plump canary. "Nice broad shoulders. Million-dollar smile. Lots of dark wavy hair. A six-footer. And"—the cat advanced on the canary—"a nice, tight bottom."

"And the profile"—Rose caught the fervor—"don't forget the profile."

"Carved out of stone. Perfect. Definitely his mother's son."

"Well now," Gwen said, "I've never met or even seen Father Ron Wheatley. But they run a head shot of Father George Wheatley alongside his newspaper column. Judging from that, the father doesn't hold a candle to his son . . . if what you say is true."

"Granted," Rose admitted. "But when you asked for the best, we told you the truth. George is head and shoulders over his son when it comes to voice, delivery, piety, magnetism, the whole shebang—"

"But then," Beth cut in, "George Wheatley is head and shoulders over just about any member of the clergy you can think of . . . whatever the denomination."

"A question then," Gwen said. "How come such a treasure is only a simple parish priest?"

"You mean," Rose said, "how come he's not where he ought to be? Well, the story is that George Wheatley turned down a bishopric."

"He even turned down the position of canon," Beth added.

"Rose passed!" Mary was looking daggers at her partner, Beth.

Beth made sure her cards were in order, studied them a few moments. "Pass."

Mary shook her head.

Without waiting to be prodded, Gwen looked at her cards briefly. "Pass."

"He just wants to be a parish priest, I guess," Rose said. "I can't think of any other reason why he would turn down such honors, such power."

"That," Beth said, "brings us back to Father Ronald Wheatley. Unmarried—and quite a catch."

"Matter of fact . . ." Rose looked at Gwen. "You two would make an ideal pair." Rose, Beth and even Mary were well aware that no matter how desirable Ron Wheatley might be, Gwen was the more physically flawless of the two.

For a moment, all four women sat lost in an envisioning of the wedding of Ron Wheatley and Gwen Ridder.

Father George would undoubtedly o.
tos of Ron and Gwen, he heartstopping i.
study of perfection in white—would be clipp
sured by young ladies each of whom wished i
just like that.

Back to reality. This wedding hadn't happened.
even met. It might never happen. But if it didn't Gw.
miss their guess!

"One club is the bid," Mary reminded. "Everyone e.
Want to play it? Or give it to us and move on?"

"One bids are tough to make," Gwen said.

"Oh, let's give it to them and move on," Rose said.

"Okay," Mary said. She gave her team twenty points and b.
a sigh of relief. She didn't really think she could have pulled i.
minimum seven tricks.

Rose gathered the cards, and began in leisurely fashion to shuffi.
them.

Gwen removed the tray holding the remains of the tea sandwiches.
As she did so, she thought about what she'd learned this evening.

If George Wheatley had turned down advancement, what effect
might that have on his son's advancement? She would have to launch
her crusade slowly and carefully. She would begin by making an appointment to see Ron: She would take instructions in the Anglican religion.

She smiled to herself. Her beauty would stun him. But she would
play it cool. To this point in her life she actually remained a virgin.
Losing that would have been a terrible price to pay to jump-start a
relationship.

No, Gwen Ridder would offer herself purely and intact to
whomever she eventually would marry.

This opportunity seemed heaven-sent. If Ronald Wheatley was all
these girls made him out to be, she, his wife, would make sure he
became a bishop—just in case he himself had missed the point and the
boat.

He would be astonished at her biblical knowledge. Why, he himself might not have actually read the entire Bible all the way through.

rse it was hard to tell, when one read scattered passages, some ne or another of the books, and others in no particular logical ronological order.

How could she miss? With her looks and her germane knowl- e—dare she term it erudition?—she was tailor-made to become his e. After which she would begin the campaign to raise him to the inence ordained for him.

He would be a bishop and she would be the bishop's worthy consort.

Go with what you know. She was very sure that she was doing just that.

Nothing would stop such an eminently qualified couple.

ELEVEN

R ON AND GWEN WHEATLEY CONTINUED to sit in silence.
It was the familiar conclusion to angry, bitter words.

This capped the end of a most frustrating and ill-fated evening. If anything, Gwen was angrier than Ron had ever seen her.

Staring holes in the kitchen table, Ron's mind returned to happier times. The times at the very beginning.

A phone call had started it all.

She was interested in the Episcopal Church. Could she perhaps begin instructions?

Of course she could. They made an appointment.

As he hung up the phone, he reflected on her voice. It was the most charming and feminine sound he'd ever heard. He was eager to discover what frame and what personality comprised that voice.

He certainly was not disappointed.

It was a Thursday night in the dead of winter. He hurried to answer the door.

There she stood. She almost sparkled. She wore a white coat with artificial fur at the collar, sleeves, and hem. The coat curled around her form in an attractive swirl. Her pillbox might have been a tiara, so well did it set off her face and hair.

She had never been in his church. Of that he was certain. At least not while he was officiating. He couldn't possibly have overlooked her.

They sat across from each other in the rector's study. She had been directed to this parish and to him by a friend. And, no, she didn't think he knew her friend. The friend, in turn, had heard of him from a Mrs. Rogers, a parishioner. It finally came together. He knew Mrs. Rogers.

They set up a series of appointments so that she could understand what the Episcopal Church was all about.

He had no idea what brand of perfume she wore, but the delicate fragrance lingered after her departure. He sat there a long time, alone, enchanted by the scent.

In subsequent visits, she gradually explained her upbringing, her very superficial religious upbringing. He learned that, while she was not E. Power Biggs, she did play the organ and the piano.

He could see how useful that accomplishment might prove in his parish. And—need he confess it to himself—in his life.

She overwhelmed him with her grasp and knowledge of Scripture.

She was perfect. At least as perfect as he could imagine.

In due time she was ready to become an Episcopalian. Actually, she was ready far in advance of her formal qualification. Ron prolonged the instruction period because he enjoyed her company so much. He needn't have worried; she was in no hurry to leave his presence.

So she was accepted into the Church, but kept seeing the pastor. In time they began a serious courtship. He was much more open in revealing himself to her than she was to him. He didn't learn until much later in their marriage that she had layers which only time would reveal.

The beginning, when they first met, was like a fairy tale. He knew nothing of those layers. He wanted to open himself to her, to let her see his ambition.

He recalled particularly a conversation they'd had just before they announced their engagement.

Almost as if confessing a sin, he told her of his goal: to become a bishop. For Gwen, that was the cake under the frosting.

Because he had been so hesitant to speak of this seemingly secular goal of climbing the ladder of success, he now remembered that conversation almost verbatim.

It had been a warm summer evening. They were sitting on a park bench.

"There's something you ought to know about me," Ron began. "I mean, before we get so committed to each other that there is no turning back."

"We're not there yet?" she asked coyly.

"Not quite, I think. It's about my calling."

"I've got no problem with your being a priest. You know that."

"It's more than that. Let me give you a little background—"

"If this is too difficult for you, you don't have to go into it." Actually, it was of supreme concern to her. The sine qua non.

She could help him over any obstacles that might stand between him and the office of bishop. She was sure of that. But he had to have the drive and the desire to go the full way. She sensed that he was about to tell her how he aspired to be a bishop.

She was certain his drive was genuine. That was why she had persevered with him this far. What he was about to say was of supreme consequence to her. No way would she countenance his postponing letting her in on his ambition. For it was hers as much as his.

"Ever since I was a kid," Ron said, "I've identified with my father. That's why I followed in his footsteps. I wanted to go to seminary. He encouraged me. I was pretty successful. The grades were good. The personality development was good. I never had a doubt that I could make it into the priesthood. Everything was A-okay. I had the world on a string." He paused. "Except for one thing: I could never measure up to Dad's accomplishments.

"Take that voice, for instance: It's like an organ played by angels. Now my voice is not at all bad. But people don't come from miles around just to listen to me—"

"You are incredibly handsome," Gwen interrupted. "He is not."

"He's not a gargoyle by any means. As a matter of fact, he is the embodiment of what your country parson should look like. He is comfortable. Like an upholstered chair. His genuine concern for people is consistently evident."

"He's not a saint."

"Close."

Gwen turned slightly toward Ron, relishing his impressive profile. "What does all this have to do with your priesthood?"

"It came to me in my final year in seminary . . ." Ron paused again. "I was in competition with my father. Not that rare in a father-and-son relationship . . . but a bit uncommon when both become priests."

"How so?"

"I've seen a few fathers and sons who are Fathers with an upper-case '*F*.' Usually they are clearly pleased that they are in the same religious profession. They help each other. Defer to each other. Are better friends than in the run-of-the-mill parent-child relationship.

"But that is not the case with George and Ronald Wheatley. And I don't know how the divergence came about. When I was a kid we were really close . . ." He fell silent, in recollection. "Alice did a piece on my father and me. It wasn't her fault. She was the daughter that, it turned out, my father eagerly awaited.

"But I must say, it didn't much bother me. I didn't mind it at bedtime when Dad told her stories and sang her songs. I think we avoided trouble on that level because ours was not a dysfunctional family. Dad, but especially Mother, loved us differently but equally.

"This was also the case when Richard came along. Somehow, Alice and I knew Richard would be the last child in the family. But he didn't get any special treatment because he was the baby. No more than did Alice turn out badly because she was the middle child."

Gwen shook her head slightly. "What a family! Especially compared with mine. From time to time I wonder at what my life would have been if I hadn't been an only child. In the same school of thought that you've been using, I should have been pampered, spoiled." She gave a ladylike snort. "The way things turned out, I was lucky to get out of there in one piece. "Do you know how lucky you are to have the family you have?"

"Of course I do. But no family . . . no one but God . . . is perfect."

"Agreed. But I still don't understand what this has to do with your priesthood?"

"I was coming to that." He picked up his retrospection. "All that time, when I was a kid, admiring my father, everything was fine. If anything, I was extremely proud of him, his natural attributes, his talent, his accomplishments. That attitude remained all through my years in seminary.

"But after I was ordained, it was as if he threw down the gauntlet. 'Outdistance me if you can,' he seemed to be saying.

"Well, I tried. I gave it my best shot. And I found some measure of success. In all fairness, I accomplished more than just about any other priest—excepting only George Wheatley.

"He's the one who had the column in a large metropolitan newspaper. He's the one who had the radio program on a powerful station serving a good part of southwestern Ontario as well as a large section of southeastern Michigan.

"My father had talent to burn. He had only one way to go: to become a bishop. He never mentioned the high office. But it was his for the asking. He didn't even have to acknowledge it.

"Now, you see, I've been flirting with the same goal. But I've known all along that my quest was futile."

"Futile? Why? You would've been the next best thing to your father. There is more than one diocese that needs a bishop."

"I know. But I—discreetly, of course—talked it over with some influential members of the Church. In effect, they told me to cool my engine . . . that I didn't stand a chance."

"But why not?"

"A dynasty. They were afraid of establishing a dynasty. Which could happen if my father were made bishop and then I were to become a bishop, too. And then what about little Alice? Suppose she were to become a priest—and a very competent one, too? There would always be the chance that the electors might eventually turn to her.

"They referred to the Kennedy clan. Joe, the oldest son, was being groomed to be President. He died a war hero. But Jack stepped right in. When he was assassinated, Bob ran, and might well have made it.

"Teddy got the message: It was open season on Kennedys.

"Forget about the death, the assassination. Our hierarchy simply doesn't want a dynasty. When Dad was made a bishop, Alice and I could kiss any similar aspiration good-bye."

"But then," Gwen said, "to everyone's amazement, he turned it down."

"Yes. The time came. The offer was made. And to everyone's surprise he turned it down."

"And you were back on track."

"Yes. The obstacle was rolled away. They wouldn't have to worry about a dynasty. So, my campaign started fresh. My path was clear.

"Now, I'm a shoo-in . . . as long as I continue to do all the right things that a bishop-in-waiting should do."

Ron looked at the kitchen clock. They had been seated in silence for almost three quarters of an hour. For each of them their respective recollections had been like viewing the rerun of a movie—a movie of their past.

Gwen's early life might have been unique in its peculiar circumstances. Her knowledge of a wide range of religious hymns contributed form to her extraordinary familiarity with Sacred Scripture. She saw herself as the wife of an important clergyman. She did not want the ordained life for herself. That would be too confining. She would function better as the power behind the throne. So she had to be most judicious in selecting her consort.

He would have to be the type who could ascend the ecclesiastical ladder to a prestigious level. At the same time, he would have to be malleable to her guidance.

It was not an easy challenge. But she found her prize candidate—and landed him.

Her nominee's father could have been an obstacle to her grand plan. But before Gwen even appeared on the scene, as if by a miracle, Ron's father had taken himself out of the race, leaving the field clear for Ron. Enter Gwen, whose sails caught the wind, and it was full speed ahead for both of them.

And now—! Now George comes up with this . . . this cockamamy notion to desert the Church in favor of the Romans.

Once more Ron's friends in power would tell him that his chances were buried . . . nil. 'The acorn doesn't fall far from the tree' argument. Ron would, after all, be the eldest son of a defector. How could the electors be confident that, having followed in his father's footsteps before, he would not follow in them again?

No argument would be sufficient to sway them. Ron was not the only possible candidate for the office. Yes, he would have made a good, perhaps even a superior bishop. But if not he, others could fill the bill most adequately.

Who could have known that the old man would defect? And that his defection would create yet another impediment?

This is where they were at the moment: Ron and Gwen, all dressed up and no episcopal vestments to wear.

Gwen was unsinkable. She believed firmly that if a door was shut, one should look for an open window.

But all this had sapped Ron's strength. Thus their verbal battle this evening. She had to firm up his resolution.

There must be a way.

❧

No doubt about it, Ron's spirits were at rock bottom.

He had wanted for so long to be a bishop.

He had counted his lucky stars that he had found Gwen. Or vice versa. It didn't matter; the point was that he had a life's companion who was all but tailor-made for her role. And to top it off, she entered fully into his ambition to go places in the Church.

They had shared this roller-coaster ride. Yet she seemed as resolute as ever. He marveled at her endurance. It was due mainly to her steely determination that they would continue to go forward.

That didn't matter to Ron.

It was time for him to take the reins and do something on his own. Something effective for a change. Something that would prove to her that he was his own man. That he could play the role of the leader in this twosome.

What did it say in Scripture about one who wanted to be a bishop? Something from Timothy . . . Ah, yes: "This is a true saying, if a man desire the office of a bishop, he desireth a good work. A bishop then must be blameless, the husband of one wife, vigilant, sober, of good behavior, given to hospitality, apt to teach; not given to wine, no striker, not greedy of filthy lucre; but patient, not a brawler, not covetous; one that ruleth well his own house, having his children in subjection with all gravity; for if a man know not how to rule his own house, how shall he take care of the Church of God?"

There was more. But this was the pertinent excerpt: "If a man know not how to rule his own house . . ."

How true.

Am I going to be the leader of this house as the Bible describes what I want for myself and, now, for Gwen?

There could be only one answer.

Gwen sensed that the time for remonstrating was long past. Now was the time to shore up their resolve. "There are so many things that could happen," she said. "Do you really think your father can bend himself to the rules and regulations that the Roman Church is going to throw at him?"

"I hadn't thought of that," Ron admitted. "It doesn't seem likely. But I don't really know. So much has happened that I can't comprehend."

"Well," Gwen offered, "think of the possibilities. Suppose he finds that in practice, the Romans are going to have a very low degree of tolerance for his opinions. Remember, a lot of things that he's been able to do and support as an Anglican priest are opposed by the Romans. From the highest levels some of these things have been condemned so strongly as to irrevocably be out of the question.

"Things like contraception, remarriage after divorce, and maybe biggest of all, women priests. Can you see him turning one hundred and eighty degrees on things like these?" She shook her head. "It's not going to happen."

Ron thought about that. "As far as I can tell, he's creating a dilemma for himself. You're absolutely right: I can't imagine him giving in on a single one of those issues.

"But Dad's no fool. In fact, he's one of the brightest, most intelligent men I've ever known. I'd put him up there—especially in this kind of situation—with Thomas More."

"How is that possible?" Gwen tossed her head.

"Oh, it's possible. I'm quite sure of that. He is extremely good at sidestepping and splitting hairs.

"I mean, everybody knew that Thomas More was 'guilty' of not recognizing the king as head of the Church in England. And that he opposed the king's remarriage after the divorce. But as 'certain' as they were they still couldn't pin More down. Only someone else's perjury would defeat him.

"I must confess," Ron continued, "I don't know how he's going to somehow bridge the distinctions that separate our Churches. But he must at least have a plan.

"Gwen, he's going to have to take theological studies for the better part of a year. These things will have to come up. His professors must be aware of the beliefs of the Church he's leaving. How will he get past their eagle eyes?"

"I don't know chapter and verse," Gwen said. "But that's all theory. There won't be any—what would you call it?—a practicum, where he'll have to tell a woman who genuinely and desperately wants to be ordained that there's no hope of that ever happening. Nor is there any Roman bishop who would wink at such an ironclad Roman ruling . . . no such bishop exists to whom Dad could refer such a woman. No"—she shook her head definitively—"I'd be willing to bet he'll never be able to get past the intense scrutiny he'll get, especially from some of those fundamentalist conservative Catholics.

"Besides," she continued, "even if he were to somehow be able to get past the conservatives and the hierarchy, what would be the cost to him?"

"What do you mean?"

"In health. This campaign that seems inevitable would have to take a lot out of him. How long can he hold up under the gigantic pressure? He's not young. He hasn't got a lot of reserve. He could end up in a nursing home—or worse."

Ron rubbed the stubble on his chin. He was well past five o'clock shadow. "God, I hope that doesn't happen. I don't want my father to be humiliated—or to be ill, and maybe even confined. I don't hate him. But I hate what he's doing to himself—to you, to me. If it came to that, I'd rather see him go quickly."

"You mean die?"

"Well, yes. It sounds outrageous, I know. It's just that sometimes a quick death solves some problems that can't be solved in any other way."

A smile appeared at the corners of Gwen's mouth. She looked pleased, as if she'd stumbled across a solution to the problem. She yawned. "Come on," she said, almost inaudibly, "let's go to bed."

The answer to everything: Let's go to bed.

At times Ron thought about Gwen and bed all day long. Well, perhaps not literally *all* day long. But, he had to admit, much of the day.

If all else failed, bed was always where every game was played— except conception. For various and differing reasons, the two had agreed from the outset that they would have no children. Not unless both genuinely agreed to do so—either by adoption or having their own.

Once that had been decided, neither had ever brought up the subject again.

The conversation tonight actually was an articulation of Ron's thoughts on the matter of his father. En route home, he had pondered the same ideas Gwen had expressed just now. The three possible conclusions to Dad's conversion: disgrace, insanity, or death.

Ron had reluctantly settled on death as the most reasonable conclusion: The kindest thing to do for his father would be to end this charade. That was pressure enough if this was to be solely his responsibility. But now, amazingly, Gwen seemed to have reached the same conclusion.

Leaving Ron smack in the middle.

Monkey in the middle.

He wanted the office of bishop so much he could taste it.

He'd had it once on a silver platter, made possible when his father had turned down the office.

Odds were that his father's intended defection had again stolen it from Ron.

But what if Father Wheatley were dealt a mortal blow? Ron could then renew his quest. He would again be in the running. His actions and convictions would demonstrate that he himself was no traitor. Plus, as the principal bereaved—next to his mother—the offer of a bishopric would be an approved if not expected show of sympathy.

To put that in practical terms, a nominating committee somewhere would put his name on the slate; supporters would quietly advance his cause (while he maintained a studied pious unawareness), and *voila!* He would be elected bishop of a significant diocese.

He worried about the pressure that was building. It demonstrated once again that Gwen wanted this honor for him no less than she wanted it for herself.

Somehow fate had put him in the middle. He might fumble with a final solution to this scenario. But should he falter, Gwen would not let him abandon the course.

He had much to think about.

He had much that needed to be planned.

If a man desire the office of a bishop, he desireth a good work.

But first, to bed.

TWELVE

I N DUE COURSE, GEORGE WHEATLEY WAS RECEIVED into the Roman Catholic Church. This one, holy, Catholic, and apostolic body did not impose the indignity of rebaptizing him. But it did reordain him a deacon. He continued the process of study that would prepare him for the Roman priesthood.

In Cardinal Mark Boyle, George found a prelate who was willing to sponsor him, incardinate him in the archdiocese, give him the faculties necessary to operate validly and licitly in the archdiocese, and, finally, pay him a salary. The eventual amount, should he be successful in his quest, was negotiable. That didn't overjoy the ordained and celibate Roman priests. Since convert priests such as George were married, the practice was to pay them considerably more than priests who had no family to support.

George selected Notre Dame University for study in the Roman teachings in the fields of Liturgy, history, and dogmatic, moral, and spiritual theology. Some of these studies paralleled Episcopal teaching. Some diverged violently—usually toward the conservative Anglican approach. But, of course, history is written by the winning side. And in coming over to the Romans, the convert priests were approaching, in effect, the winners.

Through all of this, Nan was the most affected. More than Ron, more even than Alice, and surely more than Richard, Mrs. Wheatley suffered most because she internalized all the familial conflict. She supported both her husband and her children. Even though two of the three offspring stood poles apart from their father.

By the present time, the date of Father's Wheatley's scheduled ordination, Alice had come to understand all that had transpired between today and that evening many months ago when her father had announced his decision.

At first, against her better judgment, she had bargained with God. She would promise this or that sacrificial penance if only the Lord would make her father see the light. In time she realized that her objective would not be attained. God had heard her prayers, and the answer was no. God would not abrogate George's free will.

From that time on, she drifted away from her family. Mostly, she separated from her father. It was a deeply painful break. She could not forget and, try as she might, she couldn't forgive.

In the few moments that she held Sue's hand, Alice relived in her memory the tragic fragmentation of her once united family. She kept trying to find some way of putting Humpty Dumpty together again, but she kept running into immovable walls.

The last thing in the world she wanted was her father's death. She fought against the belief that that was the only way out of the maze. Was there no other way? Was that the only path to eventual peace—the only resolution to the heartbreaking situation?

No, it couldn't be! And yet . . . and yet, it seemed so.

She shook her head. She didn't want to think about that anymore. She was with someone who loved her unconditionally. She should have been able to find solace in Sue. But that was denied and part of the blame lay at her father's doorstep.

Making love with Sue brought a measure of peace. As was her habit, Alice drifted into a dreamless sleep.

That left Sue wide awake to drift owl-eyed through the early morning hours trying not to move and thereby rouse Alice from her shallow slumber.

Tonight, Sue had a surfeit of thoughts as she waited for sleep to take her, too. She was profoundly disturbed that Alice would think they should part. It had been the furthest thing from Sue's mind.

She was perfectly willing to have Alice as anything from a spouse to a significant other. She preferred a marriage. But she could understand Alice's serious difficulties in that resolution what with both her bishop and her potential parishioners.

So, all right, they would continue to be secret lovers, remaining in the closet.

But then came Alice's father . . . Father Wheatley . . . *Roman* Father Wheatley. The straw that broke Alice's back.

He would not ratify her relationship with Sue. Not that such ratification would have amounted to anything legally. But if anyone in the media were to ask him, he would tell the truth as he saw it. He already had made his mind known: He could find no biblical or scientific approval of such a relationship.

It might, as Alice feared, be a final refutation. Her father, whose opinion was accepted as Gospel by a great number of people, would not approve—and, thus, would be on record as condemning his own daughter's lifestyle.

Sue scarcely could sit by and see her lover humiliated. Granted, the whole kit and kaboodle didn't really mean that much to her; she could live with anything society would throw at her personally. But she was not determined to be a priest. Additionally, she felt that Alice was correct in expecting priests to be above sin—especially sins of the flesh.

Something had to be done about Alice's father. Something more effective than today's debacle.

Sue knew she had hours before sleep would come. She would use her time productively, pondering the problem: What could be done to stop Alice's father from delivering the final blow—his ordination in the Roman Church—to his daughter?

THIRTEEN

M R. AND MRS. LEON HARKINS SAT SILENTLY in the kitchen of their modest east-side duplex. They were finishing their traditional late Sunday afternoon dinner. They said nothing because there was little left to say.

They had no children. Neither Leon nor Grace had any close family. The few still-living cousins were scattered outstate.

They had a dog and a cat that had declared a truce and coexisted by ignoring each other. Perhaps they were imitating their master and mistress. The cat—Puss, of course—was a tabby; the dog, Lucky, was a Jack Russell mix. The cat identified with Grace, the dog with Leon.

All of them, dog, cat, and humans, finished eating almost simultaneously. Leon forked down the last of his apple pie, pushed back from the table, and walked somewhat unsteadily into the living room.

Grace watched him leave, then rose to clear the table and wash the dishes. Not for the first time, she thought that if there was anything to reincarnation, she would choose to come back as a man, a man who would eat large dinners prepared by the little woman, unbuckle his belt, collapse into a comfortable chair, and belch lustily. The woman could do the dishes.

Playing the man's role was exactly what Leon was doing.

Utilizing the remote, which he did so well, he clicked on the television. Surfing, he hit upon a PGA tournament. Golf was pleasant if one didn't have to walk all over creation chasing a little white ball. It was perfect in the living room after a large dinner. Stretched out in comfort in his recliner, he found the game soporific.

He was snoozing when Grace entered the room and took in the all-too-familiar scene. She picked up her knitting. The needles clicked, adding length to an eternal scarf. TV golf was good for this, too.

Puss jumped onto Grace's lap and burrowed a shelter for herself under the knitting. Lucky was content to lie on the carpet and rest his head on Leon's slippers.

The game marched on. From time to time, Grace, whose fingers had memorized the pattern, glanced at the TV. Sometimes the screen displayed nothing but blue sky; viewers had to make an act of faith that somewhere up there a golf ball was in flight.

Grace kept a clean, near immaculate home. When she married, some forty years ago, she was excited at the prospect of having children, lots of them and soon. She would be a good mother and an even better grandma. She would dish out strict discipline, but with an abundance of affection. The phrase "tough love" had not yet been coined when she made her resolution.

But fate was to deal her a different hand.

Leon had just retired from the Ford Rouge plant. He welcomed retirement, though he had no specific plans—at least no ambitious plans such as adding on to the house, or doing freelance repair work. He was good at that. But he wanted to leave all that physically demanding stuff behind.

Down deep he knew what would occupy most of his spare time. He would devote countless hours to his gun collection. His basement housed a veritable arsenal.

High on his small list of things to do was to volunteer at his parish of choice, St. Mary's, in Eastpointe. The Harkinses did not live within the boundaries of St. Mary's. But St. Mary's was the sort of parish that most suited Leon. Grace went along for the ride; to her a parish was a parish.

Switching parishes was easily accomplished nowadays. Before the loathesome Vatican Council, attending a parish outside one's own church boundaries entailed a lot of red tape. One had to have a credible reason to switch parishes, as well as a note from the home pastor giving permission to switch allegiance.

Today, the average pastor is happy when a Catholic joins his parish, whether that Catholic lives within the boundaries or elsewhere. To hell with the red tape!

As far as Leon was concerned, St. Mary's Eastpointe was not the perfect parish one could have found routinely before the Council. Now, as he occasionally grumbled to his wife, all hell was breaking loose. In this range of bad choices, St. Mary's was somewhat more than merely acceptable.

But while he pledged allegiance to St. Mary's and was active there, he kept a weather eye on some of the more deviant of the maverick parishes. Chief among these, in his view, was the venerable St. Joe's downtown.

Leon could find parishes—too many!—most of them in the inner city, that played fast and loose with Liturgy that was marginal at best. Some as bad, and, amazingly, even worse than St. Joe's.

But no one, no parish could compete with the admixture of Liturgy *and* the pastor that constituted St. Joe's.

Who are they trying to fool? Leon would snort from time to time. More often than not the rhetorical question would be addressed to no one but himself.

Once upon a time the Harkinses had belonged to St. Joe's parish. They didn't live within the parish's boundaries because at that time St. Joe's had no territorial boundaries. It had been designated a national parish. Specifically, a German national parish, open to anyone of German descent. Frank was German on his mother's side. Grace was German and Polish.

They continued to be conscientiously active in the parish until the neighborhood changed. The primary change was in color. Frank knew—or thought he knew—what that augured. It was time to pull up stakes.

The Harkinses moved to Center Line, a northeastern Detroit suburb. Unfortunately, Frank found no Center Line parish suitable for his patronage. He tried the neighboring suburb of East Detroit. Just what the Vicar of Christ ordered. So "right" was East Detroit that it eventually changed its name from East Detroit to Eastpointe. It wanted no part of predominantly African-American Detroit.

But Leon could not get old St. Joe's out of his system. Even after Vatican II, things were not so bad. Although Leon did have his doubts when Father Koesler was sent there. Koesler had a reputation for being liberal. Of course, in the aftermath of the Council, many of the younger to middle-aged clergy had such a reputation.

But Koesler had withstood inspection. His congregation ran mainly from middle-aged to elderly. They wanted a prayerful, reverent Liturgy. And, largely, that was what they got.

Then came the unfamiliar clergyman from the Southwest. Born in the Deep South, his ministry was to the poor and black. He worked his way west to Dallas—and from Dallas to Detroit.

The out-of-towner did not come with a ready-made reputation. But he quickly began to build one.

Leon made it a habit to attend Mass at St. Joe's almost every week. He also attended Mass at St. Mary's in Eastpointe—just to make sure he had attended a valid Mass. Leon was definitely a belt-and-suspenders type.

It did not take the new priest long to recruit neighborhood residents who had not been "churched" for many years. Young business-people who now gave up extra sleep on Sundays to attend a Liturgy that involved them.

And those kids with their drums and guitars, jazzing up what should have been a respectful few minutes with God.

As for the greeting of peace—well! It grew to be out of hand—just completely out of hand. Everybody—except Leon—milling about, talking loudly, hugging instead of merely shaking hands.

What had old St. Joe's done to deserve these desecrations? It had housed a black man in a white man's color.

Oh, he was black all right. Father Tully was black. Leon knew all about that. If he hadn't learned it on the streets of Detroit, he surely was exposed to the culture in all his years of working side by side with blacks, and, more to the point, blacks who were trying to pass. With their do-rags and their lotions and creams. Oh yes, as much as Father Tully tried to pass himself off as a white man, Leon could tell: This was a black man. Oddly, the term mulatto never crossed his mind.

From time to time, Leon thought something really ought to be done about the disgrace that went on there week after week.

But what?

He began his crusade by writing letters to the priest who headed the Downtown Vicariate.

At first he received personalized responses from the Vicariate office. Letters from a Sister Somebody . . . one of the few women religious left. His only contact was by mail; he hadn't a clue as to what she looked like.

Her handwriting was tiny but extremely legible. He guessed she was elderly; that would explain the small script. Saving paper, saving money. Older nuns would have had such habits—and probably still did.

Her letters attempted to address his complaints. She explained—again and again—that St. Joseph's Liturgy was well within the rubrics. There were—yes, there really were—limitations on what was permitted in today's Church. But due to questions regarding the Masses at St. Joe's—particularly the folk Masses—the parish had been monitored—several times—and all was kosher ("liturgically correct" were her exact words).

She suggested that he try another parish, perhaps one in the suburbs. It certainly wasn't that the sort of Mass he was comfortable with wasn't being offered in many Detroit-area churches. They were out there and since he felt so strongly about it he certainly was free to join just about any parish he wished.

She wrote some seven consecutive responses to his objections. She searched for different ways of saying the same thing. Finally, she had to conclude that Leon Harkins was not going to be satisfied until St. Joseph's Liturgies conformed to the hyperorthodox standards set by Rome. She also knew that as long as Father Tully was pastor, St. Joe's would be faithful to the minimum standards set by the Vatican.

So the response to Leon's complaints to the Vicariate office metamorphosed into nothing more than a series of form letters. Leon was disgusted.

There was a hiatus during which Leon seethed. Nonetheless he continued to attend Mass at St. Joe's. Not often; he couldn't stand the racket and what he considered the offhand approach to this core sacrament of the Roman Catholic Church

Like an itchy scab, St. Joe's Liturgy was a magnet that lured him back time and time again to survey and assess the damage.

Of course not all the Masses were of the folk variety. On Sundays at least one Liturgy was offered in a staid fashion—occasionally even both Liturgies fell within a decent parameter. Still, enough liberties were taken—by Leon's lights—in the Saturday Mass to satisfy the casual, less finicky Catholic.

Leon began writing to Father Tully. He mentioned his correspondence on the Vicariate level—hoping that such a record would demonstrate the dedication and resolve of the writer.

History repeated itself. At first, Father Tully replied in a sympathetic, understanding way. Encouraged by Tully's responsiveness, Leon fully expected things to change. But nothing did. If anything, there was even more noise and commotion than before . . . if that was possible.

It surely seemed a lost cause. Leon could think of no other course than appealing to the head honcho himself, the Cardinal Archbishop.

Contacting the Vatican would only be a waste of postage. Even Leon realized the Pope had many concerns far more pressing than how a Mass was being offered in an insignificant parish in the heart of Detroit. If anyone asked the Pope about the state of the Church in this core city parish, he would respond with a wrinkled brow and the word, *"Where?"*

But it stood to reason that a bishop—for that was what Mark Boyle was beneath the red silken robes, a bishop—would be both informed and concerned over what was going on in one of his parishes. He was the shepherd, and one of his sheep, in the form of a single parish, was lost.

Not only that, but the archbishop could, with a single sweep of his pen, rid St. Joseph's of that fraudulent priest. No one need know that the priest was black masquerading as white. Leon would not be vindictive. He just wanted that priest out and the parish to return to its proper state of orthodoxy.

Trying to make contact with the Cardinal did not prove effective. Age had sapped the elderly prelate of any inclination to enter this combat zone. He passed Leon's letter along to his secretary, who, in turn, sent it on to the Office for Christian Worship.

That left the matter back at square one.

The official for Liturgy sent Leon a covering letter along with numerous small pamphlets spelling out orthodoxy in the varieties of worship available in this post-Vatican II Church.

Leon bothered to finger through the pamphlets, even though he foresaw their contents. The problem with all these bureaucrats is that they never lift themselves off their chairs and go out to see what's going on and who's doing it!

All they had to do was to attend the Saturday afternoon mockeries and watch this distraction of a priest pass himself off as white. But no, all these uppity churchmen and churchwomen could do was write generic gobbledygook communications, and when they'd exhausted that, send form letters and mindless publications!

It was so simple; Leon just wanted to do the will of God. God surely frowned on what was going on in that historic church.

He was about to regretfully take himself out of the game when one evening while watching a rerun of the TV drama *Law and Order* he was inspired.

The plot revolved around a stalker. The viewer was encouraged to view the stalker as the villain. Leon had to rejigger that plot. Sometimes—and this was one of those times—it became necessary to right wrongs. And if anyone were to rise to correct the wrongs in that parish, the authorities had made it clear none of them would do the job. The hero of this real-life situation would have to be Leon Harkins or no one.

He watched that episode carefully in the best spirit of emulation.

How did the protagonist—the villain in this telecast scenario—carry out his campaign?

For one, he assembled a multitude of publications—magazines, newspapers, pamphlets, etc. Get one's message in order, then play cut-out, pasting letters on notepaper to spell out bold threats.

Also the stalker needed pictures—mostly, it seemed, to allow him to stay fixed on his target.

There were few pictures of Father Tully available. There were plenty of pictures of St. Joseph's church. Some he photocopied at the library. Some he took from brochures.

As for the quarry himself, Leon surreptitiously took photos. This was the most thrilling part of his adventure. Sneaking around, aiming the camera, and pushing the button was the next best thing to sneaking up, aiming a gun, and pulling the trigger.

Then there were the phone calls. Leon found a spy store that sold a voice-altering device. It could speed up or slow down the sound of one's voice, completely masking the identity of the speaker. Leon had seen devices like this used on TV shows. He hadn't realized he could actually buy one. But, sure enough, for a little more than sixty bucks, he could play in the major leagues of spydom.

So far the threats had proved empty. They fell on deaf ears and blind eyes. Most frustrating of all, Leon couldn't tell for sure whether they were even reaching Father Tully.

Of course, Leon had no knowledge of the possible effect of the threatening letters. He couldn't be present when—or if—they were opened.

Were they opened? Were they just thrown in the wastebasket? Were they thrown in the wastebasket unopened? Did Tully laugh at the threats? Had he gone through this before? Was he frightened by them?

As for the phone calls, at first, Tully had merely seemed concerned, although impressed at the professional manner in which the caller masked his identity. Eventually it became obvious to Tully that the caller was not going to lighten up. It was then that Leon noted, to his satisfaction, an apprehensive tone creeping into the priest's voice. And now, lately, after hearing only a few guttural words, Tully would hang up, slamming the phone down on its receiver.

That encouraged Leon greatly. He knew then he was reaching Tully. Yet still nothing happened to that cursed Saturday Mass that so displeased Our Lord.

Nonetheless, Leon vowed to continue. Nothing would stop him. He would keep it up until he wore down the priest and forced him to pull up stakes and Go!

But in his inner heart, Leon knew this priest was not going to give up. No, he could and would wait Leon out.

Leon tried not to think of this inconclusive future. This priest held all the important cards. He had no intention of straightening up, reforming, or mending his ways. He was leading the parish down a primrose path, and no one was going to stop him. Leon was self-condemned to frustrating failure.

There was only one alternative: If the priest would not leave voluntarily, he would have to be forced to vacate. And how, Leon asked himself, do you do that?

The day had long since passed when an undesirable was ridden out of town on a rail, tarred and feathered. There was a great deal to say for the Ku Klux Klan. But the organization had lost all or most of its clout. Too bad; this—a black man posturing as white—was right up the KKK's alley.

Father Tully seemed impervious to every removal plan Leon could imagine. The priest couldn't be intimidated or scared off. Leon's best efforts, his most zealous threats at terrorizing, did no more than make Tully angry. Taking the priest by the scruff of the neck and marching him back to Dallas—or anything in that vein—well, the very idea was impractical and silly.

Of course Tully might die . . .

When he was feeling especially frustrated, Harkins would consider murder. But he never entertained the thought for more than a few seconds at a time. One did not kill anyone, much less a priest.

It will happen. If you wait long enough, Leon told himself, *everything happens*. But to have to wait that long—well, that was impractical to a practical man like Leon.

Somebody was yelling. It was the TV announcer. Some golfer had come within an inch or so of a hole in one. Leon wiggled in his chair. The dog lifted his head from Leon's slipper, looked around, and saw Puss's paw emerging from the bottom layer of Mrs. Harkins's knitting. All was well. He lowered his head again into the instep curve of Leon's footwear.

Barely roused by the momentary excitement, Leon opened his eyelids a crack to see the fans gathered around the green. They had witnessed what was almost history being made.

Suddenly, the golf scene vanished from the screen. Gone was the peaceful setting, the vivid green of the manicured grass, the bright golfing attire. Instead there was the interior of some building. It looked as if there had been a fire. Plenty of dust and rubble.

Grace Harkins emitted a startled squeal. "Is that what I think it is?" She pointed at the screen.

"What?" Leon shook off his torpor. "What happened?"

"Shhh," Grace stage-whispered. "I want to find out what happened."

The camera panned over the area, pausing to focus on a poignant scene. The solemn tones of an unseen reporter were heard. "Floyd"— evidently directed at the anchorman back at the studio—"we're here at historic old St. Joseph's church on the northeast outskirts of downtown Detroit.

"Just a short time ago, this was to have been the scene of a ceremony welcoming George Wheatley, the popular Episcopal priest and preacher, into the Roman Catholic priesthood. He was to be ordained here in this church. But as the ceremony was about to begin, a bomb exploded in the sanctuary . . ." The camera played about the broken, toppled statues, and the rent and blackened paintings.

"The police," the now visible reporter said, "tell us that there has been one fatality, a visiting priest . . ." He consulted his notes. "As far as we know, there were no other injuries. That alone may qualify as a miracle. And what better place for a miracle than in this ancient parish church. St. Joseph's parish—in an earlier building—was one of the first churches established by Antoine de la Mothe Cadillac in Detroit.

"I have with me, Floyd"—the picture widened to include an obviously shaken man—"an eyewitness who was seated near the area where the bomb exploded. He is Thomas McNerney, of Rochester.

"Mr. McNerney, tell us, please, in your own words, what you experienced here today."

McNerney's eyes were wide with shock. "It was awful! I was talking to a guy from my home parish in Rochester. Then I heard this horrible roar. I had a ringing in my ears for a long time. Matter of fact, I still hear the damn ring—oh, pardon my French."

The reporter shrugged the impropriety away. "And then . . . ?"

"And then I turned around so I could face the altar. Statues were falling and smashing. It was awful! It made me think of hell."

"Did you see the priest who was felled by the explosion?"

"There was so much smoke . . . I guess I was more interested in the statues and the paintings. But then I did see this figure in black . . . in the corner. I could tell it wasn't no statue. But I didn't realize it was a human being until this Father and another guy, I guess it was a cop—anyway they came running into the sanctuary here and went right to him—I mean to the body." He shuddered as if with cold. "It was awful."

"I see. Well, before that, did you see anybody in the sanctuary? Somebody who maybe shouldn't have been there?"

"I didn't see nobody. I was talkin' to this guy from my parish. Then it went kerflooey! A big blast. Maybe, because the altar sort of held the blast inside the sanctuary, it saved a lot of lives. I can tell you, I wouldn't be standin' here talkin' to you if whoever planted that bomb hadn'ta put it up against the altar." He shuddered again. "I hate to think what woulda happened if anybody was on the other side of the explosion. I mean, besides the poor guy who got blown away."

"That's St. Joseph's!" Grace said needlessly. "We used to belong there." She turned to her husband. "You still go there, don't you, hon?"

"Yeah. But on Saturdays. Not on Sundays."

"Well, it's a good thing you didn't go today. You coulda got hurt."

"Or killed . . . like that priest!"

"So"—the camera again focused on the reporter—"what really happened here? We have learned that the priest who lost his life in this sacred place was just visiting. He planned on attending the ordination ceremony of The Reverend George Wheatley. He appears to have been an innocent bystander. Apparently something in the altar area may have attracted his attention. Curiosity led him up the sanctuary steps—and to his death.

"We have a police officer here who can fill in some of the gaps in this story." Again the lens widened to reveal another figure standing next to the reporter. "This is Officer John Nader." He turned to the policeman. "Officer Nader, can you tell us what happened here? As much as you know at this point?"

"The investigation," said the uniformed officer, "is just beginning. One thing we know: The procession was late in starting. We are not at liberty at this point in time to divulge why the procession was delayed. But if it hadn't been late, all those clergym— uh, -persons would have been in their places. They would have been in the direct line of the explosion. Whatever the reason, it was just plain lucky that the delay halted the procession before it entered the church."

"I see. What can you tell us about the priest who was killed?"

"His name was Farmer—Father Joseph Farmer. Earlier, he was sitting in one of the front pews. For his own reasons, he didn't want to be in the procession. Apparently something caught his attention. That something may have contained the bomb. Our first order of business is to find what attracted his attention . . . if such an object is still identifiable."

"Speaking of that procession again," the reporter said, "you mentioned to me off-camera a likely scenario. Can you tell us about that?"

"Well, yes. That altar is made of granite. It's built something like a packing crate, like you'd use for packing and moving. There's a slight indentation in the middle of the side that faced the rear of the sanctuary. So the greatest force of the blast would be channeled right in that indentation. Anybody standing near the center of the altar would receive the full force of the explosion."

"And what would that do?"

"Anybody standing there . . . well . . . pardon the reference, seeing we're in a church. But, anybody standing there would end up like that priest who got killed. And if that priest had been a little closer to the center . . . well, we'd have picked him up with a blotter."

"And," the reporter said, "have you identified who would have been on that spot at that fatal moment?"

"Yes. The Reverend George Wheatley would have been dead center. And Father Tully, the pastor, would have been right next to him."

The camera swung back to capture the reporter's face staring into it. "So there you have it, Floyd. To recap: Just a little while ago, a powerful explosion occurred in St. Joseph's church in downtown

Detroit. It caused serious but confined damage. One person was killed by the blast. He was a priest, Father Joseph Farmer, a missionary priest who had spent much time conducting services in this city. As far as we know, no others were injured.

"The police, particularly the Bomb Squad, are beginning their investigation to find the person or persons responsible for this horrible crime.

"An accident of timing apparently saved the lives of numerous clergypersons. It caused the cancellation, or at very least postponement, of a ceremony inducting The Reverend George Wheatley into the Roman Catholic priesthood.

"Father Wheatley is extremely well known and well liked in this community. He writes a weekly column in the *Detroit News*, and hosts a local radio talk show. He is much loved by many people he has helped.

"Father Wheatley has been taken to the rectory, the priests' home, for questioning and debriefing, along with several others who were to play principal roles in this afternoon's rite.

"We will keep you informed of details as they develop. And now, back to you in the studio, Floyd."

"And there you have it," said Floyd, now on camera. "We return you now to the golf match still in progress."

There was a stunned silence in the Harkins living room.

It was not infrequently that violence, often senseless, erupted in the big city. But that that violence occurred in a church was very much out of the ordinary. That, plus the fact that Leon and Grace were extremely close to the church and the parish of St. Joseph, invested this news announcement with special interest.

A bomb in a Catholic church? Unimaginable.

"Is nothing sacred?" Grace asked of no one.

Leon did not reply. His eyes were once again following the golf match. But his mind was far distant from the greens.

Just minutes ago, Leon had been thinking that it was inconceivable to kill a priest. The question was: If it is impossible to rid God's

149

chosen people of this stye in the eye of the Church by any other means, is it permissible to murder him? The answer was: Of course not. Don't be a damn fool!

Suddenly, it appeared to be open season on priests. Someone, for whatever reason, had killed one by accident—allegedly—and just missed killing two more deliberately.

It was like the four-minute mile. It was a given that that record could never be broken—until Roger Bannister did it. Fifteen feet was the untoppable height limit for the pole vault. Six feet for the high jump. And on and on. Records, achievements, almost anything can be improved upon. Records were made to be broken. Impossible dreams become possible.

The irony of today's disaster was that someone almost did the trick—if you could believe that cop at the scene of the crime.

Leon was going to get all the newspapers he could find. He would watch every TV news program starting tonight and running through at least tomorrow. He would have to gather all the data surrounding this event. He would have to plan with greater precision than he had ever invested in any previous enterprise.

Concentrating intensely, he gave serious thought to precisely what had gone on at St. Joe's today.

What if the thing had worked exactly the way it seemed to be planned? The perpetrator likely would have involved not one but two priests. Which one—if only one death was intended—was the real target? Which one was a stalking horse? Which one was taken along for the ride?

This special challenge faced the investigating police as well.

The cops would have to find a bond that might link the two priests. Maybe the perpetrator really intended to kill both priests. Lacking that bond, which of the priests was the real target?

What a marvelous mystery! That could keep the cops busy till doomsday.

Meanwhile, Leon's challenge was to find another occasion when more than one priest might be the intended victim. That could be really tough. But he'd give it a try. Yet he couldn't waste too much time building this straw horse. Within a relatively short period, he would have to go after Father Tully.

Who said a priest can't be murdered? Well, Leon had—earlier this very day.

❧❧❧

"What's got into you, Leon?" She'd actually stopped knitting.

"What? What!" He did not want to be distracted from plans that had to be carefully and discreetly laid.

"You're not watching the golf match. I can tell."

"Can you watch it? After what we've just seen?"

"Well, no. I guess not."

Leon hoped that he could silence his wife. His imagination was trying to work overtime. To do this successfully, he wanted—needed—quiet. He didn't care whether Grace got absorbed in thoughts of murder in St. Joe's church, the golf match, or her knitting. Just as long as she left him in peace.

"I don't think it's healthy for us to dwell on the trouble at St. Joseph's," Grace said. "After all, I know how you feel about Father Tully. You probably wish that he was the one who's dead. That's not nice."

She knew how he felt about Tully.

It's true, thought Leon. He didn't share everything with his wife by a long shot. But obviously she was plugged in to his feelings toward the traitor-pastor.

Would he have to kill Grace, too? To shut her up during the investigation that would inevitably follow the second killing?

He was so fortunate that whoever had planted that bomb had set it up so that there were two possible victims. The cops would have a lot on their plate.

Once he killed Father Tully, the police wouldn't have time to concentrate on that death in any exclusionary way. The Wheatley bombing would still demand their attention. This was a lucky break for Leon. Particularly if he could get the two men together again and, hopefully, kill two birds with one stone.

But what if Grace stuck her nose into this business?

He'd have to really think this thing through.

"I'm going to turn the TV off," Grace announced. She had been talking nonstop all this time. No wonder he was confused. He needed silence. But he knew from experience that she would just switch the TV off and turn herself on. He couldn't have that.

"I'm going to turn it off," she repeated. "Then we can talk."

"I'm going to the basement for a while," he said. "You go ahead and knit. I've got some stuff to work on."

He rose and left. She didn't attempt to stop him. They were playing an oft-repeated game.

The nice thing about this, Leon thought, as he descended the basement stairs, was that if he killed his wife it would be a necessary evil. Yes, that was it: a necessary evil. To the best of his recollection, that's what they'd called such a secondary effect in parochial school.

Come to think of it, the same could be said for that Wheatley man. Although on second thought he would try not to take Wheatley out if he could avoid it.

But of one thing he was certain: Killing Father Tully would definitely be God's will.

FOURTEEN

DINNER WAS WINDING DOWN at the Koznicki home. Hosts and guests were enjoying coffee and dessert.

Father Koesler had held center stage throughout the meal. He was the only one in this group who had known Father Joe Farmer. And, as it happened, Koesler had known Farmer very well.

Responding to the questions and to his memory, Koesler had begun at the end. For he had been the last one to speak with Farmer before the fatal explosion.

But now he tried to keep it on the light side. There really had not been a dark side to Joe Farmer. If he had not become a priest, he might have been quite successful as a traveling salesman. In a sense, that term described him fairly accurately.

He was on the road pretty regularly, mostly throughout the Midwest . . . one of the last of the old-time preachers who proclaimed his version of Catholicism.

When it came to the essence of Christianity—Jesus Christ—Joe Farmer was not forceful. When it came to the Commandments, the rules and regulations of the Roman Catholic Church, the position of the Pope as solitary, supreme, and singular in authority, he was not wimpish.

In fact, Koesler told his listeners, it was this very mission Father Farmer was working on when, apparently, curiosity had led him to pay the ultimate price. He had voluntarily entered the enemy's fortress to gather material for an upcoming retreat to be conducted for a group of conservative Catholics. A group who would be shocked by such revelations as Father Farmer would put before them.

From that point, traveling backward in time, Koesler regaled the diners with anecdotes he had amassed from personal memories and hearsay tidbits.

During a break in Koesler's reminiscences, Wanda invited every-one to take his or her coffee to the living room so she could remove the table dishes. The first dish she reached for was a bowl still half full of spaghetti and meatballs.

"I don't know how you do it, Wanda," Koesler said. "You had precious little time to prepare to feed this small army. You weren't expecting anyone other than your husband."

"Oh, I got used to this years ago." Wanda smiled. "Walt used to bring home his police buddies and they would go on and on and on. They'd discuss their cases, their work, law enforcement in general.

"Actually, I was lucky that I had planned on spaghetti for dinner tonight. You can add to that forever."

"And you even have leftovers . . ." Koesler gestured toward the bowl Wanda was holding. "This is almost as good as the miracle of the loaves and fishes."

Everyone laughed except Zoo Tully, whose brow knitted as he tried to find some relevance between such a miracle and a police inves-tigation.

"Wanda . . . everybody," Koesler said as he looked around the group. "I must apologize for running off at the mouth. I haven't given anyone else a chance to say anything."

"Don't feel bad, Father," Wanda reassured. "Your stories are much more appealing than Walt's used to be. Body parts all over the place," she mused in reminiscence, "heads separated from necks, extremities hacked off . . . and all of this while our kids were trying to eat!" She shook her head.

"Now you folks move out of here and let me get to work."

"Wanda," Anne Marie said, "please let me help."

Some wives are adamant in wanting to work the kitchen area alone. Wanda was not of that number. "Sure, Anne Marie. You come along. I'll appreciate your company. The menfolk can cluster around the living room and tell their stories."

And so things began to move. Dishes from the table and three men and a teenager to the living room.

Young Richard Wheatley was not particularly impressed by Father Koesler. After all, he was just another priest. And Richard, what with his father and his brother and his sister and their extended circle, usually felt he was being smothered in priests.

But Inspector Walter Koznicki and Lieutenant Zoo Tully . . . well, they were another species. They were *cops*. Granted, the inspector was retired . . . but everyone seemed to treat him as if he were still on the force.

Rick had never been this close to cops before. He hardly ever saw a cop outside of TV or the movies. He wondered if these cops were carrying real guns. He had the impression that police officers kept their "rods" under their pillows when they went to bed and in the shower when they were bathing. He wondered if he could be bold enough to ask to see them.

He decided against that. Too presumptuous.

"Any word from the church?" Koesler asked.

"No," Tully responded. "They'll still be gathering evidence. I don't expect to hear from anyone till later tonight. But they'll check in. They're good officers."

"The best!" Koznicki agreed. He had once headed the Homicide Division and, with understandable loyalty, was still proud of its officers, many of whom he himself had trained.

"Do you think," Koesler asked, "there is any possible chance that poor Father Farmer could have been the intended victim?"

Tully shook his head. "All things are possible, as the saying goes. But no, that idea is as close to impossible as you can get."

"There was a timing device controlling the bomb," Koznicki continued. "While the bomber could put a time value on the explosion, there was no chance the perpetrator could know, or even guess, that Father Farmer was going to be at the altar. In fact, he should not have been there. He was not in the procession. He was not taking part in the Liturgy. He had a place down front—his Roman collar got him preferential treatment in this instance—he should have remained there."

"Then . . ." Rick spoke up tentatively; he wasn't sure his participation in this conversation was welcomed. " . . . does anybody have any idea who the victim was supposed to be? Father Tully? My dad? Or both?"

"That is the question," Koznicki said. "No doubt about it."

"That will be determined as the investigation moves along," Tully said. "It should be among the earliest facts we uncover. This much seems certain: Either our perp wanted to kill both men or he wanted one of them bad enough to wa—" Tully pulled up short, suddenly all too aware that he was talking to the young son of the man who could have been the intended victim. Under the circumstances, the verb "waste" did not seem appropriate. "—uh, to target both of them to get the one he really wanted."

Wanda entered, carrying a steaming coffeepot for those who wanted refills. As she made her way around the room, she said, "This must be a terrible shock to you, Richard . . . and also to you, Zoo. If it hadn't been for an accident, your father, Richard—and your brother, Zoo—would be dead now. And our dear friend, here, Father Koesler, could be badly injured. I'm sure the rest of us will pray for Father Wheatley and Father Tully as well as for Richard and Zoo."

"Amen to that," Koesler affirmed. Rick directed an appreciative smile at Mrs. Koznicki.

"Thank you. Thanks a lot," Tully said. "But I doubt very much that the delay was an accident."

"Yes," Koznicki commented, "it stretches credulity too much. I believe that to be too convenient to be a coincidence."

"Uh-huh," Tully agreed. "The phone call came just in time to stop the procession. That delay saved lives and limbs."

"And," Koznicki said, "the person who requested Father Wheatley to hear his confession never showed up."

"That call could be one of the most important features of this case," Tully said. "It opens up the possibility that the perpetrator might have had a coconspirator," he added.

"Why is that?" Rick was spellbound at being in on an investigation of murder and attempted murder. Even—or especially—since his father was part of it.

Koznicki smiled. He was amused that the young man was so obviously fascinated by a real-life major felony.

"That scenario"—Koznicki was like a careful teacher—"rests on the assumption that—let us call him Perp One—that Perp One and Perp Two collaborated on this venture. Perhaps they cooperated on making the bomb. Or perhaps not; the bomb was such a simple device that one person could easily have assembled it alone.

"But whether they cooperated on that or not, they were in this together. Maybe one planted the bomb at the altar while the other was a lookout.

"Now you may wonder why the police would posit the involvement of at least two people. It is that phone call, and only that phone call, that may indicate a conspiracy.

"This way Perp One plants the bomb and waits for the timing device to set off the bomb. Meanwhile Perp Two is having second thoughts. He knows, of course, what time the bomb is set to explode. He also knows when the procession is slated to start.

"As the time draws nearer to the planned assassination, Perp Two becomes frightened, or—in any case and for whatever reason—is getting cold feet. He wants to call it off. But how? He cannot march up to the altar, tuck the bomb under his arm, and nonchalantly walk out. By this time, the congregation is settling down. He would be grossly conspicuous. There were ushers, possibly even security people all over the place. Surely one or more of them would stop him to ask why he was removing something from the altar.

"He couldn't just run into the church to hold up the procession until the bomb exploded: How could he explain knowledge of the device without incriminating himself?

"Actually, according to this scenario, he proved himself very clever. He put a call into the rectory, asked for and got Father Wheatley. Counting on the good Father to respond affirmatively to what he termed an emergency, he was able to stall the procession until it no longer was in harm's way."

With that explanation, Koznicki spread both hands, palms up, indicating he'd finished.

Rick closed his mouth, then opened it just enough to whisper, "Wow!"

It was Lieutenant Tully's turn to smile. He recognized the voice of the officer who had been his own mentor. And, in fact, the scenario just outlined by Walt Koznicki was under investigation even as Koznicki's guests sipped their coffee.

"Of course," Koznicki observed, "this is but one theory about what had happened in St. Joe's church just a few hours ago. It could just as well be the work of one perp working alone. But that hardly lends itself to an easy explanation for the phone call."

Father Koesler was once again impressed by the deductive powers of this man who had spent the better part of his lifetime solving real-life mysteries.

Of course, the police would have to solve the question of the phone call that saved the day—that saved everyone, except, of course, poor Father Farmer.

As far as Koesler was concerned, Inspector Koznicki's explanation made sense. He had noticed the smile on Lieutenant Tully's face during Koznicki's exposition. Koesler correctly guessed that the police who had been on crowd-control duty outside the church, as well as those who had been rushed to the scene after the explosion occurred, were even now checking things out exactly as Koznicki had just detailed.

Wanda and Anne Marie entered the room. Each was drying her hands with a small towel.

"What about your brother, Lieutenant?" Rick asked. "Is he safe?"

At mention of his brother, Tully's jaw tightened. "As safe as we can make him. A lot of this he brought on himself."

"Dear," Anne Marie said, "don't be too hard on Zachary. He knew we'd get involved if we found out about the threats. He was only thinking of us."

"It's not that simple, honey. He's got a brother who's a cop. I'm not an untrained do-gooder who wants to meddle in stuff that shouldn't concern me. I'm a professional. Checking out threats is part of a cop's job.

"Even if I'm in Homicide, I'm still a police officer. It was just plain stupid to keep those letters and calls to himself. He's gonna hear from me about this. He will not do this again." He nodded grimly. "I can guarantee that."

"What about Richard's question, Zoo?" Wanda asked. "About the safety measures?" She herself knew the answer from the numerous times her husband had explained the standard procedures of similar situations, to her and to others.

"Safety?" Tully repeated. "We'll make Zack—and Father Wheatley—as safe and secure as we can. But it'll be minimal protection. The only way we could come close to maximum security is to confine them—in a hotel room or even a specially outfitted cell.

"But," he addressed Rick, "neither my brother nor, I'm sure, your father would stand for a procedure like that. So we've got a couple of surveillance teams, one stationed outside my brother's rectory and one outside your father's house. Bottom line: I hope your dad and my brother will get a good night's sleep." He paused, reflectively. "I'm not sure they will . . . after all they've been through today . . . even with the security."

"Perhaps," Koznicki suggested, "it would be good for you to tell everyone, as I'm sure they are interested, what you expect will happen now."

"What I expect?"

"What happens," Koznicki prompted, "when a police officer or those near to him are involved in something like this."

"Oh . . ." Tully cleared his throat. "I was sure you'd all know; it's one of the rare things that movies and TV get right.

"Well," he proceeded, "cops tend to close ranks, circle the wagons, whatever, when one of their own is in trouble. You must have seen packed church services for funerals of policemen—firefighters too—who've died in the line of duty."

Heads nodded.

"It's pretty much the same when someone close to a cop is threatened or killed. In this case a lot of Detroit and neighboring city cops will do everything they can, from actively investigating to keeping their eyes and ears open.

"That's why Walt and I expect a pretty fast resolution to this case. But I'm still sore at Zack for keeping all that pressure to himself. There's nothing much we can do about the past phone calls. They're gone. But to throw away all those threatening letters . . . well"—his jaw tightened again—"that's just incredible."

"So have we begun to work the phone?" Koznicki asked. "I mean, in case the calls start up again in the wake of the bombing?"

Tully nodded. "It's one of those things I was just talking about," he explained for Rick's benefit. "About how my friends on the force—and even a lot of the guys and gals who just want to help out—will get on this thing and ride it.

"Ordinarily, we would have started the ball rolling on this phone business bright and early tomorrow. Now, normally, it would be the responsibility of the complainant to cut through a lot of the red tape. Nothing special one way or another about that. The victim, of course, wants everything done yesterday. But, for our own sanity, if something can be set in motion within a reasonable time, we want to handle things during what passes for business hours.

"But not with this case." He looked to Koznicki. "You tell them, Walt."

Koznicki nodded. "If I can guess where you intervened—at which point you became involved—I will just begin at the beginning.

"There is," he proceeded, "a series of steps that the customer would take if threatening calls are received. The customer—in this case your brother—contacts the local police and files a report."

"Of course in this case," Tully interjected, "there's no problem: Several of my squad *are* the local police."

"Next," Koznicki continued, "your brother—who is already in contact with the police—is given a Police Report Number. He may be required to sign a release form—"

"My brother," Tully said firmly, "will not need to sign such a form."

"The police will suggest," Koznicki said after a moment, "that your brother call the Ameritech Annoyance Call Bureau. The police will see to it that he has that number.

"Armed with this information and documentation," Koznicki continued, "the AACB will put a trap on the line."

"If," Tully said, "the AACB prefers to do all this sometime tomorrow during business hours, the police will convince the AACB it would be better done tonight. *Now*, as a matter of fact."

"Of course," Koznicki proceeded with his explanation, "it is always possible the operation will require a court order. Just to be on the safe side, whichever police officer is closest to being friends with a judge will phone him or her first and then pick up the court order."

"In this particular case," Tully said, "I would probably get the warrant because the only local elected official who doesn't owe me a favor is one of the Drain Commissioners. But a court order has already been obtained, or I would have received word."

"You mean," Koesler said, "that these steps you're explaining have already been initiated?"

"Uh-huh." Tully smiled. "The judge and the warrant—that's merely belt-and-suspenders. It could be messy when we catch this guy if the whole thing were to fall apart at that crucial moment. We could fool around with Ameritech Security or a Subpoena Group. But we wanted something foolproof."

"So the process," said Koznicki, as he took over the explanation once again, "is just about in place. The customer—again, the lieutenant's brother—phones the AACB, located in Redford, requesting that a trap for all future calls be placed on the line.

"Father Tully gives the Police Report Number to the AACB and follows the instructions he is given to log calls for the investigation.

"Finally, the AACB provides specific call information to police for the investigation. The police will contact Father Tully as soon as the next threatening call is made."

Koznicki was inwardly pleased that he could still rattle off the details of an investigation "by the numbers."

"Do you think," Anne Marie directed her question at her husband, "this will do it? Are you positive? It's Zack's life we're talking about."

"Right now," Tully responded, "it's our best shot. I'd bet my last buck that the guy will call again. He's called so many times in the past. And the important thing is, he's been getting away with it.

"He may or may not send another pasted-up letter. If he does, we'll be ready to use every means we've got to identify him: fingerprints, the type paper used for the letter and envelope, and so on. That'll take more time. But we'll do it." He looked at his wife reassuringly. "Don't worry, hon; we'll get this guy one way or the other. But my money's on the telephone trap."

"How about my father?" Rick asked.

"Your father," Tully said, "is another thing entirely. He hasn't received any threatening mail or phone calls—or so he says. The only contact we know about is that one call he got earlier this afternoon. The one that delayed the procession. But he says he couldn't identify the caller.

"What I'm hoping is that the guy who's been harassing my brother is the same one who's responsible for today's bomb. If that's so, and we catch the guy who's been calling and writing my brother, we'll also get the guy who's after your dad.

"Meanwhile, we're going to do everything we can to protect both men. As I said, neither of them is going to stand for being locked up and treated like a household plant. But we'll do our best."

Wanda rose from her chair and took the towel from Anne Marie's now dry hands. The two women headed back to the kitchen. Wanda had paid little attention to what was said after Anne Marie asked about the effectiveness of the phone trap. From long experience as the wife of Walt Koznicki, she already knew the answer.

Wanda and Anne Marie were no strangers to each other. Before Zoo Tully married his first wife, he had been like a son to the Koznickis. That affiliation repeated itself after his first wife divorced him, as well as later, after his significant other left him.

Then he married Anne Marie, and he seemed to finally be doing what the Koznickis hoped he would do: learning from experience. One of the major changes of lifestyle Wanda had noticed was that Zoo apparently no longer shared the details of his work with his wife.

It was just the reverse of Wanda's relationship with Walt. They shared quite totally with each other. It was more than a merely matter-of-fact nonholding back; rather it was that each wanted the other to know what was going on.

They shared the dangers as well as the triumphs. Thus, were Walt to mention a phone trap, Wanda would immediately know what was involved and the chances of success. Whereas Anne Marie had been pretty much in the dark until a few minutes ago when the impromptu team of Walt and Zoo had explained it all.

Now the general feeling was that this dinner gathering was over. The guests shifted in their chairs, and references were made to what a busy day tomorrow would be.

In the midst of the valedictories, Anne Marie's voice took on an urgency that was, at that moment, unique. "Zoo, honey, can you take a look at the disposal?"

Tully chuckled. "That's about the best I could do: look at it."

"I thought you were good at this sort of thing. We've known each other long enough so I was sure you were good with your hands."

For one fleeting moment, an off-color remark rose to Tully's lips. He caught himself. "You weren't paying that much attention, sweets. My MO for fixing things is to discover that the machine or appliance is out of gas. Or that the plug is out of the socket. But a disposal? Out of my league."

"That must be why you're such good cops," Wanda said. "Your job requires no mechanical aptitude whatsoever."

"Stop picking on me," Walt joked.

"Isn't there anybody here who can help our hosts?" Anne Marie pleaded. All eyes turned to Father Koesler.

"Don't look at me," Koesler protested. "We learned in the seminary that that's why parishes have janitors."

"I think I might be able to fix it," Rick Wheatley said in an unassuming voice.

Koesler was reminded of the biblical account of the feast at Cana. Before Jesus had worked any of His miracles, He, His disciples, and His mother were invited to a wedding. The hosts had served their wine generously. So much so that the supply was running low. Noticing this, Jesus' mother simply stated the fact: "They have no wine."

Jesus explained that His time had not yet arrived; it was too early for Him to intervene in such a situation.

His mother was not one to take no for an answer. She told the waiters to do whatever her son commanded.

There followed the first of Jesus' miracles—and one of His most famous. He told the waiters to fill six large stone jars with water, then to take them to the chief steward and await the steward's judgment.

The steward's comment after tasting the water-turned-to-wine: "Most people serve their good wine first. After the guests have had an abundance of that special wine then anything would suffice. But you have saved the best wine until last."

Or, as the late Fulton Sheen put it figuratively, "The water saw its creator, and blushed."

From the unlikeliest guest came the solution to a nagging problem. Rick probably was not going to make the disposal whole by means of a miracle. But it was in this company at least a minor miracle that someone with know-how could step forward to help.

"I am afraid this is my fault," Walt said. "That disposal has been acting up since we returned from our trip. I should have called the plumber."

"Just give me a couple of minutes," Rick said. Then, feeling he might be perceived as cocksure, "I didn't mean to give the impression that I can fix *any*thing. There are a few things that stymie me. Or I may not have the right tools. But I'll know once I take a look at it."

Those at the kitchen door stepped aside, creating a path for Rick. Koesler, thinking he might learn something of future use, took a step to follow him into the kitchen. "If you don't mind, Father," the boy said, "I work better if nobody's looking over my shoulder."

The priest backed off. Good-naturedly he patted the young man on the back. "It's all yours, Rick."

Those in the living room had time to engage in the briefest of small talk before Rick stuck his head through the kitchen door. "I need a hammer and a screwdriver, please."

"I'll get them," Wanda said. "Poor Walt here doesn't even know where they are."

Everyone laughed but Walt Koznicki, who reddened and smiled ruefully.

Now armed with the basic tools, Rick disappeared again into the kitchen, followed by no one. In just a few moments, the sound of the faucet going full blast was heard, followed by the clear hum of the happily purring motor. Everyone was duly impressed.

"Mrs. Koznicki, have you been missing a bone?" Rick appeared, holding up a fair-sized, circular bone that had once been part of a generous cut of rib-eye steak.

Wanda looked embarrassed. "It must've fallen down the disposal—"

"And lodged in there," Rick said. "I just fished around till I felt it. The disposal should work okay now."

"I can't thank you enough," Wanda said. "On top of everything, you've saved us from a repair bill much bigger than that bone."

Rick grinned. "You fed me tonight . . . and very well, too."

"It must be nice," Wanda said, looking pointedly at her husband, "to have somebody around the house who can take care of such emergencies." She smiled at Rick. "I assume you inherited your talent from your dad. It must've been handy for your mother to have him around . . . before the three of you children arrived, I mean. Or is it your mother who has the mechanical ability?"

Rick grinned again. "Neither. We kid Mom and Dad about it from time to time. We tell Mom that we can understand how she could've brought the wrong baby home. But . . . three?"

"You mean . . ."

"My parents are like all of you. Oh . . ." Now his was the face that reddened. "I'm sorry: I didn't mean to sound so smart-assy. Please excuse me."

His hosts and the other guests all laughed heartily.

When the laughter died down, Rick said, "If you think I'm good with my hands, you should see my brother and sister. They can build or fix anything. I'm learning from them all the time."

"So," Wanda said, "your folks are lucky . . . or at least they'll stay lucky till you move out. Then they'll be back on their own. Have they learned anything from their talented children?"

"I don't think so. They're like . . ." He was about to add insult to injury, but he caught himself. "They're like so many people who give up too easily. But, yes, when I move out they're going to be right back where they were before we three came along."

With that, the guests donned their outerwear and headed toward the front door. "Come on, Rick," said Anne Marie, "we'll take you home now."

"We'd better," Zoo said to Rick. "Walt and I are the only ones who could get you through the surveillance team."

FIFTEEN

D ON'T CHANGE THE CHANNEL. I wanna see this."
The bartender shrugged and took his hand from the remote control.

It was late Sunday evening. Besides the man on the bar stool, there were only two other customers. The couple, at a table in the far recesses of the room, seemed to be having an odd conversation: The man was steamed; the woman appeared disinterested.

The bartender studied the couple almost clinically. Chances were that tomorrow a newspaper headline would announce yet another homicide in a city that once had the distinction of being known as the Murder Capital of the United States.

If such were to be the case, if the newspaper headline was valid, cops would shortly be in here rounding up facts and witnesses. Just as well for him if he cooperated and gave the officers better than average information based on careful observation.

From long experience—how many similar scenes had he witnessed over the years?—he figured she was the guy's ex-wife or his soon-to-be ex-girlfriend. He was trying to reconcile. She was having none of it.

The bartender mentally constructed a likely outcome. She walks out on him. He follows her out. She starts walking nonchalantly down Washington Boulevard. He shouts after her. She continues to walk, without looking back. He pulls out a gun and fires several times. He is no marksman. He's lucky—or unlucky—that one of the bullets hits her in the head, fatally.

The bartender calls 911. The EMS gang gets here in a jiffy. They cart her off. Receiving Hospital pronounces her DOA.

The bartender ends up being the prime witness. He accepts the role; it's part of the price of admission.

❧❀❧

The bar, Jim's Place, is depressing. The odors of alcohol, cigars, and cigarettes permeate the room. The cleaning lady will be here in a few hours. She'll sweep, dust, mop a little. The odors and much of the grime will remain.

What this place needs, thinks Jim Davis, owner and mostly sole barman, is a crowd.

That's what used to happen here on a regular basis back in the seventies and before. When downtown Detroit was alive and kicking.

At five, six o'clock, people from the office buildings had joined people from the majestic Hudson's flagship store and those who staffed Washington Boulevard's Airline Row for Happy Hour before heading home in a relaxed alcoholic glow.

Downtown was where all the first-run movies were shown. Downtown had good—even great—restaurants. Downtown was where friends met friends under the Kern's clock, the oversized time-piece hanging from the third major store after Hudson's and Crowley's.

Whether those halcyon days would ever return and rejuvenate the city on the Detroit River was anyone's guess. Jim Davis was just marking time until he could retire with Social Security and Medicare. But his memories were vivid. Jim's Place had been an intimate bar on swanky Washington Boulevard, Detroit's antecedent version of Los Angeles's Rodeo Drive.

Now Washington Boulevard resembled a scene from the apocalyptic movie *On The Beach*: drab and deserted. Where classy shops had once displayed highly desirable attire for both men and women, now there were only boarded-up windows and third-rate merchandise. And whoever had erected those revolting monkey bars should have been forced to climb them endlessly.

On those occasions when the slogan *City of Champions* was valid because the Lions, the Tigers, the Pistons, and/or the Red Wings took a divisional title or a championship, there was a run on downtown.

But such occasions were sadly rare.

Davis would point out that Sunday nights were not typical because, of course, you couldn't measure downtown business by Sundays. Workdays and Saturdays were definitely better than Sundays. Not that much better. But better.

The man at the bar was unknown to Davis. That meant that this was probably his first visit. Davis recognized each and every one of his clientele. A memory for names and faces was a profitable talent in any business, and perhaps more so for bartenders.

The TV news update that the stranger wanted to see ended. It was commercial time.

"This your place?"

"Yeah, that's right."

"That your name: Jim?"

"Uh-huh. Yours, stranger?"

"Uh . . . Rybicki. Stan Rybicki. How come you said 'stranger'?"

"You ever been in here before?"

"Uh . . . no. But there must've been . . . I don't know—what? This place must be about forty years old."

"Yeah, about forty years."

"Forty years! There must have been hundreds . . . thousands of customers in here. You expect me to believe you remember everybody?"

"I got you right, didn't I, Stan?"

"Well, yeah, I guess you did."

Silence. Davis polished a glass that didn't need polishing. It was something for his hands to do. Smokers, particularly those who've broken the habit, need something to do with hands that no longer finger a cigarette. It didn't much matter to Davis that he no longer smoked. If what they said about the dangers of secondhand smoke inhalation was true, his customers would give him cancer almost as surely as he could do it himself.

There would be many periods of silence that both Davis and Rybicki would find comfortable. This was one such silence.

"Maybe I missed it," Rybicki said. "Did that TV guy say there would be more updates later on?"

"If he did, I didn't hear him. You interested in something special?"

"Yeah."

"The early news comes on at ten."

"Yeah."

Silence.

"You don't get downtown often?"

Rybicki snorted. "Why?"

"Oh, nuthin' special. Just that you knew I was here for forty years. But I don't remember ever seein' you before. Is all."

"I used to work down here."

"Yeah? Where?"

"The chancery building."

"The chancery building?" Davis grew animated. "That's practically across the street. Headquarters for the Catholics in Detroit. Well, more'n the city—the whole archdiocese. Takes up about six counties."

"That's it."

"Were you a priest?"

Rybicki almost choked. "You think everybody who works there is a priest?"

"You kind of look the type."

"What does the type look like?"

"I don't know exactly. The combination: white hair; portly; red face; easy way with liquor."

"I think it was just 'cause I mentioned the chancery. Good ol' 1234 Washington Boulevard. One of downtown's most famous addresses. It's true: Most of the jobs there belonged to priests, or monsignors, or bishops. But there's always a few jobs held down by ordinary guys like me."

Silence.

"How long you work there?"

"About twenty years."

"I must be losing my touch. You worked across the street for half the time this bar's been here and I don't know you!"

"Not to wonder. I just didn't come in here. Or any other bar."

"You work and go home?"

"You got it."

Silence.

"You work this place by yourself?" Rybicki asked.

"I got a guy for lunch and dinner Monday through Saturday. Sundays you could fire a cannon in here"—he spread his hands and inclined his head toward the almost empty room—"and not hit anybody."

"Dinner. You got dinner?"

"Burgers and trimmings. That's it."

"Could you whip me up one?"

"Sure."

"Medium and everything on it."

"You got it."

Davis disappeared into a room behind the bar. Soon the evocative aroma of frying meat and sizzling onions wafted out. Davis did not reemerge. Evidently he preferred tending the burger through to the bitter end.

Rybicki glanced at the couple at the far end of the room. His impression was that the woman was about ready to leave. She was sipping the last of her wine.

The man was crying. Noiselessly, but crying nonetheless.

Rybicki frowned. Men shouldn't cry . . . at least not in public. It was creepy. He had the urge to march over to their table and give the guy a shot upside the head. That'd give him something to cry about.

But he didn't make a move. Granted, the guy had maybe thirty years on Rybicki. But Rybicki had maybe thirty pounds on the guy. So he wasn't afraid. Not for a moment. He just didn't want to get involved. He would just munch his burger and nurse the Miller Lite.

Davis returned, set the burger plate before Rybicki, and shoved the condiments on the counter toward him. Rybicki squeezed on a touch of mustard. That was all. He bit into the burger. Heavenly. The meat was thick and pink and juicy. The onions were just singed—al dente. And only three bucks. Three bucks for a perfect burger. He vowed that given the chance he'd be back with some regularity. But he wouldn't be recommending this find to anyone; he'd keep it as his own private oasis.

Davis glanced at the couple. He saw what Rybicki had seen. Davis felt no urge to intervene in any way. His only concern was that there be no bloodletting in his bar.

"So what'd you do in the chancery? You not being a priest or anything?"

"I ran the elevator."

"That's it?"

"It was busy. Lots of people came to the chancery. Mostly guys who worked there. Priests who ran the various departments in the archdiocese: the Tribunal, the Propagation of the Faith, Catholic schools, Catholic cemeteries . . . like that. I started there a little bit before Cardinal Mooney died.

"You couldn't tell he was so near death. He went off to Rome to help elect a new Pope. But he died just before the Cardinals were locked up in the Sistine Chapel for the duration.

"He was a class act, he was." He nodded in recollection. "A real class act."

"You got to know him?"

"Saw him just about every day. Going and coming. It didn't take him long before he knew my name . . . and used it. 'How are you, Mr. Rybicki?' he would say. Yup . . ." He nodded again. " . . . a real class act."

Silence.

The couple at the far table were quiet—both of them.

Good. Davis was all for quiet. Especially from people like that couple.

They had entered the bar about two hours ago. She'd ordered a white wine, which she was just now finishing. He was nursing only his third beer.

Davis didn't care. They could sit there till closing time as far as he was concerned. As long as there was no trouble, Davis was the soul of indifference.

"A real class act," Rybicki repeated.

"What was that?" Davis's concentration wobbled. He had forgotten what Rybicki was talking about.

"The guys who used to work in the chancery. Starting with the bishop . . . and on right through the ranks."

"You think it's gone downhill now?"

"Oh, yeah. You know, when I was running that elevator you had to have an appointment to see the boss."

"That so?"

"Every morning they gave me a list of names that I stuck up on the wall of the elevator. These were the guys who had an appointment and who could get out on the second floor. That was the boss's floor.

"Some of the movers and shakers—not just in the Church, but also the business community—would get off on two. I got to know them pretty good, too.

"Then in the late sixties, early seventies, the crybabies started comin' in. Usually I would recognize them from seeing their pictures in the papers and on TV. Peaceniks, flower children—those guys. Hair all over and dressed to slop pigs." He made a face. "Disgusting!"

"That why you got outta there?"

"Partly. Anyway, because I got to know a lot of the brass—mostly Ford and GM guys—I got a job as a security officer at GM headquarters on Grand Boulevard."

"And you lived happily ever after?"

Rybicki did a double take. Was Davis making fun of him? After a moment he decided not. Rybicki was a mesomorph. Had he been playing pro football in the present, he would have been an interior defensive lineman. Even at his present age, people shied away from the casual insult. "Yeah," Rybicki said at length. "I've been doin' okay. All things considered."

"So what brings you downtown on a late Sunday? Reliving old times?"

"Nah . . ." Rybicki was glum. "I wanted to see that sonuvabitch they were gonna ordain today."

"Huh?"

"You know . . . you musta read about him in the papers."

No reaction from Davis.

"On radio or TV?" Rybicki couldn't believe that anyone in the metropolitan area wasn't aware of the unique Catholic religious event that had been scheduled for earlier this day.

Apparently there was at least one oblivious person. And Rybicki was talking to him.

The barkeep picked up another clean glass and began polishing it. " 'Fraid not."

"You don't read the papers?"

"Sports . . . some comics."

"No TV news?"

"Sports. Maybe the weather. That's about all my customers talk about. I reckon I don't have to be up on anything else."

"I guess it figures," Rybicki said, almost sadly.

"So what was going on that got you down here?"

"It's kind of complicated."

"Try me. I'm a quick study."

So Rybicki related the tale of the noted Episcopal priest—noted, apparently by everyone but Davis—who'd left the Episcopal priesthood and was supposed to have been ordained in the Catholic Church today.

"Today? *Supposed* to be? What happened?"

Rybicki told him about the bomb.

"That was on TV?"

"Yeah. That was the news update you were gonna turn off a little while ago, but I ast you to leave it on . . . remember?"

"Yeah . . . I remember you asked me to leave it on." Davis whistled softly. "Man, this is gettin' bad if I'm not payin' any attention to a bomb going off in a church in Detroit!"

"Well, that's what happened."

"Why would anyone want to knock off a priest? Especially with a bomb?"

"For starters he—this new guy—likes the idea of women priests." He looked at Davis sharply. "How would you like to go into a Roman Catholic church and see a woman up there in vestments, saying Mass?"

Davis smiled. "I was raised a Catholic . . . even went to a parochial school for a while. Tell you the truth, thinking back, I'd rather see and hear a woman doin' it than some of the men I remember."

Rybicki waved away the remark. In doing so, he almost knocked over his glass of beer. "Get serious," he said. "Besides women at the altar, this guy—this Wheatley—is gonna bring his wife in. They'll be living together." He shook a warning finger at Davis. "Now don't come back with a smart-alec remark like, 'Husbands and wives generally live together.'"

"I know you'll believe me when I tell you, you took the words right out of my mouth."

"I thought so. There's no use talking to you." Rybicki rose as if to leave.

"Don't go," Davis said. It wasn't the first time he'd had to placate a disgruntled customer. *Why didn't I keep my mouth shut?* "I promise: no more smart-ass remarks. I really oughta be up on something like this. I got a hunch you can give me straighter stuff than the media will."

"Well, okay." Rybicki sat back down on the bar stool. "The thing that pisses me off is that all these hippies and yippies who used to crowd into the chancery are gonna think they won. They wanted women priests. They wanted married priests. Now they found their hero in this Wheatley guy. Hell, his daughter's even gonna be a priest. And he's *married*." He made it sound like some loathsome disease.

"So with this one guy, they've achieved a couple of their main goals. What comes next: abortion; annulments on demand; getting together with Lutherans, Baptists, what all? I can just see these turkeys the way I used to see them at the chancery. The only reason I put up with 'em then was I knew they were doomed to failure." He sneered. "I knew they could never win. The Catholic Church was the mighty fortress!"

"Man," Davis managed to get a word in, "you are really worked up over this."

"Damn straight I am!"

"Bad for your blood pressure."

"I don't give a damn!"

Davis was getting a bit uneasy about Rybicki. Somebody who says he doesn't give a damn, after making it obvious that he definitely *does* give a damn . . .well, in a situation like this, it could mean that this guy feels, "What the hell; I've got nothing to lose." And with that sentiment, the sky's the limit—up to and including even murder.

"Whoa . . ." Davis warned. "Isn't it possible that the guy . . . what's his name?"

"Wheatley."

"Wheatley . . . that he's like an innocent bystander in this thing. Okay, so maybe he wants to switch religions. So maybe he can't see anything wrong with women priests. But look: All he can do is submit his case. He can't do it on his own. No more than the flower children of the seventies—the ones that used to drive you up the wall—could.

"I mean, I'm no expert, but isn't it pretty much up to the Church whether or not to let him have his way? It's like the hairy kids years ago. They wanted all this stuff. But you didn't get so worked up because—as you said—they were doomed: The Church wouldn't let them have their way.

"So now it's a different story. Now the Church is getting out of their way . . . am I wrong?"

Rybicki was silent, pondering.

"I can see your point," he said finally. "But it doesn't seem to help me. I mean, you can't bomb the whole screwed-up Catholic Church. What you *can* do is blast one small corner of it. Just to get the attention of Rome. Yeah, all the way to the Vatican with a bomb set off here in southeast Michigan. Right here in Detroit's core city."

Silence as both Davis and Rybicki mulled over each other's words.

Suddenly a commotion from the only other people in the room—the odd couple. The man shouted something—it was unintelligible—at his companion.

Wouldn't you know, thought Davis; only three customers in the place and every one of them poses a potential problem.

Davis didn't know which deserved the bulk of his attention. He finally returned his focus to Rybicki, while remaining alert to the couple. "Look, I don't have any firsthand knowledge of the bombing this afternoon. Right now all I know is what you told me. Were you there? I mean when the bomb exploded?"

"I was there," Rybicki said with a tone of self-satisfaction.

"Well, how did you feel about it . . . I mean, when the bomb went off . . . and afterward?"

"I was rocked at first. I didn't expect any explosion. It was deafening. Scary, too," he added after a moment.

"Well," Davis pursued, "what about after? After the bomb?"

An odd smile crossed Rybicki's face. "I felt glad . . . happy. I thought whoever did it oughta get a medal."

"You gotta be kidding! I mean, you didn't know what the damage was. You didn't know whether the priest was dead or alive. You didn't know how many people—how many *Catholics*—had been injured or killed. How could you feel happy?"

"It wasn't like that," Rybicki protested. His face twisted. "An' I don't take kindly to bein' accused of not givin' a shit who got hurt. Sure I hoped that nobody else got hurt. The point is, I figured that if somebody tried to get the sonuvabitch with somethin' as big as a bomb, well then, he probably got him.

"And if some others got hurt or killed . . . well, there's worse things than death."

"That's crazy, man," Davis said. "This is human life we're talking about. You can't wish that much misery on somebody. My God, the guy's a priest! Ain't anything sacred?"

Rybicki leaned over the bar. He was a large man; when he extended himself his face was only inches from Davis's. "Listen, my friend: The bogus priest may have survived this attack this afternoon. But he can't be so lucky that he continues to dodge the bullet every-time someone tries to kill him."

Davis instinctively leaned back away from Rybicki's strong presence. "Friend, you make it sound like there's an army out there waiting to kill this priest. That can't be so . . ."

"Maybe not an army . . . but there's lots of people who'd gladly buy into a lottery for the next chance to get rid of the guy. We're not so very many, but"—Rybicki's voice dropped to a harsh whisper— "we're committed. We'll do it!"

With that, Rybicki downed the last of his beer, slammed the glass down on the bar, spun about, and strode out. He walked such a straight line that any cop checking him for sobriety would be satisfied.

It had been a disturbing conversation. Jim Davis was a peaceable man. He was that way by nature and had made pacification a principal practice. Operating a bar, especially in downtown Detroit, called for this. Many's the argument he'd had to mediate. Many's the fight he'd had to break up.

176

But this Rybicki, he was a rare bird. His quarrel was with the Catholic Church. Davis did not get many beefs like that.

And as for killing that priest, how much of that was for real and how much was the beer talking? Judging from his long experience listening to customers whose basic attitudes were colored by alcohol, Davis would wager that Rybicki had just pumped himself up and was no real threat.

Davis turned his attention to the remaining couple. He couldn't understand why the woman had stayed this long. She'd given every indication that she didn't want to hang around with the guy. Was she just baiting him? Some women did that . . . oftentimes to their eventual sorrow.

Suddenly she stood, picked up her purse, and walked purposefully out of the bar. Closely followed by her erstwhile companion.

Davis listened carefully. He half expected to hear a gunshot. But . . . nothing. All was quiet.

Too quiet.

Ten o'clock. Time for the local nighttime news on Channel 50.

The anchorwoman gave a big introduction to the most startling news story any area channel would feature anytime. A bomb had gone off in a local historic Catholic church this afternoon. Old St. Joe's, a place of prayer almost from the first days of the founding of the city of Detroit, was the scene of a bomb explosion that had destroyed part of the sanctuary and killed a visiting priest. After a commercial break, a reporter would be back with all the details.

Well, thought Davis, at least that Rybicki guy was right about the church bombing. He hadn't made that up.

But Davis wasn't about to wait around for the commerical break to end. It was past closing time. He began locking up. He'd be able to pick up the details on the eleven o'clock news after he got home. And tomorrow, nice and early, there'd be the newspaper.

As he turned the deadbolt, he wondered if he would ever see or hear of Rybicki again.

SIXTEEN

Most nights, before retiring, Father George Wheatley watched the eleven o'clock TV news. This evening he was early by an hour: He watched the ten o'clock news. That finished, he clicked the off button and watched as the screen zeroed into a white dot, and then darkness.

He walked slowly and deliberately around the house, checking all the locks. As he reached the front door he could see through the window the unmarked police car at the curb directly in front of the house.

Nothing had happened except for the arrival of his son, Richard, driven home by Lieutenant Tully and his wife. That, thought George, might rank as the safest ride in the city.

Richard briefed his parents on all that had gone on at and after the dinner at the Koznickis'. Then, not at all sleepy, he headed for his room and a little computer nonsense, as well as some homework before bed.

Neither George nor Nan had been hungry. They'd each had a bowl of cereal, merely to accompany their vitamin supplements.

They hardly said a word all evening. At about nine-thirty Nan kissed George on the forehead and went up to bed. George would've accompanied her, but he waited to see how the news treated this afternoon's explosion.

There were many shots of the interior of the church, especially the sanctuary. The damage did not seem widespread. The bomb's effectiveness appeared to have been limited to the section between the altar and the rear of the sanctuary, with emphasis on the area nearest the altar. Just where he himself would have been standing. He and Father Tully. George shuddered.

Now he would go to bed. Not because he was sleepy. Tired, yes; sleepy, no. He was going to retire because it was time to do so. He well knew what that meant: a long, lonely night of turning this way and that.

At times like this, he tried to convince himself that lying down, quietly resting, was good for one . . . even if sleep was delayed. The way he felt right now, it looked as if it might be an all-night delay.

That could be unfortunate. Tomorrow likely would be a most busy Monday. This thing had to be investigated. The culprit had to be apprehended. Plans had to be rescheduled.

George wanted to be ordained in the Roman Church. That hadn't changed. He wondered whether his sponsor, Cardinal Boyle, would still want to go through with it. After all, the Cardinal wouldn't want to establish an atmosphere wherein it could be open season on the clergy.

George knew that the Cardinal must even now be mulling over the possibilities. No use trying to figure how it was going. Tomorrow would be soon enough. And that was only a few hours away.

Everything was secured. His surveillance team was in place. Wheatley stood very still, gazing through the window at the officers. He couldn't actually see them. But they were there, that he knew.

They would do whatever was humanly possible to protect him, his wife, and his son. But there were so many windows and doors in this rambling house. It was too large for his diminished family. On the other hand, if ever he *was* ordained, he would be expected to move into St. Joe's rectory, which was also too large for his family. Meanwhile, he was grateful for the roof over their heads. Grateful to the Episcopal Church of Eastern Michigan, which, in recognition of the years of distinguished service George had given the Church of his birth, had permitted the Wheatleys to stay on in the rectory until George's future was firmly and irrevocably settled.

He wandered upstairs. He paused at Rick's door. He knocked softly several times, then pushed the door ajar.

The young man, in pajamas, and seemingly wide awake, was seated at his desk, which was almost covered with open books as well as a couple of legal pads. As George opened the door wider, Rick looked up apprehensively, then relaxed somewhat as he saw his father enter the room. "You all right, Dad?" He seemed genuinely concerned.

George smiled. "I'm hanging in there, son. How about you?"

Rick smiled. "I'm okay, I guess."

"Catching up on the homework?"

Rick nodded. "Sort of. But I can't seem to get what happened this afternoon out of my mind. It's kind of hard to concentrate."

"Want to talk about it?"

Rick thought for a few moments. "I don't think so. I'm getting tired, which means I'm moving in the right direction."

"I'm sure your teachers will be aware of all you've gone through today. I think they'll cut you some slack."

Rick began closing the books on his desk. "It always happens this way. I put off the homework and then something comes up and I don't get a chance to do it. I figured the Mass and the reception would be over by early evening. I guessed wrong. I should've taken the time to get this stuff out of the way. But in my wildest dreams I couldn't have expected . . ." His head drooped.

"Nobody could have. Hit the sack as soon as you can. If you need me for anything, just let me know. I'll be sleeping lightly—if at all."

George shut the door and headed for the master bedroom. He paused at the door of the room his daughter, Alice, used to call hers. How many hours he had spent with her, telling her stories, singing her songs . . .

He gave her door a gentle push and it opened slowly. He walked in and sat on the bed, just where he had sat so many times, so long ago.

Anytime he was asked which of his three children was his favorite, he always breezed off an answer along the lines of "They're all equally my favorite." Indeed he did love all his children totally, each for different reasons.

But in his heart, he knew that Alice, always his little girl, held the edge.

Why did she so oppose his decision to affiliate with the Roman Church? He had explained his reasons at length at the family gathering that had turned out to be their final meeting before the ceremony ordaining him to the Roman diaconate.

He had known beforehand how Richard and Ronald would react. Richard largely wouldn't give a darn. He just wasn't that involved with any organized religion, not even his own Episcopalianism.

As for Ronald, George was well aware that he had been competitive almost all his young life. It was a private joke between George and Nan. First Ronald played at offering Mass or leading prayer. Later he would find anything that his imagination could conceive as a microphone, and he would imitate George's technique in doing the radio broadcast.

At age five or six Ronald could have told anyone who cared to ask that when he grew up he was going to be a priest. It was cute.

After college graduation, Ronald, as expected, entered seminary. His classmates let him know repeatedly that while he was his father's son, he did not—and never would—measure up to his father's accomplishments.

That's when the competition became almost palpable.

George encouraged his son's clerical aspirations. The father didn't have a jealous bone in his body. This did not mean that George's own high standards did not remain constant. Aware that the boy's gifts were not as effective as his own, still he was proud of his priest son.

George kept watch over his son and the boy's religious career. So he was aware that Ron had begun entertaining thoughts of running for bishop. Quietly exploring appropriate dioceses, making himself very visible (but not too obvious). Where he knew a member of the nominating committee, he might just quietly, over martinis, let drop that he would not be averse to having his name included on the list of those under consideration. George did not think that ambition was healthy.

Occasionally he would try to talk to Ron about this. But each time Ron would somehow work in the text of St. Paul's letter to Timothy, Chapter 3: "This is a true saying. If a man desire the office of a bishop, he desireth a good work."

And each time, George would bow to Scripture. But he would admonish his son that while it might be pardonable to desire a bishopric, running for the position in much the same way as a politician compaigns for political office was *not*.

Then, too, a bishop in the early Church was hardly the same as a bishop today. Bishops in apostolic times often were prime targets for persecution and even death at the hands and whim of the Roman state.

Then came Ron's marriage to Gwen.

George would readily concede that she was quite the most beautiful young woman he had ever met. More beautiful, even, than Nan in her younger years.

George had to wonder why a woman with Gwen's attributes would choose to marry a priest. Not that there was anything questionable or wrong with marrying a priest. But a woman such as Gwen could have had almost any man she set her sights on. For instance, she could have married more money in five minutes than Ron would make if he were granted five lifetimes.

It was a mystery George never did solve. But then he had never been introduced to Gwen's background in any depth.

Ron was given Gwen's history because she didn't think she could get away with not sharing it with the man who would be her husband. Also she thought it important that he know where she was coming from and thus why certain things were a sine qua non for her.

Once Gwen came into Ron's life, he became doubly dedicated to becoming a bishop. He coveted the office for many reasons. Not the least of which was to best his father at something, something substantial. Then, upon his marriage, he wanted the office because his wife demanded it of him.

Ron, and surely Gwen as well, saw George's conversion to the Roman Church as an exceedingly significant obstacle to their goal. Right or wrong, they opposed it to the extent of severing relations with George and Nan. Both parents were saddened. But, in the final analysis, that was Ron and Gwen's decision. George felt called to the course he was on.

However, as hurt as he was by Ron and Gwen's cutting themselves off from him and Nan, George was grieved many times over by Alice's reaction.

Now that he was sitting on her bed remembering the private times they had shared, he felt the crushing loss of her love and support. Her reaction had been unexpected, but once that reaction became manifest, he could understand why she felt the way she did.

After all, he, her father, had introduced her to the special love of both their lives: the Church, their priesthood, and the Episcopal tradition, or, as Anglican theology had it, Scripture, Tradition, and Reason. It was all one package. That's the way he had taught her. That's the way she believed.

To take away one of those three foundations was like trying to take the milk from bread pudding.

And then her father did it. He removed the Episcopal from this three-legged foundation. With the abscision, her house of cards came crashing down.

Her peers in seminary let her know early and repeatedly that Father George Wheatley was a traitor and a defector. Some students actually shunned her. On the other hand, her staunch intimates protectively circled the wagons of their friendship.

In any case, no one was in any way neutral about what had transpired.

Alice was torn. And by this time her father knew it. He wished and he prayed for the Holy Spirit to gift Alice with understanding.

No matter how sticky things became between father and daughter, he was convinced that what he was doing and the way he was doing it was God's will. Just as he had come to his most difficult decision through prayer and penance, so he would stay the course. But he was heartbroken at the loss of his daughter. All he could do now was to hope that she would soften as time passed. He knew he would work tirelessly to bring this about.

Softly he hummed the melody from *Madama Butterfly*. *"Un Bel Dì."* One fine day, Alice would return to him. By happy coincidence, the aria was a favorite of both of them. Neither could have known, years ago, as Alice snuggled under the covers while he sang it to her, that such a day would come—a day when they would be estranged.

But it would all come together. He knew that God, in His generosity, would make it so. And that would indeed be *Un Bel Dì.*

He was crying. He knew not how long this had been going on, but he could feel the heat of each tear that found its path down his cheeks. He took a handkerchief from his robe pocket, wiped his eyes, and blew his nose.

Dwelling on thoughts such as these was a distraction he could ill afford. He was convinced he was doing the right thing. Damn the torpedoes; full speed ahead.

He left Alice's room, closing the door behind him. He walked the few feet to his bedroom, trying to be as quiet as possible. Nan's breathing was soft and regular; he assumed she was asleep. He slid into bed and pulled the bedcovers over himself, being careful not to disturb Nan. A lateral sleeper, he turned onto his left side.

He tried to surrender to sleep, but his brain refused to cooperate. It teemed with images of the traumatic events of just a few hours ago. If he had not taken that phone call, he would now be tucked in a hospital bed with tubes running into or out of appropriate orifices, and other tubes introduced into newly created orifices. Nurses would be hovering over him. Life support systems would be beeping, sustaining his bodily functions—his very existence. Or, he would be dead.

He felt overwhelmed by all these fantasized devices holding him immobile. Claustrophobia struck with a vengeance. He perspired freely.

He turned onto his right side, facing Nan. The sheets under him here were cool, a restful contrast to the spot he had just vacated. But he worried that if he got into a bout of tossing and turning, he might wake Nan.

Still his mind was a maelstrom. He thought, as he had so often lately, about so many things.

He pictured the priestly company he would soon be part of. The Roman priests who for one reason or another were rejecting him. Those who could not abide the very thought of women priests. It was so obvious that he supported that innovation: He'd flaunted his daughter's attendance at an Episcopal seminary. Others of his future brethren who had made the promise of a celibate life looked at him with resentment: He would be able to do all they did canonically while enjoying the consolation and pleasures of a wife and family.

Ron. *Father* Ron. George's priestly son. Had he erred in leading Ron toward the priesthood? In encouraging Ron instead of waving him off? Would George's affiliation with the Roman Church really cripple Ron's campaign for becoming a bishop? Is it always a good work for a man to desire the calling of bishop?

Was Ron being spurred on to attain this position by beautiful Gwen? While George did not completely understand what made Gwen tick, he was aware that she generally got what she wanted. She could be a formidable pressure should Ron's determination begin to flag.

He worried perhaps most about Alice. Her contemporaries could be cruel. One might expect better—more understanding—from seminarians. But seminarians, as well as priests and bishops, were human. They might fear the like-father/like-daughter possibility. With that they could, and probably did, make her life miserable.

Alice . . . his darling Alice. She, more than anyone—with the exception of Nan, of course—he wished would understand the path he had chosen.

All of this made him second-guess his move yet once more. His situation gave a new depth to the word ambivalence. But he had been over this countless times in prayer and in any number of rationalizations.

He wasn't getting any closer to sleep. He rolled over on his back. It was not his normal sleeping position. On the other hand, it made it easier for him to think, if thinking was the best he could do right now.

"Having a hard time of it?" Nan whispered.

"Did I wake you?" George returned the whisper. Why they were whispering was anyone's guess. With Richard occupied in his room, they were, for all practical purposes, alone in the house. But somehow, this late at night, whispering seemed appropriate.

"I haven't been asleep . . . just intermittent napping."

"I haven't been sleeping either."

"I know." Nan's smile, unseen by her partner, was ambiguous.

"I've been bouncing around. I tried not to wake you."

"It's all right. We've had a full day."

George nodded. "So much of what's happened has been focused on me. I'm afraid you've been neglected. How have you been holding up?"

"As well as can be expected, as they say in hospitals. I'd be a lot happier if my pulse rate would slow down."

"It's really reached you, hasn't it?"

"My life is so mingled with yours I can't help feeling all the things that affect you."

A long silence followed. So long that one or both of them might have fallen asleep.

"Still with me?" George tried to pitch his whisper so softly that if Nan was asleep he would not wake her.

"Yes." Pause. "You've been thinking of those closest to you who might have had something to do with that bomb, haven't you?"

George turned his head in her direction. Air exited his pillowcase in a whoosh. "How could you have known that?"

"How long have we been together? How close are we?"

George was well aware that over the years they had steadily grown closer. Frequently they had the same thoughts simultaneously. On review, it was not at all miraculous, let alone odd, that she would share his unspoken thoughts.

"You were thinking of your comrades, priests in the Episcopal as well as the Roman Church . . . weren't you?"

"You're right, of course."

"Do you really think that's possible?"

George was silent a moment. "All things are possible."

"Maybe. But, honey, we're talking about *murder*. And, granted, we know many in the clergy who are not worthy of the title 'a man—or woman—of God.' But can you really, sincerely imagine anyone in the clergy who would stoop to cold-blooded murder?"

"Until today, dear, I would have agreed completely with you. But *somebody* planted that bomb. It had to be premeditated all the way. I think they refer to it, at least on TV, as Murder One." He had intended the reference to television's infatuation with murder mysteries as a light touch calculated to soften this rather morbid, if low-keyed, conversation.

But Nan didn't laugh. She didn't even smile. This was life they were talking about . . . her husband's life. She did not want to be a widow. Ever. Surely not this soon.

"One thing for certain, I think," George said. "We're talking about a very small percentage of the clergy. Of those we know personally, there couldn't be more than an extremely small percentage who would seriously consider such a great evil as murder . . . and an even smaller percentage who would follow up on or carry out such a consideration.

"I mean, most of the clergy—Episcopal and Roman—aren't that deeply involved in my decision. The Anglicans feel they're losing me, and, by and large, most of them are not happy about that.

"Still speaking in generalities, the Romans resent the salary I'll be receiving. But much more, they'll resent my family—particularly you and Richard.

"But that's as far as it goes: resentment. They not going to *do* anything.

"Although," he said, after a moment's thought, "I suppose there are a few who might indeed do *some*thing."

"You haven't mentioned the laity," Nan said.

"No, I haven't. Only because—with no statistics to back me up— I can't see the laity getting that perturbed. Oh, maybe some heated discussion over the dinner table or at a parish meeting. But still . . ." He shook his head. "No, I don't see the laity making this their cause."

"But, darling, there's always the lunatic fringe—on both sides of the aisle."

"Yes. I'm quite aware of that. The angry letters that I get in response to some of my columns, and the wild phone calls that come into the radio station. But . . . no, I just don't think so.

"People who assassinate, I think, realize that they put their future in jeopardy. The men who shot John and Bobby Kennedy, Martin Luther King, Jr., John Lennon, Ronald Reagan, and the girl who attempted to kill Gerald Ford—they're all behind bars or have died in captivity.

"Assassins almost always throw their own lives away in the commitment of their crime. Besides, in any case, what can be done about it? The most convenient weapon is a gun. And this country has guns all over the place—"

"I know what you're going to say, dear: Something to the effect that if people want to kill somebody, they'll be able to do so—as long as they don't mind what happens to them afterward."

"Well, that's true, isn't it?"

"I suppose."

Both lay motionless staring at the barely visible ceiling. They could hear the water running in the bathroom down the hall. Rick was getting ready to retire, whether or not his homework was completed.

"Besides," George said, "Lieutenant Tully is doing his best to guard us. Two of his men are just outside the house now."

But Nan wasn't thinking of the guards. The running water called her attention to Richard and their other two children. The hardest part for Nan in this entire enterprise had been the reaction of Ron and Alice. She knew this affected George, too, but not as deeply, she felt, as it did her.

She and George had, of course, talked about this—many times— in the past. But the added consideration of today's attempted murder made it now imperative to get this into the open and air it out. This was as good a time as any. "How do you feel about the kids?"

"The kids?"

"In all your thinking, planning, have you thought about the kids being involved in this at all?"

Silence.

"To be honest," he said finally, "the thought has crossed my mind. I try to rid myself of such considerations as quickly as possible. It couldn't be."

"Dear, don't you think that we underestimated their reaction to your decision? We knew they'd be surprised and somewhat negative, at least in the beginning. But we never thought their resentment would be so deep or that it would last so long—how long now?— nearly a full year.

"All this time and their bitterness is so deep . . . deeper than it was in the beginning . . ."

Nan sighed. "I know . . . Do you think Richard is play-acting? I mean, this thing hasn't seemed to bother him in the least."

George laughed softly. "Richard? With Richard you get what you see. I think he's enjoying all that's happened—with the exception, of course, of the bomb.

"No, I'd be very surprised if Richard doesn't come out of this smelling the roses.

"I must confess," he said after a moment, "I don't grasp Alice's problem. I know she's taking a ribbing at school over this. Not only from some of the seminarians, but even from some of the faculty . . . which surprises and disappoints me.

"But Alice should have the backbone to rise above that. It puzzles me. It's almost as if there's something else going on . . . something she wants kept secret. Something she's afraid will come out with all this publicity." He, too, sighed. "I trust in the Lord to reveal what's troubling her . . . so we can do something to help her."

For the past year or so Nan had quietly shared George's concern with regard to Alice. She hadn't communicated her worry to him. He had a heavy enough burden as he began the process of his submission to the Holy See. Nan was so intimately caught up in that journey that she had found no time or opportunity to take the matter up directly with Alice.

"Last and by no means least," Nan said, "is Ronnie. He has, from the beginning, had a most difficult time coping with your decision."

"Yes, I know. But he's jockeying for bishop. We've talked about this before—you and I. I don't approve of what he's doing. But he's my son . . . my firstborn. In a limited way, I've tried to advise him on this matter."

"You have?" Nan almost sat up. "I didn't know that. You didn't tell me." Far more surprising to Nan than that George had advised Ron was the fact that her husband had not discussed it with her. The two prided themselves on their intercommunication, especially in such important matters as this.

"I'm sorry, dear." George had had no compelling reason for not talking it over with her. He had just considered his limited counsel as merely minor, if largely unaccepted, guidance in the face of Ron's ambition. "I just told him," George went on, "to be most careful that the powers that be did not become aware that he was running for the office of bishop. It would be the kiss of death. At least by the book, the office is supposed to seek the man or woman, not vice versa."

"When was this?"

"Oh, long ago. Before he married Gwen."

"How did he take it—your advice, that is?"

"You mean did he resent my meddling in his campaign? I think not. He may have perceived this even before I brought it to his attention. In any case he seemed surprised that I would attempt to help him. He knew I didn't approve of what he was doing. I didn't. And I don't. But, he *is* my son. He's my firstborn," he said again. He hesitated. "We are close, Ron and I."

"I know."

"Not perhaps as close as Alice and I. But I never got the feeling that either Ron or Richard was jealous about that."

"They aren't," Nan assured him. "I think—I truly do—that you have been an excellent father to each and every one of them."

"That means a lot, coming from you. I mean, I know you would be frank with me on a matter like this."

Nan squeezed his hand. The gesture was an affirmation of what he had just said.

"If I'm concerned about anyone in the family, frankly, it would be Gwen," George said. "She has always seemed exclusively dedicated to achieving her goals in life. She thinks things over carefully, lays her plans, and from that point on, she's a juggernaut."

"I agree with you completely," Nan said. "I must admit I was astonished that a girl like her would choose to marry a priest."

George was smiling. "What do you mean, 'a girl like her'?"

"She's gorgeous," Nan declared. "Quite the most beautiful girl I've ever seen."

"I agree."

"Oh, you do?" It was Nan's turn for frivolity.

"In the sense of 'Look, don't touch,'" George explained somewhat feebly.

"What I meant," Nan went on, "is that she could get pretty nearly any man she set her cap for. If her prime concern was money, she could have married anyone: Donald Trump, Bill Gates, whomever."

"So, what's a girl like Gwen doing married to a simple parish priest?"

Nan shook her head in the dark. "I didn't mean to be denigrating. There's nothing wrong with marrying a priest . . . after all, I did."

"Not only did you marry a poor, humble priest, but you've just been describing yourself."

"What?"

"One day," George predicted, "Gwen will look just as you do now. When we were married, I thought you were the most beautiful woman I'd ever met."

"Don't get me wrong, dear"—Nan was close to blushing—"I enjoy a compliment as much as the next girl. But even on my best day I couldn't hold a candle to Gwen. You, my darling, have eyes that are blinded by love. And I thank God for that."

"We are two lucky people who fell in love. And grew in love."

"You're right about that, sweetheart. We married because we were in love. But I think Gwen married Ron because he was bishop material. Anyway, that's *my* evaluation. And all that did was to increase the pressure on our boy to make good."

Now Nan did sit up. "You don't mean you think Gwen could be involved in some sort of plot to kill you!"

"No. No. Not that. Nothing to do with murder. It's . . . it's just that I think she's high-pressuring Ron to get in there and fight. Get to be a bishop.

"You know, all Gwen's early life was spent associating religion with poverty. Her father was a preacher . . . and dirt poor. I think she wants to put together a combination more to her liking. She is determined to link religion with power and prestige. *She's* not going to be the daughter of a Raggedy Andy preacherman; she's going to be the wife of a bishop. And not just the bishop of Timbuktu . . . more like New York or L.A."

"You think she's planning that far ahead?"

"If I had a last buck, I'd put it on that. She's got a plan; and she needs to move it along on schedule. My going over to the Roman Church she probably sees as a glitch that can be repaired."

Nan slid back down in the bed.

The two were silent, but still not close to sleep.

"Well," Nan said finally, "there *was* a bomb."

"That surely is true. There was a bomb."

"And it was intended for you."

"Granted again."

"Any ideas on who might be responsible?"

"Putting together all we know, I'd have to say it was someone very—or at least quite—familiar with Liturgy. He—or she—had things timed pretty tightly.

"The person would have to be intimately involved in at least some facet of religion. It's pretty clear someone does not want me to be a Roman Catholic priest—for whatever reason.

"I don't want to believe that it could be an Episcopal or Roman priest. That, I think, would just break my heart.

"Yours, too, I'll wager," he added, after a moment.

"I can't bring myself to think it's a priest either," Nan said. "It's got to be a fanatic of the right or left. I'm just praying that the police get whoever it is soon. Very, very soon."

"Amen to that!" George affirmed. "Right now, for all we know, this thing might be over."

"Do you think so? Nan grasped at the tenuous hope. "Do you really think so?"

"Sure. Why not? He took his chance. It failed. He probably put a lot into this plan. I wouldn't be surprised that he's given up after the first try. Now that he's seen the effect of his efforts."

"That's a happy thought." She hugged herself. "I'm just going to hold on to it." She turned onto her side. "Let's try to get some sleep."

"A splendid idea." But he didn't turn to his side. There were other things to ponder.

"And," Nan added, before what was to be a fitful sleep, "let's not forget the person who made that phone call and saved all those lives. Whoever he was, we are beholden."

Yes, George thought, *that just might be the trickiest mystery of the day.*

SEVENTEEN

L EON," GRACE HARKINS CALLED from the top of the basement steps, "come on up. It's time to go to bed."

"You go ahead, Gracie. I'll be up soon."

Grace Harkins wasn't worried. She was concerned.

Her husband was a creature of routine. Their life together conformed to a staggering series of routines. Before she was married she'd always been spontaneous. After marriage, initially there was a struggle. Her spontaneity, and many other similar traits, slowly fell by the wayside. And, inevitably, routine won out.

That's why she was concerned now. Normally, Sundays were packed with one established routine after another.

First there was Mass. Then a substantial breakfast. The many-sectioned newspaper was casually read. It was too large and too multifaceted to be absorbed from first to last page.

Usually, Leon just scanned headlines and glanced at the captions under the pictures. Sports was the only section in which he invested a measure of thoroughness.

That was followed by a nap.

After the nap there had to be at least one, if not several, televised sporting events. Commercial television's great gift to weekends was to fill them with sports coverage. And the sports reciprocated by shamelessly overlapping each other.

Once upon a time sports events sharply demarcated the seasons. Fall was football, winter was hockey, spring was basketball, and baseball was summer. Sports such as golf and tennis were more in search of a climate than a season.

That was then. Now, sports fell all over each other in search of network gold that trickled down from commercial investment. The end result was that people like Leon Harkins need never be without televised sports no matter what time of year it was.

Late Sunday afternoon dinner would be a lesser meal due to the filling brunch. Not infrequently, football widows were still challenged to schedule dinner for half-time break. To pull this off with perfect timing was just that: a challenge; from the so-called two-minute warning to the actual halftime, a good twenty minutes to a half hour could elapse, courtesy of all those commercials.

Sunday evening's TV offerings routinely led to a reasonable bedtime.

Which was why Grace Harkins was now concerned. Instead of sporadically napping in front of the TV set throughout the evening as was his wont, Leon had descended to the basement. He had been down there for hours now. He had broken his Sunday evening routine all to hell and gone.

And then, in response to his wife's summons, Leon had done nothing more than put her on the back burner.

It had all started with that graphic film of the bombing of St. Joe's church. Yes, Grace nodded to herself, that was definitely it. There were, she felt, many ways one could have reacted to that story—none of which would be to spend the entire evening in the basement.

Written-in-stone routine had filled this Sunday until that ominous event on TV.

Grace was concerned, not so much that Leon had spent the evening in the basement, but that he'd fractured his routine. This would trouble her, thus interfering with her own routine of falling asleep as soon as her head hit the pillow.

But . . . Leon was the boss: Leon giveth routine and Leon taketh routine away.

❧❀☙

Meanwhile, in the basement, Leon had made his well-considered selection. Having so many from which to choose, he'd had to measure what this particular weapon would be asked to accomplish.

The single- and double-action Taurus fit his hand like the proverbial glove. It came with a key that activated the trigger lock.

194

And what was all this complaining about gun safety laws? If all handguns were as safety-conscious as this one, any of the complaints made by these knee-jerk liberals would be seen as just plain silly.

Leon had spent hours this Sunday evening cleaning and oiling the weapon and its leather holster. He practiced repeatedly, drawing the revolver from the holster below his left arm.

Of course this was not going to be a shootout at the O.K. Corral. The concept here was simple.

Over the months that he had been communicating with Father Tully about the goings-on at that dear old parish, St. Joe's, Leon, himself such a creature of routine, had become familiar with Tully's routine.

Tomorrow, Monday, would be the ideal moment to strike.

Tully began the morning with Mass at eight-thirty and finished the Liturgy at about nine-fifteen. Leon would not make his move during or immediately after Mass. Some things must remain sacred.

Then the housekeeper would serve the priest breakfast.

Not then. There'd be a witness.

After breakfast, about ten-thirty, Tully would sort out the Sunday collection, then deliver it to the bank. This could be an ideal time to strike—except that often Tully was accompanied on this mission. Tony, the janitor and general handyman, found this a convenient time to do his own banking. And, on occasions when the collection had been generous, money bags could be heavy; Tully could use the help.

Banking completed, after dropping Tony back at the rectory, Tully would stop off at the women's holding cells in Police Headquarters. This had proved an extremely fruitful time to visit with some ladies who were extraordinarily sorry. Admittedly, their sorrow, more often than not, sprang from having been caught and arrested, rather than from having sinned. But any sort of sorrow, Tully had learned, was a good place to start and perhaps build upon.

After all that had been accomplished, Tully would return to the rectory for lunch.

That was the time.

According to Leon's surveillance, Tully was never accompanied by anyone when he returned for lunch.

That may not have been the optimal time, but as far as Leon's investigation revealed, it was good enough.

The revolver had never looked better. Not even when it was brand new. Leon passed it back and forth from hand to hand. It began to feel more natural in his grip.

Carefully he loaded each chamber with a .357 round, then secured the weapon. It was ready.

It would be extremely effective at moderately close range. It would do a lot of damage.

He had fired the weapon previously, but always at an inanimate target. Tomorrow he would hunt big game. He would teach all so-called priests a lesson: not to fool with the sacred Liturgy.

Leon had planned most carefully. He'd first considered doing something like this when he'd become convinced that he was getting the royal runaround from the chancery as well as from the parish.

But it was the incident this afternoon that opened the door for him. Somebody had been brave enough to cry halt with the aid of a bomb. Okay, so it hadn't done its job. Someone else had to pick up the torch. And that someone was Leon Harkins.

His cry was that of the crusaders: "God Wills It!"

EIGHTEEN

M ONDAY MORNING.
A dismally gray day in Detroit. Meteorologists reported scattered clouds and some sunshine in the far northern suburbs. But the sun was having nothing to do with the city, nor with Metropolitan Airport, the base for many of the forecasts.

Washington Boulevard, once the stylish center of downtown, made its quiet prediction that it never would return to its elegant past.

In the same general area, on the eastern outskirts of downtown, stood historic St. Joseph's parish, whose sanctuary had been severely damaged in yesterday's bombing. In the basement of the rectory, Father Tully was consecrating bread and wine for holy Communion.

It was 8:55 A.M.

Two men in clerical attire were walking across Washington Boulevard from a car park toward the chancery.

On the ground floor of a building across from the chancery and slightly north of the Church administration headquarters was a bar and grill called Jim's Place. Jim was cleaning his place of the modest trash his few Sunday customers had left behind. He would never get rid of the stale odor, but he could sweep, mop, and polish. The cleaning woman never quite got it all.

Out of the corner of his eye, he saw two black-clad men walking away from him toward the chancery. He had no idea who they might be. They were, he noted, the only people on the boulevard at this hour.

Jim Davis was about to redevote his entire attention to cleaning when one of the men, the shorter of the two, turned to check for traffic. There was none. But Jim caught sight of the man's profile. He was sure he recognized the man. But from where? It was someplace recent. Where, where . . . ?

It came to him: this morning's paper. One of the two clergymen who'd been the alleged targets in yesterday's bombing.

The whole bizarre conversation with that nut came back. On a hunch, Davis looked up and down the boulevard. There was one car, standing at the curb near the north end of the street, pointed toward the south and the chancery. Could it be the nut's car? Smoke was coming from the exhaust, so its motor must be running.

Davis turned away from the bow window. Getting too involved could mean unwanted trouble. He resumed his cleaning. It would be a while before the bar was open for business.

"It was good of you to come with me, Bob," Father George Wheatley said.

"I've been with you through this whole process," Father Robert Koesler responded. "I'm going to be with you to the conclusion. Besides, I'd be surprised if you got much sleep last night after all you went through yesterday. I thought you might appreciate having a friend around."

"No . . . you're right; I didn't." Wheatley wished devoutly he had had a more restful night.

They entered the outer doors of the chancery and walked toward the elevator along the corridor that the chancery shared with the Catholic Bookstore and the offices of St. Aloysius parish.

"Second floor, please," Koesler directed the operator.

"Your names, please?" the very large, very black man challenged. Koesler knew that on the best day of his life he would never physically take on this gentleman.

He gave the operator their names. Wordlessly the man checked them against the list affixed to the control panel—the list of those who would be allowed to exit on the second floor.

The second floor comprised a reception area, the offices of the Cardinal Archbishop and his secretaries. The entire floor was quiet. Even the lighting was indirect and soft.

They waited only briefly before one of the secretaries said, "The Cardinal will see you now."

As they entered his office, Cardinal Boyle stood to greet them. After they shook hands, he motioned toward the chairs at a low, round table.

Wheatley had not met with the Cardinal often. On each previous visit the priest had marveled at how frail the prelate appeared. His hair was wispy white, and his frame was so fragile one felt that he would break if hugged. His very existence seemed linked with that of the Pope. Both had been influential at the Second Vatican Council—but in opposite directions.

They had proceeded on divergent paths. As an instance: Boyle had founded the Call to Action, a liberal organization that championed the laity's role in the Church. The Pope endorsed those who condemned and opposed the CTA.

When Wheatley, Koesler, and Boyle were seated, the Cardinal asked if either of his visitors would like coffee. Neither did. They got down to business. Which definitely was the Cardinal's style.

"Terrible thing, yesterday," Boyle said. "Tragic . . . poor Father Farmer."

"It was indeed a terrible thing, Eminence," Wheatley replied.

"I've been briefed on what happened," Boyle said. "But not by anyone who was actually present." It was an invitation to these two priests, who not only had been eyewitnesses, but who, each from his own vantage, could put most of the events together like a jigsaw puzzle.

Koesler and Wheatley took turns describing what had happened, trying to keep events in chronological order.

Throughout their painstaking recap of what took place, Boyle sat in profound concentration. The lines in his face deepened.

They climaxed their description with the explosion. At that moment, Wheatley had been ready for the procession up the aisle. The head of that cortege had just begun to move. Koesler had been hurrying to take his place in line.

Immediately after the explosion occurred, Koesler turned and dashed up the aisle, along with Lieutenant Tully. They were among the few who actually saw what the bomb had done to Father Farmer.

Meanwhile, Wheatley had been hustled back to the vesting area, where he would be as protected and safe as anyone could assume possible. After all, an incident of extreme violence had just occurred. No one knew then, and no one knew yet, exactly who had done what— or why.

The two priests concluded their co-narration. The Cardinal sat almost motionless, his only movement the fingering of a cuff link. He always wore French cuffs when in clerical garb.

"It would seem," Boyle said in his scholarly fashion, his soft voice overlaid with a tantalizing hint of his Irish ancestry, "the most intriguing element of this entire tragic event is the phone call you received, Father Wheatley."

"Yes, Eminence," Wheatley replied. "As I said, the voice was muffled—deliberately, I'm sure."

Koesler, whose mind was frequently apt to wander, wondered about that. Why would anyone bother to muffle a voice unless it was someone Wheatley knew? Or could it be because the caller's normal voice was distinctive enough to be identified? Or had the caller wished to disguise his voice just on general principles?

"Strange," Boyle commented. "Strange that you should honor this request for confession . . ."

"I just didn't see it that way, Eminence. The caller seemed desperate. And I thought: What's so important about a procession that it can't wait a few minutes to help a desperate soul?"

Boyle's face creased with smile lines. "I would hope you would feel that way."

"Besides"—Wheatley relaxed in the warmth of Boyle's understanding—"if I had not waited for the man, I would not now be here talking with you."

Nothing was said for several moments. Wheatley's statement was a consideration to be meditated upon.

"Well," Boyle said finally, "that brings us to what we intend to do about this."

Koesler and Wheatley looked at each other. The Cardinal's statement lent itself to many interpretations.

"You mean," Koesler asked, "are we going to go ahead with Father Wheatley's, uh, reception into the Roman Catholic priesthood?" Koesler could not bring himself to call this procedure an ordination. As much as anything else, Koesler had built a friendship with as well as an admiration for Wheatley. Thus the noun "reception."

Boyle nodded. "Yes. That would be the basic question. Yesterday's attack, among other things, indicates that there is physical danger accompanying this ordination . . ." Obviously the Cardinal did not have a problem with the term. " . . . at least here in Detroit."

"Excuse me, Eminence," Wheatley interrupted, "you're limiting this 'danger' to Detroit?"

A hint of a smile crossed Boyle's face. "We have a reputation—which, parenthetically, I do not feel we deserve—of being a hotbed of liberal what-have-you's, from radical liturgists to liberal theologians . . . literally liberation theology."

"I'm aware of this reputation." Wheatley swallowed a comment that it was this very reputation that had attracted him to begin his projected mission in this archdiocese. As far as he was concerned, this reputation was richly deserved. As a matter of fact, he was counting on just that.

He knew this archdiocesan reputation was due largely to the fact that the Cardinal was able to coexist civilly in the same sphere as those with whom he did not see eye to eye on a variety of issues.

A lot of sparring lay ahead for Boyle and Wheatley. Both knew it. Once Wheatley was admitted to the Roman presbytery, the sparring would begin.

"Prescinding from the accuracy or inaccuracy of this reputation," Boyle said, "the image is there. It is rare that this difference of opinion expresses itself violently. But it *does* happen. Never more notoriously than as in yesterday's bombing.

"What I mean," the Cardinal continued, "is that perhaps we ought to look about for another, perhaps smaller, diocese for you to function in. Perhaps that would be a safer atmosphere in which to work."

Silence for several seconds.

"Eminence . . ." Wheatley spoke slowly and forcefully. "I have spent countless hours studying everything I could find about various dioceses in which I would want to minister. I did not choose lightly. For a great number of reasons, my attention always returned to Detroit—"

"Is it," Koesler broke in, "that you want to work in a diocese led by Cardinal Boyle?"

Before Wheatley could reply, Boyle shook his head. "I shall not be here forever, even though it may seem that way."

"Yes," Wheatley said firmly, "I would prefer having you as my bishop. But I am perfectly willing to work in a diocese that you *had* led. Detroit will bear your stamp long after you finally get the chance to retire."

"Or die," Boyle said.

"Well, all right," Wheatley responded. "Or die."

"Father Wheatley . . ." Boyle fixed the priest with a penetrating look. " . . . my reservation to your incardination into Detroit revolves solely around your safety.

"I am well aware of all the talents you bring with you. You would be an extremely valuable asset to this or any other diocese. But I want you to have another look at what you may encounter here. Violence surrounded you yesterday. It may again. You would not be thought a coward if you chose to go elsewhere."

"I would be branded a fool if I chose to go elsewhere," Wheatley said with conviction.

Boyle appeared convinced. "Very well, then. When shall we schedule your ordination?"

Wheatley shrugged. "Next Sunday? I think it would demonstrate that we haven't been intimidated. Of course, it could not be at St. Joseph's." He paused. "How about the Cathedral?"

Boyle hesitated, but only for a moment. "Yes, of course. The Cathedral it shall be."

Koesler and Wheatley moved as if to stand. But Boyle continued speaking and the two priests settled back into their chairs.

"Last evening we had a meeting of some of the archdiocesan staff. Ned Bradley, our director of Communications, advised that whatever our decision in this matter, we should call a news conference for tomorrow—Tuesday."

"That sounds good," said Wheatley.

"Then it's agreed: We'll schedule it for ten tomorrow morning. It will be at the Gabriel Richard Building across the street. Let's say you stop in here first, Father Wheatley—about nine-thirty?—and we can discuss our approach to the media."

"Fine."

They parted, and Koesler and Wheatley took the elevator down to the street floor.

"Sorry to have gotten you involved in that, Bob. I didn't need the backup I thought I would."

"Don't mention it. As long as we're here now, how about some coffee? There's a coffee shop just a block away."

The cell phone buzzed. "Yeah," Sergeant Phil Mangiapane answered briskly.

"Phil?"

"Yeah, Zoo." Mangiapane recognized his lieutenant's voice immediately.

"What's the status of my brother?"

"Everything seems fine. There was a little confusion when the parishioners realized they weren't gonna be able to use their church for a while. Your brother got 'em into the rectory basement."

"No signs of anything out of the ordinary? Besides the switch from church to basement, I mean?"

"Nope. All is well, Zoo. Father Tully's having breakfast. Al has gone to get something for us. Don't worry. First sign of anything we'll let you know."

Tully hung up and immediately punched another number.

"Moore," Angie said into her phone, somewhat less briskly than Mangiapane's bark.

Sergeant Angie Moore, with Sergeant Bill Foley, was on surveillance of George Wheatley, which surveillance now included, since they were together, Bob Koesler as well.

"Reverend Wheatley make his appointment downtown okay?"

Angie recognized Zoo Tully's voice. "Yeah, Zoo. The appointment's finished. Incidentally, Wheatley's picked up some baggage."

"Who?" Tully abhorred surprises. And having anybody hanging around Wheatley qualified as a surprise.

"Father Koesler."

"That's okay." Tully was relieved. If anything, he wanted Koesler to be part of this investigation. "What's happening?"

"They went into a coffee shop on Michigan Avenue. It's an in-between time, so right now they're the only customers. Where are you?"

"Headquarters. And ready to roll."

❦

Father Tully had just finished a light breakfast: cold cereal with a banana, and coffee.

Tony, the janitor, entered the dining room. "You want me to come with you?"

"We don't have anything heavy to bank. I can handle it. On the other hand, the cops who are keeping me company probably would appreciate it if I'm not alone."

Tony shrugged. "I got nothin' else to do now until the police finish up in church."

"Okay, friend. I'll give you a buzz when I'm ready to go."

Tony went off to the garage to fix an automatic door that wasn't being automatic. In the parking lot was one car. Its motor was not running. He did not take it as a police car. It was not marked. Probably one of the congregation who had stayed after Mass and was now about to go off to work.

Tony was wrong about the parked car. It belonged to the City of Detroit. Inside the car a pair of detectives munched on what passed for their breakfast.

It was nine-thirty.

❧❀❧

In the average Detroit restaurant it would be so rare as to be almost unique if the only customers were two priests in clericals. But not at Carl's Corner.

The corner of Michigan Avenue and Washington Boulevard was top-heavy with the administrative offices of the Archdiocese of Detroit. Housed either in the chancery—1234 Washington Boulevard—or in the Gabriel Richard Building—305 Michigan Avenue—were approximately eighty archdiocesan offices.

So it was by no means strange that a goodly number of priests could be found walking around that corner with the two buildings only a couple of blocks apart.

It was just after the early rush hour at the coffee shop. Those starting work at eight or nine had already stopped by for their morning caffeine jolt and were now at their office tasks, looking forward to the ten A.M. break, when Carl's would once again host a rush.

The two priests took their cups to a table in the back so they would not be distracted by any incoming or outgoing customer traffic.

"How is yesterday affecting you?" Koesler asked.

"Radically," Wheatley responded.

"Has it made you second-guess yourself? I mean, just a little while ago you were pretty positive with the Cardinal."

"I guess emotionally I'm sort of ambivalent. I was rocked yesterday when the bomb exploded. And it didn't get any better afterward. This morning, I feel a bit calmer.

"It's just that we were completely unprepared for what happened. The lack of forewarning—the unexpectedness—was the scariest thing. Now we've got the security of morning to calmly reassess the event . . .

"Maybe it's over. I couldn't say that yesterday with any sort of confidence. But now . . . maybe. I've got a hunch."

"I sure hope you're right."

"What do you think, Bob?"

"I pretty much agree with you. It may just be wishful thinking, but . . . well, yesterday's occurrence was so carefully prepared that . . .

well, when such a seemingly well-laid plan failed, I can see that the perpetrator might not want to give it another try."

"I feel good that you agree. Yesterday there was no police presence—just the traffic cops outside the lot. No reason for any special need for the police then. But now? They're going to be all over the place."

The counter clerk hesitated in his work. The voice of the shorter priest was so impressive. He was sure he had heard it before. Actually, he hadn't. He did not listen to heady programs such as a religious-based talk show. But Wheatley did have a resonant voice.

Seated as they were in the rear of the coffee shop, they could see out of the large windows, while anyone outside would have great difficulty seeing them in the interior.

There was little to see, though. Few pedestrians went by. And those who did seemed intent on getting to their destination or on claiming their rightful corner where they would panhandle the whole day long.

NINETEEN

A T POLICE HEADQUARTERS Lieutenant Alonzo Tully busied himself with administrative tasks that were his responsibility, but
which he was in no hurry to finish.

Patrolman Vernon Dietrich sat down alongside Tully's desk and
offered him a Styrofoam cup filled with steaming hot coffee. Tully
accepted the cup with thanks. He didn't really want it, but he would
sip it anyway, just to keep his hands busy.

"Any word from the Techs?" Dietrich asked. "Prints and stuff?"

Tully shook his head. "Prints, yeah. Some of them must go back
to Gabriel Richard himself, or maybe even Cadillac. They didn't have
a thing on keeping the place especially clean."

"Be better if we had some idea of who we're chasing."

"Yeah," Tully agreed. "The best lead they've got going so far is
that the bomb may have been behind one of the floral pieces."

"We lookin' for a florist?"

"Could be. But which one? Flowers were ordered from two different shops. We checked both of 'em, and they both look clean.
Nobody at either place seems to have even the slightest motive. But
we'll keep pressing them.

"On top of that, quite a few parishioners brought in flowers and
put them anywhere they wanted around the altar and the statues."

"Ward interviewed a priest who claims that he returned some vestment that he'd borrowed," Dietrich said. "So far nobody's come up
with it. For his sake, somebody'd better find it—or its remains—pretty
soon."

Tully tried the coffee and decided it was too hot for mortal
tongue. He set the cup on the corner of his desk. "I wish that bastard
would make one of his crazy calls to my brother . . . or even send one
of his pasted-up letters."

"That'd have to be special delivery, no?"

"Yeah. I'm just on edge." Tully found a somewhat clean spoon in one of his desk drawers and stuck it in the cup. Maybe that would cool the coffee to potability.

❧❀❧

Father Wheatley returned to the booth with refills for both of them.

"I don't know how you feel about it," Koesler said, "but it bugs me."

"What's that?"

"Attitude! My Church's attitude about your priestly orders."

"Oh, that."

"Yeah, *that!* I look on you as every bit a priest as I am."

"Thanks, Bob. I appreciate that . . . I really do."

"If you're so aware of this attitude, how do you put up with it? I mean, so many Roman Catholic officials are treating you more as a seminarian than as a priest. It's demeaning."

Wheatley shrugged. "A price, I guess, I just have to pay.

"I want into the Roman priesthood. It's supply and demand. Rome gives every indication that it is not so eager to accept converts from the Anglican priesthood into the Roman. In this entire big country of ours there is one Cardinal and one Chicago-based priest actively involved in this procedure. That's not nearly the investment of time, personnel, and money the Roman hierarchy is pouring into recruitment of standard seminarians.

"But"—he smiled at Koesler—"don't give it another thought, Bob. I want this. I'm willing to pay the price."

Koesler blew lightly across his coffee to cool it. "There isn't that much separating us."

"And yet," Wheatley countered, "there is so much."

"There's Leo XIII's letter . . ."

"*Apostolicae Curae,*" Wheatley supplied.

"The Pope insisted that Anglican orders were 'absolutely null and utterly void.' But most everybody who's looked into the matter recently would deny, or at least question, his conclusion."

"And I," Wheatley said, "am among those who have studied and reached the same viewpoint: a repudiation of his conclusion. Are you aware of George Tavard's 1990 work: *A Review of Anglican Orders: The Problem and the Solution*?"

Koesler thought for a moment. "I'm not sure I am."

"He concluded that Leo's teaching was in error due to historical mistakes in research and, as Tavard expresses it, 'by theological pre-suppositions that were inadequate yet hardly avoidable in the neoscholasticism of the late 19th century.'"

Koesler was impressed that Wheatley could quote this off the top of his head.

Wheatley read his thoughts. "Impressed that I can quote verbatim? Just one indication of how serious I am about this step I'm taking."

"I know how serious you are about what you're doing. But you shouldn't have to swim upstream to get there. It just seems so obvious from where we are now that there is at least a justified doubt about Leo's decision of over a century ago. Current theologians, using extremely diplomatic language, are claiming the Pope erred when he denied the validity of Anglican orders. And that this error was committed because he based his opinion on faulty research."

Wheatley nodded. "I know all that. But you and I both know that the wheels of the Roman Church grind slowly. I may well be dead and buried a very long time before that Church acknowledges the validity of my present orders. And"—he smiled—"I don't think I can wait that long."

"Well . . ." Koesler shifted his chair so he could face George directly " . . . that brings up once more the fundamental question in this whole matter: Why should you feel you must wait for *any* decision?

"I've heard you speak to this question before, George. To be frank, the reasons you give I've never found completely satisfying. You know beyond a doubt that you are a priest and that you don't need a Roman dispensation and ordination to prove it.

"Before you made this move toward Rome you had a very successful ministry as an Episcopal priest. Why muddy the water? Why go through this often demeaning procedure? Can you explain it all one more time for me?"

Wheatley smiled and nodded. "My friend, I don't know that I can make my decision crystal-clear to you . . . or to anyone. But it's clear in my heart.

"Maybe it's best explained by something Jimmy Carter once said. I was impressed by it . . . so impressed that it's become a sort of mantra for me. He said, 'I have one life and one chance to make it count for something.'"

He smiled quizzically. "It's not much, is it?"

For a few moments, Koesler was deep in thought. "It doesn't have to be much . . . or lengthy. It says a lot."

"It did for me."

Koesler reflected briefly. "You don't feel your life was counting for enough in the Episcopal Church?"

Wheatley's head tilted. "Almost. Not quite.

"Try it this way: It wasn't that my life as an Anglican priest was not counting for enough. Rather, I felt that my life—or what's left of it—might count for more in the Roman Church.

"You see, movement is a sign of life. And my dear Episcopal Church has plenty of momentum. If things look as if they're slowing down toward a dead stop, there's always Bishop Spong to stir things up. And once he inevitably leaves the scene, there'll be someone else to take his place . . . challenging us to think, to pray more intensely, and act out our prayer.

"The Roman Church, on the other hand, was crawling slower than a turtle until that charismatic character, John XXIII, happened along. In a few years, John's aggiornamento blew in the fresh air for a century or more to come. The Roman Church was moving and living."

"And then"—Koesler took over the narrative that was so familiar to those who lived in that time—"John's successor, Paul VI, took over and culminated the Council. But then he dug in his heels, and ever since, it's been a pitched battle between those who hold that the Council went way too far and those who see the Council as a preliminary for continuing change."

"And," Wheatley said, "I belong to that latter group. I believe in progress and in the Anglican Communion. I am used to it. In all due modesty, I have a popular column, as well as a thriving radio program. And I have been promised that I may continue with both of them."

"Do you have it in writing?" Koesler was only partially joking.

"I know what you mean. I know that at least a couple of Detroit auxiliaries are not in the same ballpark as the Cardinal. But I know how to walk a tightrope. I can go forward.

"If I can make a dent in the armor of the naysayers in this pivotal diocese, I think I will make my one-time-around life count for something."

"A bit of excitement at your parish yesterday."

It was the bank manager's way of straddling a fence. As far as Mr. Warren was concerned, there was good news and bad news about the bombing at Old St. Joe's.

The death and injury numbers were blessedly low for such violence. On the other hand, a priest had been killed and considerable damage done to a portion of the church.

Bradley had been expecting Father Tully and his maintenance man. Father Tully always showed up on Monday mornings to bank the church funds, and not infrequently Tony accompanied him on his own personal banking business.

Of course, there was always the chance that yesterday's tragedy might have derailed their routine. Nonetheless, Warren had his greeting ready. Better be prepared with some concerned opener, even if it turns out not to be needed.

"Plenty of excitement." Tully waited until a teller buzzed him into the inner sanctum beyond the counter. He hefted the bag containing checks, currency, and coin onto a shelf. The money would be checked against the deposit slip later when the heavy Monday morning bank traffic had thinned out.

Warren regarded the bag with a practiced eye. "Not up to your usual deposit, is it, Father?"

No sooner were the words out of his mouth than Warren realized he had blundered. An ordination Mass would not include a collection.

Many of the parishioners who would otherwise have attended the earlier Mass—to which they would have contributed—had instead attended the ordination Mass. In any case, St. Joseph's collection was normally small by comparison with more affluent parishes. So, what with one thing and another, naturally, today's deposit was a fraction of the normal deposit Father Tully—and before him Father Koesler—would regularly have made.

Warren tried to cover his gaffe. "How are things going presently, Father?"

"I'm tempted to say things are going as well as can be expected. The police are finally pulling out. Of course it is somewhat unnerving to be the target of an assassin."

"You were a target?" Warren was truly surprised. "The news account this morning was somewhat unclear. It was my impression that the Episcopal priest was the target."

"That's what the police are checking into. Was it Father Wheatley? Was it me? Was it both of us? Was one of us the target and the other had to be taken out accordingly?

"And then, of course, there's the traditional question: Whodunit?"

"My heavens!" Warren exclaimed. "I had no idea it was so complicated. Shouldn't you be . . . someplace? Like in protective custody? Is that what it's called? All I know is what I see on TV and read in the paper."

"I guess 'protective custody' would be the operative term. But I've gone over this with my brother—"

"Your brother the Homicide Detective?"

"Yes." Tully wondered what other brother it could be. As far as he knew, he had only one brother and that brother was a police officer. "John F. Kennedy—and probably others, too—said that if someone is determined to get you he probably will. That's sort of how I feel. I guess the easiest way to kill somebody nowadays is with a gun. And God knows there are enough guns around."

Warren, a member in good standing of the National Rifle Association, made no comment. His hero was Charlton Heston. And it was knee-jerk, bleeding-heart liberals like Father Tully who were bent on disarming our great country.

But it was easy for Warren to keep his personal convictions separate from his professional duties. He would overlook the implications of the priest's remark. "Does this mean that you will be taking no precautions at all?"

"Just enough to satisfy my brother, the lieutenant. I guess I've got a couple of officers following me around. That represents Alonzo's minimum, and my maximum, negotiated commitment."

"You mean there's someone tailing you now?" Warren's interest rose several degrees. Outside of bank business, his contact with police procedure had been pretty much limited to radio, movies, TV, a few mystery novels, and the occasional nonfiction crime book. But this— this was real-life adventure. He peered from side to side. "Are they here? In my bank?" Warren was definitely engaged.

Father Tully was amused. "To tell you the truth, Mr. Warren, I don't really know. All I do know is that I agreed with Alonzo to put myself under some surveillance. I don't know what they look like or where they are . . . only that they're probably around someplace." He looked around, then back to Warren. "I guess they could be in your bank."

The manager was agog. "Oh, dear. In my bank! Oh, my—there *is* somebody I haven't seen before . . . over there . . . in that corner. Do you think he could be a policeman?" Secretly, Warren did not discard the possibility that the stranger just might possibly be the assassin.

"Well," Tully said, "I guess we'll see you next week."

Warren said nothing. His gaze was riveted on the unidentified man who might bring excitement and intrigue into the banker's otherwise dull life.

Tully gathered Tony, who had finished his own transaction.

Tully was pleased with himself for having brought some adventure into a banker's experience.

He was running a bit late. Nothing serious, but he would have to hurry along to catch up with his scheduled routine.

It was eleven A.M.

According to Leon Harkins's research, the bogus priest Tully was just returning to the rectory, where he would let Tony out of the car. Then he would go into the rectory to check the morning mail. Unless something in the mail demanded immediate attention, he would leave it until the afternoon or evening.

Most important, he had to get to the jail for his eleven-fifteen visit. The inmates, or nearly all of them, had been treated shabbily, usually by men, throughout their lives. The basic service he provided the women was a reliable masculine presence. He could counsel, he could absolve, he could just listen. But most of all he had to be on time. It was amazing how important punctuality was to the inmates.

So at eleven-fifteen A.M., Leon Harkins could envision Tully arriving to talk to the incarcerated women.

Harkins was off only by a minute. The women prisoners would forgive Father Tully. They had ways of learning what had gone down while they were off the streets. In the case of the St. Joe's bombing, they might even have heard the muffled roar of the explosion—the church was that close to police headquarters.

One minute usually doesn't make much difference in the affairs of mankind. But considering the tight schedule Harkins was on, it could be crucial.

Grace Harkins was concerned.

Normally, by this hour, her husband would be up and around and underfoot. She'd talked to other wives whose husbands had retired; many of them had this same experience. The men, at least in the Harkins's neighborhood, were at loose ends after retirement. They hadn't planned anything that would occupy them. They missed their jobs, even if they claimed to be glad to get away from them.

But this morning Leon had stayed in bed much later than usual.

Grace had begun her day at the regular time, about six A.M. She said her Lenten prayers and began tidying up the house, dusting and straightening up as needed.

Periodically she would call up to Leon. Each time, the only response was a barely audible grumble.

This day would be climactic for him. He was through being pushed around. The worm had turned. Leon was about to take matters into his own hands. He was going to kill a priest.

It sounded strange when he said that simple sentence to himself. *I am going to kill a priest.*

Weird.

Little Leon had been an altar boy. He remembered how painstakingly he had learned the Latin responses to the Mass. He never understood what he was saying. But he knew this: His Latin was as good or better than that of the priests who mumbled their way through the Liturgy.

Some of the priests he'd known while he was growing up were hardly edifying. But whenever he expressed reservations, his parents had been quick to remind him of how difficult a life the priests—and nuns, for that matter—lived.

He envisioned himself in his youth. His hands and face, neck and ears, scrubbed to pass inspection by his mother. Dressed now in a black cassock and a carefully laundered surplice. His hands pressed together in a prayerful manner. His Latin, quite precise and articulate. His mother kneeling out there in the congregation. Beyond his knowledge, his mother praying that her one and only son would become a priest.

Actually, he himself hoped for this. But his teachers discouraged his trying for the seminary: His marks were not promising. He was not dumb. Just slow.

But he loved the Church and admired its priests. That is, until that damnable Council and the new breed of renegade priests it spawned.

Now he was about to do something about it. He was not offering himself as a sacrificial lamb. His plans called for him to escape capture. But he had to face the possibility of being arrested. Maybe even killed.

Never mind. He was going to strike a blow for the betrayed Church . . . Christ's Church.

He practiced drawing his gun out of the holster some more. He was getting quite good at it.

He studied the framed motto hanging on the bedroom wall. It was something President Carter had said that radically influenced Leon. So much so that he'd had his wife cross-stitch it. *"I have one life and one chance to make it count for something."*

Leon Harkins's one chance was only about an hour away.

TWENTY

THE COFFEE SHOP was beginning to fill up.

Still, there were no other clerically attired customers. A few patrons, on entering, did a double take when they spotted not one but two clergymen. Those more familiar with downtown just assumed that the priests had business either in the Gabriel Richard Building or the chancery.

In any event, the two priests were left to converse undisturbed. In days of yore they might have been interrupted with requests ranging from "Would you bless my rosary?" to "Would you pray for my uncle?"

If either of the two was likely to be recognized it would be George Wheatley; his photo ran with his column in the paper.

If any of the patrons did identify him, none approached. For which both priests were grateful.

"You mentioned the opposition you expect from at least some of the clergy and laity of the Roman Church," Father Koesler said. "And you mentioned that you were used to walking a tightrope. Is that the way you intend to handle the opposition—by walking that tightrope?"

Wheatley nodded. "At least partly."

"Do you have a patent on that rope?" Koesler was smiling. "I can think of a lot of guys, including me, who'd love to get hold of it. You might make millions."

Wheatley shook his head. "No patent. The formula is sitting out there waiting for anyone who wants it."

"*I want it!*" Koesler said, in a rare show of emotion.

Wheatley chuckled. "Okay, okay. It's kind of a triple formula. I wouldn't be surprised if you were already familiar with it. I kind of stumbled into it and adopted it."

"So?"

"So, it was attributed to Melanchthon by a gentleman named Bowles, who had the aphorism inscribed over the doorway of his house. And it reads . . ." Wheatley paused to refresh his memory. *"In necessariis, unitas.'"*

"'In necessary things, unity.'" Koesler translated the simple Latin.

"'In dubiis, libertas,'" Wheatley continued.

"'In doubtful things, liberty.'"

"And," Wheatley concluded, *"In omnibus, caritas.'"*

"'In all things, charity—or love.' A simple formula, isn't it? But open to a lot of interpretation," Koesler added.

"I agree it can be kicked around a lot. But among fair-minded people, it can be very helpful in situations when a strict consensus can't be reached."

"And that happens a lot," Koesler noted. "But how does this saying help a divided body like the Church?"

"Well, here we get back to the things that divide us. As far as Anglicans are concerned, there aren't that many things graven in stone. We might say, 'Let's try this for a century or so and see what happens.'"

"I know where you're going with this one. The Roman Church will hang on to a dogma or moral teaching for dear life. Then if there's any change at all—which is rare—we introduce it with the catch-all, 'As the Church has always taught . . .'"

Wheatley nodded. "The point of all this, Bob, is that there are precious few things the Anglicans hold to be necessary. By 'necessary' I mean compulsory, or set in stone. The closest we come to that is our Catechism, in the Book of Common Prayer. And even those few 'musts' are diluted when you include all that Bishop Spong and others of like mind have got going . . ."

"Whereas there is a large-sized catechism for Catholics—full of 'necessary' things that are a sine qua non for unity," Koesler interjected.

"Indeed," Wheatley agreed. "So that leads us into the doubtful area where, according to our motto, there must be liberty—freedom. Freedom to inquire. Freedom to test. And freedom to change."

"And this is what you hope to introduce into the Roman Church?"

"Part of what I intend to try to do, yes. The main difficulty, of course, will be in limiting as far as possible the 'necessary' things. That can happen only gradually at best. Step by step, dogma by dogma, law by law."

"I think I understand," Koesler said. "The object is to move as much as possible from the 'necessary' column to the 'doubtful.' 'Cause then there'll be an increase in the freedom to explore."

"Exactly! Some doubtful items will rise once again to necessary things, to which we owe unity. A lot of doubtful things will remain and be added to. These things we'll be free to explore. The job of exploring them will return to Roman theologians, who have been stifled by a hierarchy who simply will not let go of the reins."

Neither Koesler nor Wheatley could drink another drop of coffee. But neither wanted this conversation to end.

Only two of the few tables in the shop were occupied. The priests sat at one. A well-dressed young man studying notes on a legal pad sat at another. The rest of the customers were carry-out trade.

Convinced that they were not inconveniencing any patrons who would prefer to occupy a table, the two priests continued their ecumenical discussion.

"I think I understand better now, George. But as your mission grows clearer, it begins to sound as if you're about to begin an episode of *Mission Impossible*."

"Really? How so?"

"Okay. The one that comes to mind is the Pope."

"I'm not surprised. We want the Pope."

Koesler's eyebrows raised. "You *do*?"

"Yes. As the first among equals."

"The other equals are the bishops—Episcopal, Roman, Lutheran, and so forth?"

"That's it. The way it was in the 'good old days.' When, right off the ground, in Antioch, Paul accused Peter of waffling in his approach to the Gentiles. Paul wasn't excommunicated, or suspended, or forbidden to teach. On the contrary, it was Peter who changed his methods.

"The Apostles and the early disciples recognized Peter as the chief of the Christian community. He was the leader. And, as Jesus carefully taught, to be the chief, the leader was to be the servant—"

"I know, I know," Koesler cut in. "You're referring to the Last Supper."

"Of course. Jesus set about washing the Apostles' feet. Peter objected, and Jesus said that if He did not wash Peter's feet, he, Peter, would have 'no part' with the Lord. So Peter asked, in effect, to be washed completely—'also my hands and my head.' Then Jesus told the Apostles that they did well in calling Him 'Master.' But if He, Master, acted the part of a servant, He was giving them an example. The Apostles were appointed to serve the new community. Peter was the first servant. Not much like the current successor to the throne of Peter."

Koesler smiled. "That's just the point, isn't it?"

"Yes. Over the years—over the centuries—the Papacy has grown away from what it was in the beginning."

"So how are *you* going to change it?"

"I don't know," Wheatley confessed. "Maybe it won't happen in our lifetime."

"Maybe it won't happen ever."

"Maybe it won't. But if it doesn't, the fact that the Papacy will be the same when I leave the world as it was when I entered it does not alter my purpose."

"It doesn't?"

"I know I am called," Wheatley said. "That is the clear message that came through to me in prayer. I don't know what exact goals I will have until the Lord makes His calling clear. I doubt that my target will be the Papacy. This I do know: If the Papacy is the field the Lord wishes me to work in, my goal certainly will not be to destroy the office—if ever I even could. No, my mission will be to do what I can to bring it back to its roots."

"Well, God bless you, George. If you do accomplish that, we may, indeed, see a Pope who is first among equals. I wish you success."

"Thanks for your good wishes, Robert. But I can't see the Lord steering me in that direction. More likely I will be laboring in a smaller ministry."

"Like women?"

"Women?"

"Women priests."

"I'll raise the ante, Bob: women bishops."

"Women bishops! Even some Anglican dioceses won't accept women priests, let alone bishops."

"I know. But it could happen. Some twenty-five years ago the ordination of women was an impossible concept for Anglicans. That same degree of impossibility continues to exist today in the Roman Church."

"That's so, isn't it?" Koesler recalled. "Some fearless women— and a couple of retired Episcopal bishops—changed that. They got together, couldn't find anything against it any way you look at it—so they just up and did it."

"Can you imagine how the Roman Church would react to an event like that?" Wheatley quietly savored the idea.

"Yeah, I can, actually. The Vatican would find some reason—any reason—to declare such a ceremony null and void—not to mention illicit and illegal."

"Now, probably . . ." Wheatley nodded. "But in time . . ." He didn't complete the thought, yet his expression registered hopefulness. "The point I'd like to make, Bob, is simply this: The women and the bishops who participated in that ordination took a big chance, and definitely made their lives count for something.

"And that's precisely what I want for my own life. Not necessarily to be instrumental in opening the Roman priesthood to women. But *something*. Does it mean much at all if the Romans will not accept another word, transubstantiation, for the essence of Eucharist? Anglicans are not very technical on this point. We do what Christ did. We believe what He believed. Christ is present in the manner He intends. Anglican theology of Eucharist today is about the same as that of your beleaguered theologian, Father Schillebeeckx. Anglicans *do* have tabernacles just as Romans do. So, what's in a name?"

"I think I see what you're driving at. That type of argument does seem petty and pointless. But it goes on and on, doesn't it?"

"Yes. And it keeps us from addressing substantial differences that really do divide us." He paused to reflect. "Maybe this defines the importance of the third passage of that precept: 'In all things, love.' The love of people who are already joined in the love for Christ should make it possible to brush aside all our differences, whether petty or substantial.

"Maybe that's my calling: To help in shifting some things presently perceived as 'necessary' into the 'doubtful' category, where they can be freely discussed without insisting that change is impossible. And to help make sure that everything—quite literally *everything*—can be discussed in an environment of love."

"Sounds good to me, George. More than good: inspiring."

"It's what I perceive will be my calling. After we clean up this mess, of course . . ."

"Mess?" Koesler, wrapped up in Wheatley's dream, had forgotten what was on just about everyone's mind. "Yes, of course, the mess: Who is responsible for the bombing in St. Joe's?"

The ambience was all wrong. It was just a room with a couple of chairs. No other furnishing. That it was a room in Detroit Police Headquarters explained the spare decor.

This was Act Two of the routine worked out by jail guards, inmates, and Father Zachary Tully.

In Act One, the priest preached a *fervorino* to a congregation of women, many of whom attended the chapel service only as a welcome alternative to sitting in their cells. The group included, among others, Catholics, Baptists, members of The Church of Where It's at Now.

Act Two was an invitation to any of the group who wanted to consult with the priest for a more or less traditional Sacrament of Penance or just to talk to someone from the outside.

One of the latter members was presently informing Tully what was new in her life. When not in the slammer, she was a lady of the evening who was picked up periodically by the police and sent through the system. She consulted regularly with Tully. But only when she was locked up, as she now was.

"It seemed like a good idea, Father. I mean, I wasn't goin' anywhere for a few months. So I took the course," she explained.

"The course in cosmetology?" Tully had to make sure they were talking about the same thing. She had a tendency to wonder off the subject.

"Yeah, Father, that's it."

"Did you complete it?"

"Yup. Went right through. From beginning to end."

"You mean you got your diploma?"

"Yup."

'So now you're a licensed cosmetologist."

"Yup."

"Well, congratulations." Tully was genuinely pleased. He firmly believed that almost everyone who was repeatedly arrested for transgressions such as prostitution could do well in the legit world.

"But," Tully said, "you must have gotten your diploma during your previous stay in jail . . . when was that now?" Tully searched his memory for the date of her most recent previous incarceration.

"Three months ago," she supplied.

"That figures," he said. "I haven't seen you in about half a year. So you must've spent pretty much all your time on that course. And that's why you weren't visiting me here."

"That's right, Father. My prison counselor thought the course was a good idea. So I took it. It seemed to make her feel good."

Tully's pleasure mounted. It didn't matter whether he or a counselor had worked the miracle of rehabilitation. This young woman had been set on the straight and narrow road.

Then, a conclusive thought struck Tully. "Wait a minute: If you got your cosmetology license three months ago and got your freedom at the same time, how come you're back in here? The last time I looked, practicing cosmetology is not a crime. You *did* get a job in a beauty shop or the like . . . didn't you?"

"Me fix other broads' hair?"

"That's the idea. What happened?"

"Land a glory, Father, I can make more money flat on my back in one night that I can make at a beauty shop in a whole week."

Not much surprised Father Tully anymore. But this story held a surprise for him.

She had not come to him for absolution. Long ago the two of them had determined that she was not a Catholic, nor was she particularly interested in any of the organized religions. No, as long as she was in jail and constrained from being otherwise occupied, she just enjoyed talking with him.

The priest and the unrepentant sinner exchanged words of farewell, after which she left the room.

No one else entered in her wake. Tully was about to get up and leave when another woman appeared in the doorway, looking sheepish.

"Did you want to see me?" He motioned her forward. "Come on in."

As she entered the room, he looked at her more closely. She looked familiar. But as far as he could recall, he had never seen her here—

Then he remembered. She had been in the news the past few days. She had shot her husband. In itself, such an act was not unheard of in Detroit and environs. Father Tully would have paid no particular attention to the event except that her husband had been a deacon. The permanent kind who opts to stay in that position—unlike the transitional deacon, who remains at that level for a year or so and then advances to the priesthood. Even with that Catholic connection, Father Tully had merely skimmed the newspaper account and gone on to the sports pages.

She sat down and demurely crossed her legs at the ankle. "I'm Clare Watson."

"I know. I saw your picture in the paper."

"Did you read the article that went with the picture?"

"Not carefully." He found himself somewhat embarrassed at having preferred the sports section to the news pages.

"That's okay. They didn't report the story very well. If you don't mind, I'd like to tell you what happened—as objectively as possible."

Tully checked his watch. It was eleven forty-five. Plenty of time to hear her story and get back to the rectory for lunch at twelve-thirty.

"Sure. But before you begin, did you want to make this part of a confession? If you do, nothing you tell me would I tell anyone else. The seal of confession, you know—"

"I know, Father. I've been teaching in a parochial school. I'm not so sure I'll be doing that anymore . . . what with shooting the bastard and all."

He thought her termination at the parochial school was a safe bet.

"Well, Father, sometime back—maybe a year or so ago—I was pretty sure my husband had somebody on the side. I wasn't absolutely certain, but there were lots of unexplained absences. He would stay late at the office and that would happen more and more often—oh, and Father: Let's make this a sacramental confession. One can't be too safe."

"That's true. Go on."

"The thing sort of escalated. It went from staying late at the office to taking trips out of town—"

"There's no possibility these things could have been on the up and up?"

"Of course that was possible. I don't want to give you the impression that I didn't go along with his absences. Our sex life was fine, so it never entered my head there could be somebody else. The only reason he might have a gripe in that department was that he wasn't home often or long enough to have sex regularly.

"That," she continued, "plus the fact that he's a salesman for a local radio station. His draw isn't very high. A guy in his position makes most of his money on commissions.

"Up until this started to happen—his being away so much—the income was good. But once he was allegedly 'working late' and going on 'business trips,' his paycheck started going downhill.

"Now how would you figure that, Father? If he's putting in all that extra worktime, you'd think he'd be pulling down a fatter check . . . no? But it was going the other way."

"It doesn't make sense."

"I want to tell you, Father, that I was getting sick and tired of eating alone, spending my evenings alone, taking care of my little girl alone. Oh, did I mention we have a child?"

"No. How old?"

"She just turned six. She's in first grade." She made a face. "I don't think he even knows how old she is.

"The whole thing began to run me down something fierce. And all the time, Father, our sex was incredible. That's what threw me. How could it be another woman? But what could the reason be? Why was our income suffering while he was putting in hours—days!—of extra worktime?"

"'Beats me," Tully said. "Sounds like you needed a marriage counselor."

"Exactly! But do you think he would go? I could have gotten him into the Twelve-Step program of Alcoholics Anonymous faster than to a marriage counselor. And Greg doesn't even drink."

Tully stifled a laugh.

"But I finally got him to go with me. I laid an ultimatum on him. And would you believe it: He came on to her . . . the counselor! Second session.

"She was used to the maneuver. Called it 'transference.' What surprised her was that he was a deacon. I guess she expected a religious person to be holy."

"No guarantee there," Tully said.

"Anyway, it did come out . . . the bimbo he was seeing."

"Then he *was* seeing somebody."

"Yeah. And the one he's seeing is married—well, she's not completely married."

"Not completely?"

"She's getting a divorce so she can marry Greg, my husband."

"Isn't there something wrong here? You're still married to him."

"I know. He told her he'd get a divorce . . . that the time was not just right. Actually, the sex between us was so great he couldn't bring himself to break it off. So I helped him to make the thing work by filing for divorce."

"Just out of curiosity, is he still a practicing deacon?"

"He was until I shot him. Then he was fired. Defrocked, I guess they called it. And that's not all."

"There's more?"

226

"The woman he's been running with—the woman he's going to marry—she used to be a nun. She was a nun for fourteen years. She even taught in a parochial school, like me."

"But not in your present school?"

"No. Another one. But that's not all."

"There's *more*?"

"Her husband, he used to be a priest."

"A Roman Catholic priest!"

"Yeah. He left the priesthood to marry her.

"He left the priesthood to marry her," she repeated, "and now my husband is leaving me to marry her!"

"Incredible. Let me just run through this thing once more to see if I've got it straight: You are divorcing your husband, the deacon, because he wants to get married to an ex-nun who was married to a former priest."

"That's pretty much it."

"And"— lly was having a difficult time holding everything together and not collapsing in laughter—"you want to confess that you shot your husband?"

"No. The bastard deserved far worse than that. He came over to tell me he was going to fight for custody of our little girl."

"No kidding!"

"Yeah. So I got the family gun. I was going to shoot him in the gonads. I thought that was a particularly appropriate spot to hit him. But then I just couldn't do it. So I shot him in the foot. I figured that it might keep him from putting it in his mouth so often."

"Then, you'll excuse me, but why did you come to see me? You said you don't want to confess. Did you want absolution for shooting your husband?"

"No. I already said the bastard deserved at least that."

Careful, Tully reminded himself; she hasn't asked for any advice. Not yet. Let her conscience be her guide. "Well, then, what *can* I do for you?"

"I've been contacted by a literary agent."

"You've—! A book? You've been here only a couple of days. They want you to write a book?"

227

"Well, I wouldn't exactly write it. They suggested that I tell my story to Lowell Cauffiel and he would write it. He's a terrific true crime writer. What I want you to tell me is, Do you think making money for shooting my husband is . . . uh . . . unethical?"

"You may not have to concern yourself about that. I think there's a law against profiting from a crime."

"*If* you're found guilty. We're figuring I'm going to be found not guilty."

"So . . . unethical?" Father Tully's face wrinkled as he pondered this. "I don't think so."

"Oh, that's good news, Father. I already talked to Mr. Cauffiel once. I kind of sketched the story. I even suggested an illustration for the dust jacket."

"Oh? And what's that?"

"Well, when my husband was studying to be a deacon, all the would-be deacons' wives had to take classes for a few weeks to learn what would be expected of us.

"To make a long story short, we wives were supposed to be supportive and nonpublic. So, with that in mind, I suggested a picture of a jockstrap for the cover of my book." She smiled. "What do you think, Father?"

"It sounds like a grabber."

No sooner were the words out of his mouth than Father Tully realized he was guilty of a very bad pun. But it was too late to take it back.

They agreed there was no absolution needed. Father Tully wished her well and blessed her, mentally shaking his head at her seeming lack of repentance for her deed. The two of them then left the room, he to return to his concern about an assassin, she to her cell.

He took the stairs. They were a compelling alternative to one of the truly slowest elevators in Western civilization.

On the way down he met another priest who was headed up the stairs. The pastor of downtown St. Mary's parish, a neighbor of Old St. Joe's, was eager to get the bombing story from the horse's mouth. After all, the bomber might well have mistaken St. Joe's for St. Mary's. Crazier things had happened in Detroit.

As they conversed, the Angelus sounded in St. Mary's tower. It was just twelve noon.

Leon Harkins continued to practice drawing his gun from its holster. He was getting quite good at it.

Leon was about to leave for his appointment with destiny.

Should he send one more message to his prospective victim, Father Tully? He debated with himself. Would it be overdone? Would it be inappropriate?

He knew that Father Tully would not be at the rectory by noon. Probably he would be just about to leave the jail. The rectory answering machine would record any phone message.

If Harkins were to fail in his deadly objective, he himself might well be killed. In which case Father Tully would live to hear his message. However, if Harkins were to succeed, Father Tully would be dead, but the message would survive, taunting the police, who would not be even close to figuring out who did it.

He adjusted the device that would mask his voice. He dialed the rectory number. The phone rang five times before the answering device picked up. The recording detailed the Mass schedule. If this was an emergency there was an alternate number to call. If the caller merely wanted to leave a message, wait for the beep and carry on.

B-e-e-p.

"Father Tully . . ." Harkins spoke in a normal tone, knowing that the masking machine would slow the speed of his voice to the point where his identity would be well disguised. "You have had all the warnings I am going to give you. If you can hear this, I have failed. But others like me will follow in my footsteps. I have given you all the reasons why I have come for you. We need not go into them again. Farewell, Father Tully. We will meet again before God."

Hawkins hung up. He would say nothing to his wife. If she had the slightest idea of what he had in mind, she would do all in her power to prevent him from carrying out his plan

No, nothing would stop him now.

It was 12:02. Father Tully was still in conversation with his neighboring pastor.

Koesler and Wheatley at long last emerged from the coffee shop. They were now standing next to Wheatley's car in a nearby parking lot.

"Would you like me to accompany you to the news conference tomorrow?" Koesler asked.

"Thanks, but no, I don't think so. I don't want to trouble you. Goodness knows I've been through enough of these over the years. I'll meet with the Cardinal beforehand. I imagine he'll want to settle on a schedule for my ordination. I can give the media that information, anyway.

"As far as anything else related to the bombing, I don't really know all that much. I'm afraid what little I do know will not satisfy their curiosity. Sorry about that. But, as you Romans occasionally put it, *'Nemo dat quod non habet.'*"

"Nicely said. It brings me back to my seminary days. We sneezed in Latin." Koesler fingered the keys to his car. "Do you feel as creepy as I do about not knowing the identity of the bomber?"

Wheatley nodded somberly. "Uh-huh. I hope it's all over now. Still, it's unnerving to know there's someone walking around freely who wants—or wanted—to kill me. It makes me reflect on my own mortality. It's unsettling, to say the least."

"Turning seventy did the same for me. Death is not all that real when you're in your twenties—even your fifties."

"But if someone is trying to kill you, that does bring a measure of reality." Wheatley fingered his key ring. "Trying to guess *who* that someone is has become an obsession with me. The closer that *someone* may be to me, the more frightening the whole thing becomes."

"'Closer'? You can't mean Alice or Ron!"

Wheatley's face was pained. "Just a thought. Touching all bases, as it were." He hesitated, as if trying to decide whether he was putting an unwarranted burden on his fellow clergyman. Although Father Koesler was of a different background, and their friendship was of a more recent vintage than that of the majority of Father Wheatley's Anglican cronies, still he had come to value that friendship, as well as trust Koesler's judgment.

"Don't exclude Gwen," George said quietly. "She would like me out of the way—out of Ron's way."

Koesler looked puzzled.

"Ron wants—badly—to be a bishop. Gwen wants him to be a bishop—as much or even more than Ron himself wants it." He looked fixedly as Koesler. "What do you suppose his chances are now that his father is 'deserting' to the enemy?

"No," he said sadly, "my son and his wife are *not* happy that I may have cost him—them—their bishopric."

Koesler didn't know what to say. So, as he usually did in such circumstances, he uttered a non sequitur. "On the brighter side, I'm beginning to look on whoever made that call as your guardian angel."

Wheatley winced. It was a momentary reaction, but Koesler caught it. "What is it, George? What's wrong?"

Wheatley hesitated. "Nothing. Just that if that *was* my guardian angel I hope he stays alert."

Wheatley climbed into his car and rolled down the window. "Thanks again for the offer to accompany me tomorrow. Let's stay in touch."

It was twelve-ten.

"Manj," Lieutenant Tully shouted into the phone, "I was just going to call you."

"Zoo, I got somethin' I gotta tell you—"

"In a minute. We got the phone call! The guy who's been calling my brother just phoned a few minutes ago. His name is Leon Harkins. Lives on the near east side. Our people are talking to his wife right now."

"Good God, no! Zoo, your brother: We lost him."

"Zack? How could—?" Time enough later to fix guilt. Right now he had to find his brother. The assassin was on his way for the kill. "Where are you?"

"Here at 1300. I'm in the elevator comin' up to our floor. Geez, Zoo, everything was goin' right on schedule. Al and I were parked out front. Father was supposed to leave here between twelve and twelve-ten. When he didn't show, I left Al in the car and went in to look for him. The women's guard said he left a bit early. Bottom line: I don't know *where* he is."

Father Tully was growing antsy. The other priest was buttonholing him for all the details. Zack had no idea that while he was stuck in the stairwell, a massive search of the building was about to start.

"Listen, Manj"—Zoo Tully was as close as he'd ever come to naked panic—"start a floor-to-floor search. Almost everyone here knows what Zack looks like. I don't know what could've happened to him. I'm sure he didn't try to lose you. Harkins is after Zack. I can't think he'd be stupid enough to try to hit him in the station. He's probably figuring on a confrontation at the rectory. I'm heading there now. Get on this end of it, Manj: Now!"

If there were any speed records in the category of leaving HQ, jumping in a car, and heading for an emergency, Zoo Tully broke them all now.

En route, he called the cops at the Harkins's home. They were attempting to get additional information from Mrs. Harkins. She was trying to help. But she was too frightened to be of any real aid. However, they did have a description of Harkins, and several photographs. And Mrs. Harkins was able to tell them what her husband was wearing when he'd left the house earlier.

"Okay, from what we've got, you're looking for a male Caucasian, slender build, five feet nine, one hundred fifty pounds, wearing a herringbone fedora, trench coat, black trousers, and black shoes."

"Right."

Tully's radio crackled. It was Mangiapane. "We got the whole building on it, Zoo. And we're sending backup after you."

"Good. I've got the rectory in sight now."

"I don't know if backup'll get there in—"

"There's a guy on the front porch. It looks like he's ringing the doorbell."

"If it's him, you're probably on your own, Zoo." Mangiapane, normally cool and offhand, couldn't keep the worry from his voice.

"It's the guy. He fits the description."

"No sign of your brother there?"

"No. I hope to God he isn't here. I'm going in."

"Good luck."

Tully was driving an unmarked car. He had not used the flasher or the siren. He might have been a parishioner with business at the rectory.

He got out of the car and began to walk nonchalantly toward the porch. "Having trouble getting in?" he called out.

Leon Harkins tilted his head sideways as if trying to recall who this familiar-looking man might be. Recognition crossed his face. "You're the brother. You're the cop." He shrugged. "If I've got to get through you to get to him—so be it."

Harkins's right hand was resting against the second button from the top of his trench coat. With a well-practiced motion the hand slid inside his coat. The fluid gesture continued as he drew the gun from its holster. In a split second the gun had cleared the coat and was being raised, pointing at Tully.

It all happened in the blink of an eye.

Tully cursed himself for not having drawn his gun the instant he got out of the car. It was a fatal mistake—he knew that the minute he saw the barrel of Harkins's gun rising to aim at his chest.

Though it was too late, Tully went for his gun anyway.

Then a strange thing happened. Harkins didn't fire. His gun remained pointed directly at Tully's heart, as an odd combination of fear and fury suffused his face.

In that moment, that fleeting instant, Tully fired. The sharp crack ricocheted and reverberated through the downtown canyons.

Harkins toppled over the porch railing. His body lay motionless.

The scene resembled a tableau.

Then, Tully moved toward the inert body. At every step, he kept his weapon carefully aimed at the downed man. But Harkins would move no more.

Tully went down on one knee. He slipped on a pair of plastic gloves. He felt for the carotid pulse. There was none.

Damn!

In all his years on the force, Tully had fired his weapon at a human being only twice. Each time, the shooting had been justified. And each time the shot had been fatal.

From experience, he knew that it would take time to get over the shock of having taken a human life. And the fact that he'd fired in self-defense made little difference.

Sirens sounded in the distance, loudening rapidly as they converged. The skirls punctuated into silence, as the blue-and-whites carrying Tully's backup arrived and screeched to a stop. It was clear the threat was over. The officers gathered around the central scene.

A sergeant squatted alongside Tully, who was still down on one knee. Both studied the dead man.

"You okay, Zoo?" The sergeant spoke without moving his gaze from the corpse.

Nor did Zoo look up from the body of his would-be killer. "I've been better." No point in bravado here. In any case, it wasn't Tully's style. He had been badly frightened, and was still shaky. "I thought I was done for. He had me cold. He just stood on the porch with his gun pointed straight at my chest."

"Any idea why he didn't fire?" For the first time the sergeant looked directly at Zoo.

"Yeah, I got one now." Tully pointed at the revolver lying harmlessly in Harkins's limp hand. "Here . . . just above the hammer—the lock? The poor bastard probably forgot to release the lock. He didn't fire because he *couldn't*. The trigger was locked. For a while, I thought it might have been suicide by cop . . ." Tully was referring to cases where somebody wants to end his life but hasn't got the guts to do it himself, so he points his weapon at a cop, forcing the cop to shoot him in self-defense. "The thought crossed my mind that he might've been doing that. But"—Tully shook his head—"he left me no choice. How could I know that trigger was locked?

"Besides," he added, "it all happened in seconds."

Another squad car pulled up. Mangiapane and his partner were the official occupants. In the rear sat a somewhat bewildered Father Zachary Tully. "We finally found him, Zoo," said Mangiapane.

Zachary took in the scene. Organized bustle. The small yard in front of St. Joe's rectory was swarming with police, technicians, and bystanders. "What happened?"

"You're late," his brother answered, with the shadow of a smile.

"I got pinned down in the stairwell by my neighboring pastor. He wanted to know everything that happened here yesterday, and I mean *everything*. I couldn't get away from him." His half-grin was ironic. "And to think that I took the stairs because your elevator is so slow . . ."

"Get down on your knees," Zoo said, "and thank God for that slow elevator and that nosy priest. If they hadn't held you up you would've gotten here on time. And if you had, you'd probably be lying here dead"—Zoo looked down at the body—"instead of this poor bastard."

For the first time, the priest looked carefully at the victim. "Leon Harkins," he said in slow recognition. "The poor tortured soul. He lived for his Church, and died trying to save it from me." Zoo looked up at his brother. "Actually, he was trying to save it from itself."

He made the sign of the cross over Harkins. "I'll just step in and get the oils, and anoint him before they take him away." He looked up at Zoo again. "If that's all right?"

Zoo nodded. Father Tully disappeared into the rectory so abruptly that Zoo was unable to say what he was thinking: *Why are you praying for a dead man?*

A morgue attendant appeared. The technicians were finished with the deceased. It was time for the autopsy. "Are you done, Lieutenant?"

Zoo was about to release the body when he remembered his brother off in search of some oil. "No. Just a little while longer. I'll let you know."

He turned to see his brother coming down the porch steps. His lips were moving, but no sound was coming out. He was praying silently from a pocket-sized book. As Zack stood over the body of his would-be assassin, Zoo leaned over to look at the book his brother was using. It was open to a section titled, "Prayers for the Dead." Appropriate, thought Zoo.

Once Zack had anointed Harkins's forehead and closed his prayerbook, Zoo nodded to the attendant, who, with a partner, picked up the body and headed off toward the morgue wagon.

Zachary looked fondly at his brother. "You saved me, didn't you?"

"You could say that. But it wouldn't be the whole story. Something weird is going on."

"You got a minute to come in the rectory? We both need to wind down a bit . . . don't you think?"

Zoo hesitated. "Okay," he said after a moment, "I've got some reports to fill out on this shooting. But I can spare a couple of minutes. Do you have anything to drink besides altar wine?"

It was an inside joke between them. Zachary stocked nothing but inexpensive wine, and beer.

"What's wrong with altar wine? Ours is delivered by Catholic teamsters."

"Don't worry about me. You're the one who'll need a little internal help."

They settled into the rectory parlor. Zachary took a bottle of red wine from a cabinet and poured a couple of fingers into a glass. Zoo waved off any wine. For the interrogations about to come, he wanted to be cold sober.

He looked at his brother somberly, then slowly shook his head. When he finally spoke, it was almost as if he was thinking out loud. ". . . by overwhelming odds you should be a dead man now."

The gravity of his tone prompted Zack to return to the bottle and add a little more wine to his glass.

"I know you didn't take this threat to your life very seriously. You should have reported those calls and letters. To me. And I don't care whether you didn't want to involve me or trouble either of us. Anne Marie is no namby-pamby shrinking violet—and I'm a professional—a law enforcement officer—*and* your brother. You weren't doing your-self—or us—any favors . . ."

Zoo went on to bring Zack up to date: the intercepted telephone call wherein Harkins gloated over how he was going to kill Zack. The race to apprehend Harkins before he caught up with Zachary and made good his threat. Finally, the gun—rendered useless because Harkins had forgotten to unlock the trigger.

In the face of Zoo's unbroken narration, Zachary was forced to agree that he was one lucky man—although he preferred to term it Divine Providence.

"I don't know what it is with you guys," Zoo said. "You seem to have somebody the rest of us can't see watching over you. That your guardian angel?"

"You could say that."

"Yesterday you and Wheatley would have been blown away—lit-erally. But a mysterious phone call saved both of you. Today, you would've been killed if an inquisitive neighbor hadn't kept you past your time at the jail."

"What about the gun with the locked trigger?" Zachary protested. "He couldn't have killed me with that gun."

Zoo smiled sardonically. "Once Harkins knew what was wrong with his gun—and he knew it the instant he tried to pull the trigger—it would've taken him no more than a few seconds to unlock it. With me, he didn't have that extra time; I got him before he got me. It's as simple as that. You were unarmed. You would've been killed."

Zack Tully's health was sound. He was not yet old enough to take death seriously. For the first time in his life he had been brushed by mortality. He was surprised now to find himself alarmed by the inevitability of it. He tried to keep his face—and his voice—expres-sionless. "I'm glad he didn't get either of us." But the offhandedness of his statement was belied by the almost imperceptible tremor in the hand that held the wineglass.

Zoo gazed at his brother with a variety of emotions: relief, com-passion—and yes, he silently admitted—love. Aloud he said only, "The next time you see Father What's-His-Name from . . ."

"St. Mary's," Zack supplied.

"St. Mary's . . . well, the next time you see him, thank him for all of us."

"Unfortunately," Zoo said to Mangiapane, "we did not bag two birds with one stone."

"So I heard."

"Harkins was not the bomber. We were looking to the guy who was harassing Zack as being the same guy who set the bomb." Zoo looked almost disgusted. "But his wife . . . his widow—she claims the two of 'em were watching TV yesterday—eating, or snoozing, or watching TV."

"Yeah, I know," Mangiapane commiserated. "The guys found an arsenal in his basement . . . but no bomb fixings. Plus a pile of magazines and newspapers he cut up for the letters he sent your brother."

The two men looked at each other, silently sharing the identical thought: Whoever had set off that bomb was still out there.

TWENTY-ONE

S TAN RYBICKI TURNED OFF HIS RADIO. He had a lot of news to digest.

What was that man's name? Leon Harkins. Yeah, that was it.

Stan wondered had he ever met this Harkins guy. At a political or religious rally, maybe? Maybe. He certainly wasn't one who came to mind at mention of his name. Stan would have to wait till Harkins's photo was shown on TV. Or until a fuller account of the incident appeared in the newspaper.

Whoever he was, this Harkins guy had balls. Imagine taking on the brother of a cop!

On top of which, he'd gone after the wrong guy. Of course this Tully priest had been making a shambles of the divine service what with his guitar Masses and encouraging extreme Liturgies discouraged by the Pope and the whole Vatican hierarchy. While that was certainly bad enough, at least he wasn't destroying the core of the things that the Church had always taught.

But this Wheatley guy! He was the one who was going to give vestments and altar breads and chalices to females and pretend that they could do the most sacred thing in all of Catholicism!

And as if that wasn't more than enough, this guy Wheatley, this— oh, there were no words for it!—he was going to trot headlong into the rectory, where he would live right out in the open with his wife and kids.

As the Church has always taught, the law doesn't demand that men remain single. Only those who want to be priests: *They* have to be celibate.

So there's nothing to the argument that the Church forces priests to live single lives. The Church doesn't force anybody not to marry. But if you want to be a priest, the rules are the rules.

Bottom line: Harkins went after the wrong guy. And that blunder had been a total foul-up: He'd failed to off the guy. And even if he *had* shot and killed Father Tully he most likely would've gotten killed himself. It didn't take an atomic scientist to figure that the cop would surround his own brother with protection.

The radio said that the cop—Lieutenant Tully—actually was the one who killed Harkins.

So what has the poor schlemiel got to show for his efforts? One guy—the guy he should've gotten—not even injured. And that poor innocent priest . . . what had he ever done to deserve being blown half to bits? Rybicki shook his head. So then he goes after the other guy—the wrong guy—who walks away without even a bruise.

Rybicki rocked back and forth in his easy chair until he got enough momentum to swing his large body up into a standing position. He walked to the kitchen and got a beer from the fridge. He twisted the bottle cap off.

Still, he reasoned, Harkins ought not to be ridiculed. At least he'd had the gumption to do *something*. And something certainly needed to be done. Mainly, the right thing needed to be done. Somebody had to turn this stuff around and take effective steps to make people know what was going on. The common people were going to let all this happen and it'd be over—an accomplished fact before they even knew what had happened to their dear religion.

Rybicki thought of all those noble men who had ridden his elevator, doing their jobs way back when. The good old days.

Most of those guys were gone now. But they'd be spinning in their graves if they could see women up there on the altar! If they could know that some priest was fooling with his wife before getting up to say Mass!

He could see the religious hippies who'd barged onto his elevator and tried to get off on the sacrosanct second floor to confront the archbishop. No—no way! Rybicki tossed his head. They never got past him, by God!

They'd argue that St. Peter was married 'cause it said in the Bible that Jesus cured Peter's mother-in-law. But they never considered that once Peter got serious about following the Lord, the Bible never mentioned her again—and certainly never mentioned any wife. Peter just got called to celibacy a little late.

Well, you big lug, Rybicki reasoned with himself, what are you going to do about it?

He didn't want to die. He liked living. Of course, life wasn't perfect. And, of course, he did want to go to heaven. And getting rid of Wheatley was certainly a ticket to heaven.

But not just yet.

Maybe there was a way of doing this without a personally fatal confrontation. There had to be some way of getting rid of Wheatley without risking his own life.

Movement—that was the ticket.

Wheatley was scheduled to hold a news conference in the Gabriel Richard Building. According to the paper, that was set for tomorrow morning. There had to be a way of parlaying his intimate knowledge of the chancery and the Gabriel Richard Building into a plan that would get rid of Wheatley once and for all.

Movement . . . something involving movement.

"You never told me about this!"

"There was never any need . . . until now."

Alonzo Tully and his wife, Anne Marie, sat across from each other at the kitchen table. Each had a cup of freshly brewed coffee. Anne Marie and her coffee were steaming. "For the kind of thing you did today, they should have given you a commendation, a medal . . . something!"

"They did. They gave me some days off."

"They're not days off!"

"Restricted duty. It's just a term . . . another name for time off."

"You could've been killed!"

That stopped Zoo. He'd been making a conscious effort to forget what had happened just hours ago. Yes, he could have been killed. And he would have been had Harkins remembered to release the safety. That mistake was all that had stood between a live Lieutenant

Tully and his body on a slab in the morgue. "Honey, we've been over this. You know there's danger in my work. I carry a lethal weapon. So do the bad guys."

"I know. And I know we've talked about it. But it never was for real until now. And it scares me."

"To be honest, it scares me, too. It didn't when it was going down. Then, the adrenaline was pumping. Now, it's time to cool down. That's what I'm doing here at home with you."

Anne Marie wiped tears away with the back of her hand. "Tell me again, sweetheart, what you have to do now. Can't they give you a break and overlook some of the red tape?"

Zoo shook his head. "Honey, you gotta remember this procedure has been built up over years of trial and error. And besides, I already got one break."

"And that is?"

"The procedure is, I was supposed to be taken immediately to headquarters. That's so nobody—mainly the media—could throw any questions at me, or ask for a statement. My guys gave me a couple of minutes with Zack."

"Then what?"

"They took my gun. It's part of the investigation. They'll test it and identify it as the weapon that killed Harkins. Then they gave me the Garrity Warning—"

"That something like the Miranda Warning?"

"It's sort of the Miranda Warning for cops. I have to make out a PCR—that's the Preliminary Complaint Report. Nothing said in that can be used against me—because I am ordered to make the report.

"The rest of it is pretty routine. The Board of Review investigates, and the department psychiatrist examines me. I even get to be interviewed by a department chaplain—" He noted her lifted eyebrow. "No, I didn't request it; it's compulsory in these situations.

"Then I get to confer with our union representative, and our lawyer.

"Bottom line: Once I get clearance from the Board of Review and the psychiatrist, I can resume normal duties."

"And until then?"

"Tomorrow, I stay home. The next day, I'll go on desk duty. But it'll probably be three or four days before I'm allowed back out on the street." He paused momentarily. "Honey . . . see, odds are strong—very strong—that there'll be litigation. There almost always is . . ."

"But what can anybody sue you—or the department—for? What you did seems like a classic case of self-defense."

"They'll argue that Harkins's weapon was locked . . . so that, in effect, I killed an unarmed man."

"But you couldn't know the gun was locked!"

"Baby, I said they'd sue . . . I didn't say they'd win."

Both had been sipping their coffee. What remained in the cups was cooling. Anne Marie hotted up their cups.

"All this is by the book," Zoo said, "so it doesn't trouble me."

"Then what *is* troubling you?"

"I'm going to be off the streets just when I most need to be on active duty."

"How come?"

"Harkins wasn't involved in the church bombing. That we know. That means the bomber is still out there. He's frustrated: Not only did he fail but the guy who followed in his steps also failed. This can get to be like a shark's feeding frenzy.

"Today's surveillance was mostly a personal favor to me. Realistically, we can't afford that kind of bodyguarding indefinitely.

"I could do it. With a few people from my squad we could give Zack and Wheatley pretty good protection. But not only am I off the street, I am not allowed to participate in any investigation of this case. And that prohibition is the strongest of all: I'm off this case . . . period!"

Anne Marie reflected on this. "I can understand why the department is cautious about the possibility—"

"Probability," Zoo corrected.

"All right, *probability* of a lawsuit. And I can see why the department is supercautious about protecting you . . . and itself. But giving you desk duty and keeping you from this case? That sounds as if you're being punished. And I don't think it's fair."

"Experience," Zoo said firmly. "The school of hard knocks. The department wants to be supercertain there are no loopholes. We want to be prepared for the worst. But"—he smiled—"here you've got me defending the department. You're clever: You're supposed to be on the department's side: keeping me out of action . . . and out of danger."

"I do feel that way, hon. It's just that I know how this tears you up. I do want Father Wheatley to come out of this alive. And especially I want Zack to be safe. It's just that I know that you're the best officer to bring them through this alive and well. I guess . . . I'm just torn . . ."

"So am I. But I know me. I'm going to be a bear for a few days. I just hope I don't make life miserable for you . . ."

"You won't. I'm on your team. I guess," she concluded, "the only thing we can do is pray."

"That's your department, babe." He grinned. "I'll just count on your prayers." He stood. "Why don't you finish making supper while I watch some TV? Maybe I can find some mindless violence on the tube. Nothing I want more now than watching some TV cops blowing away an infinite number of bad guys."

She patted his hand, and turned to her task. She put a prepared dinner in the oven. Ordinarily, she would've put together a superior meal. But tonight she neither had the time, nor was she in the mood.

About prayer? She loved her husband. She loved everything about him. With him she felt protected and loved in return.

If there was one thing she could add to their lives it would be faith—faith enough for both of them. Faith in God, and communication with Him through prayer.

She would continue to work at that for as long as either of them lived.

Zoo was too good a person not to know Love Himself.

Nan Wheatley sat quietly in the comfortable living room. She, like her husband, was grateful to the Episcopal Church for giving them leave to remain in their old rectory until . . . until what? Until the Wheatleys would move into St. Joseph's rectory, leaving behind—but no, she mustn't dwell on that.

Uppermost in Nan's mind were thoughts of her children. Alice, having been questioned at length, was finally free to return to Dallas. However, she had decided to stay in Detroit until this affair had run its course.

Richard, for the duration, was staying with one of George's relatives in Windsor, just across the Detroit River, in Canada.

Ron was carrying on his ministry as well as possible, though in a distracted fashion. Part of that distraction was due to Gwen.

Nan had never really liked Gwen. Her reservations sprang from Gwen's ambitions to climb socially, and the pressure she inflicted on her husband to do likewise. But beyond that, Gwen's ambitions for her husband's advancement were fixed on nothing less than his becoming a bishop. An office not easily attained, particularly if actively pursued. Knowing Gwen's background of extreme poverty infused with very fundamental Christianity, Nan could understand her daughter-in-law's ambitions. She could understand them, but she could not ignore what those ambitions were doing to Ron.

Ron and Gwen and Richard had also been questioned about the bombing.

As a result of the investigation thus far, Lieutenant Tully had been able to ascertain that not Alice, Ronald, Gwen, nor Richard had an established alibi for the time immediately preceding the explosion.

Actually, Richard seemed to need no explanation for his whereabouts during that period. If anything, he was merely bemused over all this commotion surrounding a switch in Church affiliation. Outside of his concern over this threat to his father, Richard seemed a carefree teenager.

Ronald and Alice were another question. They were bitter over what they saw as George's defection from the Episcopal faith. As, by extension, was Gwen.

Presumably, each of them could have a viable motive. Even if those motives might possibly differ one from another. And, given the comparative ease of assembling a timed pipe bomb, in Lieutenant Tully's eyes, any of them could have had the means—although there might be some question about Gwen's competency in that realm. To Zoo, it was all conceivable; to Nan Wheatley, it was unthinkable.

Of course one had to keep in mind that the majority of conservatives—particularly the inculcated ones—were just plain angry—some few to the point of fanaticism.

Angry that their Roman Catholic Church would welcome an Anglican priest and his family, and that this priest from a "heretical" sect openly espoused female priests. It was almost too much for a Catholic of the "old school" to bear.

Episcopal traditionalists were similarly affected. Father Wheatley was abandoning the Church, as well as the countless faithful he had counseled, comforted, and instructed over a great many years. He was, to some, a traitor.

Then there was Father Morgan, whose reportedly returned vestments still had not turned up. Nobody had seen him around the altar before the explosion—but then, who had really been paying attention? Who knew *who* had been anyplace around the altar?

Nan stood above all this. She remained the adhesive that held her fragmented family together. Her first love was directed to her husband. Very closely following this was her concern for her children.

Neither George nor Nan had had much of an appetite at dinner. Both had done little more than pick at their food.

Things were beginning to settle down now. Though they still reacted with anxiety and concern over the danger and excitement of Sunday's bombing.

After all these years together, Nan could tell that her husband was presently a bundle of nerves, though he gave no outward indication of this. For one thing, he had been puffing on his ancient pipe. George had given up smoking years ago. But he had not gotten rid of his various pipes. They were like old friends, even if they were deadly. That he was smoking one now confirmed Nan's suspicion that inwardly George was seething.

"Outside of the obvious, dear, is there something particularly bothering you?"

George laid his pipe in an ashtray and slipped a bookmark into the book he was reading. "Just that I worry about Father Tully. I don't want anything to happen to him."

"Nothing will, darling. He made it through today's threat. And considering what happened, I think you'd have to call him a survivor."

"Easy enough to say. But from what we know, providence—or luck, if you prefer—saw him through it."

"But, George, you must remember: The dead man wasn't the bomber, just someone with a grudge against Father Tully."

"Oh, I know Mr. Harkins was not the bomber. His widow could testify to that. But that's just the thing: There isn't any doubt in my mind—nor yours, I'll wager—that I was the prime target on Sunday. Whoever did that wanted to kill me badly enough to risk killing one or more others to get to me."

"No, dear, the bomber isn't the sort to go after Father Tully as a lone target. I doubt that Mr. Harkins would have even thought of attacking Zachary if not for what happened Sunday. Oh, Harkins would be frustrated and complain about his pastor and the 'new' Church in general. But I'll bet that's as far as he would have gone if it hadn't been for the example in St. Joe's church. I fear it may be open season on Church functionaries." He closed his eyes, under a brow that appeared knitted in pain. "I fear it."

"And I do not," Nan stated firmly. "I am convinced that once we get you through this, it'll be over and done with. In fact, I feel that it's behind us even now. I don't think our mad bomber will attempt to strike again."

"You think so?" George was ready to grasp at any straw.

"I do, indeed. In fact Mr. Harkins may just be the scarecrow in this."

George looked puzzled.

"Don't you see," Nan explained, "now that the police are aware of this possible threat, they are a deterrent force. What happened to Mr. Harkins could happen to anyone who tries to harm you—or anybody else—in similar circumstances . . ." Her voice trailed off, and she fell silent.

George retrieved his pipe from the ashtray. He dumped the dottle, tapping the bowl; then cleaned the inside of the bowl, shook in a fresh plug of tobacco, tamped it, lit it, and sucked in. Smoke paused for a moment over his head, then spread to the room's four corners.

Nan appreciated the aromatic odor. She did not appreciate what it was doing to her husband's lungs. "There's something more, isn't there?" she prodded.

George affected to be occupied in coaxing the tobacco to ignite. Actually the pipe was doing quite well.

"I know there's something more," she pressed. "It'll do you good to get it out."

He puffed more vigorously. By now the smoke was wafting throughout the room. The heat made his mouth uncomfortable.

"Well . . . yes," he admitted at length. "But it's just useless speculation . . . nothing anyone can do anything about."

"Nevertheless, it's troubling you. Won't you tell me?"

"Hmmm. It's just that this whole thing has grown like Topsy. It seems to have taken on a life of its own."

"Pardon?"

"The process of leaving the Episcopal Church was worse than I had imagined . . ." He paused momentarily. "But the call seemed so clear. I did not much care for abandoning Anglicanism. I did not appreciate having to go back to school and 'learn' from people who knew less than I did. I certainly hated the idea that I would not be allowed to have a pastoral ministry. 'Special services' like the chancery, jail ministry, even the seminary, are what's being demanded of me." He paused again. "I suppose I should be grateful they're letting me keep the radio program and the column. In short, this whole business has proved very depressing." He sighed.

"But I knew this was coming. No matter how discouraging, the call . . . Christ's call for me to make this difficult move . . . was stronger than the impositions I've had to undergo."

In all their years together, Nan had never heard her husband mention a specific "calling." Not to the priesthood. Not to the newspaper. Not to the radio program.

This gave her more reason to believe that George felt he had experienced some sort of divine intervention in his life.

"To be perfectly open, Nan, everything I've mentioned: the reaction of both Roman and Anglican conservatives, the demeaning process I've been put through—none of this has been more oppressive than the deep-seated opposition of Alice and Ron.

"I knew they would be terribly upset. But I thought that would be only their initial reaction. I was certain they would get over it."

"They may yet, dear. They may simply need more time."

"Do you think so? It seems so discouraging. I didn't want to hurt them, God knows that. But it would be the last straw . . . if they were to turn away from me forever. The last straw."

"You'll see, dear. In the end, they'll stand with you. Just give them time."

"I don't know." His eyes welled with tears. He wiped them away before they could escape down his cheeks. "Maybe I was wrong about having some sort of call. Why would the Lord single me out of all the people who could better accomplish this task? What if I'm wrong? It's not too late . . ." The pipe, still hot from the smoldering tobacco, rested, forgotten, in his hand. "Darling, what do you think? Should I back out? I've just been ordained for the diaconate in the Roman Church. I haven't been ordained to the priesthood yet. There's still time to get off the track. You are closer to me than anyone on earth: Should I call it quits and salvage what I can?"

Yes, you should, Nan thought.

From the very beginning she had not been sold on this momentous project. Of course, the move would bring great hardship for her. But she had proved that she was able to make the necessary sacrifices. No, it was George she worried about, much more than herself. Yet even she could not have foreseen the events of the past two days. The whole thing had gotten out of control.

Who could have guessed that one man—a priest, an innocent bystander—would be killed, and another man, bent on murder, would be shot down? And what was yet to come?

But this was not the word George was seeking from his wife. She knew her husband well. At this point, he wanted—he needed—the support and the encouragement that only Nan could provide. A negative response would only further grieve him.

In the end, she gave him what she knew he needed.

"Things have always been demanding for those who strive to do God's will. Starting with Jesus Himself. Just let your imagination wander through the ages. Think of those who have sacrificed themselves for a noble goal. History is full of examples. I'm sure the Lord is pleased that you have answered His call.

"Besides, dear, we haven't far to go. In less than a week we will be launched on another ministry. I think it's going to be thrilling. A challenge that will be a joy to meet. And in the very near future, our children will be around us again.

"It'll work. You'll see. Now, no more doubts. We will stay the course."

A smile was trying to break through his countenance. "Nan, darling, what did I ever do to have you share my life?"

"We must have been pretty good to have found each other. I cannot imagine life without you."

"Nor I without you in this life and the next."

Nan left her chair and walked across the room. She perched on the arm of George's chair. He laid aside his pipe. It smoldered in the ashtray. She slid her arm across his shoulders and rested her head on his.

"God's in His heaven," George said. "We are together. All's right with the world."

TWENTY-TWO

TUESDAY MORNING. The weather was typical for a Lenten day on the verge of spring. It wasn't so much raining as misting. Not quite demanding an umbrella so much as a rain hat. A damp chill hung in the air. The perfect climate to encourage a late winter cold.

Radio, television, and print newspeople were filing into the Gabriel Richard Building on the corner of Michigan Avenue and Washington Boulevard.

The weather was cheerless. But it could not compete with Jim Davis's wretchedness. As the longtime proprietor of a downtown bar and grill, Davis should have long since gotten used to the reek of stale tobacco and alcohol. This morning, however, the only thing that kept him from being sick to his stomach was that he wasn't pregnant.

It had begun yesterday.

Before he left home for work, his wife had given him one important but simple task: Mail the mortgage payment. It was the final day to send it in without incurring a penalty.

But yesterday afternoon an old classmate had dropped in at Jim's Place to chew the fat. The friend stayed and stayed. Old football games were replayed. Old teachers were fondly or bitterly recalled. Perhaps once every two years Davis had a drink. Yesterday was that biennial day.

The result: He had forgotten to mail the house payment. And because the mortgage company had been swallowed by an out-of-state concern, he couldn't even hand-deliver the payment—not unless he wanted to drive to Minnesota.

His wife was furious. And he had the world's foremost hangover.

He had hated having to get up and go to work this morning. However, given the choice of staying around the house listening to a nonstop sermon on adult responsibility, or heading for the relative peace and quiet of Jim's Place—well, it was a no-brainer.

All in all, a doubly dreary day.

Customers would trickle in later. For now, Davis elected to sit by the window looking out on Washington Boulevard and give the sickening pounding behind his eyes a chance to die down.

As usual at this time of day and in this weather there were few cabs and even fewer pedestrians. Nearly everybody who worked downtown was already at work. Those who had no work huddled in doorways or under overhangs, trying to keep dry.

Davis's bleary gaze steadied on a car that was idling a short distance up the street. Wasn't that the same car he'd seen yesterday at just about the same spot? Again not parked, just idling.

Yesterday he'd thought the driver might have been Sunday evening's oddball patron. Davis's face contorted as he tried to focus. As far as he could tell, the man just sitting in his car now was the same guy who'd been sitting there yesterday morning. Yeah . . . the guy who'd gone on and on about that church bombing.

Davis tried to recall the patron's name. But it was simply too much effort. His brain seemed the organ slowest to recover. What was that guy doing hanging around a near-deserted corner in downtown Detroit anyway?

It's probably nothing, he decided. He lurched to his feet. Time to ready Jim's Place for the faithful few.

At least he had mailed the goddam house payment—along with the fee for tardiness.

Stan Rybicki's fingers drummed the steering wheel.

He was quite certain what he wanted to do. He had to depend on fate to have a chance at doing it.

Yesterday he had almost succeeded. For a brief few moments he'd had the Wheatley man in his sights. But another priest was with him. That wouldn't do at all.

Rybicki had circled the block periodically, trying not to attract undue attention. But the two priests had stayed in the coffee shop—and stayed and stayed. And, after all that, when they did finally emerge, it turned out that Wheatley had parked in a lot adjacent to the shop.

He'd had no real chance.

Today, however, held more promise.

According to news reports, a press conference concerning Wheatley's future was to be held in the Gabriel Richard Building.

The boss—that would be Cardinal Boyle—would probably want to confer with Wheatley beforehand . . . possibly even accompany him to the press conference. Rybicki waited. Fate would be his guide. If God gave an opening, Rybicki would strike. If not . . . He shrugged. God's will be done.

There he was.

Parking in the same lot as yesterday. Rybicki could not mistake the dumpy figure, swathed in a misshapen black raincoat. Even with the black hat pulled firmly down over his brow to ward off the misting rain and sharp wind whipping in from the Detroit River.

The fly in this ointment came in the person of another black-clad man—probably another priest, but not one familiar to Rybicki—who pulled up and parked next to Wheatley's car. Now he walked along-side Wheatley across Washington Boulevard toward the chancery. No way of knowing whether the unknown priest would be accompanying Wheatley to the news conference, or whether he had just happened along coincidentally.

There was only one more chance. If it failed, Wheatley's fate would have to be at the very least postponed.

Rybicki watched the two clerically clad men disappear into the chancery building.

Sometime—sometime soon—Wheatley would have to go from the chancery over to the Gabriel Richard Building, where the conference was scheduled. To get there, he'd have to cross both Washington Boulevard and Michigan Avenue.

If, in doing this, he would have company . . . well, it would be God's will.

Right now, Wheatley was undoubtedly conferring with the Cardinal. It would not be a long meeting; the conference was due to begin in a few minutes. The newspeople must already be assembled; no last-minute arrivals were scrambling in.

In a short while, Wheatley would ride down in the elevator. The elevator that Rybicki himself had operated and watchdogged all those years.

He waited. For the moment, there was nothing else he could do. But pray.

It was a brief meeting. Almost pro forma. Cardinal Boyle was not feeling well. The violent events of the past few days had done him no good. He said very little. Nor, for that matter, did Father Wheatley. The director of the Department of Communications did all the talking. All Father Wheatley need bother with was (a) complete ignorance with regard to who was responsible for the bombing or why it had occurred; the matter was in the capable hands of Detroit's Homicide detectives. And (b) Wheatley's ordination ceremony would take place this coming Sunday in Blessed Sacrament Cathedral; admission would be by ticket only.

And that was it.

A pretty meager briefing, Wheatley thought. But it didn't trouble him; he'd dealt with the media in the past. He and they would get along all right.

The director then excused himself from attending the news conference. He had several calls to return, a couple of which might prove important. Wheatley remained unperturbed; he did not need anyone to lead him to 305 Michigan Avenue.

On the ride down on the elevator, Wheatley considered how the conference would go without the director's hands-on presence. The main thing that had to be emphasized was that no one without an invitation was going to be admitted to the ordination ceremony.

Even so, Wheatley reflected, security would not be airtight. They simply did not know who was responsible for the first attempt on Wheatley's—or, perhaps, Tully's—life. It could have been a relative, a friend, or even another—though ideologically opposed—priest. Or— who could tell?—a professional assassin. A ticket might well be given to a murderer and withheld from an innocent person who just wanted to witness history in the making.

Wheatley's ride aboard the chancery's elevator was over. He walked through the empty vestibule and let himself out the door to Washington Boulevard. He paused, pulled his coat collar up around his neck, and his hat brim as far down as possible.

It was still raining. Perhaps a little harder than when he'd entered the chancery. He stepped out onto the boulevard and headed for Michigan Avenue.

Stan Rybicki jerked upright in the driver's seat.

He tapped his foot against the accelerator. The engine was running.

The heretic was walking alone right into harm's way.

Perfect.

God had provided the sacrifice.

It was God's will!

Wheatley arrived at the corner. He glanced briefly down Michigan. He barely turned his head; he didn't want to get his glasses wet. There was no vehicle turning from Michigan onto Washington Boulevard. He headed across the boulevard toward the median. He crossed the median, then, as he was about to continue into the street, he glanced up, this time to his right. No traffic. Just a parked car. He stepped forward.

The car's engine roared. Not unusual in itself; maybe there was a stalling problem . . . had to rev the engine to get it going.

Rybicki released the brake and pressed the accelerator to the floor.

The car shot forward.

Wheatley knew instantly something was terribly wrong. He had no time to think of anything beyond that. The car struck even as he started to turn his head.

His body seemed to float gracefully through the air. Something like an acrobat in a circus. It turned a complete somersault before crunching into the wet pavement.

And there he lay.

The car was a block down Michigan Avenue before Rybicki slowed and turned off the main thoroughfare. Although he had fixated on his target, he was quite sure there had been no witness.

It would take a while for his pounding pulse to slow to normal. But he had done it: He had stopped his Church from betraying Herself.

Rybicki was wrong about there being no witness.

Jim Davis was sweeping near the front window when he heard the snarl of the motor and the squeal of the tires. He looked up, saw the car strike the victim, and witnessed the body make its artful turn in the air.

Davis, and probably he alone, knew exactly what had happened.

His first inclination was to detach himself from this mess. People rarely got into trouble keeping quiet.

But there was something particularly heinous about this. In Davis's catalog of evil, vehicular homicide, or the attempt thereat, ranked high.

He had heard about, even in a few instances seen people being killed. It wasn't that he was particularly squeamish about murder per se. But it was one thing to kill expeditiously—a gun, a knife—and another to inflict a slow, painful death. Running someone down with a car was so deliberate, so premeditated. And odds were that the victim would not be dispatched quickly. More likely there would be much suffering before the victim's lingering departure.

All this and more impelled Davis to immediately call 911. After which he pulled on an old raincoat and a rubber fireman-style rain hat and dashed down the boulevard toward the inert figure.

Before he reached the victim, a blue-and-white, siren wailing, sped past him and screeched to a halt alongside the inert form.

Just as farmers are so accustomed to barnyard noises that they are more or less deaf to the normal moos, quacks, oinks, and clucks, Detroiters are so accustomed to sirens that the sound rarely even registers on their consciousness. However, if the wail stops abruptly in the near vicinity, that is apt to grab one's attention. And so it was now: Office workers lined windows, and those on the lower floors began spilling out onto the sidewalk.

One officer radioed for backup and an ambulance. He bent down to reassure the victim, then turned to help his partner with crowd control and restricting and preserving the crime scene.

Davis, on seeing the police arrive, had slowed his run. Now, approaching the supine man, he heard a muffled sound. Wheatley was saying something. But Davis could not make it out. He knelt and bent his ear to Wheatley's lips.

"Who did this?" Yes, that's what the priest was murmuring over and over. "Who did this?"

One of the officers turned and noticed Davis. "Hey, buddy, get away from there. Come on, now . . ."

Davis got to his feet.

"Did you see this happen?" the officer asked. As usual, he expected no cooperation. So he was surprised when Davis replied, "I saw the whole thing."

While this exchange was going on, the other officer was questioning members of the growing crowd. No one had been at a window when the impact occurred. A few said they'd seen the car as it turned the corner and sped away. But there was no consensus as to the make, model, or year—although all agreed that the vehicle was a dark color.

No matter: Davis's interrogator had struck pay dirt.

Davis described Stan Rybicki's lingering visit to Jim's Place last Sunday. How Rybicki had intimated violence against Wheatley. Davis added that he had seen Rybicki—or at least he thought it was Rybicki—parked down the street yesterday as well as this morning. Davis had been at the front window when Rybicki's car struck Wheatley.

"What was the make?" The officer was scarcely able to recover from such serendipitous cooperation.

Davis was able to identify the make, model, year, color, and even—amazingly—the license number. And, miracle of miracles, even the driver's name had come back to him. The pub owner did everything but make a citizen's arrest.

The officer, marveling, took it all down, along with Davis's name and number.

By this time, the scene resembled a movie set. The initially small group of onlookers had grown to a sizable throng. An ambulance and several other blue-and-whites had arrived, all with flashers flashing and sirens ablare.

Davis's questioner gave his information to Sergeant Mangiapane, the ranking officer on the scene. All of them were near ebullient over the unusually specific information dropped in their laps.

Wheatley, now unconscious, was loaded into the ambulance, which, siren and flashers again activated, headed for nearby Receiving Hospital.

Mangiapane was about to follow the ambulance. Before leaving, he asked the first officer on the scene, "What did the Davis guy say Wheatley was mumbling?"

"He said he kept asking, 'Who did this?' Over and over."

"Kind of odd . . ." Mangiapane scratched his head. "Usually, it's 'How bad am I hurt?' Or 'Am I gonna make it?' I don't think I've ever heard anyone worry about IDing the perp.

"But I can tell you one thing," he added, "Zoo Tully is gonna be one sore dude."

"I'll admit I was pretty damn sore when I heard about it," Zoo Tully said.

Anne Marie was refilling the coffee cups. On hearing her husband describe his earlier condition as "sore," she turned so the others could see her exaggerated if silent mouthing of the word "furious."

Zoo caught the furtive aside. "Okay, okay," he admitted. "Maybe furious. But I cooled down after a while."

Anne Marie pointed at herself.

Zoo laughed. "All right: Annie talked some sense into me."

By this time, everyone was chuckling.

It was about ten P.M.Tuesday. Seated around the Tully dining table were Walter Koznicki, Father Koesler, Father Tully, and his brother Zoo.

All had been occupied with the same matter—the attempted murder of Father George Wheatley and the speedy arrest of Stan Rybicki.

Inspector Koznicki had joined Zoo Tully at headquarters, looking on as the wheels of police procedure ground flawlessly. Neither of the two men could actively participate. Tully, on desk duty, was excluded from working the case until a verdict came down on his shooting of Leon Harkins. Koznicki, of course, was retired.

Father Koesler and Father Tully had spent most of the day at Receiving Hospital, trying to comfort Nan and the Wheatley family. The two priests were joined in this effort by several others, including an equal number of Episcopal and Roman priests.

Now, the day done, Zack, Koznicki, and Koesler were winding down at the Tullys' condo at Zoo's invitation.

"What is the latest on Father Wheatley's condition?" Koznicki directed the question to both or either of the Fathers who'd been in attendance at the hospital from mid-morning on.

"It's been changing slightly all day long," Father Tully said. "A CAT scan didn't show much. At least they couldn't find any serious brain damage. He drifts in and out of consciousness. The doctors suspect a concussion. When he does come to he has lots of confusion. He seems dazed. He has trouble remembering his age and other incidentals. It's hard for him to recall the accident.

"But you've got to remember," Tully cautioned, "that I'm giving you a sort of summary of briefings from several doctors." He turned to Koesler. "Did you get anything more, Bob?"

Koesler shook his head. "I think you covered it pretty well, Zack. In general, the thought seems to be that he was lucky—very lucky—to have survived the impact. As of right now, it seems to be a waiting game. I've heard doctors describe situations like this as waiting for nature to heal something. After that, it's a case of following nature's process and patching things up." Koesler looked thoughtful. "The doctors did say that George seems withdrawn . . . indifferent; unusually quiet—and quite depressed. But"—he sighed—"that would be expected, I guess, from the injuries he's sustained and all he's gone through."

"The department must be glad," Anne Marie said, "that they don't have to start from scratch in finding the guy responsible for all this."

"Yes," Koznicki confirmed. "Seldom does it go so easily."

"It could've gone easier for my man," Anne Marie said, glancing at her husband.

Koznicki seemed almost embarrassed. "I am sorry. I did not mean to imply that killing a man intent on killing you was easy. Only that in both affairs, the cases were closed so rapidly."

"Oh, I know, Inspector. It's just that I worry about Zoo so much." Again she gazed at her husband with love and affection.

"Hey," Zoo countered, "didn't your friend, Shakespeare, say 'All's well that ends well'?"

"Okay, okay . . ." Anne Marie wished she hadn't made the comment that had started this.

The others were now either smiling or chuckling outright.

"Besides," Zoo added, "if Leon Harkins hadn't cashed in at St. Joe's, he was still headed for some hard time."

"Oh?" Zack looked puzzled.

"We had him on a twenty-year felony."

"For what?"

"Extortion. For threatening to kill you if you didn't do what he wanted. I'm pretty sure that any judge would have given him the full term."

"And this Stanley Rybicki . . ." Anne Marie wanted to get off, and stay off, the matter of Harkins and Zoo's role in that scene. " . . . he would have been hard to find?"

"All day long," Zoo said, "we would have been gathering evidence—skid marks, paint samples—and somewhere—with luck—we might have latched on to a witness."

"But," Koznicki added, "Mr. Rybicki went from incredible luck to no luck at all."

"The problem, of course, remains," said Zoo. "We still don't have the bomber, or—an even tougher nut to crack—the guy who made the phone call. We know it wasn't Harkins. He was home all Sunday. His wife swears to that. And from everything the bartender reported, Rybicki *was* at the church—but he didn't plant the bomb . . . or make the phone call.

"Rybicki isn't fighting the hit-and-run charge. But he does deny any part in the bombing."

"So," Koznicki said, "the heart of this matter has yet to be solved: Who planted the bomb? And who made the call that changed the whole complexion of this crime?"

There was a long silence as each present consulted his or her own thoughts.

"This has been a difficult time," Koznicki said finally. "Perhaps it would be good to call it a night."

It seemed an idea whose time had come. The guests rose to begin preparations for departure.

"I guess," Father Tully said, "I don't have to ask for your prayers for Father Wheatley."

All—except Zoo—mumured assent. Zoo had nothing against Wheatley. He just had no faith in prayer. If he had, he undoubtedly would have stormed heaven with prayers of gratitude for his escape from certain death the day before.

Just as the guests were about to leave, Zack came up with another question. "What was it Father Wheatley kept saying over and over before he was taken to the hospital?"

There was no immediate response.

"I believe," Inspector Koznicki volunteered in the absence of any other reply, "it was something like, 'Who did this?'"

"That's strange, isn't it?" Anne Marie said. "At that moment, if I had been the victim, I'd be a lot more concerned about my condition and staying alive than knowing who hit me. But, as the Fathers said, maybe he was just confused—and, of course, scared."

Koznicki noted a change in Father Koesler's expression. The priest's eyes glazed and his mouth dropped open slightly. Koznicki had seen a similar expression on his clerical friend more than once. Koznicki had often thought that if Koesler were a comic strip character it was at such times that a lit lightbulb would appear over the priest's head. For such an expression usually indicated that the priest had gotten a sudden idea. An idea that could lead to the solution of the crime at hand. Something that could answer a question, solve a problem, or clear up a mystery.

Good-byes were offered, and one by one the guests left.

Koznicki hoped Koesler's singular expression might once again prove fruitful. From experience, he knew that the next several hours would be critical in the success or failure of Koesler's inspiration. For Koznicki also knew that the lightbulb signified the first step toward the solution; that everything had to fall into place before his friend would, à la Sherlock Holmes, set the scene for the denouement.

Time would tell. But, short of a phone call from Koesler, Koznicki would be at the hospital to witness the next act in this ongoing tragedy.

TWENTY-THREE

*W*HO DID THIS?*"*

Father Koesler pondered this question all during his drive home and still later while he brewed a large cup of tea. He had virtually ceased making coffee since no one except him seemed to find it potable. His tea was more readily accepted. Though he himself could not tell the difference as far as quality was concerned.

As for George Wheatley's repeated question, Koesler could surmise only that Wheatley thought he should know his assailant.

Was that possible? It would be a major surprise if George *had* known Stan Rybicki, the actual driver of the attack vehicle. Of all the likely culprits in the church bombing, Rybicki's name had never come up, not even as a remotely possible suspect.

Who did Wheatley think—who might he think—had been the driver? Obviously, George thought the driver and the bomber were one and the same. George was wrong, of course. But, if Koesler's analysis and conclusions were correct, it now seemed that Wheatley may indeed have had his own suspicions. Suspicions that he had shared with no one—or at least no one in the Homicide Department or in the close clerical circle. And if Koesler was correct in his assessment that George Wheatley thought he might know who was responsible for all this, why wouldn't he confide his suspicions to the proper parties?

Koesler pondered this at length, his mind twisting and turning—examining, then discarding hypothesis after hypothesis in turn.

Could it be—?

No; it was unthinkable!

And yet . . .

And yet. Sherlock Holmes's oft-repeated dictum leaped to mind: "When you have eliminated the impossible, whatever remains, *however improbable,* must be the truth."

Could George Wheatley suspect someone in his own circle? Someone near to him? Someone *very* near . . .

Yes, that would have to be it: Otherwise why keep his suspicions— his gut feeling—to himself?

Koesler went back to square one: All those who were closest to George Wheatley—Nan, Ron, Alice, Richard, and Gwen—were conversant with the Bible. Was this leading to a biblical clue?

Koesler rose, took his Bible from the shelf, and returned to his chair. He didn't open the book, but just sat, holding it in his hands, as if expecting an answer through some sort of literary osmosis.

He set his memory to scanning a stream of consciousness. What biblical incidents would come to mind relating to conflict between husband and wife? Between father and son? Father and daughter? Father-in-law and daughter-in-law?

The first thing that came to mind was Jesus' story of the Prodigal Son. The young profligate who demanded, then squandered, his inheritance. Wiped out financially and emotionally, he returned, shamefaced and groveling, to his father. The father was overjoyed at his son's return—so overjoyed that he ordered a feast in celebration.

Koesler could find no compelling connection between fact and fiction here. Not even in the hostile reaction of the faithful son, who resented the forgiveness and undeserved reward accorded his repentant brother.

Next, Koesler's scanning mind stopped at another story told by Jesus, about two brothers, directed by their father to work in the family enterprise. One brother agreed readily, but, in the end, loafed all day long. The other brother at first refused to work, then had a change of heart and did as his father had bade him.

Again, this parable seemed irrelevant as far as whoever it was George Wheatley suspected. George did have two sons, but Koesler was not aware of any such similar or analogous reaction on the part of Ron or Richard to any of George's commands.

Koesler's memory slipped into the Old Testament.

David the King.

David surely had a most serious conflict with his son, Absalom. Both David and George Wheatley were noteworthy for a great ability to love. Both loved their sons dearly. Absalom tried to overthrow his father and usurp the kingship. So much and so deeply did David love his son that he lost all interest in what was happening to himself—and the kingdom. His sole concern was for Absalom.

But David came out of battle unscathed, whereas Absalom was killed. George Wheatley could, or should, have been killed in the explosion. But neither Ronald nor Richard had been physically harmed.

Nevertheless, Koesler felt he might be getting closer to the core connection.

The characters who next came to mind were Abraham and Isaac, the two participants in possibly one of the most moving stories in the entire Bible.

Isaac was the only child of Abraham and Sara. The child was born in Sara's great old age and Abraham's decline. All of Abraham's hopes for the future were concentrated in Isaac.

But God demands that Abraham sacrifice his son as a burnt offering. God is testing Abraham's faith. And Abraham almost superhumanly proves his faithfulness. The Bible tells how Abraham, Isaac, and some servants collect the ingredients for the ritual holocaust. But something is lacking—an animal to be the sacrificial offering. Isaac asks about that. Abraham assures his son that God will provide the sacrifice. When they reach the site, the wood and the altar are prepared and—undoubtedly to Isaac's horror—the son is bound as the sacrificial animal. Abraham is about to kill his son when, at the last moment, an angel intervenes.

Koesler sat very still. He felt he was getting closer. Yet something—some things—were missing; for a perfect analogy it needed other elements.

He thought very deeply until another possibility came to mind. And, for the first time in Koesler's ruminations, this example included a young woman.

The story was in the book of Judges. It involved the illegitimate son of Gilead, an Israeli chieftain. The son's name was Jephthah. Gilead had other sons, all legitimate. These forced Jephthah into exile because he was the bastard of the litter.

Jephthah became a mercenary warrior who attracted some like-minded lowlifes. As a group, they were very successful, and profited from many raids.

Jephthah had pretty much forgotten his previous life. And then the tribe of Ammonites went to war against Israel. The leaders of Israel came begging to enlist the aid of the man they had expelled. Their mission was crucial.

At length, Jephthah agreed to lead them into battle, under the condition that should he win the war he would become undisputed leader of all Israel. His terms were accepted.

Jephthah counted as much on God for victory as on his troops. He promised God that should He grant victory, Jephthah would offer up as a sacrifice the first person who came to meet him when he returned in victory. His vow was a pretty safe one; after all, he had but one child, and certainly no way would she be the first person he would set eyes on after the battle.

Wouldn't you know it: When Jephthah returned to his house in a victory parade, it was his daughter who came forth, playing the tambourines and dancing. At sight of her, he rent his garments and cried, "Alas, daughter, you have struck me down and brought calamity upon me. For I have made a vow to the Lord, and I cannot retract.'"

Nor does he. After a two-month interval, during which the daughter puts her life in order, her father fulfills his vow and sacrifices his only child.

Obviously the stories that Koesler had summoned up bore certain similarities to the tragedy that had struck George Wheatley. Still, none of them came close to being a perfect match.

In the biblical narratives that Koesler could bring to mind, the father is always the principal figure. But it is the daughter, the sons, who are the victims, or near-victims.

In the real-life drama, as far as George Wheatley was concerned, the scenario was upside down: George himself was first the near-victim, then the actual victim.

So what did Koesler have for his pains? A complete washout . . .

He was ready to give up and call it a night. He half rose from his chair to do just that when another thought struck: If the Bible stories were upside down, what would happen if they were turned around? Koesler sat back down.

He went back over the five examples, turning them around, upside down, backward, and forward from their original biblical messages.

Then it hit.

One story did have everything. Oh, it wasn't a perfect match by any means . . . but the essentials were there.

Most of all, it satisfied Koesler's absorption with the mysteriously timely phone call that had caused a delay sufficient to save Wheatley's life, as well as that of Tully—and who knew how many others.

It wasn't a flawless blueprint, Koesler admitted to himself. But it was a solid hypothesis. A hypothesis that needed to be tested.

Who better? Koesler dialed the number for Walter Koznicki.

From the tone of Koznicki's voice, it seemed that the inspector had been waiting for, indeed expecting Koesler's call.

The priest explained his rationale for the conclusion he had reached.

Koznicki agreed totally. Koesler's conclusion might be no more than a theory. But it was a sounder theory than anyone else had come up with. It needed one more hearing; one more brain to run it through.

It was too late tonight, and even tomorrow might be too early for George Wheatley to be of any help. Nonetheless, the retired priest and the retired Homicide detective made a date to meet at the Intensive Care Unit of Receiving Hospital at eight A.M. tomorrow, and then go from there.

Neither Koesler nor Koznicki slept well that night.

TWENTY-FOUR

Promptly at eight A.M., Father Koesler exited the elevator and stepped into the corridor leading to the ICU waiting room. He was amazed at the sight that met his eyes. An overflow crowd spilled out of the waiting area into the corridor. Members of the media mingled with relatives and friends of the injured man.

Koesler's clerical collar afforded him a grudging path through the crowd. Still, it was slow going as he made his way toward the waiting room. When he reached the door, once more it was his collar that gained him entree.

With Koesler's height, he had a fair chance of getting a glimpse of most of those present. Specifically, he was looking for Inspector Koznicki and/or any of the immediate Wheatley family. He located the inspector with little trouble; his height also made him easy to spot. Koesler did not spy any of the family. They must, he assumed, be seated somewhere in the far corner of the room.

The ICU door was opened by a young woman in nursing uniform. Instantly the crowd surged forward a step or two. There was no room to advance further.

"Is there a Father Koesler here?" the nurse asked.

"Yes." Koesler waved a hand in the air.

"Please follow me."

There was a commotion on the part of the media mostly. Of course they wanted access. Of course none would be granted them. But now that something was going on, they felt impelled to act.

Koesler followed the nurse through the door. "How is he?"

She shook her head. "His condition has deteriorated somewhat. The doctors don't want to do anything invasive at present. It's now that we count mainly on his will to live. He asked to see you. That's a good sign. But he's aware how critical his condition is. Don't stay too long. And"—she turned a steady gaze on him—"try not to excite him."

She ushered Koesler into a fairly good-sized room that appeared smaller than it actually was. This, Koesler thought, was due to the life-support system and monitors that encompassed the patient.

There was no sound save the whisper of oxygen and the soft ping of the heart monitor.

Koesler had been in many a hospital room over the years. He was no stranger to ICU facilities. The fact that George Wheatley was hooked up to a near cobweb of tubes and wires was not surprising. Nor did any of this equipment speak to a healthy person. George Wheatley was badly injured. He looked and acted it.

The nurse left the room. The whistles, beeps, and pings would keep her well informed of the patient's condition.

"George . . ." Koesler spoke a bare decibel above a whisper.

Wheatley opened his eyes and focused on Koesler. A quarter of a smile was all he could muster. "A . . . a little while ago, one . . . one of my . . . Anglican buddies . . . gave me . . . the Ministration to the Sick. I . . . I hope you don't mind."

"Of course not. . .

"George, are you sure you want to talk? Maybe it would be better if you just rested. You did get bounced around quite a bit."

Wheatley rotated his head slightly to the the right, then to the left. Quite obviously he wanted to communicate something. No matter if it cost him dearly. "That phone call . . ." He spoke haltingly, effort-fully, his words barely audible.

"Maybe we'd better get into that later." Koesler, of course, knew to what phone call Wheatley referred. But as eager as he was to test his theory, he was reluctant to cause Wheatley more grief.

"Now." George sounded like an angry man who had run out of patience. Actually, he was just trying to conserve his energy so he could continue to communicate.

"Okay. You were called to the phone just as the ceremony was about to begin. It turns out you are notorious for not being able to ignore a ringing phone. We assumed that whoever called probably knew that. We also assumed that it was the caller's purpose to detain you long enough so that you would not be injured by the explosion.

"Since no one showed up to go to confession to you, we connected the bomber to the caller. But whoever he was, the caller did not consider the possibility of an inquisitive Father Farmer.

"You have said all along that you did not recognize the voice on the phone . . . that it was muffled and not distinguishable. It was clear enough to be understood, but not to be identified—"

Wheatley appeared agitated. He broke into Koesler's narrative. "I . . . couldn't . . . be . . . sure."

"But you had a suspicion?"

George nodded slowly, painfully. "How . . . did . . . you . . . know?"

"Everytime I was with you and the question of the caller's identity came up, you seemed to grow ill at ease."

Again a bare smile. "Yes."

"I'll save you the trouble. Did you think it might have been Ron?"

"Might." George emphasized that he couldn't be certain of the caller's identity, though, of course, there was a possibility. "But . . . why?"

"That has puzzled all of us," Koesler said, choosing his words carefully. "The question of who made the call began to become more important than who planted the bomb . . . if they were indeed not one and the same person."

"If . . . Ron . . . why?"

Koesler, careful not to dislodge any of the tubes or wires, moved his chair closer to the bed. "Last night, on a hunch, I tried to match what happened to you with some biblical event. Almost everyone who is either related to you, associated with you, or is an actual suspect in this case has some familiarity with the Bible, to a greater or lesser degree."

Wheatley nodded as vigorously as he was able. Koesler took this to mean that George himself had already been down this path. Unsuccessfully.

"I won't bother you with all the dead ends I ran into. But think for a moment of Abraham and Isaac."

George was, of course, quite conversant with the famous story. But even after several moments' thought, his expression indicated that he saw no connection.

"Turn it around," Koesler said. He allowed several moments for George to do this. "Now, pretend that the son was on a divine mission to sacrifice his father. Assume that instead of Abraham being told by the voice of God to kill and offer Isaac as a burnt offering, Isaac is told to sacrifice Abraham.

"In Abraham's case, God was testing Abraham's faith. In your case, you were about to betray your faith. Driven by the voice of God—and perhaps one other person . . . but we'll get to that later— Ron prepared to make of you a sacrifice.

"Once Abraham passed the test—proving beyond all doubt that his faith was strong enough to actually kill his own son, an angel stopped the proceedings, and Isaac was saved.

"Ron had one test for you. A test that would convince him that you didn't really believe in this heretical Roman Church. If you passed this test, you would be spared. Just as, if Abraham passed *his* test, Isaac would be spared.

"Your test came down to your identity as an Episcopal priest.

"Ron planted the bomb—something I'm sure he will regret all the rest of his days. Then he placed a call for you, timed for just as the ceremony was about to begin. Ron well knew how you couldn't resist answering a ringing phone. He tried to mask his voice so that you couldn't be certain to identify him.

"He told you he was desperate. Actually . . ." Koesler stopped to think for a moment, then nodded as if to himself. "Yes," he continued, "when it comes down to that, he *was* desperate. Anyway, he told you this was a life-or-death request. He had to go to confession to you. And he had to do so *now.*

"And here is where your test of faith occurred.

"He and you were ordained Episcopal priests. In becoming a Roman Catholic you were forced to renounce that ordination. You

271

were about to be ordained a priest for—as far as the Roman Church was concerned—the first time. If that was what you really believed, it would not be possible for you to comply with the caller's request; you did not have the power to absolve. You were not yet a priest. You were minutes away from being ordained a priest.

"If this was your understanding of what was about to happen, you could not have absolved this stranger at that time; if you could not go through with his request at that time, you would ipso facto be admitting that your Anglican ordination was invalid and that you thus could not hear his confession then.

"I think instinctively you agreed to grant his request. So what if the procession would be delayed slightly; the welfare of a human soul is clearly worth more than a brief postponement.

"Once you agreed, Ron's test was over. You passed. And in passing, and waiting in vain for a penitent to show up, you saved yourself. Just as in passing his test of obedience, Abraham was able to save Isaac.

"In a way, there even is a similar conclusion to both stories— though no one could have foreseen that. Once Abraham passes his test, there *is* a sacrificial animal caught in nearby bushes. That animal becomes the victim. And once you passed your test, Father Farmer, as innocent as any sacrificial lamb, becomes the victim."

Wheatley nodded slowly in comprehension. As Koesler had expounded his theory, George could see the inevitable conclusion. And he agreed that Ron certainly had made the call and probably had also planted the bomb. Clearly, he had saved the designated victim. But, in either case, Ron had committed a crime.

"Then . . . the car—?"

Koesler shook his head. "No, it wasn't Ron. The driver is in custody. He is a traditionalist—" Seeing the question in George's eyes, he added, "No, not an Anglican. A Roman Catholic who seems to have some sort of pathological resentment against what he termed the 'tainting' of his Church by an Anglican 'intruder.'"

George, eyes now closed, nodded slowly. Then his eyes opened. "The other . . . person, you said . . . was in . . . on this . . . ?"

Koesler sighed inwardly. "I don't know if that will ever be proven. But Gwen—" He stopped as a spasm of pain crossed Wheatley's face.

Koesler could not tell whether Wheatley's pain was physical or emotional—or both. But as Wheatley gestured for him to continue, Koesler went on. "I don't know, but I think that Gwen—maybe even more than Ron—was responsible for this whole thing. Remember, as we were leaving the coffee shop, you said, 'Don't exclude Gwen; she would like me out of the way.' If Ron *is* involved in this, I think you can bet that Gwen had a hand in it as well."

George Wheatley was the embodiment of sorrow. "Will . . . Ron . . . and Gwen . . . be charged?"

Koesler nodded. "The police are awfully good at this. What I will report as a result of our talk now will help them close the case more quickly than they might otherwise have."

"Of course . . . you . . . must tell." He fell silent. Koesler allowed him this peace.

Then: "My . . . family?"

"They're in the waiting room. At least I assume they are. I didn't see them. But then, I'd only just arrived when the nurse told me you wanted to see me. Would you like me to call them?"

George, eyes again closed, nodded.

Koesler summoned the nurse and passed on George's request.

One by one, the family entered. Koesler backed away, giving them space to gather around the bed. Alice clutched George's right hand, and rested her head on his arm. Richard fingered George's toes beneath the sheet as a mute statement that he was there. Nan glided between the tubes and wires to hold her husband in her arms. It was the Pietà in human flesh.

Mary's Jesus had just been taken from the cross and was dead. George was still living. But, Koesler feared, not for long.

George rested his head against Nan's shoulder. "Where's Ron . . . and . . . Gwen?"

"We couldn't reach them," Nan said. "Rest, darling; you'll need all your strength to fight this."

Everyone was in tears. Including Koesler. Through blurred vision, he thought he saw George turn his head toward the wall.

George Wheatley had already received the Anglican version of the Roman Sacrament of Anointing, which the Roman Church gives in cases of illness or impending death. There was no longer any reason for Koesler to stay. His presence would merely intrude on the family's attempts to show their love for their husband and father. He quietly departed.

TWENTY-FIVE

Easter had come and gone.

This year's celebration of the glorious Feast of the Resurrection was somewhat altered for Father Koesler. He was mindful of George Wheatley's Anglican attitude of ranking Christmas above Easter. Behind this was the belief that it was more important that Jesus came than that He died.

Koesler would never be convinced of that. But he had to admit that the body of Christmas music—sacred and pop—was far, far greater than "Easter Parade" and interminable alleluias.

Koesler had thought about George Wheatley and his family countless times since the priest's death. Not the least because Koesler would never be certain whether Wheatley's death had come as a result of the injuries suffered in the hit-and-run, or from the assaults on his spirit inflicted by his own flesh and flood—his own seed, to wax biblical. Had George, his heart broken, just given up and handed himself over to a loving God?

In any case, tonight Koesler would recall and go over the sad details one more time, if only because Walt Koznicki and his wife had not been present for the events that followed Wheatley's death and burial.

The inspector and Wanda had left the day after Wheatley died. They had scheduled visits with their various offspring, most of whom had settled along the Western seaboard.

Tonight's dinner was being hosted by Father Tully at St. Joseph's rectory. Tully remained both the pastor of Old St. Joe's and the sole inhabitant of its rectory.

The assemblage consisted of Koesler, Walt and Wanda Koznicki, and Zoo and Anne Marie Tully.

Father Tully led the Koznickis on a tour of the refurbished sanctuary. Work had been completed only a week ago. The Koznickis were the only guests who needed such a tour; the others had watched the work in progress.

Now all were seated in the spacious old living room, which, in times past would have been referred to as the parlor, or the drawing room, depending on one's socioeconomic status.

Anne Marie, as the host's sister-in-law, assumed the duties of hostess and passed around crudités and dip.

"We had to pack and begin our trip just a few hours after poor Father Wheatley died," Wanda said. "Of course we tried to keep up with the story as we traveled. The national media did report on events surrounding his death. But there were little or no specific details. So"—she turned to Koesler—"would you bring us up to date, Father?"

Father Koesler began the narration, leading off with his going to the Bible for inspiration and finally coming up with an analogy between the story of Abraham and Isaac and the actions of George and Ron Wheatley, only in reverse. Then putting that together with George's suspicion that the voice on the phone was, indeed, that of his son.

"Of course," Koesler said, "there was no question about our conversation falling under the seal of confession. We were just talking and comparing notes and hypotheses." He fell silent for a moment. "Watching George's family gather about him was one of the saddest experiences of my life."

Zoo took up the story at that point. "Father told me about his talk with Wheatley. The Bible story gave the good Father"—he inclined his head in Koesler's direction—"the clue he needed to arrive at the truth. Which, of course, was useless to us as hard evidence. However, Wheatley's admission that he thought the phone call was made by his son, Ron, did give us enough to go for a warrant."

He smiled. "Fortunately it was an ideal time of day to find a judge who would issue it.

"When we got to Ron Wheatley's home, we found one wretchedly miserable, really sorry man, and a packing wife. We had to Mirandize the priest . . . he was that eager to confess. In the basement we found the leftovers of the bomb: powder, pipe, parts of the time-piece—the whole thing. That and the priest's confession wrapped up the case against him.

"But the wife was something else. She wouln't say a word without her lawyer.

"We didn't have a case against her. Even if we believed she was as guilty as her husband, none of the evidence pointed to her." He shook his head. "Of course one word from her husband and we could've slapped the cuffs on her in a minute.

"We didn't think she had any part in actually constructing the bomb. But we were convinced she'd put plenty of pressure on her husband to plot murder." He winked at his wife. "A real Lady Macbeth.

"Anyway, that's why she was packing: She couldn't be sure Wheatley wouldn't implicate her—so she was outta there.

"But he refused to say a word against her. No matter how hard we pressed him, he wouldn't budge. We had a principal but couldn't nail her."

"'Principal'?" Koesler had never heard that term used in this context.

"Some places," Zoo explained, "call it 'accessory before the fact.' We call it 'principal.'"

"Ron Wheatley's lawyer informed him," Tully continued, "that spousal immunity would protect him from having to testify against his wife. And we just couldn't shake him. So—the beautiful lady skates."

"Where is she now?" Wanda asked.

"Getting a divorce. It'll be easy. Her husband is cooperating completely . . . probably part of the self-punishment he's heaping on himself," Tully said. "It worked for him once; maybe it'll work again."

Wanda looked puzzled. "What do you mean, 'It worked for him'?"

"It worked in the final analysis," Tully explained. "He started out being booked for Murder One. There wouldn't have been any question about the sentence. It would've been life, without parole. But they plea-bargained it down to Murder Two. That's a sentence of twelve-to-twenty years.

"That's when the self-punishment—repentance—call it any way you want—comes in. He started helping the other guys in the lockup. Praying for them, praying with them, counseling them.

"Anyway, what with that and one thing and another, the judge said she was convinced that his remorse was, as she put it, 'genuine, substantial, and compelling.' So she reduced the sentence to ten-to-fifteen. With the truth-in-sentencing on the books, we know he'll serve at least ten years."

Wanda still looked puzzled. "Didn't it make any difference that poor Father Farmer was not the intended victim? I mean, Father Wheatley didn't want to kill Father Farmer . . ."

"It makes no difference, love," Walt said. "It is called 'transferred intent.' It is the same as killing the intended victim."

Wanda, looking thoughtful, nodded understanding.

"I forgot to ask you, Zoo," Father Tully said, "what about that vestment that Father Morgan said he left in the sanctuary? That never turned up, did it?"

Lieutenant Tully shook his head. "Easy to see how it could have been destroyed in the blast—or disappeared in the ruckus afterward. Anyway, whatever your Father Morgan was doing in the sanctuary, he isn't our bomber. We've got our bomber."

"We've got the bomber *and* the caller," Zoo continued. "Ron Wheatley admitted planting the bomb. He claims that once he got started on this project, he couldn't call a halt to it. Personally, I think he just couldn't stop the wheels from turning because his wife wouldn't let him. But on that count, he clams up."

Zoo fell silent for a moment, going over these events in his mind. "Ron Wheatley was taking a chance on getting away with planting the bomb," he said at length. "He wore denims, carried a large floral piece, and walked out as soon as he'd deposited it—and the bomb—at the altar. He figured that the one or two people who might know him—Fathers Koesler and Tully, who had met him only once or twice—wouldn't recognize or even notice him in that guise. And if by some fluke he *was* recognized, at that point he could easily abort the plan.

"He figured his father wouldn't be in the church proper that early before the ceremony.

"Then he changed from his denims to his clericals in a public rest room at the Milander Center—just a few blocks from St. Joe's.

"And another precaution: He called his father from a pay phone."

Silence followed, as all present went over these events in their own minds. Most of their questions had been answered, the events explained.

"Remember," Lieutenant Tully added, inclining his head toward Walt and Wanda, "at the party at your house? Young Richard Wheatley was talking about how neither of his parents could fix anything; they both were total klutzes when it came to working with their hands. And then he said that he and his two siblings—all of them—could fix anything. Each and every one of them could put anything together.

"Well, *I* should've put it together: That was a clue that could have pointed us in the right direction immediately." He grimaced as he shook his head. "I blew it."

"Don't be so hard on yourself," Anne Marie said. "It just opened things up for Father Koesler to come up with a really imaginative solution." She turned to Koesler. "I think that's really clever, Father: how you turned that Bible story around and backward to discover who made that phone call."

Koesler almost blushed. "Well, Ron was playing God—literally and figuratively." He smiled. "Beware the one who plays God—or is the custodian of God's will. That's the one to keep an eye on."

Anne Marie wouldn't let Koesler off the hook. "And, Father, I think you gave a great eulogy at Father Wheatley's funeral."

"That was at the Episcopal cathedral, was it not?" Walt observed. "Why there?"

"Nan arranged that," Koesler replied. "She would have it no other way. And I agreed with her. I got the clear impression that she never quite believed in what George was doing in the Roman Church. But she saw her place as standing with George. However, inside she was aching. Her heart never left the Anglican Church. How George would be buried was her call. The Roman Church excursion was over when George died in her arms. She had no place to go but Home.

"Nan was the one who invited me to deliver the eulogy. I was honored."

"Tell me, Father," said Anne Marie, "where did you get that description of Anglicanism—the one that you used in the eulogy? I notice it was also printed on the prayer card."

"George shared it with me," Koesler replied.

"We had not heard of this," Walt said. "What is it?"

"I've got the card," Father Tully offered.

Koesler nodded.

Zack took the small prayer card from his coat pocket and read aloud:

> *"Anglicanism was and is at its best Catholic, for it holds the Catholic essentials. It is Protestant because it rejects the papal innovations in faith and order. It is traditional, for it looks back to the past for the body of its creed, for the great facts of the Christian revelation on which it is based, and to the great march of the Church's history, from which it draws its precedents. At the same time, it is modern, for it seeks ever to make this creed and these facts tell with force in the minds of this modern age."*

The room was silent as Father Tully stopped speaking. He looked around at his family, both his related family and his family of friends. "That's from a biography of Joost de Blank, an Anglican archbishop who was a leading fighter against apartheid." After a moment, he added, "It is a pretty magnificent statement."

"Yeah," said Father Koesler to himself. Aloud, he said only, "Amen."